D0866670

PEABODY INSTITUTE LIBRARY

Danvers, Mass.

WHISTLE IN THE DARK

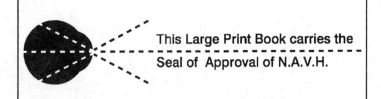

This Large Print Book carries the
Seal of Approval of N.A.V.H.

WHISTLE IN THE DARK

EMMA HEALEY

WHEELER PUBLISHING
A part of Gale, a Cengage Company

Farmington Hills, Mich • San Francisco • New York • Waterville, Maine
Meriden, Conn • Mason, Ohio • Chicago

GALE
A Cengage Company

Copyright © 2018 by Emma Healey.
Wheeler Publishing, a part of Gale, a Cengage Company.

ALL RIGHTS RESERVED
This is a work of fiction. Names, characters, places, and incidents are products of the author's imagination or are used fictitiously and are not to be construed as real. Any resemblance to actural events, locales, organizations, or persons, living or dead, is entirely coincidental.
Wheeler Publishing Large Print Hardcover.
The text of this Large Print edition is unabridged.
Other aspects of the book may vary from the original edition.
Set in 16 pt. Plantin.

**LIBRARY OF CONGRESS CIP DATA ON FILE.
CATALOGUING IN PUBLICATION FOR THIS BOOK
IS AVAILABLE FROM THE LIBRARY OF CONGRESS**

ISBN-13: 978-1-4328-5863-6 (hardcover)

Published in 2018 by arrangement with Harper, an imprint of HarperCollins Publishers

Printed in the United States of America
1 2 3 4 5 6 7 22 21 20 19 18

To my mother, Kathryn Healey

THE END

"This has been the worst week of my life," Jen said. Not what she had planned to say to her fifteen-year-old daughter after an ordeal that had actually covered four days.

"Hi, Mum." Lana's voice emerged from blue-tinged lips.

Jen could only snatch a hug, a press of her cheek against Lana's — soft and pale as a mushroom — while the paramedics slammed the ambulance doors and wheeled Lana into the hospital. There was a gash on the ashen head, a scrape on the tender jaw, she was thin and cold and wrapped in tinfoil, she smelled soggy and earthy and unclean, but it was okay: she was here, she was safe, she was alive. Nothing else mattered.

Cigarette smoke drifted over from the collection of dressing-gowned, IV-attached witnesses huddled under the covered entrance, and a man's voice came with it.

"What's going off? Is that the lass from London?"

"Turned up, then," another voice answered. "Heard it said on the news."

So the press had been told already. Jen supposed that was a good thing: they could cancel the search, stop asking the public to keep their eyes open, to report possible sightings, to contact the police if they had information. It was a happy ending to the story. Not the ending anyone had been expecting.

The call had come less than an hour ago, Hugh, wrapped in a hotel towel, just out of the shower (because it was important to keep going), Jen not dressed and unshowered (because she wasn't convinced by Hugh's argument). They had never given up hope, that's what she would say in the weeks to come, talking to friends and relatives, but really her hope, that flimsy Meccano construction, had shaken its bolts loose and collapsed within minutes of finding Lana missing.

Even driving to the hospital, Jen had been full of doubt, assuming there'd been a mistake, imagining a different girl would meet them there, or a lifeless body. The liaison officer had tried to calm her with details: a farmer had spotted a teenager on sheep-grazing land, he'd identified her from the news and called the police, she was wearing the clothes Jen had guessed she'd be wearing, she'd been well enough to drink a cup of hot, sweet tea, well enough to speak, and had definitely answered to the name Lana.

And then there she was, recognizable and yet unfamiliar, a sketch of herself, being colored in by the hospital: the black wheelchair rolling to the reception desk, the edges of Lana's red blanket billowing, a nurse in blue sweeping by with a white-coated doctor and the green-uniformed paramedics turning to go out again with a wave. Jen felt too round, the lines of her body too thick and slow for the pace, and she hung back a moment, feeling Hugh's hands on her shoulders.

He nudged her forward. Lana's wheelchair was on the move and Jen felt woozy, the scent of disinfectant whistling through her as they got deeper into the hospital. She hadn't anticipated this, hadn't been rehearsing for doctors and a recovery, had pictured only police press conferences and a funeral, or an endless, agonizing wait. The relief was wonderful, the relief was ecstasy, the relief made her ticklish, it throbbed in her veins. The relief was exhausting.

"How are you feeling?" she asked Hugh, hoping his answer would show her how to react, how to behave.

"I don't know," Hugh said. "I don't know yet."

They spent several hours in the ER while Lana had skeletal surveys and urine tests and her head was cleaned and stitched and some of her hair was cut. Her clothes were exchanged for a gown, and her feet, pale and chalky, stuck out naked from the hem. Jen wanted to hold those feet to her chest, to kiss them, as she had when Lana was a baby, but just above each ankle was a purplish line, like the indentations left by socks, only thinner, darker. The kind of mark a fine rope might leave. They made Jen pause, they were a hint, a threat, and they signaled a beginning — the beginning of a new doubt, a new fear, a new gap opening up between her and her daughter.

The police noticed the marks, too, and photographed them when they came to take Lana's white fleece jacket, now brown and stiff with blood. There was so much blood on it that Jen found herself wondering again if her daughter was really still alive.

"Head wounds, even relatively minor ones, bleed a lot," a doctor said, seeing the look on Jen's face.

There was a pat on the shoulder and another offer of coffee. This was followed by a great deal of waiting, and then of walking, and Jen found her boots were rubbing, though they'd been perfectly comfortable crossing fields and tracing woodland paths a week ago. And finally they were in a ward, Lana in a bed, the drip hung up and heat packs renewed. She was asleep, or, if not quite asleep, then in some fog of her own. The day had been blue and bright, but now the sun was low, the air cold. A ladybird had got inside and kept throwing itself at the window with that particular beetlish noise, a whirring tap, an itchy sort of sound. Ladybirds had been waking up for over a month, coming out of hibernation because of the warm weather; they'd had three in the bathroom at home and Jen had dithered over whether to kill them or not because they were all definitely harlequin ones and therefore invaders, imposters, villains who threatened local wildlife.

She didn't dither now but crossed the room and crushed the beetle in a tissue.

"Meant to be bad luck to kill a ladybird," a woman said. She was on the cusp of being elderly, with gray-white hair cut very short and several layers of clothes stretched tight across her back, and she was sitting by the

11

bed of a small child, knitting.

The color of the cardigan she wore (teal) and the color of the wool she was knitting with (dark turquoise) were so close it seemed as though she were adding to her own clothes as she went. There was something mythical about this, fairy-tale-like, which stopped Jen from telling her to piss off. She dropped the tissue into a hazardous-waste bin and sat down again.

She had painted a ladybird at the beginning of the week, mixing crimson and burnt sienna for the shell, dropping the paint lightly onto the paper. It seemed like a lifetime ago, or — perhaps more accurately — it seemed like a moment she had imagined during a sun-drenched daydream. Lana had painted the beetle, too, nestled inside a cowslip, but the red paint had bled into the pale yellow of the flower and she'd been annoyed and ripped the paper.

Lana had destroyed lots of her work over the holiday, despite Jen begging her not to. There were a dozen ragged edges in her sketchbook, the remnants of pictures that had gone wrong.

"Hello." A man wearing the doctor's uniform of a checked, rolled-sleeved shirt tucked into chinos greeted them, and Hugh stood up, his own unchecked, unrolled, untucked shirt a little more crumpled, a little tighter over the belly.

"I'm Dr. Kaimal. Can you open your eyes for me, Lana?" He spoke with a deep, rich voice, tilting his head as he shone a light into Lana's eyes.

Hugh stepped forward and Jen knew he wanted to save her from this last bit of discomfort. Lana blinked and groaned, her head shrinking back into the pillow, her movements jerky when the doctor asked her to squeeze his fingers and submit to another blood-pressure test. Each action seemed almost beyond her, and Lana's head fell forward when he was done.

"It's all looking pretty good," the doctor said, pocketing the little torch. "We've got her temperature up, which we're pleased about. She's dehydrated and disorientated, obviously, and there are some infected scrapes, but the laceration on her head isn't nearly as nasty as it looks. What we'd like to do is keep her in overnight for observation and give her some fluids and antibiotics. All right?"

"What happened? Can you tell?" Jen asked.

He grimaced slightly. "She might have had a fall but, apart from bruising, there are no other injuries. She's been very wet for some

13

time and her skin is quite sore, and of course she's been cold. She should be able to tell you when she's a bit stronger." He paused a moment. "Am I right in thinking the police have already spoken to her?"

"She told them she got lost," Jen said. "They want to speak to her again, when she's better."

"Right. Well." The doctor nodded at them both, dividing his nods between them equally. "Someone will be back to check her in an hour."

The sun had sunk behind a building and all the previously golden edges were now gray. The relief Jen had felt at seeing Lana again was turning into something else, and though she mostly wanted to bundle her up and rock her and feel the weight of her and do anything she could to convince herself that her daughter was really okay, there was a thin thread of dread within her, too. She was frightened to tug on it but knew she wouldn't be able to resist for long.

"How did you get lost?" she said to Lana, who opened and shut her eyes.

Hugh sat down slowly, listening, concentrating.

"Was it an accident?"

Lana moved her head in what might have been a nod.

14

"You didn't go off deliberately?" Jen asked, and her daughter's reply could have been a yes or a no. "You weren't trying to hurt yourself?"

"Please," Lana said. The word was painful.

"Okay." Jen smoothed a hand along the edges of Lana's blood-matted hair. "Okay. You sleep."

And she kept her mouth shut, though the questions rattled around her head, and she kept her hands steady, though she wanted to shake her daughter awake and demand an explanation. A desperate rage ran through her like a wick. It scared her, this anger, unfocused and physical, and she wasn't sure she could trust herself.

"Is she really here, Hugh?" Jen said. "Is she really all right?"

He nodded. His hands were clasped as if he'd been praying, the fingers interlaced, and he moved them about as one, resting them on his knees, his thighs, his stomach.

"And whatever happened, she'll recover?"

"Yes." He lifted the joined hands and then stretched up and over to support the back of his head.

"She'll be fine?"

"Yes."

"And we won't blame her?"

15

"No," Hugh said, letting his hands spring apart. "No, of course we won't."

"No, of course we won't," Jen repeated. She sat back.

Lana's name had been written on a whiteboard above the bed and someone had drawn a flower with a smiley face next to it. The ink had become powdery around the dotted eyes so it looked like the flower's mascara had run. Jen got up to wipe a finger under the marks, but she couldn't get them to look even and kept neatening and neatening until she'd rubbed the eyes away entirely. The face looked happier without them, she thought, annoyed to find the blue of the marker had got under her nails.

MAN OF GOD

On the painting holiday her hands had been covered in ink and paint, and they had used brushes and reed pens, small squares of thick, absorbent paper and huge rolls of wallpaper. They were encouraged by the course tutor to rub mud from the fields onto their pictures, to crush coconut-scented gorse flowers into their sketchbooks, to note the smells and sounds of the landscape on the edges of each painting.

Jen told herself she would carry on with

16

this expressive work when she got home to London but could already predict how she would make one half-hearted attempt and never find the time again. It was the place that made it possible: the bright studio and the footpaths into the hills and the dining hall where all the meals were provided.

They'd booked the course in January when being outside was painful and they couldn't imagine daylight lasting beyond four o'clock in the afternoon. It had been something to look forward to: a week in the country at the end of May, a week for walking and art, for self-improvement and, possibly, even some mother–daughter bonding after the last two years of conflict. Time together without social workers and doctors and psychiatrists.

They'd gone shopping for art materials and proper walking gear. Watercolor palettes, putty rubbers, paintbrushes with water reservoirs in the handles, and masking fluid. Waterproof trousers, fleece jackets, thick socks and boots. The shopping trips had been fun and Jen had taken this as a sign that the holiday would be a success. But, as the day for departure drew nearer, Lana had become less enthusiastic.

"I think it's unfair that Dad can't come," she'd said, and, "How much walking will

17

we have to do? What if I can't keep up?" and, "What if everyone else is an amazing artist and I'm shit?" and, "Who else will be on the course? Will it all be adults?" and, "It's miles away. How long will it take to drive there?"

In the event, they didn't drive. Hugh had needed the car so they took the train. And Jen thought the journey might be a good time to start to "reconnect" and "open up the lines of communication," but while they were waiting in the station, Lana said again the phrase Jen had come to dread.

"I want to kill myself." Her voice was flat and quiet, toneless and powerful.

Jen spent a couple of seconds trying to formulate an answer but, somehow, before she could speak, the conversation moved on and she found she'd missed her chance.

"Those are the shoes I like," Lana said, pointing. "See? That woman in the blue."

"Yes, they're nice," Jen replied, her mind gasping for air while her real breathing stayed even.

"But my feet are too ugly," Lana told her, looking down, rather cheerily, Jen thought. "Too veiny. You have to have smooth brown feet for those shoes."

"Oh, I see," Jen said, not knowing how to get back to the beginning of their exchange, not knowing if she *should* try to get back to it, and thrown, as usual, by the speed in the shift of her daughter's emotions.

On arrival, they found that Lana was the youngest of the group by thirty years but, once that was established, she didn't seem to mind and Jen felt proud of her daughter, chatting away, working hard on her pictures in the studio, helping the older amateur artists get through gates and climb over the more difficult stiles. She complained only once about the basic accommodation, the cold linoleum floors, the occasional wood louse, the fact that the shower block was a separate building down a dark gravel path. And she'd seemed less tired than usual, not hanging on Jen's arm but striding off to find the best spot for a picture. She never repeated what she'd said at the station.

Jen was pleased Lana had thrown herself into the activities so wholeheartedly, but she'd been keen to have Lana to herself and was vaguely irritated by the way the other people on the holiday demanded her attention. The class was full of interesting characters, or so everyone kept saying. Almost all of them were female. There was a pagan and a tarot-card reader and a Reiki practitioner; there was a woman named Peny who insisted they make sure they were pronouncing her name with only one *n,* as she could tell if they were using two, and another woman who was currently engaged in designing motifs to decorate her own cardboard coffin.

"Someone should write a novel about us," they kept saying, which made Jen wonder if any of them had ever read a novel.

Stephen might have, she supposed. A watercolorist in his midforties, he tended to avoid evening activities in order to "catch up on some reading," and Jen thought more highly of him for a couple of days. But then it turned out that the reading he was doing was part of the training he had undertaken for the ministry of some obscure Christian sect called the New Lollards Fellowship. The books mostly had fuzzy pictures of waves on them, or sunsets confused by curling typefaces, and her estimation of him fell.

It turned out his previous hobby had been family history and he'd unearthed an ancestor with a link to the church, and although he'd spent his life as an uninterested agnostic this connection had convinced him to become a member.

Jen found this idea seductive and wondered how her own life might be altered by discovering the occupations and interests of her predecessors. But she had a sneaking suspicion that she'd never manage to be as committed, or suggestible, as Stephen.

By the third day of the holiday he'd begun to use any opportunity to "save" his fellow painters, attempting to explain how the Bible had been wrongly interpreted, to convince them that his was the one true religion, to defend his church's preoccupation with Hell, which they believed it was possible to visit.

"I don't remember that being in the Twelve Conclusions," said Peny, who wasn't a pagan or a Reiki practitioner but did have a degree in theology.

"We are not connected to the Lollards of Wycliffe," Stephen said. "We take that term 'lollard' to mean 'heretic' in the best way."

He was by turns tedious and infuriating. Despite this, there was something charming about him, boyish and cheeky. The other women often asked for his opinion of their work and were readier to laugh when he was with them. Jen couldn't exactly bring herself to dislike him, until he began to spend all his time with Lana.

This seemed to happen suddenly. Jen would find them walking together at the back of the group, Stephen holding brambles out of her way, or retying the arms of her jacket around her waist. They shared a series of jokes which Jen only half caught, and in the studio he had a habit of throwing pieces of Blu-Tack at Lana, making her squeal. This flirtation (what else could she call it?) worried Jen, especially when he began to talk to Lana about the Right Path and Sin and Saving Souls. Lana listened intently and asked questions, and seemed to be genuinely interested, and Jen imagined that Stephen's smile when he met her eyes had a hint of triumph.

But, to Jen's relief, Lana wasn't particularly susceptible to the religious arguments and was quite annoyed when she found him trying to convert other visitors during a group trip to a National Trust property.

"People don't come here to be stalked by religious fanatics," she said.

Stephen didn't seem to be upset by her categorization but gave a roguish smile. He appeared to be generally impervious to Lana's criticism, however insulting she made it, and it was Lana who always walked away, agitated and incredulous.

THEOLOGICAL ARGUMENT

STEPHEN (*smiling, his tanned walker's knees displayed by khaki shorts*):

Forgive me, but you're being naive, the world is only ten thousand years old. Those fossils have been planted to test our faith.

LANA (*leaning forward and trembling slightly*):

That's a load of crap and you're insane.

ALTERNATE UNIVERSE

Someone, usually a nurse, came every two hours to shine a light in Lana's eyes and take her blood pressure, and she seemed to fall into a disturbed sleep in the meantime, trembling and frowning as if she were still having an argument with Stephen. Jen wondered what her daughter was really dreaming about, and whether she should wake her.

"When can we ask what happened?" Hugh asked a nurse as the light balance tipped from outside to inside and their reflections appeared on the window.

The nurse, tucking a clipboard under her arm, looked confused behind her glasses. "When she's awake?" she suggested.

"So that would be okay?"

"Yes, I should think so."

"What are you asking that for?" Jen said,

23

when the nurse had gone.

"They always check on detective shows," Hugh said. "I thought you had to."

"But we're not police. We don't need permission to talk to our own daughter."

"I didn't think it was about permission," Hugh said. "I thought it was about not inhibiting recovery."

"How can it *inhibit recovery* to ask where she's been?"

He turned a weighty look on her. "In detective shows, any questioning they do always inhibits recovery."

They sat watching the bed for a moment, as though it were a television screen. Jen was uncertain whether or not she should feel for Lana's hand under the blankets; just how delicate was she after her ordeal? Whatever that ordeal might have been. She held Hugh's hand instead, despite being irritated by his insistence on following the procedure of TV detectives. A few minutes later an older nurse appeared from behind the curtain like an actor.

"Hello, sir. Hello, ma'am," she said, very formally, but with a jauntiness that made Jen think she was mocking them.

"Hello," Jen and Hugh said, looking at her as if they expected a performance. Their united voices were rather half-hearted, an

24

audience that hadn't been warmed up yet.

The nurse had cropped hair and a Chinese name, and her voice was already familiar: Jen had heard her jollying patients along in the rest of the ward. She rolled a blood-pressure machine away and came back again, her walk a heavy shuffle, her thick-soled shoes loose on her feet. They were black slip-ons, scuffed and well worn, the shape of her toes clear in the leather. Reassuring shoes, Jen thought, the shoes of a good nurse.

"So what we got?" she said. "Dehydration, cuts, bruises. Nothing too serious, hey? And she said no to the forensic examination. So. So. The doctor thinks tomorrow she can go home."

"Great," Hugh said, sounding like he'd just been told there was a table ready for them in a popular restaurant.

"What does that mean?" Jen asked. "The forensic-examination part?"

"It means she thinks she doesn't need one."

"Great," Hugh said again.

Jen felt like elbowing him. "But, sorry. What is a forensic examination?"

"It's," the nurse said, pausing to raise her eyebrows high, "a rape kit. The police asked. They talked to you about it?"

"No," Hugh said. "I don't think they mentioned that."

He sat perfectly still, and Jen copied him, though her brain was cramping with questions. What had made the police think a rape kit was necessary? Had Lana said something to them? And why had she turned it down? Because nothing had happened? Because she was embarrassed or ashamed? Jen briefly felt another version of herself, in another universe, reacting to the alternative answer, reacting to the news that Lana had said yes to a rape kit. The Hugh and Jen in the other universe also sat perfectly still, but their internal organs had shrunk and the world around them had grown large. Jen had to work hard to keep herself in the right universe, to remember which she belonged to.

"Well, okay. Good sign, no? Good sign," the nurse said. "You don't worry now."

"Right, we'll try."

"Yes. Yes, good. Where you from?"

"London," Hugh said.

"And what's that?" The nurse patted a plastic bag on top of the bedside locker.

"Sketchbooks," Jen said, struggling to concentrate. "I had them with me . . ." In fact, she had clung to them over the last four days, feeling as if the half-finished watercolors and smudgy charcoal drawings connected her to Lana.

"Can I see?" the nurse said.

Jen was inclined to say no, as the police had already been through them, looking for clues, and the pages were slightly dog-eared, some of the pictures stained and muddy from handling. But it seemed rude to refuse when she was showing an interest and the nurse's fingers were delicate and clean-looking, so she just nodded.

"Oh, *very good*. And I can see where this is." The nurse held up a picture of a stone circle known as the Nine Ladies. "Your daughter do these?"

"Actually, they're mine," Jen said. "The other sketchbook is Lana's."

"You're a talent, aren't you?"

She flicked through Lana's sketchbook more quickly, nodding and mentioning each location. "Now, I know this place," she said, and, "I recognize that church," and, "That view, I know." But mostly she just held up each page and repeated the same sentence: "Where's that? Where's that? Where's that?" as if they were flash cards for a geography test — historic and architectural sites of the Peak District — rather than a sketchbook.

Jen answered as best she could, though the names of some of the places were

27

already forgotten. It began to seem absurd, and she and Hugh looked at each other when the nurse had left the ward. They were still holding hands, and he bounced hers up and down now.

"Where's that?" he said, parroting the nurse.

"Under . . . I'm underneath," Lana said in her sleep, startling them.

THE PAPER

Hugh went down to the foyer to buy a paper, though the last thing Jen wanted to see was the news. There had been a picture of Lana on the front page of the local gazette and of two national tabloids, and the sight of that photo reproduced in soot-like ink had been as disturbing as anything she'd experienced. It had made her daughter seem really lost, like those other children on the news, the ones who never come back, who become a byword for gruesome death, or a joke in the routine of a shock-reliant stand-up comic. She had focused on the layout of the article, the off-center image, the awkwardness of the margins, the slightly unaligned adverts at the bottom of the page, convincing herself that, if the design wasn't

perfect, the story — her story — coul(
be true.

There was very little to focus on wit
the hospital — everything was neat :
regular, set at right angles, and matching
so Jen looked at the reflection of her o
face in the darkened window to find a bi
asymmetry, something soft and imperfe
Behind her, Lana's shape was slight a
marbleesque, like an effigy.

People often said she and Lana look
similar, though neither of them could see
Lana's hair was lighter, her face longer. Je
eyelids were heavier, her lips thinner. M
was her mother's copy. Lana was Hugh
But it was the smile, people said, it was tl
smile that highlighted the family reser
blance. They always shrugged at that. Th
had the same shrug.

"Your daughter, is she?"

It was the knitting woman who spoke. Je
had forgotten she was there; the tapping o
the needles had receded to the level of
ticking clock, a background noise.

"On holiday, weren't you? It was in th
paper," she said, as if warning Jen that ther
was no point in denying it.

"A painting holiday."

"Yes, I heard it said. From London, are
you?"

"That's right."

"Wouldn't live there, I wouldn't. Wouldn't bring up children there, neither. Dirty place."

"Well, I suppose it depends on what you mean by dirt," Jen said, thinking of the fields of sheep dung and cow pats she'd walked through the week before.

There was no break in the click of the knitting needles or the steady addition of stitches and yet the woman didn't take her eyes from Jen.

"Is this your" — Jen glanced at the bed — "relation?" she finished, unable to guess at the age of the woman or the sex of the child under the stiff hospital sheets.

"Four days she was missing," the woman said, ignoring the question. "And no idea where she went. That was in the paper, too."

Jen didn't answer, not understanding why the woman was summing it up for her. Did she think Jen hadn't noticed? Was she getting some sort of kick out of repeating the story?

"Terrible, terrible," the woman added, but the sympathy sounded false.

"It was," Jen said, and she felt she'd made her voice firm, authoritative, but the woman didn't react. "What are you knitting?"

"Lampshade," the woman said, though

Jen was sure she'd misheard. The knitting paused for a moment and the woman counted stitches under her breath.

"Think she'll tell you where she's been when she wakes up?"

"Yes, of course."

"Don't you believe it."

"We're very close," Jen said, though this was a kind of lie. What did she mean by "close"? Close enough to have a screaming row, close enough to cry in each other's presence, close enough to sit for hours in silence while Jen waited for some sign that she could leave to go to work, or have lunch with a friend, or just make a cup of tea without the fear that Lana would be dead when she came back.

When was the last time Lana had wanted her company? When had she last confided in her? The holiday had been a study in keeping her mother at arm's length: slipping away by herself to sketch, talking to pretty much anyone in the group except Jen. She wouldn't have been surprised to discover Lana had gone off in the middle of the night just to get away from her.

And then there was the boy. The son of the holiday-center manager. Matthew. Jen had hoped that Lana would talk to her about him; she'd had her own holiday

31

romance once, when she was eighteen. That had been on a painting holiday, too. But there were just shrugs and sighs and accusations of being embarrassing when Jen asked where they'd been in the evenings.

"They keep things to themselves at that age," the knitting woman said. "I know teenagers. Had four myself."

"Each child is different." Jen could feel her lips tighten around the words. "My elder daughter wasn't secretive." Though perhaps this wasn't entirely accurate, either; when Meg had told them she was gay, they hadn't exactly been expecting it.

"Got another one, have you?" The woman sounded surprised.

Jen felt rather exasperated and, wanting to end the conversation, started to leaf, pointedly, through the sketchbooks again, setting the same views against each other, her own more exuberant pictures against Lana's careful drawings.

"There'll be a storm this evening," the woman said, glancing out of the window.

Jen looked at the sky, hoping to spot whatever it was that had tipped off this daughter of the soil and, thinking she might learn some country wisdom, asked how she knew.

"It was in the paper," the woman said.

Holiday romance 1979

He'd been blond. Unusual in Spain, noticeable, and later he'd explained that he was half Austrian, his hair inherited from his father. Jen remembered very little now, except the feel of his hands on her arms, the warmth of his body as he stood behind her during a painting demonstration. The heat of him and the heat of the sun were the same in her memory: it was the first time she'd been abroad, it was the first time she'd had sex.

His name was dark to her now, but the brief — very brief — courtship remained undimmed. There had been a series of gallant acts, of easel-carrying and shade-searching and ice-offering. He'd brought her a sea daffodil from the beach, a white, star-shaped flower that smelled faintly like a lily. She'd included it in a picture, a good picture, using wax to preserve the white of the paper, and he'd asked if he could keep it, rolling it up and tucking it into his rucksack.

Mostly he'd been quiet, speaking only when they were at the back of the group, or after the classes had finished for the day, and near the end of the holiday she'd suddenly realized he was married to the hotel owner, a smart, rather matronly, older woman who'd been kind when Jen had arrived after a badly delayed flight. She should have been shocked, upset, guilty, but she couldn't manage it in that languid atmosphere.

The only thing she regretted was giving away that picture. She'd tried several times to re-create it with an English daffodil but never managed to produce the same effect.

Holiday romance 2015

Matthew was cheerful, sandy-haired, and outdoorsy; he smelled of worn walking boots and toothpaste. He'd been eight years old when his dad had become the holiday-center manager, and some of the older staff still tried to ruffle his hair, though he was too tall for them to do it without an awkward stretch. At sixteen, he seemed surprised at his own height and unsure how to carry himself. He talked a lot, with a sort of stutter, repeating words and phrases, and most of his speech contained a question. He'd been visibly working up the courage to say hi to Lana since they'd arrived two days earlier.

"I was going to, I was going to go badger-watching?" he said, as everyone filed out of the hall after dinner.

"Okay," Lana said.

"Do you, do you want to come?"

"Okay," she said again.

"*I'd* like to see some badgers," Jen said.

"Oh," he said. "Yeah, I guess, I guess you can come, too."

"Ah, I see. Not to worry, I'm sure I can see some badgers another time."

"Cool," he said.

He had a blanket with a waterproof lining, and Jen tried to work out if this was chivalrous or calculating: was he saving Lana from the damp ground or preparing the way for intimacy? Either way, it was good, she decided, it was healthy, it was normal. Jen turned away as the two teenagers walked off together.

The badger-watching spot was at the edge of the grounds. One of the center workers told Jen that spliff ends were sometimes found there, but mostly the kids around here were good kids and cleaned up after themselves. They took peanut-butter sandwiches and dog food and sat quietly and waited for the thrill of white-striped faces in the gloom.

Jen wondered if she should follow them, just to make sure, but she resisted the urge.

35

And Lana had come back safe and sound. That night, at least.

AWAKE

Hugh was asleep, slumped sideways over the bottom of the bed, an empty paper cup precariously balanced on his knee, when Lana woke properly.

"Dad," she said, moving her toes under the sheets and almost patting his head with them. "Poor Dad."

"Poor all of us," Jen said. "We've been so worried."

"Sorry."

Jen had known her daughter would be confused, unsure where she was, in need of reassurance, but it was worse than that: Lana seemed only half there and could barely manage more than one syllable at a time. Her head rolled on the pillow and the red of the cut that ran through her hair flashed at Jen. She tried to keep her eyes away from it, from the parts of Lana that were still matted with blood, from the scrape on her cheekbone and the crack in her tooth, but it was impossible not to feel a burning on her own scalp, a throbbing in her own cheek, an ache in her own teeth. When Lana's hands appeared from under the covers the sight of the broken nails and ragged cuticles sent a phantom pain running up Jen's arms.

"Are you hurting?" Jen said.

"Always."

It was an echo of the conversations they'd had before, when Lana was blocking the door to her bedroom, or pulling her sleeve down over her arm to hide whatever marks she'd made there.

"What happened?" Jen asked, trying to soften the desperate edge to her voice.

"Can't," Lana said, squinting as if the room were full of bright lights.

"Can't what? Can't tell me?"

She shook her head. "It's . . . a blur."

Hugh's paper cup finally toppled onto the floor and, no longer held in place by its ethereal weight, Hugh drooped further onto the mattress, letting out a sharp snore.

"But these bruises," Jen said. "How did you get them? Did someone hurt you? Did you fall?"

"Must have."

Jen felt under the bed for the cup, reaching into the dark and grabbing for it. Her fingers were jittery. She had pushed her hand, her arm, into some other dark space recently. Yesterday? Two days ago? Time was unsettled in her memory — there was the abyss while Lana was gone and there was now. She crushed the cup and pushed it absently into her bag, finding the small bottle of perfume Hugh had given her for Christmas. It smelled of something bright and sweet, of mandarins or orange blossom. It also smelled like four days of despair, and she knew she'd never be able to use it again.

Lana held her wrist out for the perfume and Jen sprayed a little on her, thinking of it as an act of truce, though they weren't really fighting. She watched as Lana brought the wrist to her nose and sniffed.

"Nice. Thanks," she said, letting her arm flop back onto the bed.

Jen stared at the arm, the hand, the nails. "Were you trapped somewhere?" she asked. "Caught in something? Were you in a fight?" She moved her gaze to Lana's pale, doughy face. "You said something about . . . You said you were underneath, when you were sleeping."

"Ugh."

"You don't remember that?"

"No."

"Leave her alone now, Jen." Hugh's voice was deadened by the mattress. "The questions can wait."

"How long have you been awake?"

"Define 'awake,'" he said, sitting up. "I've

been vaguely conscious for about twenty seconds."

"I'm just asking Lana if there's anything we need to know."

"Well, I'm just telling you that you can do that later."

"She's angry," Lana said.

Jen sighed. "No, Lana, I'm not. I'm upset, confused, exhausted, I've hardly slept this week for worry, but I'm not angry."

"Okay," Lana said, with what might have been a smile. She closed one eye and then the other, shifting between them until she could keep both open at the same time. "I'll expect more questions, then."

"Yes, do," Jen said, feeling as though battle lines had been drawn.

Continuous stationery

To prove there was no animosity (or to lull her daughter before another attack), Jen bought, at the hospital shop: a KitKat (which would go uneaten), a mindfulness coloring book (which would be left black and white), a set of felt-tip pens (the caps would never be removed), and, in a moment of levity, a pack of novelty moustaches (Lana would attach the orange "Walrus" one to her upper lip and stare challengingly at a nurse who was taking her blood pressure).

Carrying this haul back upstairs, Jen looked through the corridor windows at each little courtyard. In one was a sad-looking tree, all stringy branches and frizzy leaves, lit by leftover electric light. It was dismal to think of it stuck there forever, or for as long as the hospital buildings surrounded it, lonely and isolated, with no access to the landscape beyond. The sight had not affected Hugh, though.

"You keep grinning at everyone," Jen said, greeting him as he came out of the loo at the end of the corridor. "Stop grinning."

"Sorry," Hugh said, grinning.

"What's the matter with you?" she asked, stopping at the entrance to Lana's ward.

"How d'you mean?"

"You're . . . giddy. Laughing at things that aren't funny, humming to yourself."

"I'm happy to have my daughter back." Hugh looked at Lana through the doorway to her bay. She was sitting up in her hospital bed, eating a red-colored jelly. "Happy to have found her alive and safe. Aren't you happy?"

"Yes, but she's been gone nearly a week, and we still don't know what happened to her, where she went, or why. It seems inappropriate to be so jolly all the time."

"We've been through it, though, Jen," he said. "That's the thing. It's like trial by fire or whatever. After everything we've been through with Lana, the fear and guilt and those excruciating therapy sessions, I couldn't see how it would ever get any better. Then the worst happened, or nearly the worst, and we thought we'd lost her, but we got through it and came out the other side, and so did she."

He sighed, and it was nearly a giggle. Jen wondered if he was hysterical.

"Do you see, though?" he said. "It's all over."

She stared at Hugh for a moment. "You think Lana won't have depression anymore? That she's been cured somehow?"

"Not cured — that makes me sound ridiculous. But yes, I think we've reached a tipping point. What are you scrabbling in your bag for?"

"My phone's buzzing," Jen said. "It's Meg. Will you take it? I want to get back to Lana."

"All right. I'll get something else for us to read while I'm at it."

Jen didn't remind him she'd just been to the shop and she kept her lips together while Hugh checked he had his wallet and kissed her on the head and answered the phone and finally left. But her teeth were already parted as she walked through the ward, her tongue poised, and as soon as she sat down next to Lana's bed she began.

"Just tell me, truthfully, did you deliberately go off?" she asked.

Lana sighed and put her empty jelly pot down. "I can't remember, Mum."

"What time did you leave the center? It must have been after I'd gone to sleep."

"I really can't remember."

"Were you alone?"

"I can't remember."

"Why did you go off, Lana? What were you feeling?"

"I can't remember that, either."

"Did that boy have anything to do with it?"

"Oh, that boy, that boy. You keep going on about *that* boy. I kissed Matthew, like, twice. This isn't *Romeo and Juliet* — he has nothing to do with anything."

This wasn't going well, Jen realized, she was only making Lana annoyed, making her exhausted, but still, she had to ask; there wasn't much time before Hugh came back.

"How did you get the cut on your head?"

"I can't remember." Said with a flat tone, looking at the ceiling.

"How did you crack your tooth?"

"I can't remember." Slightly ironic, as if this were a tedious game.

"If you can't remember anything, how did you know to turn down the forensic exam, the rape kit?"

"Oh, Jesus, Mum, there are some things you just know, okay?"

"Okay. Fine. Good." Thank God, she said to herself, promising not to think about the rape kit again. "Were you angry with me?" This was the important question: Was it my fault? Did I make this happen? Do you blame me? Should others blame me, too?

Lana looked angry now, her chin jutting, her jaw locking. "Mum, I can't remember," she said.

"Weren't you scared?"

"I can't remember." Her consonants were hard and biting.

"You must have been inside some of the time. Where were you?"

Her voice rose. "I can't remember."

"Not even an impression? Was it dark? Warm? Lonely? What?"

Lana looked at Jen for a long moment before opening her mouth. "I can't remember."

Jen felt they could go on like this forever, her own words constantly bridged by Lana's identical sentence. She imagined their conversation being printed on an endless piece of paper, on one of those printers from the eighties with the holes along each side, the stack of paper uncurling as it was fed through the rollers.

Pausing a moment, she heard the clack of the woman visitor's knitting needles and began to blame her, to think of her as the cause, the creator of this terrible pattern of speech.

"How did you lose your phone?" Jen asked, unable to stop herself.

The knitting needles tapped together. *I told you so I told you so.*

"I can't remember," Lana said.

"Did you meet anyone at all?"

The woman's bangles jangled as she unwound the ball of wool. *I know teenagers.*

"I can't remember," Lana said.

"What were you trying to do? What were you hoping would happen?"

There was a crack as the woman put down her knitting and stretched her back. *Think she'll tell you where she's been when she wakes up? Don't you believe it.*

"I can't remember," Lana said.

"Here we are." Hugh had come back with paper cups and an armful of magazines. "You used to read these ones, didn't you?"

he asked Lana. "I looked for *Jackie* magazine, but apparently they don't do that anymore."

"That was stopped in the nineties," Jen said. "I doubt Lana's even heard of it."

"Oh. Well. 'Cute Boy Confessions,' " he deciphered from the cover. "Sounds . . . fun."

The magazine was in plastic and there were various things sliding about inside it: a cat-shaped rubber, some popping candy, and a set of lip balms. Lana ripped the plastic open and unscrewed a lip balm's cap. The scent of artificial strawberries escaped and the chemical smell was the final trigger for Jen's behind-the-eyes headache. She sipped at her coffee and slumped in her seat and watched as Lana retreated behind the garish, hectic pages of the magazine.

"Can I talk to you for a sec?" Hugh hadn't sat down and was beginning to walk backwards out of the ward, narrowly missing an orderly with a dinner trolley.

Jen got up to stop him bumping into something.

"You need to call Meg," he said, lowering his voice as they got into the corridor. "Not now, but tomorrow morning. You need to give her a call. God knows what's got into her. Oh, that seems an unfortunate way to have put it."

"Why?" Jen said, putting her coffee down on a windowsill.

"She says she's pregnant."

"Pregnant. Meg?" She pictured her elder daughter, the tall, brown sensibleness of her, the straight fringe and the neat shoes and the slight, sturdy figure in between. "How?" she said at last. "Or do I mean who? No, I definitely mean how."

"She made some arrangement with her friend Tom," Hugh said. "He donated his sperm."

"Directly?"

"No, and, apparently, I shouldn't have asked that, so make sure *you* don't when you speak to her."

Jen felt rather faint, and wondered if the nurse would object to her getting into one of the beds. "And she's telling us this now?"

"She'd planned to tell us today, after her second scan," Hugh said, "so she thought she'd stick to the schedule."

Which was like Meg; she tended to stand by her decisions, no matter what. Jen and Hugh had often discussed this trait, wondering where she'd got it from, as neither of them was particularly good at keeping up routines or remembering their promises.

"Second scan? When was all this decided?"

Jen asked.

"Months ago. She's twenty weeks gone."

"Good God." Jen joined her coffee cup on the windowsill and leaned against the glass. It was cool on her shoulders, but she didn't trust it not to open suddenly and send her plunging down to join the trapped tree in the courtyard.

"Exactly what I said."

"Trust Meg to be halfway through it all before she includes us."

"Exactly what I thought."

"I'm going to have a grandchild," Jen said, not quite sure what she was feeling.

"We both are."

"I'm going to be a grandmother."

"Oh, for heaven's sake, Jen," Hugh said. "Stop grinning."

SELF-SACRIFICE

She was surprised to hear she was grinning, as that implied an unalloyed joy at the news her daughter was pregnant. And although the prospect of a grandchild *was* joyous, she was frightened by the idea of Meg giving birth. It was an ancient fear, an ancestral, female fear. It was this fear that had caused the eleven-year gap between Meg and Lana.

47

After Meg's birth Jen had decided not to get pregnant again. Not because her labor had been so terrible (it hadn't), but because she felt she'd got through it unscathed by sheer luck, and that her luck wouldn't hold for another baby.

On the maternity ward in the days after, she'd watched the other women, watched them wincing as they shifted in their chairs, or hobbled to the bathroom. They'd looked so shattered, so bruised, while their husbands had spring-stepped about, showing the babies to their relatives, rosily pleased. It was disturbing to Jen that one half of each couple had become a sort of sacrifice, and she didn't want to be a sacrifice. She didn't want Meg to be one, either. She wished Meg's girlfriend was carrying the baby.

SELF-SUFFICIENT

Lana, then, was an accident. And Meg had known it. She'd given them a pitying look when Jen and Hugh had told her she was going to have a younger sibling, as if they'd demonstrated that they couldn't manage some simple task. This judgment wasn't entirely unfair. Having avoided getting pregnant for ten years, Jen had started to believe conceiving was beyond her, the conscientiousness with which she took contraceptives had dwindled, she and Hugh had grown complacent.

So perhaps it was this proof of their irresponsibility that made Meg decide to cook for herself. Two weeks after Lana's birth a tired but not terribly sore Jen (her luck had held for this second birth and she'd come through it unscathed again) found Meg in the kitchen at six o'clock, waiting while a bowl of baked beans rotated in the microwave.

"You should have told me if you were hungry," Jen said.

"Why?"

"So I could make you something to eat."

"But *I'm* making me something to eat."

"I know. But . . ." *But you're eleven,* Jen wanted to say. She watched as Meg fished two slices of toast from the toaster and buttered them and poured the heated beans on top and sat down at the table, laying her cutlery on a piece of folded kitchen towel. A bunch of Michaelmas daisies had been put in a vase and arranged near her plate. Jen was about to remark on it when the baby began to cry and she went to feed her, and by the time she came back everything was stacked neatly in the dishwasher, the vase carried upstairs to sit on Meg's desk.

Hugh had thought it sweet, said she obviously wanted to be helpful, to be responsible, now there was a new baby in the house, and Jen had tried to be as lighthearted as he was about this show of independence, this pulling away.

The next day at six o'clock Meg was grating cheese for a baked potato, and the day after that she was washing mushrooms, which she drizzled with oil and sprinkled with crushed garlic and slid into the oven.

"Careful," Jen said over the roar of the fan.

"Don't worry, Mummy," Meg told her. "I'm quite capable."

Unlike you, was the subtext, Jen felt. Each evening the meals-for-one seemed to get more elaborate. An omelette dotted with green peppers and feta, a salad covered with homemade herb dressing, a pile of toasted pita bread, served with cucumber-and-yogurt dip.

"Don't you like my cooking anymore?" Jen asked finally. "Are you worried I won't have time to make you something you want?"

"Have you become a vegetarian?" Hugh joined in.

"No, I just thought this was best," Meg replied. "This way, you won't have to worry about me."

"But we're still your mummy and daddy. We're still here to look after you."

"Okay." Meg didn't seem convinced. She folded her paper napkin and sat down to eat, alone.

In the weeks that followed Meg seemed to be busily arranging her life in order to get out of her parents' way. She joined a home-work club, which meant she never asked them for help anymore, she passed a cycling-proficiency test and found a group of other children to bike to school with, she spent her pocket money on licorice tooth-paste, pomegranate molasses, and a tiny appointments diary.

Then, one Saturday morning, Jen discov-ered her loading the washing machine. "Did you have an accident? Overnight?"

Meg dropped the handles of the washing basket. "Of course not. My hamper was full, that's all."

"I've got a bit behind," Jen said, trying to take over the task. "I'm sorry."

"That's okay." Meg gently pushed her away. "I can do this, Mummy. I know how it works."

And so Meg began to do her own wash-ing. And Jen noticed that a bottle of fabric softener appeared next to the machine, and the unfamiliar smell of gardenias drifted about the house, and Meg nearly always wore matching socks.

BUTTERFLIES

Jen found she was wearing odd socks as she slipped into the camp bed that the nurse had made up next to Lana's. She was glad to lie down, but wasn't planning to sleep; she hardly even closed her eyes, feeling sure that, if she did, her daughter would sneak away again and they would have to restart the cycle: the shock and despair, the hope and searching, the suspicion and relief.

Something made a shadow on the wall above her head, two long, thin shapes, crossing again and again. Tree branches outside the window, or knitting needles, perhaps. But the knitting woman had left while Jen was in the bathroom getting ready for bed. She mentioned her absence to Lana, who said she hadn't noticed her earlier, and Jen began to wonder if she really had been mythical, if the sleep deprivation had made her hallucinate. How infinitely depressing, she thought, if the best her imagination could do was conjure a belligerent, gray-haired woman armed with knitting needles and a knowing manner.

The pull-out bed wasn't particularly comfortable. It was plastic-creaky, low, and short, and there was a dim blue light which blinked in the ceiling and appeared to be mysteriously linked to a constant beeping somewhere along the corridor, but lying awake in the dark next to her daughter was bliss.

"You're not going to ask me questions all night, are you?" Lana asked, and Jen promised to be quiet. Knowing she could put out a hand and find the warmth of an arm or shoulder or back was enough.

Anything was better than the last few nights, the hours after the searches had been stopped for lack of light, when she and Hugh could only wait for morning, for sunrise, for another chance to discover a clue, a trail, a lead, their hope perpetually diminishing.

"Are you awake?" Lana whispered now. "Can I? Can I have your hand?"

Jen put it up, waving it into the shadowy space above her, and felt a jittery, internal flutter as Lana caught it in her own. "Is it the storm?" Jen asked. The knitting woman had been right: there had been a crash of thunder just after Hugh left for the hotel.

"No. It turns out I'm not so keen on the dark. Weird, huh?"

53

"Do you think that's something to do with where you were?" Jen said. "Sorry, I didn't mean to ask."

"It's okay. The answer's still the same, anyway."

"I don't remember?"

"Right."

After a few minutes Jen's hand began to go numb, held above her body like that, her fingers chilly in the warm and unchanging temperature of the ward. She sat up and gave Lana her other hand, though it meant she wouldn't be able to lie down again. There was a tap-tapping in the corner of the room and when she turned her head she thought she saw the hunched shape of the knitting woman lit up by a flash of lightning, but there was no one there, and the tapping was just a regular drip from a gutter outside the window.

Lack of sleep had made her see things before. During a week of very late nights and early mornings in her last year at art college, a face had appeared in the Celtic-motifed curtains, a very definite, three-dimensional, moving and looming face, which might have distracted her if she hadn't had an immovable and looming deadline to focus on instead. Once her project had been handed in, she'd fallen into bed and slept for fifteen hours, and the face had never come back.

Years later, when her father was dying, she'd had a late-night telephone conversation with one of her brothers, who'd afterwards sworn he hadn't spoken to her and, sure enough, when she checked, there was no record of the call, though she could have given an almost verbatim account of it. And then there was the man she'd met on the train when she was a sleep-deprived mother and Lana was a baby, a man she always called Rumpelstiltskin in her head. She was certain sometimes that she'd conjured him from thin air.

There was a rumble of thunder, soft through the hospital's insulating walls and double-glazed windows.

"Just after I found you were gone," Jen said, "when I definitely knew you weren't in the loo, and hadn't gone skinny-dipping with that boy, I thought I saw you."

"Yeah?" Lana said.

"Yeah. I thought I saw you on the top of a hill, looking back down at everyone, watching us begin the search. It can't have been you and, if it had, I wouldn't have been able to tell where you were looking, but it gave me a fright."

"A fright? Why?"

"I felt like you were saying goodbye." Jen's back was aching now so she switched hands again and turned to lean against Lana's bed. "I felt like it was a message."

There was a long silence, and Jen thought Lana might have fallen asleep.

"What made you think that? What made you think it was me?" Lana asked finally.

"I just knew it was," Jen said, reliving briefly the ominous feeling the vision had given her. She had been able to see Lana's facial expression, too, though, obviously, it would have been impossible over that distance, and she'd had the sense that Lana could hear her as she spoke to Hugh.

"Which hill was it?" Lana said.

"The one where we painted the butterflies that first evening." Jen turned to peer at the half-lit planes of Lana's face. "Was it you, then?" she asked. "Up there?"

"Of course not." Jen heard her take a breath in and hold it. "I love you, Mum," she said in a rush as she released the breath, and Jen thought perhaps she'd fallen asleep and was dreaming.

Lana's hand was rough in hers — the chipped nails, the scabbing blisters on the palms — and Jen felt again some echo of her daughter's pain run through her own limbs. This pain was meaningful. It meant she should try to guess at, to imagine, what Lana had been through. It meant she should avoid guessing or imagining. It meant something terrible had been done to Lana. It meant she had done something terrible to herself. It meant she was telling Jen everything she could. It meant she was hiding something. It meant too many things.

She stopped trying to determine the meaning and remembered painting on top of the hill. It was a vivid memory because she had carefully studied the view, and drawn the view, and painted the view, and she'd noticed so many details, the orange-tip butterfly on a purple rhododendron flower, and the beetles crawling through the clover, and the silvery undersides of the whitebeam leaves. It was vivid, too, because of the notes they were encouraged to write along the edges of their sketches. *Cool breeze, the excited whistling of curlews, smell of cut grass, the ground spongy under my feet.* These had been Jen's notes. But Lana had written: *I've got a headache.*

The police had gone through the sketch-books and drawn Jen's attention to the sentence, wanting to know what Lana had meant. But the only annotations Jen had been aware of were the crude sad faces that Lana had drawn over the top of the pictures she thought were unsuccessful, before she tore them out and crumpled them up.

"You liked the holiday, didn't you?" Jen asked now. "You didn't find it too frustrating? Or stressful? Or like school?"

"It was great," Lana said, but she didn't sound completely sincere.

Jen pictured Lana's fingers, which seemed unfamiliar now they weren't a child's fingers, now they were slender and lifeless rather than chubby and eager. She saw them drawing a sad face and crushing the paper into the shape of a giant sweet wrapper. And then. And then? Nothing, no disposal. The paper just vanished from her mind, and she couldn't see it being slipped into a pocket or scattered on the wind.

"What did you do with the pages you ripped out of your sketchbook?" Jen said, knowing she shouldn't be asking. "The police wanted to know where you'd thrown them. They weren't in the bin in the studio or in our room."

Lana struggled up, her body curling from the mattress. "You're still annoyed about me ripping up my sketches?" she said, sounding almost amused. "I'm sorry I tore them up. Okay?"

"I'm not annoyed. I just wondered where they'd gone to."

"Hoping to rescue them?"

"Well, it would have been nice to look back over them. They might even have jogged your memory."

Lana's scarred hand tightened on hers. "They might have," she said, "but it's too late now. They're long gone."

Idea for a detective novel

One day, when she had time, Jen was going to write a novel. A crime novel, she thought, with a female detective, a female detective who was also an artist. And one of the clues would be in a sketchbook. In the last chapter, it would turn out that the name of the murderer was written on one of the sketchbook pages in clear wax, and this name would become visible only when a deep blue watercolor wash was painted over the paper with a soft, wide brush.

Jen didn't tell anyone her idea for fear it would be stolen.

Right to reply

There were other things to write in the meantime. Starting with replies to the dozens of messages from friends and relatives. Every time she looked at her phone, though, Jen felt writing a novel would be easier. Because, what was she supposed to say? She couldn't explain the events of the last week. She didn't know where Lana had been. She was unable to say how her daughter was doing, or even how she, Jen, was feeling now. She didn't need them to do any cooking or cleaning. She had no suggestions of other ways they could help. And the last thing she wanted was a long telephone conversation, or an inquisitive visitor, or an obligation to go out for coffee.

"Just send them all the same reply," Hugh said, seeing Jen panic as yet another notification lit her phone screen. "I'll even write it for you."

Hi. All fine now. Thanks ever so. See you soon. X

"That's a bit breezy, don't you think?" Jen said. "A bit short, a bit off hand."

"Okay." Hugh took the mobile back and typed again.

To whom it may have concerned. Lana is now safe and well. Thank you for your message(s) of support, it is/they are much appreciated. However, we do not need to be mucked out or catered for. I am unable to give you an answer to your questions at this time but hope to satisfy your curiosity at some point in the future. Kind regards, Jen.

"Mucked out? Hope to satisfy your curiosity? Are you trying to lose us all our friends?"

Hugh grinned. "Too stiff that time? Too pointed? Fine, I'll try again."

"Thanks." Jen handed over the phone. "I did enjoy *To whom it may have concerned,* though."

Hello. Lana's recovering and we're going home today. We don't really know what happened yet. Thanks so much for your kind offer, but we just need some family time to sort everything out. Hope to catch up properly in a few weeks. Lots of love.

RUMPELSTILTSKIN

Many messages of support had arrived when Jen was a new mother, scribbled in cards and left on the answering machine. People offering congratulations and sympathy and help, and studiously avoiding giving advice. She hadn't known how to answer them then. Unless someone could magically make her baby stop crying, there was nothing she wanted. And hardly anything stopped the baby crying.

Except trains. She had got into the habit of taking Meg for short journeys to settle her. A car might have worked, too, but they didn't have a car in those days, couldn't afford one, so getting on the suburban line and traveling a few stops out and a few stops back had been the next best thing. And when Lana was born, Jen had done the same again, even though Hugh had bought a car by then. It was tradition, she said, it was a charm.

One night, when Lana was only a few days old and had been crying for a long time, Jen got on a train to Strawberry Hill. It was one of the old rolling stock, the type the railway companies were always promising to withdraw: freezing in the winter except just by the heater, where, if a passenger put a foot too close, the rubber of their shoes would melt. There was a breeze coming from every direction, from the rattling windows, from the open door at the end of the carriage, and her ears had begun to ache from the noise of the train.

But Lana was finally asleep, though she wasn't Lana yet; they hadn't yet been to register her birth and, in fact, Jen had provisionally named her Milly. She was a warm little lump in her arms. Two solid hours of crying had made her go purple, but she was nearly the right color again and Jen just had to be careful she didn't fall asleep herself.

It was twilight and, from the window, she could see hundreds of birds flitting in and out of trees beyond the tracks, making their way back to roosts and perches — part of a kind of feathered rush hour. Lights glowed mysteriously in a patch of woodland as the night got darker, and then there was nothing to see at all and she found she was staring at the inside of the carriage in reverse.

The train was nearly empty, but there were two heads visible above the seat backs. Jen couldn't tell if they were men or women. A smell of beer drifted along and she wondered in that anxious, distracted way of tired mothers if a baby could be harmed by the smell of alcohol in the way it might be harmed by cigarette smoke. She decided probably not and closed her eyes for a minute, pinching her hand in the zip pocket of her jacket so she couldn't drift off. When she opened them again there was a man opposite her.

She hadn't heard him sit down and thought she might have fallen asleep for a few minutes, that the train might even have stopped at a station. The man had thick, wild hair, and he held his long, pale hands between his thighs, making the shape of a V. His head was half turned away, looking towards the window, but Jen could see, clearly, that his eyes, reflected in the glass, were fixed on Milly.

Turning her daughter, she put her over her shoulder so her tiny face was away from the man. She was annoyed because she risked waking her to do it, but she wanted a better grip on her little body, wanted to be able to hug her closer. The man followed Jen's movements in the window's glass, and his teeth, the lower set, jutted forward to bite his top lip. Suddenly there was fear in the cold breeze and the heated air and the rattle of the windows.

She realized then that she *must* have slept, that the train *must* have stopped at a station, because when she looked over, casually-casually, she saw the other heads behind the seat backs had gone. She was alone with the man and her baby. The guard was nowhere in sight and she hadn't got round to buying a mobile yet (had only recently been convinced that it would be useful).

"What's her name?" the man said, pointing at Milly.

Jen told him she and her husband hadn't quite decided, but Milly was probably what they were going for. She told him it was a family name. She told him her great-grandmother had been called Amelia. And then recited the names of all the other members of her family tree, or all the ones she knew. She told him the other names she'd come up with for her daughter. She told him her husband was getting impatient at her inability to decide. She talked and talked and thought she could humanize them both by talking (there was a lot of stuff on the radio about that sort of thing then).

"Milly," the man said. "Milly, Milly, Milly."

He kept repeating the name, and Jen wished she hadn't said anything. She could never call her Milly now, she thought, because she'd heard him pronounce it in his peculiar, scratchy voice. A voice that was like a stranger running his fingers through her hair.

"No. You should call her Lana," he said at last. "Lana."

Jen quite liked the name and told him so, trying to placate him.

"Promise me, then," he said. "Promise me you'll call her Lana."

He seemed deadly serious and gave Jen such an intense look, such a frightening stare, that she promised. Then he got up and went away. Just walked down the carriage, never to be seen again. And it was odd, but Jen felt they'd made some kind of bargain, she and this man: her baby's name for his absence. So she stuck to her promise, though she never told Hugh why she'd changed her mind about Milly or why she was so definite about Lana.

Q&A

They'd all seen police stations on the television and, after Lana was discharged from the hospital, they were able to judge which programs were the most accurate. The interview room had a sofa and a coffee table and, although it wasn't exactly luxurious, it wasn't the gray, intimidating interrogation room Jen had been expecting. They were offered drinks and given biscuits, the door was left open, and everyone could choose the seat they wanted. Jen and Hugh sat on either side of Lana, like some middle-aged, out-of-shape henchmen, but luckily, no protection was needed, and the detective, a woman with a very lean face, wasn't unsympathetic.

"Are you okay to talk to us?" she asked, and Lana nodded. "Can you tell us what's been going on in your life recently?"

Lana seemed surprised at the vagueness, the casualness, of the question and Jen wondered whether she'd been expecting more of a battle and, if so, what she would have fought to hide.

"Just normal stuff," Lana said. "School and . . ." She shrugged.

"You were in the Peak District on holiday? What were you doing?"

"Yeah. We were, like, painting and drawing. It was good, actually. Our tutor took us on walks and made us try different techniques, like putting food dye in water, and using wax resist, and cutting our own reed pens."

"You were enjoying the holiday?"

Lana nodded.

"That's good. Did you like the other people?"

Lana nodded again.

"Can you tell me about them?"

"They were mostly really old."

The detective smiled. "Like over forty or something, huh?"

"Forty's not old," Lana said. "Is age something that worries you?" She sounded just like her therapist, and the tone made Jen feel uneasy. It was unnatural in the voice of a fifteen-year-old and it gave away Jen's failure as a mother, someone who'd had to fall back on professionals. The whole situation reminded her painfully of sessions in Dr. Greenbaum's office, waiting for Lana to

67

explain why she wanted to hurt herself.

"You think I'm patronizing you. I'm sorry," the detective said. "Answer this for me: have you seen anyone away from the group?"

"Like, anyone on the holiday? The people from the holiday?"

"From the holiday or anyone else. Anyone special?"

Lana shook her head and looked at Jen, who took a ginger biscuit and tried unsuccessfully to nibble at it quietly. It was sweet but not very spicy and she immediately wished she hadn't been tempted.

"What about Matthew?" the detective asked Lana. "You had a friendship with him, is that right?"

"Did my mum tell you that?"

Jen stopped nibbling for a moment.

"She didn't, but Matthew was also missing for a few hours on the Friday morning when your disappearance was discovered, so I have to ask you about him."

"Oh," Lana said. "Okay."

"Was he with you at all during the time you say you were lost?"

"Did he say we were together?" She sounded outraged, as if her reputation might be at stake.

"I want to hear what you say happened."

"He wasn't with me."

"But you would say you were friends?"

"Not really."

"He thinks you are."

"He's a bit lame," Lana said. "I mean, he's sweet, but he likes bird-watching and stuff. I only hung out with him to be nice."

"He had some pages from your sketch-books in his room. Did you give them to him?"

Lana winced then looked at Jen. "Not exactly," she said. "I left them between some rocks."

"Did you leave them for him to take? Or for someone else?"

"I didn't leave them for anyone, really," Lana said. "Or, I guess I left them for the countryside, for Mother Nature."

"But there were notes to Matthew on the pages." The detective looked down at her own notes and read out loud. *"Of course I like you. I can't sneak away. Okay. After dinner. Where are the eco toilets?* Did you write these?"

"Yeah."

"And you were addressing Matthew?"

Lana shrugged and nodded.

"So you did spend time with him, then? Alone?"

"Yeah, if you don't count the badgers."

"Has he hurt or threatened you?"

"Matthew?" Lana smiled. "No."

"Has anyone threatened you, Lana?"

"No."

"Has anyone told you to keep quiet?"

"No."

"Have you had contact with anyone? Have you made any plans to meet anyone other than Matthew?"

"No. No, I haven't, I didn't."

"Can you tell us where you've been?"

"Not really. I got" — she took a breath — "I got lost."

"Mr. Crossley — that's the farmer who found you — he said he thought you'd come from the woods. Is that right?"

"I'm not sure," Lana said. "It's a bit of a blur."

Jen had heard this all before, and wasn't sure whether it was a good sign or a bad sign that Lana was using nearly the same words. She had an idea that people who told the truth used more varied vocabulary. She put her half-eaten biscuit back on the coffee table.

"Okay. How did you get lost? Can you remember that?" the detective asked.

"Not really. I was sleepy," Lana said. "I went to the shower block because I'd left my wash bag and I wanted some lip balm. I thought I'd taken the path back to our room, but I guess I hadn't . . ." She stretched her hands out.

"Did you find the wash bag?"

"Huh?"

"The wash bag. Was it in the shower block?"

Lana was still a moment. Had she been caught out or was she trying to remember?

"I don't think it was there. I think it must have been in our room after all."

The wash bag *had* been in their room, inside Lana's suitcase. Jen didn't know if that made her story more believable.

"So you went to the shower block," the detective repeated, "and the bag wasn't there. What happened next?"

"I took the wrong path," Lana said. There was a faintly biblical quality to the sentence, which made Jen uneasy.

"Which way did you go? Left, right, straight on?"

"I can't remember. It was dark, I'm not good with directions. I just walked the way I thought and then, when I realized I'd gone the wrong way, I tried to walk back again, but I only got more lost."

"Okay." The detective wrote something down. She held her pen very loosely and had beautifully slanted writing. There was a pause while she reread what she'd written, and Jen felt Lana sit up ever so slightly.

"And did you see anyone before Mr. Crossley found you?"

"I don't think so."

"Have a think about it. We'd like you to try and be sure. There were lots of people out searching for you. You didn't see anyone? Hear anyone?" She left another long gap, but this time she looked at Lana during the silence.

The stare was determined, focused, and Lana cleared her throat and shuffled her feet, obviously uncomfortable. Shifting in her seat, she began to turn her head and then stopped herself, as if she weren't sure that her parents were allies any longer. Jen dropped her bag, trying to distract the detective's gaze for a moment, though it seemed a faintly ridiculous and theatrical thing to do and neither the detective nor Lana seemed to notice.

"Can you tell me how you got the laceration on your head?" the detective asked, after it became clear Lana couldn't remember seeing anyone.

Lana put her fingers up to her head and touched the stitches. "I think I fell."

"Was anyone with you at that point?"

"No."

"Where did you fall, Lana?"

She shrugged. "Near some rocks?"

"Can you describe the rocks?"

"Big. Gray. Rocky."

"You can't tell me anything else about them?"

"No."

"Okay. You're doing really well, Lana. Just a few more questions, all right? The doctor noticed some marks around your ankles when you got to the hospital. Can you tell me what they were from?"

"My socks."

"You're sure about that? You haven't had anything tied around your ankles at any stage? Somebody else hasn't tied anything around your ankles?"

"No. My socks were tight."

A nod and a note. "Your clothes were very wet. How did they get wet?"

"From the rain?"

The detective tapped her pen against her lips. "I don't think that can be it, Lana," she said, "because it hasn't rained heavily since the day you went missing."

"Then I'm not sure."

"Are you telling me you can't remember?"

"I suppose I am."

"Okay." She wrote something else down. "Did you take your mobile phone with you when you went to the shower block?"

"Yes."

"And did you keep it on or switch it off?"

"I kept it on. Oh, but I might have switched it off for a bit to save the battery."

"You didn't switch it off so that your whereabouts couldn't be traced?"

"No."

"And you don't have it now?"

"No, I lost it."

"Do you know where you lost it?"

"No."

"We haven't been able to find it yet, but if you could tell us where to look, perhaps we could recover it for you."

"I don't know where to look."

"All right. What were you wearing when you got lost?"

"Leggings, a fleece, a jacket."

"What else?"

"Socks, shoes."

"What else?"

"Underwear."

"Is that everything? What about a T-shirt?"

"I . . . er . . . I didn't put one on when I got up."

"What T-shirts did you have with you on holiday? Can you remember what you packed?"

"Not really."

74

"Why does that matter?" Hugh said, breaking his promise not to interject.

The detective didn't seem annoyed. "Lana wasn't wearing a T-shirt when she was taken into hospital, and a ripped T-shirt has been discovered not far from where Lana was found."

"It's not mine," Lana said.

Jen nearly asked to be shown the T-shirt, to be given the chance to identify it, but she didn't want to ask in front of Lana, to imply that she didn't trust her word. And anyway, she wasn't sure she'd recognize the T-shirt, or be certain it was Lana's. The police had been noticeably disappointed by her vague memory of Lana's clothes when they'd asked for a description during the search.

The interview went on. They talked about Stephen, and about Peny, they talked about Matthew again (Lana rolled her eyes). They talked about Lana's school and her friends and her social-media accounts, they talked about the dangers of meeting strangers on the internet (Lana rolled her eyes). They talked about her therapist and her therapy sessions and the "dark thoughts" which had led her to cut herself in the past (Lana rolled her eyes).

"How were you feeling the night you got lost?" the detective kept asking. "How were you feeling *within* yourself?"

Lana's answers got shorter and shorter. "I was pretty happy, from what I can remember," she said. "Fine. I was fine."

It was lunchtime when Lana was eventually released into Jen's custody.

"Mine?" Jen said, caught between anxiety at the responsibility and gratification at the official allocation of power. "My custody?"

But custody wasn't quite what she thought it would be. After silently swearing not to let Lana out of her sight, it turned out she just had to make sure she was available if there were any more questions in the next couple of weeks. And then they were in the car and the car was on the motorway and it was all behind them.

PRETENSE

Lana feigned sleep all the way to London: Jen knew she was feigning because she'd seen her sleep, the corners of her mouth wet, her arms twisted around each other, her legs splayed. She knew this neat, dry sleeper in the back seat of the car was a fiction.

CREASES

Lana's damp, heavy head left sharp creases on her pillow, and sometimes the lines would be visible on her cheeks at breakfast. Jen had worried about them when Lana was small — they seemed slightly sinister, pinkish marks made by a nightmare, or a creature from a nightmare — and she'd got into the habit of smoothing the pillowcases and tucking the ends down tightly before Lana went to bed. It had never been any use; the lines had always appeared again by the morning.

Since she had stopped putting her daughter to bed, she had stopped smoothing the pillow but, at the holiday center, where they shared a room, Jen had begun to run her hands over the cotton covers, to pull at the corners and press the fabric flat. And sometimes, in the middle of the night, she had tugged at the material again, easing the creases out from under Lana's sleeping face. On the last night, though, there had been no sleeping face there.

She hadn't thought to check the time, but had waited, half dozing, expecting Lana to creep back in after having a wee, to disturb the drowsy, musty air, to whisper the sheets over her shoulders, to squeak the mattress springs as she curled towards sleep. At first Jen slipped towards sleep herself, but then the cold of the night began to seep into the room and Lana still wasn't back, and the light of dawn glowed above the curtains and finally Jen sat up and shivered. None of the guests had been able to get a signal on their phones since they arrived, but she tapped the buttons anyway, listening to the low Call Failed triple beep again and again.

Feeling disorientated, scooped out, she had put on clothes, checked the loos, and then gone to the shower block. It was called the shower block but was mostly full of deep baths which seemed like they'd come from a thirties boarding house, and little wicker stools that creaked all the time, even when no one was touching them. The cubicles were almost romantic. Ivy grew against the high windows, and someone's rose-scented talcum powder had been spilt over the floor. But there was no Lana.

Jen had a sensation of clutching at nothing, though her hands didn't move, and she walked around the series of outbuildings, her steps weighty in the thin morning air. It was too early to believe it yet, but she believed it anyway. Lana was gone.

By the time anyone else was up, she was terrified, she was crying, and she was certain. The center manager called the police and the staff rechecked every building, went around the grounds, took the footpaths towards the moor, up the hill, through the wood.

Jen called Hugh while the police went through Lana's belongings. They found her phone was missing but her clothes were still there, except whatever she was wearing. Leggings, Jen guessed, and a white fleece jacket.

"You're sure she went to bed?" a policeman in an expensive-looking waterproof asked. "And you didn't hear her get up?"

Jen answered yes and no and began to feel she was lying. They asked about Lana's depression, whether she had ever attempted suicide. "Not exactly," Jen said, "but she's run off in the past, and she's hoarded pills in the past, and she's cut herself in the past." She hoped it *was* all in the past.

The policeman rang Hugh in London. Jen heard him explain that their daughter was officially missing, that the police were doing everything they could, that someone had to remain at home in case Lana turned up, and that some officers would be around to search her room.

"Do you know if she kept a diary?" he asked.

And who were her closest friends? And which school did she go to? And what was the name of her head teacher? Her therapist? Her GP? A request was put in to check her text messages and emails, a trace was put on her phone, but it was already undiscoverable. The CCTV at the bus and train station was checked. And, meanwhile, they started to search the surrounding countryside.

Staff and holidaymakers volunteered and the police began to interview people in the center manager's office. Stephen came out talking about trusting in God, a phrase which seemed to make the police suspicious, and for a few hours it seemed the boy, Matthew, was missing, too. But he turned up suddenly, standing still amid the activity, asking what was going on, asking if they were really sure Lana wasn't there.

The police took him into the office straightaway and, according to his father, they were quite hard on him.

"Matthew wishes he *did* know where she was," he said, hugging his son to his side, "but he hasn't seen her since yesterday and she said nothing to him."

There were some scrapes on his hands and knees and a bruise on his elbow which the police wanted explained, and he said he'd been for a long walk, hoping to see, or at least hear, a bittern or, failing that, a chiffchaff. To Jen, these words seemed to be made up, a fantasy, until one of her fellow painters quietly reminded her that bitterns and chiffchaffs were types of birds.

"Have you, have you tried calling her phone?" Matthew asked. "Where are they searching? Which direction?"

His questions, the naïveté of them (as if she wouldn't have thought to try Lana's mobile), and the way he leaned into his father as the wind caught his hair made Jen feel violent towards him. She walked away to call Hugh again. The police had been to their house in London but hadn't found anything useful, and he had asked Meg to come and stay so he could join Jen in the Peak District.

Everyone was doing something, had a role, a task, but Jen couldn't decide what she should do. She hadn't the focus to go out on the search, and her vision seemed to be marred by a great, dark shape that pushed all the color of the world into her peripheral vision. And she couldn't call Lana's name, knowing where it had come from; a kind of superstition stopped her, even made her imagine that the man on the train had somehow discovered them and returned to claim her daughter. A pain in her stomach made her want to sit doubled up, and Peny made her eat some toast, in case it was hunger.

There was something gleeful in the way each person bustled about and spoke to one another; they'd been given a purpose and were enjoying it. Jen could almost believe they'd conspired to make this happen. She began to interpret their words of sympathy, their certainty that Lana would be all right, as proof that they knew where she was. When Stephen came over to lead her in prayer, Jen got up and went back to her room. Their room.

She realized she hadn't looked in the mirror all day, and seeing herself was a bit of a shock. It wasn't her appearance which took her aback (though on any other day she would have lamented the grayness of her skin, the depth of the lines, the dark circles under her eyes), it was the familiarity, as if she had never expected to see any face she recognized again. She turned away and stared at the creases on Lana's pillow instead, studying the way the pale daylight caught the different facets of the crumpled cotton, and she wondered where her daughter's head might be resting now.

THINGS WILL LOOK BETTER
IN THE MORNING

Night fell and the searchers called it a day, even though Lana hadn't been found. When Hugh arrived, he was white and drawn, his voice deeper than usual, and Jen was sure he'd had a cry in the car. But he was still full of reassurances, and she appreciated it in him, though it would have made her angry coming from anyone else. When he said, "Things will look better in the morning," she believed him and didn't feel like strangling anyone. It was a relief, not wanting to strangle someone.

They booked into a hotel rather than stay on in the holiday center, and lay fully clothed on the bed. And although she didn't sleep, somehow, in the turmoil of those hours her brain made a little bit of space for a different time, for a memory of the night, thirty years ago, when she'd tried to sleep in her car.

She had been on her way back from visiting an art-college friend in Scotland and, convinced that her boyfriend was cheating on her with his copywriter, she'd decided to drive home overnight and catch him, or them, early in the morning. It had seemed like a good plan, an exciting plan, when she'd set out, but after four hours squinting against the headlights of oncoming traffic her eyes had dimmed, and stung, until pulling over had been the only option.

By then, there was nowhere to pull over except the car park of an abandoned service station, deserted except for a few rusting cars. As soon as she'd turned off the engine, the cold had materialized, as if it had been lurking in the back seat and waiting to ambush her. That whole night had been about waiting. Waiting for sleep, waiting for the energy to drive again, waiting for a knock at the window or a lunatic to break into the car, waiting until the sun rose and she could feel a bit safer.

Sleep never really came. The car was a thin tin box with a juddering window which let the night air whistle through. Even with a coat, two jumpers, and the emergency blanket her mother made her keep in the boot, she'd felt frozen, her muscles cramping and forcing her to move, her teeth chattering unless she tensed hard. But having her eyes closed for a bit had seemed important, and then suddenly it was dawn, and the tarmac was shining gold and the rust on the wrecks of cars seemed to suck all the sunlight in. Those dark, reddish streaks looked warm and she got out of her own car to lay a hand on the rough patches of metal, feeling like she was soothing some sick, gargantuan animal.

She didn't make it home until midmorning, by which time her boyfriend had left for work, and his flat looked the same as ever. She never discovered if he'd been cheating. Somehow, it hadn't mattered by then, anyway.

And when people said things would look better in the morning, Jen always thought of the rust sparkling, the dark pink heads of some tarmac-rooted weeds standing perfectly still in the windless dawn, the white flash of a seagull catching the sun as it swooped low.

Lying on the bed next to Hugh, the gold of that morning lingered under her eyelids, a liquid film: hope. She'd had to be careful not to cry it away.

The dust settles

When Jen and Hugh and Lana got home, to their once-suburban street, now classed as inner-city London, Meg was waiting for them, and the fruit bowl had been filled with red apples. Meg was twenty-six and a genius at tableaux. Her own flat on the other side of the city was full of little collections of things sitting together: a Victorian stoneware bottle might rest next to two pebbles from a Sussex beach; an antique children's book bound in yellow fabric would bear a mother-of-pearl-handled spoon; or a delicate dining chair draped with a silk shawl might support a wide, flat candleholder and a long, tapering candle. They were like subjects for a still-life painting, quiet and interesting, and they changed the whole atmosphere of a room.

Jen had tried arranging her own collections, carefully choosing and stacking the things, but when she came back to them later they always looked wrong, like a pile of junk she'd tossed aside, and she would be forced to dismantle the display, sending the elements back into obscurity.

Meg's mouth moved now without sound, twitching into the shape of a word before the lips pulled flat again and she stood, rubbing her lower back, while Hugh and Jen brought their suitcases in. Jen was too exhausted to smile but patted her as she struggled past and nodded at the offer of tea.

Lana didn't want tea but did want a hot-water bottle (which meant using all the water in the kettle), and she wasn't interested in being welcomed home, but she did need a light bulb (which meant searching the house for one of the right size and wattage).

"We can sort that tomorrow," Jen said, unprepared for rooting through kitchen drawers. "Aren't you going to tell Meg congratulations?"

"No, we can't sort it tomorrow. My desk lamp's not working and I need it," Lana said. "Oh, right. Yeah, sis. Well done for getting knocked up."

"Thanks," Meg said. "I didn't get *knocked up,* though, I had donor insemination and it was carefully planned."

"Gross."

"How is that gross?"

"*Donor insemination?* Sounds gross."

"Here's a light bulb," Hugh said, fishing one out of a box under the sink and stopping the brewing argument.

Lana took it and went straight up to her room, which Meg had neatened, and freshened with clean sheets, and brightened with a stack of art books and a vase of Fairtrade Kenyan sunflowers.

"That was sweet of you," Jen said, sitting at the kitchen table, her chest pressed against the edge, her head nearly resting on the surface. The scrubbed wood smelled faintly of onions. "She'll appreciate it when she's had some time to settle in."

"If you say so."

"You're not showing yet," Jen said.

"Not through my clothes." Meg pulled at the long, chunky-knit jumper she was wearing.

"I just realized I haven't said congratulations, either. So, congratulations."

"Don't say it like that."

"Like what? I'm thrilled, really. I'm just tired."

Hugh, who had been bringing in bags of walking boots and watercolors, and fiddling with the car's parcel shelf and checking the parking permit and discarding his mountain of "driving chocolate" wrappers, stopped to hold his mug of tea.

"You're not showing yet," he told Meg.

"Jesus, are you and Mum the same person?"

Hugh laughed. "Did you just say that?" he asked Jen, not at all annoyed, though *her* immediate, silent reaction had been indignation. Some people, she supposed, didn't have to work so hard at keeping their own identity. "And do you know if it's a boy or a girl?" he said. "When do you find out?"

"It's a girl." Meg nodded to herself, which had always been a sign she was thinking of something to say, or trying *not* to say something. "I'm sorry it's coincided with this. I know it can't seem like good news at the moment."

"We don't see it as bad news," Hugh said.

"But I have thought about it very hard. And so has Tom. And it makes sense to us right now."

"That's great, then," Jen said, sounding less than sincere, even to herself. She took a sip of her tea in case a warmer mouth might induce a warmer tone. "Is Kayla pleased?" she asked.

"Well, not exactly. She does see it as bad news. We've broken up."

"Oh, darling, I'm sorry. That's a pity."

"Yes. Anyway. What happens next?"

"You give birth, I imagine," Hugh said.

"I meant with Lana."

"She needs a rest," Jen said. "We all do."

There was a thud upstairs and then footsteps back and forth across the ceiling. Jen tensed but didn't get up. It seemed unlikely after everything that had happened that it should be Lana up there, and she suddenly felt as if they'd invited some stranger into the house, or some mythical creature, a unicorn or a griffin, which they had no idea how to care for.

"Her school's been in touch," Meg said. "They can send over the work she's missed, and a friend has offered to drop off some revision notes. I hadn't realized her exams were next year."

Jen could imagine how thrilled Lana would be to hear she was still expected to catch up on the last few days' schoolwork. There was another thud from above and a speck of dust floated down from the overhead light to land with precision on the shining skin of one of the apples. (Later, she'd find that all the furniture had been moved and Lana's bed was now up against the window. "So I can always see the sky.")

"I suppose she's under a lot of pressure," Meg said.

"A ridiculous amount." Jen stretched her arms across the table, wiping the speck of dust from the apple with a fingertip and rearranging the pile so that it formed a peak with one perfect fruit on top. "I don't remember it being like this when I was young. The day of the exam was stressful, of course, but the revision part wasn't so all-pervading. You either passed the exam or you didn't, you were clever or you weren't. There wasn't this attempt to contort yourself, your brain, into an unnatural shape."

"Oh, yes, the good old days," Hugh said. "Everything was simpler then."

"All right." Jen was half annoyed. "But, in

some ways, that's true."

"And you certainly wouldn't have had some lesbian carrying a straight man's baby," Meg said, returning the pile of apples to their original arrangement. (Jen had to admit it looked better.) "Disgraceful."

"Okay, I get it. I'll shut up." Jen smiled and let her head drop the last few inches onto the tabletop. "I'm going to sleep now," she said. "Wake me up when I'm a grandma."

THE YOUNGEST PROFESSION

There was little time to rest, though, as Jen was needed back at work on Monday. Her job was, at a passing glance, desirable, even exciting, and she liked being able to tell people she was a graphic designer. In reality, though, she adjusted layouts for newsletters and in-house magazines at a trade association and she was the oldest member of her team by at least twenty years.

"This is a great start for me," one of the newly hired children would say, a Rupert or a Tori. "I see this as a step towards achieving my goals."

Jen had given up engaging them in conversation years ago, at around the time they'd stopped inviting her to the pub ("We assumed you had family commitments"), so now she just smiled and silently hoped they'd end up having to post one of those ads on Facebook offering to design logos for £5.

Over the past few years she had found herself spending more and more time in the Ladies. This was partly down to a new sensitivity to caffeine but, mostly, she was hiding. She wasn't quite sure what she was hiding from, but disaster seemed permanently imminent. Every couple of months the sense of danger would materialize into a sentence which floated above her for a few days. *Too old for this work.* And she would be suddenly sure that they were all of them after her job.

She'd admitted this once to her friend Grace, who'd prescribed cashew nuts for paranoid-personality disorder and told her to try mentoring her colleagues, who probably wanted to benefit from her experience. As they generally knew more about design software, came to each meeting with dozens of ideas, and finished their projects in three-quarters the time it took her to complete hers, Jen doubted it. She was only glad that her boss hated fuss, hated change, and hated stupid haircuts.

PERSPECTIVE

Grace was the only person who hadn't asked Jen where Lana had been, or what had happened, or what she could do to help; she was the only person whose messages hadn't required a response. Instead, she'd just suggested eating a hundred grams of grapes a day and filling copper bowls with water, and had told Jen to sit cross-legged and repeat the phrase "I am going to see my daughter soon." Although Jen didn't follow much of her advice, and didn't have a great deal of faith in it, she did appreciate the suggestions, was pleased that someone had a plan for her. So Grace was the only person she'd messaged back willingly.

She was full of advice and homeopathic remedies and mindfulness techniques and herbal-tea recommendations. She had a tendency to use phrases like "Open yourself to the richness of life," and, "Put yourself in a place of community," and other collections of words which sounded very nice but didn't bear close attention. She was also, Jen thought, almost pathologically calm.

"You think I overreact to everything," Jen said one afternoon, lifting her coffee cup to her mouth and performing the action of drinking, even though she'd finished the liquid and was just letting milk foam fall against her lips.

"No, it's not that."

"Then what?"

Grace pulled at her nose for a moment. "I shut my cat's tail in the door once," she said.

"Oh?"

"It was awful, this crunch, the shriek and hiss of the cat, the way he looked up at me, terrified, as if he couldn't believe I could hurt him like that. It was the worst feeling ever."

"God," Jen said. "I'll bet."

"Now, whenever I think something is awkward or painful, I concentrate on that moment. Nothing compares; everything else seems small."

"Right. So you're saying I need to find a cat . . ."

"No," Grace said, showing the brief grin that was always the reward for teasing her. "I'm saying you need to find some perspective."

A FAMILY OF BRILLIANT CONVERSATIONALISTS

Perspective was hard to come by, but Jen got home on Thursday evening determined to be cheerful, reasonable, communicative.

"I just don't see why you won't talk to anyone, Lana," Meg was saying, as Jen walked in. "Have you done something bad? Something illegal? Did you hurt someone? Are you ashamed?" She had her back to the sitting-room door, but had surely heard her mother come in.

Beyond Meg, Lana sat on the settee, curled up in that way she always curled — twisted, contorted, her limbs wound around each other so she looked quite uncomfortable — and Jen wanted to say, "Wouldn't you be happier sitting straight on? Wouldn't it be easier to take that hand away from your mouth, that foot out from under your thigh?" The sort of questions she suspected Lana expected her to ask and which made her look foolish, old, and no longer lithe, and overly preoccupied by blood clots and varicose veins.

"Are you enjoying all the attention you're getting?" Meg asked. "Is that it? You want to draw out the mystery so that people find you interesting?"

"What mystery?" Lana asked, frowning fixedly at the TV. "I got lost."

"For four days?"

Jen dropped her bag in the hall and hung up her jacket, knowing she should stop

Meg's interrogation but comforted by the idea that someone else was seeking answers.

"You must have been with someone," Meg said. "Did you think he was the love of your life but he turned out to be a loser? Or did you just run away and then get scared and come back?"

"No. I told you, I got lost. How many more times do I have to repeat it?"

"I don't know how many times, Lana. Maybe until it actually sounds believable."

Lana moved suddenly, breaking her pose on the settee. "I knew you'd do this. It's just like last year, with you interrogating me all the time. You're worse than Mum." She put on a high-pitched, nasal voice. "*What's the matter, Lana? Is it boy trouble, Lana? Are you being bullied, Lana? Are you sure you're really depressed, Lana?* If I was going to talk to anyone, it wouldn't be you. Plus, Dr. Greenbaum told you you're not allowed to ask me questions and then say I'm lying when I answer them."

"Well, then, try telling the truth for once."

"Meg," Jen said. "That's enough."

"Fine." Meg stood aside as Jen came into the sitting room. "Your turn."

There was a smell like cat food and Jen wondered what Lana had been eating but, of course, didn't ask. The curtains were open to the bright day, but the densely leafed tree in front of the window made almost everything in the room take on a green hue: the scabbing wounds on Lana's head, the shadows on the underside of her upper arm and in the tight inner bend of the knee, the bruises on her elbows — they were all green, as if she, too, were a tree with patches of moss growing on its trunk.

"Have you been out today?" Jen asked.

She'd gone back to staring at the TV and didn't answer.

"Have you heard from school?"

She said nothing.

Jen began to let herself feel annoyed. There was a lighter color on the edge of the settee cushions where feet had been drawn over the nap again and again until it had worn down. That's what came of curling up in such a ridiculous way, she thought, you ruined your mother's furniture.

The room was chilly because of the wide-open windows, and Jen closed them, and the curtains, too, shutting out the sharp evening air and the distant noise of traffic.

"How was work?" Meg asked, hovering by the door, her face becoming clearer as the green light vanished.

Jen shrugged, putting her bag down.

"When's Dad getting back?"

She shrugged again.

"Great. Well, this has been fun. What a special family, full of brilliant conversationalists."

"Sorry," Jen said. Lana's attitude to questions was evidently infectious. "Let's have a cup of tea."

They went into the kitchen.

"Has she been like that all day?" Jen asked under cover of the boiling kettle.

"Yep. She either ignored me or screamed at me. Especially when I had the audacity to ask her anything, even what she wanted for lunch. She was lying in the garden most of the time. Said she was looking at the clouds."

Jen fished an emergency chocolate bar out of the back of the tea-towel drawer and ate half of it straightaway.

"What's going on? It's been a week since you got home. Dad said he thought she was better."

"He's an optimist."

"I suppose someone's got to be."

"What's that supposed to mean?"

"Don't take offense," Meg said, pinching at her forearm through the sleeve of her cardigan. "That was about me, not you."

"You're not optimistic?"

"Well, it's not likely she would go from

98

problem child to saint overnight, is it?"

Jen crumpled the empty chocolate wrapper in her fist. "She's not a problem child."

"No, you're right," Meg said, with an unpleasant smile. "She's a joy."

All the air in Jen's lungs escaped and left her feeling like a heavy, fleshy lump. She dropped onto a chair. "I'm sorry you had to stay with her today," she said. "I couldn't take any more time off work, and I couldn't leave her alone."

There was a pause while Meg dug her nails through the wool of her sleeve. "I don't care about that," she said. "The gallery can do without me for a day. What I care about is you."

"Me?"

"The way she manipulates you, Mum."

"She isn't manipulating me," Jen said. "What are you doing to your arm?"

Meg stilled. "Nothing."

"You're scratching, aren't you? Show me."

"Mum, can we get back to the point?"

"Show me your arm."

Meg grabbed her sleeve and whipped it up and then down again so that Jen only got a flash of red. The flash was enough. Raw and crêpey, the skin was marked by fingernails.

"That's eczema," Jen said. "I got eczema

99

when I was pregnant. Have you told the doctor?"

"I've got some cream."

"Well, it's not working."

"We were talking about Lana," Meg said, "about the way she affects your mood, the way she has you tiptoeing around her, the way she uses you as a walker."

"She gets tired."

"She *says* she gets tired."

"Lethargy is a symptom of depression."

"It's a symptom of something."

"She's ill, Meg. She isn't doing it on purpose."

Jen sighed. It was true that Lana's lethargy often compelled her to ask for her arm when they were out, when Jen could persuade her to go out. And it was true that Jen sometimes thought it was like being with her elderly mother, except that Lily walked about unaided. Meg had brought this up before, and seemed to think Lana was trying to claim their mother exclusively for herself. It had been mentioned in one of their therapy sessions.

SAFE SPACE

DR. GREENBAUM (*leaning back in a black, armless leather chair, the skin around his eyes crinkling kindly*):

Explain to me how that makes you feel, Margaret — er, Meg — tell me so Lana can hear it. We want you to be honest.

MEG (*straightening the lapels of her jacket*):

She's my mother, too, sometimes I don't think Lana realizes that.

LANA (*suddenly uncrossing her legs and leaning forward*):

I do realize that. I also realize that Meg only says she's gay to get attention.

MEG (*crushing the lapels in her hands*):

That's a totally mad thing to say and, if anyone is after attention, it's Lana. Jesus. People are supposed to have mother issues, not sister issues.

DR. GREENBAUM (*turning to Jen and still, unaccountably, smiling*): And does Mum have anything to share?

THE WOMAN WITH NO NAME

When had she become "Mum"? Jen often wondered.

She didn't mind being "Mum" to her children, of course; that was normal. But from other people — health professionals, especially — it felt wrong, weird, paralyzing.

"Shall we ask *Mum* in now?" Dr. Greenbaum would say as he opened the door. "What about *Mum,* what does she think?" he always asked when they discussed some new plan. And at the end of every session: "Is there anything you want to say to *Mum*?"

Jen smiled in the way she thought "Mum" would smile (closed mouth, lifted shoulders) and pretended not to find it irritating. Perhaps it was less confusing for Lana, though she suspected that her daughter wouldn't be entirely bewildered if someone called her mother Jen instead. Really, she felt it was a punishment. This is what happened if you were such a bad mother that your child wanted to die; one of the things you automatically lost was your identity, your right to an identity. She remembered once telling a nurse that she was interested in painting and the way the nurse frowned and asked what Lana thought of that, whether it was something she could include her daughter in. Hugh was still allowed his weekly piano lessons, but the implication for Jen was clear: if this is just a hobby for you, then it's selfish and you don't deserve to enjoy it.

PRAMFACE

Lana seemed determined not to enjoy anything. She'd slept or watched TV with stern concentration since they'd got home ten days ago, as if it were painful to be in the real, waking world. Hardly moving or eating or talking, she still said she couldn't remember what had happened, that she didn't know how she'd got her wounds, that she wasn't sure where she'd been.

Jen had wondered how to get her out of the house, how to engage her, how to help her participate in family life. She'd offered (normally forbidden) fast-food lunches, suggested visiting an animal adoption center, tried (and failed) to find a film at the cinema that they'd all enjoy. What she would never have guessed would work was a trip to John Lewis. And this was possibly the strangest family outing they'd ever had. Jen felt a little like she'd stepped through the looking glass as she watched Meg and Lana and Hugh wheel various prams around the polished walkways of the department store. She held on to the handle of her chosen pram and attempted to think of something useful to say.

"This one turns very easily."

"But are the wheels too wide?"

"Well . . ." Considering she'd several times got stuck against a clothing rail, she thought perhaps they were.

Lana ran along the Baby Swimwear aisle and Hugh narrowly avoided colliding with her as he swung his pram out from Primary School Uniforms. They hallooed and went on. The shop assistant leaned against the car-seat display and gave them a tight smile.

Meg had turned up on the doorstep that morning, asking for help. Meg, who never asked for help. She had bitten her lip and bounced on her toes and wondered aloud if they were free, and Jen had had the impression that Meg was a little urchin asking if another urchin could come out to play. She'd half expected Meg to wipe her nose on her sleeve.

"I need to buy a pram," she'd said, and there was a confessional quality to her words, as if this were something shameful. "Or . . . they call it a 'travel system' now. I need to buy a travel system. I don't want to go alone."

Which was how they'd ended up scooting about the baby-and-child department, each pushing a different "travel system," waving to each other as they went. Eventually, they all arrived at the center of a sort of crossroads and stopped, looking at each other's prams, peering into them as if there were babies inside, waiting to be admired.

"What d'you think, then?" Meg said.

"What were we meant to be looking for again?"

"How does it feel? Is it light enough? Is it too light? Is it smooth? Does it handle well? Everything, anything."

"This one judders slightly," Hugh said.

"That's more of an off-road model." The shop assistant shifted, began to push herself up from the shelf she was leaning on, then changed her mind.

"Off road? An off-road pram?"

"For if you live in the country, or do a lot of walking."

Hugh looked disbelieving.

"Mine is great," Lana said. "Really easy to run with."

"Not sure how much running I'll be doing," Meg said.

"What about from muggers?" Lana suggested. "Or pedophiles?"

Meg shot her an irritated look.

"Do you think it's a bit garish, with all the chrome?"

"You mean that the shininess might attract muggers and pedophiles?" Lana said. "That *is* a worry. I've heard they're like magpies."

"Would you shut up?"

Lana smiled, seemingly satisfied at the reaction she'd got.

"You can get it with black trim rather than chrome," the shop assistant said.

"Okay, let me try it one more time." Meg took the handle from Lana and wheeled away from them.

"Weird to think I'm going to have a niece," Lana said. "Do you think she'll let me look after the baby when it's here?"

"Not if you keep talking about having to run away from pedophiles," Hugh told her.

"Better than running towards them."

"Lana, mothers are anxious enough without people adding their own ideas."

"Meg? Anxious?"

"Yes, Meg. Yes, anxious."

Lana stared after her sister, and Jen stared, too, at the still-narrow back, at her still-lithe movements. It was easy to remember Meg at eleven years old, pushing baby Lana in her pram. She'd briefly had a mania for walking Lana around the park and the shopping center and, thinking that this meant she had finally accepted the new addition to the family, Jen had let her go on with the pram, let her walk twenty or so paces ahead.

A friend had asked if it was safe, but Jen never let her out of her sight, and Meg was very careful, very attentive. She would reach into the pram to adjust the blanket, to mop up dribble, perhaps just to rub Lana's cheek, and she'd jiggle the handle of the pram to soothe her sister. It had been lovely to watch. She'd even managed to get the sun visor to stay up (it had tended to sag when Jen attempted it).

"Made for motherhood," Carolyn had said when Hugh told his mother. Jen had gritted her teeth.

People would pass and look into the pram and look at Meg. Jen could see their lips move, their eyebrows rise, but was too far away to hear their words, and she often wished she were a bit closer, so she could hear the exchanges, greedy for compliments. Meg was vague when she asked. "Oh, just *What a lovely baby,*" she said. "That sort of thing."

It was only after several months of this that Jen discovered the truth. Meg had sat down on a bench across a small square and, though Jen hadn't taken her eyes off her daughters, she was still surprised by the sudden shouting.

"Next time," Meg was calling out, directing her words at a fast-retreating woman, "next time, you should think twice before jumping to conclusions. Do you hear me? You shouldn't judge people so quickly. You only end up making a fool of yourself."

By the time Jen had joined Meg, the woman was out of sight, but Meg's cheeks were flushed, her eyes shining, a triumphant grin on her face.

It turned out she'd been relishing the mistaken disapproval of passersby. The tutting and shaking of heads, the frowns directed at her and the pram, the muttered comments about teenage-pregnancy rates — they'd been what she'd wanted. She had enjoyed being mistaken for a child-mother, had enjoyed disabusing the disapproving masses.

"Are you admiring my baby *sister*?" she had asked with a saccharine smile, as an old man paused in his shuffling journey along the pavement. "My mother is over there, and she's thirty-seven. Is that too young to be a mother, do you think?"

Jen hadn't been thrilled to find that her age had been revealed to so many strangers.

"But I'm teaching them a valuable lesson," Meg told Jen on the way home.

Remembering this, Jen found she was clenching her fists. She wondered, as Meg came back through Christening Gifts, if she would be subjected to strangers' comments in the future. Not a teen mum, but a single mum, a gay mum. The thought made her anxious, agitated.

Meg looked agitated, too.

"I'm sure you won't actually have to run away from any pedophiles," Lana said, stepping around Hugh to put a hand on Meg's. "And whichever pram you choose, it'll be the right one, sis."

Meg wriggled her hand away. "Er, okay."

Lana, perhaps realizing that this didn't make up for her earlier comments, glanced at Hugh. "And if you're worried about the price, maybe Mum and Dad should buy the pram for you."

"Oh. That's sweet of you to offer . . ."

"Yes, *very* sweet of you, Lana," Hugh said, looking at the price tag.

". . . but I've already budgeted for this."

Of course she had. Hugh was obviously relieved, but Jen suddenly wished they could buy the pram for her, wished they could shop for a new pram every day.

GETTING IT WRONG

COGNITIVE ABILITY

"Do you want to look at the clothes while we're here?" Jen asked, drifting towards the escalator while Meg went to order her chosen travel system.

"No. And would you watch out?" Lana said. "You're always walking into people. Get some spatial awareness."

TECHNOLOGY

"Oh, Lana, I came across an article I thought you'd find funny. Wait a minute. I bookmarked the page on your dad's iPad."

"You know you don't have to use your whole arm to swipe, don't you, Mum? You look ridiculous."

PRONUNCIATION

"I thought we might look and see if there's a film we could all watch on Netflex."

"It's Net*flix*. Net*flix*. Oh my fucking God. It's only talked about every single day."

FOOD

"Why don't you take a photo of this for Instagram? The colors are so vibrant."

"No one is interested in a pissing scone,

Mum. That's not the point. Strawberry jam is lame."

GIVING UP

"Fine, I'll just sit quietly and try not to annoy you by suggesting anything nice."

"Great. Can you not breathe like that, though? It's super-distracting."

FEMINISM

"I wouldn't put up with that," Meg said one day, after she overheard Lana berating Jen for falling asleep on the sofa. "She's so bossy."

"*Bossy*'s a sexist label," Jen answered, automatically. "You'd never call a boy bossy."

"Fine. My bad. But I'm saying you need to discipline her."

"And how do you suggest I do that?"

"Grounding is traditional."

"Meg, if I ground her, she'll see me as the enemy, and I need her to be able to confide in me. Besides, she hardly goes out as it is. You think keeping her in, encouraging her to be more isolated, would be a sensible punishment?"

"Well, you could at least tell her off. You just put up with her being vile to you. Get angry, stop martyring yourself."

"I'm not a martyr. I do get angry. And I've told her off in the past, but you know that ends badly."

Jen's fury, when it escaped, tended to send Lana into despair. The last time Jen had lost her temper they'd been in a crowded Christmas market and Lana had suddenly disappeared, weaving her way through the masses of people and making Jen push past in a panicked search, jostling and apologizing to a long series of angry shoppers.

Another time, Lana had been ignoring Jen all day, in favor of talking to her friends on the phone. She'd wandered about the house discussing a teacher's Facebook profile, the new season of an American reality-TV show, and a project they were doing at school on the suffragettes. She kept mentioning "Emily" Pankhurst. Finally, Jen had had enough. She'd demanded Lana acknowledge her, asked if her friends were this rude to their parents, threatened to stop paying her phone bill. Before she knew it they were screaming at each other.

"And it's Emme*line* Pankhurst," Jen had said. "Not Emily."

This know-it-all remark was met with a frightening calm, and Lana had left the room. It wasn't until a cold draft made her shiver nearly a minute later that Jen realized Lana had left the house, leaving the front door wide open.

Not long after that, they'd been arguing on a train and Lana had jumped off when it pulled into a station. The doors had closed and the train had moved on before Jen could react. She'd had an agonizing journey back, not knowing if Lana would still be there, imagining her throwing herself in front of a non-stopping express. And Jen had suddenly remembered that bit of film, often played in museums, of Emily Davison and the king's horse. The halting black-and-white clip. The moment when the small body detached itself from the crowd and then disappeared under the hooves, seemed literally to dissolve on impact.

REASSURANCE

What Jen wanted to tell Lana when she was in despair: One day you'll have a rewarding job and a lovely husband and a beautiful home and sweet little children and a springer spaniel. And this will seem like a tiny blip. Think about that.

What she suspected might be more honest: One day you will be thirty-five and receiving IVF treatment and desperately trying to feed your cat a thyroid tablet and getting ready to apply for a mortgage on a studio flat and complaining about your colleague being promoted over you. And this will seem like an idyllic time. Think about that.

TESTING, TESTING

Lana obviously wasn't going to confide in her mother, so Jen was counting on her revealing something to her best friend, Bethany. But as far as Jen knew, they'd had no contact. Lana's replacement mobile hadn't arrived and she hadn't been back to school yet.

The headmistress had been very understanding and a card had even arrived from Lana's class, *Get Well Soon* on the front. The message didn't quite fit the circumstances, but Jen doubted there was a card with the words *Hope you recover from your nameless ordeal soon* available in the shops.

The messages inside, from teachers and classmates, were vague, and most of the pupils had plumped for *Hope you're okay* (or *Hope your ok*), but a couple of them were more direct, inquiring. *What happened?* asked a Jason P, and an Elsa had drawn a heart with arms and legs and said

114

she wanted *to hear the whole story.* It was reassuring for Jen to see that other people had questions, too.

Bethany had called several times the evening they got home, but Lana had been asleep, and she'd seemed strangely nervous about speaking to her friend since. If Jen could get them on the phone, if she could just get Lana to return Bethany's calls, it might mean progress.

She was sitting in front of the TV, waiting for Hugh to get home from his Friday-night piano lesson, when Bethany rang again. A few minutes later Jen heard Lana's footsteps in the hall and pressed the off button on the remote.

"That was Bethany," she said, "while you were in the shower."

"Right," Lana said, toweling the ends of her hair as she walked into the sitting room. A smell of shampoo, a cold, wet smell, invaded the warmth of the space, made it feel tainted, unclean.

"That's your friend from school."

Lana stared at her. "I know. I can't remember everything that happened in the Peak District, Mum, but I haven't lost my memory altogether. I don't need you to tell me who I am or how I take my tea."

"Yes, of course. Sorry."

"What were you watching on the telly?"

The truth was, Jen couldn't remember, but she felt too embarrassed to admit it. "The news," she said. "Are you going to call Bethany back?"

"Maybe." Lana teased a few tangles out of her damp hair, careful to avoid the area around her stitches, which still looked raw, the line of the wound running almost parallel to her part.

"She sounded anxious to speak to you."

"Oh, fine." Lana took the landline from its cradle. "It's shitty not having a mobile," she said, as she pressed Call Return and waited for her friend to answer. "When did you say my new phone would be here?"

"Monday."

"Oh, hi," Lana said, her attention slipping into the receiver, along the wires, out of the house.

Jen made her hands into a T sign, which Lana nodded at, and walked quickly to the kitchen to boil the kettle before rushing upstairs to pick up the extension in the bedroom. She caught sight of herself in the dressing-table mirror as she did so. She looked sly and angular, listening in on her daughter's conversation, her body bent over the phone, the light from the window harsh on the planes of her face. A stereotypical villain, a Richard III or a Weird Sister.

"They've said I don't have to go back till I feel like it," Lana was saying, her voice slightly metallic.

"Lucky," Bethany said.

"I s'pose."

"Oh. I didn't mean about what happened. I just meant about school."

"I know, Bambi," Lana said.

Bambi? Jen repeated in her head. Since when had she called her friend Bambi? Bethany, Beth, Bet, Bête Noir, Betty Boop, Bezza, Bell End. She'd heard all these, but never Bambi.

"So what exactly did happen?" Bethany asked.

Jen held her breath.

"I was kidnapped."

Jen held the phone away briefly so she could breathe out. She felt faint.

"Really?"

"Yeah, by these, like, mysterious men in cloaks." An upwards inflection had crept in, as if Lana were asking for permission.

Jen tried not to grip the phone too tightly; she made eye contact with herself in the mirror, as if her reflection could be relied upon for moral support.

"Oh my God," Bethany said.

"They were chanting, and carrying can-

117

dles and everything, and they tied me up and forced me to drink the blood of a hundred chickens."

"Freaky shit."

Jen settled the phone into its base then walked slowly downstairs. She made tea for herself and Lana and took the mugs into the sitting room. Her daughter was on the sofa, watching the TV with the sound turned down low; this phone, too, was back in its cradle.

"You made your point," Jen said, putting the tea on the side table.

"If you thought I wouldn't be able to tell you were listening —"

"Yes, I realize that now. Sorry."

"Nothing happened. Nothing major happened, you know," Lana said. "I was just lost."

"Okay."

Lana reached for the remote control.

"Was 'Bambi' code?" Jen asked.

Lana grinned. "I told Beth you'd be going upstairs to eavesdrop. I knew it when you kept on at me to phone her back."

"I thought it was odd."

"What's odd is that when I switched on the TV a shopping channel appeared. Not the news. A shopping channel."

"That is odd," Jen agreed. "Don't forget

118

to drink your tea."

Lana did as she was told and then grimaced. "Ugh, Mum. I haven't taken sugar since I was twelve."

"Sorry," Jen said. "Just testing."

INVENTORY

Having established that Lana's tea-drinking habits were still the same, Jen thought she should begin to make an inventory of Lana, of the Lana they'd got back. There were the old things, the familiar things: the huddled pose, the long, exasperated blink, the marks on her arms, old ones and fresh ones, the slight aniseed smell of her sweat. And there were the new things: the bandana she wore to cover the scabbed, cropped section of scalp, a sudden restlessness which made her open and shut drawers and doors and curtains, the sharpness of her shoulders and elbows, the yeasty smell of her breath, and, most disturbingly, the cracked left canine.

"Don't you think it looks a bit like an eye?" Jen whispered when she and Hugh got into bed that night.

"What?" Hugh asked.

"Lana's tooth. I wonder if it's dead. It's gone a funny color — grayish, yellowish. Haven't you noticed? And the middle of it has cracked in a long, dark slash." She made a performance of the last word, made it as onomatopoeic as she could. "It looks like a cat's eye."

"I haven't noticed," Hugh said. "Did that happen . . . recently?"

"Must have."

"Shouldn't you take her to the dentist?"

"Shouldn't *you*?"

It was too dark to see, but she stared at the space where she knew his face must be.

"Have you asked her about it?" Hugh said.

"I thought I was banned from asking any more questions."

"Inquiries about dentistry are probably allowed. You don't think it's hurting her, do you?"

Hugh had always had a special horror of the children getting toothaches, and he couldn't bear taking them to the dentist. He'd greeted their scraped knees and bumped heads and even Meg's broken arm quite cheerfully, but taking Lana to have her premolars out had left him white and shaking, and, according to Lana, he'd offered (rather insanely) to exchange places with her and have the procedure performed on himself instead. "As if that would work. As if it was just a kind of torture," she'd said, laughing, her words still soggy from

120

the anesthetic.

"I don't think it's hurting her," Jen said now, "but she will have to get it treated. It might have to come out."

She felt Hugh tense next to her.

"I don't think she'd mind that, actually. She's always said she fancied a gold tooth."

The lights of a passing car slipped through a gap in the curtains and turned about the room, making the mirror flash and the shadows of the wardrobe and bookcase lurch about. Jen got a glimpse of Hugh's tightly screwed-up face, and she put out a hand to smooth the creases away. But the light was gone by the time she made contact and her thumb caught his eye.

"Ow. Thank you for that," he said.

"Sorry."

"What were you aiming for?"

"Your cheek."

"Oh, good. I was worried you were working towards more cracked teeth to whisper about."

"Ha bloody ha," Jen said.

She turned over, partly for comfort, partly to make sure she didn't accidentally jab Hugh in the eye again, and soon began to feel as if she were drawing sleep towards her, sucking it in. Almost full, she hardly had the energy to react when Hugh sighed out his question.

"Do you think it's the tooth that's made Lana's voice different?"

Dysregulation of the Neural Hubs

Hugh decided he'd been imagining things when they spoke the next morning, but over breakfast (while Lana kept to her room) the question became a theme and, unable to ask Lana anything, Jen rounded on Hugh.

"Is her voice breathier, or more breathless?" she asked. "Do you think she seems angrier than before? Do you think she's developed a tremor? Do you think she's been picking at her scars? Do you think they're taking too long to heal? Do you think she's deliberately not eating? Do you think she's in some kind of pain and won't admit it?"

Hugh watched the too-runny marmalade drip off his toast and said no. He said no all day, while he read the paper and emptied the bins, while he loaded the dishwasher and ironed his shirts, while he made a chorizo and pork belly casserole and drank his Saturday beer. And Jen filed her nails short and repotted a little lemon tree and thought of more questions.

"Do you think she blinks too often?" she asked, settling onto the sofa.

Hugh stared at her over the rim of his glass. The clock on the mantelpiece ticked. A gurgle of water sounded through the central-heating pipes. Lana's footsteps could be heard on the creaking floorboards above.

"I thought we weren't supposed to watch her all the time, judge her all the time," Hugh said, finally. "You keep telling me that, and now . . . Too-frequent blinking? Really?"

Jen began to explain but was interrupted by the sound of something shooting through the letterbox.

Hugh sighed as he got up. "It'll just be the *Advertiser.* I'll put it in the recycling. Oh, nope," he said, at the door. "It's for Lana."

"What is it?"

He held up the A4 envelope. The address had been typed onto a fleur-de-lis-patterned sticker. "More schoolwork, I expect. She got a bundle of essay questions and chemistry equations last week. They like to keep them busy, don't they?" He looked about for somewhere to put the envelope then gave up, sitting down again and dropping the package on the floor.

"Blinking," Jen began.

"Oh, good," Hugh said, his voice dry, "I was worried that subject had been dropped."

"I read something that said rapid blinking could be a sign of dysregulation of the neural hubs."

"And what exactly does that mean?"

Jen paused. "Yes, well, I'm not absolutely clear on that point."

Hugh rubbed his face and reached for the remote control.

"But it has something to do with amnesia."

"Do you think she has amnesia?"

"Not really," Jen said. "I think she was dehydrated and confused, and now she's hydrated and obstinate, or not obstinate but doubtful, suspicious."

"Give her time," Hugh said, using another of those reassuring phrases which somehow didn't irritate when they were in his voice.

He flicked through the TV channels until he found a midway-through, black-and-white Saturday-afternoon film and settled down. The discussion was over. Jen tried to focus on the film; it was one she'd seen before. There were a lot of American men in soft felt hats threatening each other but speaking so quickly and in such a stagey monotone that the threats seemed distant. It was relaxing. But she kept seeing the envelope in the corner of her vision.

"What if it's not schoolwork?" she said.

Hugh waited for a dialogue-free chase scene to answer. "Well, what if it's not?"

"What if it's from someone . . . sinister?" She looked at the package for a long moment, the men on the television still telling each other they were making a mistake or would regret their mistake or pay for their mistake.

"You'll be glad of me one day," a man with a little painted-on moustache said. "I ain't no weak sister."

"Okay, go on, spill," said the blond leading man.

"Give the envelope here, will you?" Jen said.

"What about allowing her some privacy, and all that?" Hugh asked.

Jen ignored him, reaching for the package. Inside, she could feel a thin wodge of papers, as if several small sheets had shuffled themselves together. She ripped the flap open and tipped the contents onto the floor. Hugh switched off the TV, and there was a stark silence to accompany the slight darkening of the room. They leaned forward to survey the bits of paper, fluttering on their oatmeal-flecked carpet: press cuttings, dozens of them, newspaper articles covering Lana's disappearance. Her face was replicated on each one and the flapping of the paper in the breeze from the fireplace made it seem like she was blinking, over and over and over.

POSTERITY

Jen felt they should put the whole lot in the recycling, but Hugh wanted, unreasonably, to ask Lana's opinion. And, inevitably, that opinion was the opposite of Jen's. Their daughter looked at the cuttings, read about the police search, scanned the kind words from her school friends and headmistress, and, pushing everything back into the envelope, carried it upstairs. The next day, Jen would discover that her daughter had pinned every article to the corkboard above her desk, and the newspaper Lanas in the photographs challenged Jen whenever she went into the room.

There was a note in the envelope, too. It read: *Lovely Lana, see how important you are? Hang on to these to look back on when you're my age. Write me a letter, please. Love, Gran.*

"Of course, it *had* to be your mother," Jen

said, annoyed at not having guessed when she saw the address label. Carolyn had an insatiable passion for fleurs-de-lis. They adorned her shopping bags and scarves, topped the banisters, were stenciled on the wallpaper. Lana had once suggested she get a fleur-de-lis tattoo, much to Carolyn's horror.

And Hugh's mother was the only person who sent clippings in the post. They were usually from magazines and had titles like "How to lower your cholesterol" or "Ways to keep your prostate healthy." But she also collected anything to do with Hugh or his sister, or her grandchildren. She had once sent them a dozen copies of an article about a local cinema, after Hugh had got involved in the campaign to save it. They still had one of the newsprint photos in a frame: a brightly sunlit Hugh looming in front of the art deco façade, the angle unflattering, as it made the viewer focus on the underside of his chin.

Then there was the time he had inspected the work of an unscrupulous builder and helped to have a man prosecuted for swindling an old woman out of her life savings. When that story had been in the papers they'd got a whole sheaf of clippings, even though each one was only a few lines and none of them had a photo.

"You need to start a scrapbook," Carolyn had said, last time she phoned. "For posterity. You should get Jen to do it."

Jen, listening on speakerphone, had silently mouthed obscenities.

"I'm a building surveyor, Mum, I'm not starting a career in show business," Hugh had said. "And Jen's busy."

"I see." There'd been a ruffling sort of noise on the line. "Well, I'm proud of you, even if she isn't."

"She's right," Jen had said, after Hugh'd wished his mother goodbye and ended the call. "I should make time to create that scrapbook. I mean, you *are* a hero."

"It was nothing," Hugh had said, attempting to flex his biceps and flutter his eyelashes at the same time.

THE DEFINITION OF HEROISM

When he inspected the work, consulting building surveyor Hugh Maddox found that Mr. Bryant had failed to complete the roof-felt replacement he twice claimed he had undertaken. Mr. Maddox condemned the work as having "no purpose or value."

GHOSTING

There was no doubt that other people's mothers were a problem. Jen's friend Grace constantly complained that hers was needy and destructive and a clear case of borderline personality disorder (though sometimes she thought it was just negative Ketu, or the influence of a retrograde planet). Jen almost felt let down by her own supportive and even-tempered mother, a woman who occasionally had to acquire quirks just to have something to say.

"Invisible or able to fly?" she'd started to ask everyone she met. "Which would you prefer to be? Think carefully now, there *is* a wrong answer."

Lily had been trying out for the role of perpetual mischief-maker at the Women's Institute, and various other clubs, since her retirement twenty years before. It was a role she wasn't much suited to, but the attempt had won her many friends. Unfortunately, due to cancer and strokes, dementia and emphysema, there were few of these left, and Lily had fallen back on the company of a second (or possibly third) cousin. Peggy was one of life's organizers, and Lily occasionally joked about dying in order to get away from her, but in reality Peggy was invited to participate in nearly everything Lily did, and usually came with them to lunch, every third Sunday.

This Sunday was bright and hot and blue-skied, and the quiet Suffolk suburb, which Jen had not been lucky enough to grow up in, might almost have been taken for California in this weather, with its wide streets and big, one-story houses.

"Hello," Lily said, as Jen and Hugh got out of the car.

Her front door was already open, her handbag on the hall shelf, the windows closed and locked, the lights off.

"Hi, Mum," Jen said, stooping to kiss her. "Are you ready, or . . ."

"Not quite. Come in a minute, will you? Oh, that's the phone ringing now. It's all go this morning."

Hugh and Jen followed her into the house, which seemed smaller and darker and more full of stuff each time they visited. While they waited, Jen went about turning frames away or laying them facedown.

"What are you doing?" Hugh asked.

"I just can't bear them."

Jen had always thought school photos looked like photos of dead children, children who'd died in mysterious and gruesome situations. They were the kinds of pictures newspapers printed and broadcasters flashed up, and she'd nearly refused to buy any when Meg and Lana had had them taken. But, of course, all the grandparents had requested them and Jen had dutifully sent each year's set.

Meg's school photos were slowly being replaced by shots of her in trendy cafés or standing next to signs in New Orleans and Barcelona, but school-formal Lana was still on display. Neat, uniformed Lana, grinning widely enough to show the gaps in her baby teeth, or smiling, lip-glossed Lana, or the latest Lana, looking at the camera with that oddly familiar dull look in her eyes. This dull-eyed photo was the one that Hugh had sent to the police the day after Lana had gone missing. It was the photo the police and newspapers had chosen, despite the fact that Jen had given them more recent ones, taken a few days before: Lana on the holiday, caught looking happy and brightly dressed.

But it seemed "happy" wasn't what they wanted and, apparently, the school uniform would remind the public that she was a young girl, vulnerable, deserving of special attention. And the resolution, sharpness, and color balance were better in the school photo, they said. Insulting Jen's camera work on top of everything else.

"What's your mum going to say when she comes back in?" Hugh asked, as Jen hid the final picture.

She shrugged, looking about the room. Yes, okay, it was definitely noticeable, the room suddenly blank where it had been full of watching eyes, of the energy of early childhood, of the angst of teenage years.

"Why on earth does she have to put out quite so many?" Jen asked.

"Making up for having only two grand-children?" Hugh suggested. "She's often seemed a bit jealous of Peggy's seven."

"If only David and Graham had had children," Jen said. "They're so selfish."

"Well, she's going to be a great-grandmother soon."

"God, don't remind me."

"I thought Meg would want to be here to tell her."

"No, she has a good instinct for self-preservation. And anyway, someone had to stay with Lana."

"Sorry," Lily said, coming back into the room. "That was the nurse about my warfarin test. Oh." She stopped and looked at the dresser, the top of the piano, the bookcase, at the flattened or swiveled photo frames, but she didn't mention them. "Where are we going for lunch?" she asked.

"There's the pub on the Longton Road, or the garden center."

"Let's go to the garden center, then, but we'd better go now, otherwise all the tables will be taken by old women."

Hugh smiled.

"What about Peggy?" Jen asked. "Isn't she coming?"

"No."

"Just no?"

Lily pulled on some fingerless gloves, despite the heat, and picked up her handbag. "I told her last time I wouldn't stand for it." She led them towards the door and began the complicated procedure of locking the house. "I said, if she said it again, that would be it."

"Said what?" Jen asked, losing patience.

"What she said about my granddaughter." Lily backed into the car's front passenger seat and leaned back as Jen reached across to buckle the seat belt. "Lana is attention-seeking, she said. That's not true, I said, and I won't hear it, and if those words come up again it will mean the end of our friendship." She began to smile and then tugged her top lip down with her fingers. "I called her a troglodyte. Well, she might as well live in a cave, she knows nothing about the world."

Jen made a face at Hugh, who was sitting patiently with his hands on the steering wheel, and shut the door on the speech. But when she slid into the back of the car she found the monologue was still going on.

"To be honest, I'm glad. It's been coming for a while. I'm surprised we stayed friends for so long, I never could stand her."

Jen had instantly, shockingly, thought of her friend Grace, and couldn't help speculating about what it would take to end *their* friendship in such a definite way. She'd never realized that she might be interested in ending the friendship and felt something like a head rush at the idea. If Jen spent less time under Grace's guidance, half-heartedly being lulled by recorded meditations or trying to sync her menstrual cycle with the moon (surely it was a bit late for this, anyway), then she might have time for more useful activities. She might even go to the gym.

A man was jogging past in neon-yellow Lycra as Hugh pulled the car out onto the main road. To Jen, his presence made the day seem fresher, healthier, but Lily groaned.

"Oh, what do they look like? Rushing

about, dressed like that."

"Like people who exercise?"

"Is that so?" Lily said. "Don't drive down the road by the Christmas-tree farm this time," she told Hugh.

"Why not?" Jen asked, bundling all their rain jackets and bags together on the back seat beside her.

"Can't stand the smell."

Jen caught Hugh's eye through the rear-view mirror.

"Not a fan of Christmas now?" Hugh asked.

"Nothing to do with Christmas. It's just those trees. They smell like sweaty old animals. They smell the way that runner chap back there probably smells." She pointed a thumb over her shoulder and pulled at the seat belt.

"I don't think you'd be able to smell the trees from this side of the road, or from inside a car," Jen said.

"But I'd be able to see them, and the sight would remind me."

"Surely talking about them reminds you?"

"But not as strongly."

Jen sat back, defeated.

"I've never really liked the way they look, either," Lily said after a moment. "The way the needles grow directly out of the trunk,

135

you know? It seems normal on the branches, but on the trunk? Quite horrid." She shivered. "Deformed hairs, they look like, or some sort of disease. I can't describe it properly, but do you know what I mean?"

Hugh moved, trying to catch Jen's eye again, but she kept her focus on Lily's head, partly obscured by the headrest in front of her. The truth was she *did* know what her mother meant, though she could hardly articulate it any better. What kind of tree allowed its leaves to sprout directly from the trunk, with no branch to act as a conduit? It *was* like hair, like pubic hair growing somewhere it shouldn't, on the inner elbow or the back of a knee; it seemed obscene and made Jen feel itchy.

Itchy inner elbows reminded her of Meg, and she asked Lily for the name of the cream she'd recommended before.

"I knew you'd forget," Lily said, "so I wrote it down. Here you are." She held a scrap of paper through the gap between the front seats. "Why's Meg got eczema again all of a sudden, anyway? Have you told her to change her washing powder?"

"It's not her washing powder," Jen said. She took a breath in. Hugh was shaking his head in the mirror, but why wait? "Meg's pregnant."

"Pardon?" The seat belt snapped back into place. "Does that mean . . . ? Has she . . . ? How could she . . . ? How?"

"As far as we understand it, she's come to an arrangement with her friend Tom."

"An arrangement," Lily echoed, her voice small.

"Yes. They're not romantically involved, but they'd both like to be parents."

"So she's still a lesbian?"

"Yes."

"And she's not getting married?"

"No."

"And it was all test tubes and artificial insemination and whatnot, was it?"

"I think so."

"Well." Lily tugged off her gloves and put them away in her handbag. "*That's* something to tell Peggy."

"I thought you weren't talking to Peggy."

"I didn't have anything worth talking about before."

Lily was still speaking when they got to the garden center, where sprinklered water droplets balanced on the car park's shrubs and the smell of petrol mixed with the honey scent of yellow azaleas.

"I suppose it's a generational thing," Lily said, "keeping up a friendship like this. People just *ghost* each other now, apparently. Have you heard of that, Hugh? *Ghosting?* What you do is you stop taking your friend's calls and stop answering their messages and hope they give up on you altogether. There was a program about it on Radio 4."

As they walked into the restaurant, Jen realized she had brought one of the framed photos of Lana with them, clutched against the foldable walking stick and the spare cardigan. Lily, flicking the stick into shape as if it were a police baton, and pulling the cardigan around her shoulders, took the picture from Jen and slipped it into her handbag. They both gazed at Lana's face for a second, lying among crumpled tissues and empty chocolate wrappers, and then Lily tugged the zip shut and looked at Jen instead.

DECEPTION

At the garden center Lily pointed out the flowers that had bloomed early this year, and on the drive home Jen realized that, while she'd been distracted, all the magnolia trees in London had come into blossom. Worse than that, they had laid most of their fat, blushing petals on the sodden pavements. She felt they had gone behind her back.

The curious incident of the cat in the nighttime

The feeling that things were happening just out of her sight was growing. That night Jen felt she could smell the damp creeping into the brickwork of their house, could hear the leaves of the plants outside uncurling, could see the office interns and assistants plotting her demise.

But a moment later she realized she couldn't sense any of those things. Something had woken her, a screeching which could have been inside her head, and though she clenched and released all her muscles from toe to neck, she knew she wouldn't get back to sleep. Hugh's face was turned towards her and she kept checking to see that his eyes were shut. Somehow, finding him staring at her in the half-light was the most frightening thing she could imagine.

Which was ridiculous, because it was Hugh, and surely she should be able to think of something scarier. Masked men breaking into the house, a fire beginning in the hallway beneath their bedroom, the ghost of a murdered former resident rising from the floorboards. But no, it was only the image of Hugh's eyes shiningly open when they should be closed that had the power to make her breath catch. She got out of bed.

There was no raging fire in the hall and no masked men. Lana's light was on, and Jen put a hand around the slightly open door to turn it off, listening to her daughter's puffs of breath, grateful, consciously grateful, that she could stand here, near her, where she was asleep and safe.

The kitchen was full of the muffled, wet sounds of the boiler and the dishwasher, ordinary and reassuring. But as she left the kitchen, carrying her glass of milk, she noticed the looming quality of the stairs at this angle, at this time of night: a thrilling, frightening aspect, an ominous promise of horrors one floor up. The clinical, unmerciful white of the walls seemed ready for the shadow of something to glide over it, the silhouette of a hand with long fingernails. Beneath were the broken lines of the banister spindles and behind them a dark shape that looked like a cat sitting on the stairs.

Jen moved slightly to the left and swallowed some of the milk, sweet against the sour taste of sleep in her mouth. The shape stayed where it was, still dark, still catlike. It was an actual cat, Jen realized, its head tilted towards the first floor, as if it were looking at someone on the landing.

"How did you get in?" she whispered, moving to the bottom step and sniffing the air in case the cat had sprayed somewhere, or worse. The cat turned and meowed at her, a quiet meow, a feline sort of whisper, as if it understood that people were sleeping upstairs. Jen put a hand out and felt the hard head bump her knuckles, felt the soft fur push through the gaps between her fingers, felt the skin above her wrists groomed by a rough tongue. A low purring echoed in the hall. The chilly night suddenly seemed full of warmth.

"I'd better let you out," Jen said. "You shouldn't be here."

But instead she sat on the step and let the cat push into the crook of her arm. It was white with black ears and reminded her of a Hiroshige picture she'd had on her wall as a student. This is what she'd woken early for, she thought. This is what her mind had pushed her out of bed for, this furry reward, these few minutes of peace. "Where have you been hiding, eh? How did you get in?"

She put her glass on a newspaper, letting a drop of milk run down the outside, and the cat licked at it. The tiredness Jen thought she'd lost returned and she leaned against the wall, rubbing the cat's cheek. It closed its eyes; she closed her eyes. Perhaps this was just what happened at this hour every night, perhaps she just missed it by sleeping, perhaps it had let itself in somehow, despite the lack of opposable thumbs . . . She was too sleepy for questions. Slowly, and without grace, she slumped onto the floor and let the cat fill the gap between her limbs.

And that was how she woke, hours later, curled around a cat-shaped space on the carpet, Hugh standing over her. It was still dark.

"What on earth?" he said.

"There was a cat," she answered.

"Which is why you slept on the stairs?"

"I couldn't sleep."

"I beg to differ."

"No, I mean I couldn't sleep earlier, and then there was this cat, and . . . that's the last thing I remember. Did you let it out?"

"No. There was no cat. Just my wife giving me a fright by lying at the bottom of the stairs and looking like she'd fallen down them."

"Oh, sorry," Jen said. "I wonder where it went, then. We'd better have a look. It must be somewhere. I hope it hasn't weed on anything."

She let Hugh help her up, groaning at the stiffness in her spine, and they walked about, checking under furniture and behind curtains, opening cupboards and lifting the lids of laundry baskets. The glass of milk (lukewarm and yellowish) was still standing on the newspaper, but there was no cat.

"Are you sure you didn't imagine it?" Hugh said. "Perhaps you were sleepwalking."

"I wasn't sleepwalking. A cat definitely got in somehow."

Hugh yawned.

"Well, what do you think?" Jen asked.

"I think there are still two hours before I have to be up and I'm going to bed, imaginary cat notwithstanding."

HER INDOORS

People had a habit of accusing Jen of imagining things: she hadn't told Meg she could meet her for lunch, Hugh hadn't said he'd get the car cleaned, and Lily had never promised to give her that fondue set from the seventies. There was no point in arguing, even though she knew very well what she'd said and heard and been promised.

And then there was Meg's girlfriend, ex-girlfriend now, apparently, though Meg had still not said much about that to her mother. Kayla had a round face, an Elvis hairstyle, a septum ring, and deep dimples in her shining cheeks. She smelled of cocoa butter and wore checked shirts, carefully ironed and buttoned up to the top, and she worked at a café near Meg's gallery, one of those places with school desks instead of tables and clanging metal stools instead of chairs. She had an easy smile for everyone. Except Jen.

Meg had taken Jen to the café a few times to have coffee and toasted banana bread while they waited for Kayla's shift to be over, and Jen had always had the impression that Kayla wished her away. Not that she was ever unpleasant, but her behavior was unsettling. Kayla seemed to bring Jen her coffee and cake with a solemnity, a formality, that she didn't display when serving anyone else. Her voice was lower when she spoke to Jen, and she held her head tilted further to one side when Jen spoke to her. There was a sort of reverence, or mock-reverence, in her manner that made Jen smile too broadly at her, ask too many questions, be too enthusiastic about everything Kayla said.

"You're imagining it," Hugh would say when Jen mentioned this to him.

"She really likes you," Meg always said when Jen hinted that Kayla might be uncomfortable around her.

"Ah, the *girl*friend," Lily tended to say, with a small smile and a deep nod, but never had anything else to add.

"Who the hell's Kayla?" Lana asked, the only time Jen brought it up with her. Of course, Lana knew who Kayla was, but she was irritated at being spoken to when she was typing something on her phone.

SIGNIFICANT OTHER

Jen had been happy to find out that the donor father of her unborn grandchild was Tom. They'd known him since Meg was at primary school, a funny, diffident boy, not unattractive but strangely unable to keep hold of girlfriends. He was a lanky sort, with loose, rangy joints, and Jen associated this looseness with his lack of grip on relationships.

He was too stubborn, Meg told them when they asked why yet another girl had fallen by the wayside. He insisted on his routine, his hobbies, his obsessions. A good friend; a terrible boyfriend. Jen and Hugh had thought (a long time ago) that Meg and he were an item, before she came out. And then Jen had wondered if he was in love with Meg. It was still possible.

He seemed to be very enthusiastic about the baby (from what Meg told them) and was eagerly learning everything he could about pregnancy and giving birth and child-rearing. Jen suspected that the actual baby would throw him, though, and that he would likely always be rather shy around his own child. She suspected that would suit Meg quite well.

"Bit of a nonentity," Hugh would say when Tom came up in conversation.

"He's an introvert," Meg always said when Jen asked why she never saw him anymore.

"Oh, sweet boy," Lily tended to say, with a fold of her hands.

"Who the hell's Tom?" Lana asked, irritated again.

FANFARE

An irritated Lana was a familiar Lana; a mysteriously tearful Lana was a familiar Lana; a suddenly cheerful Lana, an unexpectedly kind Lana, an offense-taking Lana, a sullen and silent Lana, Jen recognized them all. The Lana she couldn't get used to was the rage-filled one.

"Fuck off!" Lana shouted from her bed

on Monday morning.

They had been home for two and a half weeks and today was the day she was supposed to start back at school. But when Jen went into her room, she was greeted by the smell of antiseptic and the sight of thin, blood-dotted lines etched across sallow forearms.

"Fuckoff fuckoff fuckoff fuckoff."

It was like a sort of announcement noise, Jen thought, a trumpeting, as if her exit from her daughter's room required a fanfare. This was what she thought on one level, anyway, the level that stayed *upbeat,* the level that kept *positive* and found *the good in every situation,* or, if it wasn't able to do that, then *forgave* and knew it was important *just to have tried.* But underneath were the levels that didn't keep all that textbook advice in mind, that couldn't remember or couldn't stomach it, or couldn't find space amid the despair.

She went very carefully and quietly into her own room and collected up the mugs and glasses that she and Hugh had taken to bed, and took them very carefully and quietly down to the kitchen and, balancing them against her body, very carefully and quietly opened the dishwasher. It was full. Jen looked about for somewhere to put the

147

things, but all the counters were strewn with debris: empty cereal packets and string bags of shriveling satsumas, discarded envelopes and dusty vases, Oyster-card holders and broken attachments for blenders and sandwich toasters and salad spinners.

She'd had enough, she decided; she'd reached her limit. Her arms dropped, her fingers uncurled, the mugs and glasses made a horrifyingly loud noise as they crashed to the floor. The volume and the piercing, jagged quality of the sound were so shocking that she couldn't relate it to the deliberate collapsing action her own arms had performed, couldn't attribute it to the sudden, frustrated decision to destroy something.

"What was that?" Lana called as she got to the bottom of the stairs. "What happened?"

Jen, embarrassed, grabbed a tray from its hook and stood holding it up like a shield. "I tripped," she said, "and everything slid. From the tray."

Lana lingered at the kitchen door, untying and retying the bandana around her head. "What did you trip on?" She frowned for perhaps less than a second, but it was an assessing frown, a frown that took everything in and wondered aloud, a skeptical, calculating frown. It said: *I know this is about me, but I'm not going to acknowledge it and I'm not going to stop being angry with you.*

"Tripped over my own feet," Jen said, in that breezy voice she had been trying to perfect for over a year. "Silly me."

Lana took a step forward, her mouth open, unguarded, as she stared at the wreckage.

"Be careful," Jen said. "There's a lot of glass and you've only got socks on."

Lana's mouth tightened. "That's Dad's favorite mug."

"Is it?" Jen looked where Lana was pointing.

"You broke his favorite mug."

"Well, I didn't mean to. It was an accident." Jen searched through the jumble of fragments, trying to recognize any parts which might have once formed a beloved drinking vessel of Hugh's, but although the patterns and colors were familiar there was nothing that stood out, nothing that was linked to Hugh in her memory. She was fairly certain he didn't notice what mug he drank from, let alone invent a hierarchy, but he'd gone to work early so she couldn't ask him.

"Okay," Lana said. "I'm going back upstairs."

"Okay," Jen said.

She wanted to say more, to call after her: *I didn't do this to attract your attention, you know. I didn't expect this would make you care about me or feel sorry. I didn't think about the fact that you'd be able to hear me from your barricaded room. I forgot you.* But instead she carefully and quietly picked her way through the shards of glass and porcelain and got the dustpan and brush and gathered up the smooth pieces and the gritty splinters and poured them, chinking and rustling, into the bin.

Hazardous Waste

Upstairs, Lana's bin was filled with blood-soaked cotton-wool pads and, when Jen emptied it several days later, she was reminded of the ruined white fleece jacket that Lana had been wearing when she was found.

And something else had been found. The police called to tell Jen this while she was shining a torch over the kitchen floor to check for any stray glass shards. Whatever the new evidence was, it apparently warranted another interview, and could a PC pop round to the house to follow up?

"And how do you feel about the police coming back to talk to you?" Dr. Greenbaum said the next day, during their first therapy session since returning from the Peak District. "Are you worried at all?"

"Not really," Lana said. "But it's annoying. I don't want to keep going over it."

"Ah, and here I am asking you to do just that."

"That's okay. At least you ask more interesting questions."

"I do?" Dr. Greenbaum looked amused. "That's encouraging to hear. In that case, tell me a little about the holiday, tell me how you felt on holiday."

Lana told him, repeating again everything she'd said to the police, talking about the tutor and Stephen and Matthew. Jen could hardly concentrate. There were new cushions on the low armchairs, satin-covered cushions, overstuffed and slippery against the faux-leather seat backs. She and Lana, and even the doctor, had slid into a semi-reclined position, as if they couldn't be bothered to sit up for this story, as if they'd all heard it too many times.

"And can you describe anything you painted?" Dr. Greenbaum asked, his voice slightly strained by the position of his neck.

"I can show you, if you like," Lana said, getting her phone out of her bag. "I took photos of the good ones."

"You have those? I thought you'd lost your old phone," Jen said.

"Er, ever heard of the iCloud, Mum? There aren't rolls of film inside, either. Don't know if you noticed." She passed the doctor her new phone, tentative, as if he might tell her at the last minute that he wasn't interested.

"Very good, Lana," he said, ignoring the pointed exchange between mother and daughter and flicking through the images. "Very Romantic. This is the tradition of the sublime, I suppose. Imposing landscape, beauty as terror."

"Yeah, I suppose. Actually, some of them are Mum's."

"Mum's? Very good, *Mum.*"

"Thank you," Jen said, sliding further onto her back with the effort of speech.

"I think we should put them up at home," Lana said. "Like, have them framed."

"You want to be reminded of those places?"

"I just think they're good pictures."

"Well, perhaps *Mum* can be persuaded to display them, then." He looked at Jen.

"Oh, they're not that good," she said. "But we could get some framed if Lana wants."

"Great. And what's this?" He stopped on an image. "A nun?"

"Oh, that." Lana reached for the phone and locked the screen. "It was just a painting I thought was interesting."

"Why? This is a picture of stigmata, correct? The wounds of Christ appearing on a nun, appearing supernaturally. You relate to this image in some way?"

"Yeah. It's, like, something I understand, or maybe it makes me feel understood. I don't know."

"What about it do you understand?"

"Like, the pain, I guess. Or the cuts. I mean, because of, you know, cutting."

"You relate stigmata to deliberate self-harm?"

"No. Sort of. I mean, there is a kind of a connection, isn't there?"

"Perhaps there is. Suffering, and suffering deliberately, is a big part of Christianity, is it not?"

"I don't know. I'm not really a Christian."

"Ah, well, neither am I, so we're like the blind leading the blind. A phrase from the Bible, incidentally. Though I think it has its origins in an older Hindu text."

"If you say so."

"But wearing hair shirts, practicing self-flagellation, fasting, submitting to torture, these are all things demonstrated by the saints, I know. And it's interesting to think how these practices are reflected in life today. Self-harm, anorexia, engaging in risky behaviors with sexual partners. It's interesting to me, anyway."

"Okay."

"Where did you find the image?"

"Google."

"You searched for it?"

"Not really, I just found it."

He nodded and rubbed a hand over his jaw. "What I'm trying to get at, Lana, is: Does this raise up the practice of self-harm for you? Does it make you think it is a noble thing? A sacred thing?"

Lana had her hands flat on the seat, and she straightened her elbows, making her body stiff. She seemed to be thinking. "No," she said, finally.

"It's just a way of finding context?"

"Yeah. I mean, this is really old, this painting, but she's probably my age, right? Whoever she was. She even kind of looks like me."

"Are you suggesting, then, that the cuts you make are spiritual or divine?" He'd raised his eyebrows, as if prepared to be amazed.

Jen sometimes got the impression that Dr. Greenbaum was laughing at his patients, being sarcastic. Hugh thought so, too, and tried never to say anything during the sessions. He couldn't make every appointment and, on those days, Jen missed being able to analyze the doctor's comments with him afterwards. She wondered now if Dr. Greenbaum had ordered the slippery cushions especially. Was it amusing to watch his clients attempting to stay sitting up? Or did their attempts tell him something about their personality, their mental state?

"No," Lana said. "Obviously, I don't think God cut me."

"Then are you saying that this nun in the picture made those marks on her hands and feet herself?"

Lana smiled. "That's blasphemy."

He smiled back. "You believe in blasphemy?"

"Not really."

"Has someone suggested this connection to you, Lana?"

There was a pause. Jen caught Lana's glance.

"You mentioned a man on your holiday who talked to you about religion," Dr.

Greenbaum said. "Did he talk about stig-mata?"

"His name's Stephen," Jen said, unable to stop herself, but feeling that another word might force her onto the floor, she said nothing else and braced herself against the chair, heaving her body up a little.

Dr. Greenbaum nodded but didn't look at Jen, and Lana ignored her, trained to listen only, speak only, to the psychiatrist. "I don't really remember," she said. "He might have."

"Have you felt more inclined to harm yourself because of this picture, or the con-nection you feel to this picture?"

"No. Less, if anything."

"Why?"

"Because it seems sad, or it seems stupid. Like, I don't want to be some delusional religious fanatic. They're crazy, they're creepy."

"Okay. In that case, Lana, I ask if there might not be a better image for you, a safer, more helpful image. Is there, perhaps, a bet-ter analogy for how you feel, something that doesn't reference nuns or 'creepy' religious fanatics?"

"I see what you mean."

"I think that's something you could work on between now and our next appointment.

Find an image and describe how it relates to you; write something down, if you can. And bring the image with you. And, Lana, something without blood, if possible, please. If just to shield me. I'm rather squeamish, you know."

"Okay." She laughed. "I promise I'll find an image that's blood-free."

"Then that seems a positive action to focus on. What do you think, *Mum*?" He paused for a moment then slid himself up in one movement, pulled his satin cushion out from behind him and threw it to the floor. "I hate these," he said. "What a terrible choice of fabric. My promise to you, Lana and *Mum,* is that these cushions will be gone by our next session."

Don't think

The hours after a family therapy session were often fraught. Lana always seemed to regret having said anything in front of her mother, and she'd lose her temper at the smallest hint that Jen was remembering any exchange between her and Dr. Greenbaum. And so there were thoughts Jen tried not to think when Lana was near, in case her daughter saw the questions on her face.

She had, of course, looked for images of

stigmata when they'd got home and had been horrified by the photographs of mutilated hands, of people crying blood or wrapped in gory bandages. The only comfort was the fact that Lana's picture, as she'd described it, was an old painting. And those images, when Jen searched them, were calmer, cleaner. She was grateful, too, for the irreverence of the internet, for the photographers who'd dressed up their dogs to re-create religious paintings, for the bakers who'd made hand-shaped, raspberry-jam-filled "stigmata cookies."

The thoughts she tried not to think the next morning included: How did this happen? Where have you been? When can I stop worrying? Why won't you talk? Why must you hurt yourself? And now there were more questions, new questions: Where did the stigmata idea come from? Who put it in your head? Did Stephen influence you? Do you think you need to be punished for some kind of sin? She kept her face blank but knew that Lana knew the questions existed.

She was about to leave for work, late but not disastrously late, when Lana appeared in the hall, baring her teeth but not quite smiling. That cracked canine showed at the corner of her lips and Jen felt it was watching her. She had the notion suddenly that it was someone else's eye, another being inside Lana using the tooth to look out at the world. For a minute it all made sense. That was why she kept her mouth firmly shut, that was why she hardly ever spoke or smiled, because she didn't want the tooth-eye to see out, to see who was there.

And then, of course, it stopped making sense and Jen shivered at her own mad thought.

"I did that thing that Dr. Greenbaum said to do," Lana said. "I found a picture and I wrote about it."

"That was quick."

Lana nodded and showed Jen her phone. A photograph from a museum lit the screen: a glass case full of songbirds, all posed at different angles, as if they were landing or taking off from a painted tree.

"And I wrote about how it relates to me."

She handed Jen a piece of blue-lined paper, covered in words which had been written with such pressure that they'd left raised patterns on the other side of the page, like a form of braille.

FLUTTER

My body feels like it's made up of a thousand tiny birds flapping their wings inside my skin:

159

a blue tit at my elbow, a sparrow along my thigh, a pigeon jabbing me in the belly button. I can hardly walk, I can hardly hold myself up, without the exhausting tickling of their feathers. The ticklishness is what makes me scratch at myself, with fingernails and pens and scalpels.

Sometimes, when I see a bird in the garden or a park, I expect it to fly right into me, so I'd rather not go outside.

Sometimes, I don't dare move my head, or speak out loud, in case I cause a whirlwind of wings and claws inside me.

Sometimes, questions flutter from their beaks: What is the point, they say, how long will this go on? Can you stand it for many more years, or months, or days? Where can you escape to? When will it all end?

Sometimes, I think of ways to get rid of the birds, to poison them, to fall from a great height and feel them rush out of me.

Sometimes, I wish someone would crush them out of me.

STUTTER

Jen called in sick after that, not wanting to leave Lana at home alone with her birds. They watched daytime TV and ate some of the shriveled satsumas and didn't talk, because Lana felt she had said enough (though Jen asked where the picture had come from, and if this was why she'd spent so much time lying on the garden lawn, and if anyone *had* attempted to crush the birds out of her, and whether it was Matthew and his bird-watching that had influenced the note).

As usual, the questions went unanswered, but Lana's skin made it through the day without any more marks, and nothing in the vein of stigmata, which was all Jen could hope for. And because they were both at home drinking tea from the undropped, unbroken mugs, the milk ran out.

In order to replace milk that had been unexpectedly finished, or buy something in a can which she couldn't find anywhere else (dolmades, perhaps, or haggis), Jen would go to the corner shop. The man at the counter was always friendly, smiling and nodding as though he recognized Jen, and asking how she was, but Jen felt she didn't shop there enough to deserve this and tended to assume he had mistaken her for someone else.

Thinking she would take this opportunity to try and bribe Lana with chocolate (though what the bribe might achieve was undefined), she went to the shop between episodes of *Say Yes to the Dress*. There was the familiar bleep, set off by opening the door, there was the friendly man, at his till, raised above the shop floor, and suddenly there was Lana, coming in behind her.

"What are you doing here?" Jen asked. "I thought you weren't dressed for outside?"

Lana shrugged and looked down at her slippers, and Jen glanced at the man, feeling rather embarrassed. He was still smiling.

"Milk-and-chocolate run," Jen told him. "Shouldn't, really. Diabetes and" — she struggled to think of the other detrimental effects of sugar — "cavities."

Despite these disadvantages, they grasped at the chocolate bars in front of the till, piling them onto the counter alongside the replacement milk.

"Aren't you going to have a KitKat?" Jen asked when she saw Lana's choice. "I thought that was your favorite."

"I've gone off them. What's it to you?"

Jen admitted it was nothing to her and handed the man the money. He carefully placed the change on a little plastic tray.

"You are back," he said to Lana. "It is good to see."

Lana dropped the change as she was gathering it up, and his smile fell. Jen realized they were both staring at him.

"I'm sorry," he said. "All the news-papers . . . there were photos." He waved at the wide shelf where the last of that day's unsold newspapers lay. "You are okay?" he asked, raising a thumb at Lana.

"I guess so."

"My favorite customers," he said.

Jen felt unbelievably flattered and nearly tearful, which was surely a sign that they should leave quickly. But Lana nodded at the man and raised her thumb before they left. She looked frustrated, as if this gesture had been a last-ditch effort to communicate, and Jen realized, as they walked away, clutching their haul, that Lana's voice sounded different not because of that cracked tooth but because she had begun to hesitate over words, to repeat the beginnings of sentences, to stutter.

ECHO

"Is that what you meant," Jen asked Hugh, "when you said you thought her voice was different?"

She had been listening more carefully to the way Lana spoke and had decided it wasn't quite a stutter. Rather, Lana now began her sentences twice, adjusting the volume of her words, as if she were testing the resonance of her voice every time she opened her mouth.

"I suppose so," Hugh said, "but I couldn't put my finger on it."

Sometimes, Lana started quiet, tentative, and restarted loudly. Other times, she began loudly and then began again with a softer tone. And Jen wondered what had caused her to become her own echo.

RESEARCH

In case this was some new symptom of depression, Jen went to the library during her lunch break on Thursday. Lana had agreed to go to school, had agreed to be dropped off, had been safely seen inside the gates, hugged to Bethany's side. And Jen had sat blindly in front of her computer all morning, hoping everything was okay, expecting a panicked phone call, waiting for a chance to leave the office so she could let the anxiety show on her face.

She had been going to the library during her lunch breaks for some time. Partly to get away from the young people in her office but mostly to read self-help books and health manuals on adolescent depression and deliberate self-harm (or DSH, to those, unfortunately, undesirably, in the know).

She didn't want to bring the books home, where Lana might see them, she didn't want to borrow them and have the titles come up on her loans record, announcing to the librarians what a failure she was as a parent, so she found the darkest corner of the library and skim-read in a panic.

A year ago, she'd walked into Lana's room to discover her sitting on the floor with a glass of water and a carrier bag of painkillers. She had already begun to scoop them into her mouth (though she'd insisted since that she hadn't really been going to swallow), and the sight had made Jen feel as though her body had been whittled down to a painful core.

Lana could be grumpy and argumentative, she could be lethargic, headachy, and uninterested in food, but Jen had never thought it was something clinical.

"That's just what teenagers are like, isn't it?" she'd said to Hugh.

There had followed a series of GP visits, and sessions with a social worker, and then Dr. Greenbaum, the psychiatrist. Awful, draining hours in a khaki-painted adolescent center where Lana sat with her head down and seemed not to hear any of the questions she was being asked. Jen felt there'd been some kind of trick performed on them, some switch. Lana had been replaced by another child, or told to behave strangely, for some sinister reason. Jen even looked for hidden cameras in the consulting room, realizing that this might mean she'd gone insane herself.

After months of this, she still had no idea how to react, so she went to the library, where she wrote lists of life events and triggers and biological connections, filled in and scored emotional-discomfort questionnaires, kept a mood summary and a sleep diary and an activity log, and tracked Lana's symptoms. She monitored herself for Unhelpful Thought Cycles (which always began with *I'm a failure*), and practiced conversation openers in front of the mirror in the Ladies: "I've noticed that you've been feeling frustrated recently," and, "Do you think you feel sad or angry more than you feel happy?" They sounded so reasonable in the quiet of the library bathroom, but she knew the message would get lost in the crackling atmosphere of Lana's bedroom.

One book had pages full of pencil marks, and Jen felt she was tracing the faint path of some other worried mother, a guide, a trailblazer, a Sherpa for her own personal Everest. Every time cognitive behavioral therapy was mentioned, a star had been scribbled in the margin, and Jen read the reference more closely. The sections warning readers about the dangers of medication — addiction, increased risk of suicide — were underlined and the corners of those pages turned down, and Jen could imagine this other mother, trying to make an argument for CBT, ready for a conversation with someone else, a doctor, perhaps, or the father of the child.

This other mother had ringed the challenge to praise your child five times in twenty-four hours, and Jen wondered what she'd said and how this had gone. Home-schooling was obviously something she was trying to avoid, as every time it was mentioned as a last resort the words "last resort" were bracketed. There were marks against the sections about letting your child sleep in your bed and not forgetting that children copy their parents' thought patterns, and Jen found she had created a picture of this woman with her worries and prejudices, felt close to her, whoever she was, and was disappointed when her pencil marks didn't feature for a few pages.

But then, two-thirds of the way through, she found a big tick against the diet section. Regular meals, healthy snacks, fruit and vegetables, plenty of protein, no caffeine.

This woman obviously thought she'd nailed that already, and Jen suddenly felt irritated by her smugness, and very alone.

REHEARSAL VS. PERFORMANCE

JEN (*at lunchtime, facing the mirror in the library toilets*):

Do you think you feel sad or angry more than you feel happy or optimistic?

LANA (*in Jen's expectant imagination, hugging her mother*):

I don't feel sad more than happy, but I think I do feel sad a lot. I'd really appreciate you helping me work through this.

JEN (*in the doorway of Lana's room that evening*):

Do you think you feel . . . um . . . like you want to say anything? Or what would make you happy or not make you happy?

LANA (*outside Jen's head; in reality*):

What the hell are you talking about? Can you get out of my room, please, and stop trying to spy on me?

GETTING IT WRONG AGAIN

Jen would have denied the charge of spying but, without cooperation from Lana, she had had to find other ways of acquiring the information needed to fill out the boxes in the altered-thinking log and the altered-behavior log and the sleep diary and the self-harm-triggers questionnaire. She wrote down the times Lana got up or went to bed, noted the light in her room being on at four in the morning, counted the number of hours she spent on her phone in the evening. This monitoring made her feel guilty, and she tried to quietly compensate Lana with treats (there would be no big pencil ticks against the book's diet section for her).

On the way home that evening Jen couldn't resist buying Lana a KitKat, hoping it would make her more open to a proper conversation. She weighed it in her hand in the shop, as if gauging the effect it would have on their relationship, and she patted the shape of it through her canvas bag as she stood crushed against a door on the Tube. It was only as she got to their street that she remembered Lana didn't like KitKats anymore.

When had that happened? she wondered. What had caused the change? Lana had definitely eaten a lot of them when they'd been in the Peak District. The vending machine at the holiday center had been nearly cleared out. There was something she half recalled from one of the *helping others* books, about depressed children losing interest in favorite foods. Perhaps that was it, she thought, as she let herself into the house and tiptoed up the stairs.

Feeling compelled to destroy the evidence of her mistake, she consumed all four fingers of the bar in a few swift bites.

BODY IMAGE

Jen ended up eating Meg's treats, too, during their trip to the cinema on Saturday evening.

"I got three different ice creams because I couldn't choose: salted caramel, chocolate, and coffee," she told Meg, balancing the little pots on the armrest between them. "Which one — or two — do you want?"

"Ugh," Meg said. "Even the thought gives me heartburn. I'm going to stick with water."

And so Jen barely noticed the film because she was so caught up in the pleasure of eating and the guilt of eating and the pleasure of eating and the guilt . . .

"Do you mind coming with me to the Ladies?" Meg whispered as the credits rolled. "I need you to look at something."

"Oh. Isn't it something you can ask your midwife about?"

"No. It's not exactly medical."

The auditorium lights hadn't come on yet, so Meg guided Jen out using the torch on her phone. The shoes and lower legs of other viewers were briefly highlighted as they went: trainers and jeans, brogues and chinos, lace-up leather ankle boots and mustard-colored tights. Some of the shoes darted ahead of them as they got to the thick-carpeted corridor.

"I think I have a stretch mark," Meg said, leading her mother into the too-bright toilets and shutting them both into the disabled cubicle. "But I can't see properly. I mean, it's under my bump and I can't get close enough with a mirror."

"Oh." Jen watched as she started to roll down her leggings. "Are you sure you want to know right now?"

"I'm not going to freak out, so don't worry. I just want to be prepared," Meg said. "Is it really there?"

Jen bobbed down to look at the underside of Meg's belly. There was a smell of coconut oil, and a pink line left by the seam of the leggings, but that was all. "Can't see any-thing."

"You didn't have a proper look."

Jen bobbed down again and saw through the gap under the cubicle wall a pair of lace-up leather ankle boots and some mustard-colored tights.

"There's somebody next door," she whispered to Meg.

"So?" Meg said, not lowering her voice. "We're not doing anything wrong."

Jen nodded and looked again at the taut skin. A thin, silvery line glistened above Meg's pants.

"I think there is one there. But it's very, very faint."

"I knew it. Damn."

The toilet in the next cubicle flushed.

"Damn, damn, damn," Meg said.

There was a sound of tights being snapped back into place, of a lock being slid open.

"I thought I'd get away with it. I thought I'd have a tiny, perfect bump and no one would ever be able to tell. But I'm going to be fat and scarred and saggy and permanently exhausted, aren't I?"

"No, darling. I doubt you'll even notice the mark after you give birth. And the rest of you will bounce back, too."

"I'll have to have plastic surgery. I can't

afford plastic surgery, but I'll have to have it."

"No, you won't. Meg, is something else going on? This isn't like you."

It was more like Lana, she thought. Last year, Jen had found a list of plastic-surgery procedures among a pile of Lana's homework. A price had been written next to each body part, and underneath was the total cost, the amount of money she'd need if she got everything she wanted. It came to £15,350 and included labiaplasty. The list had been discussed with Dr. Greenbaum, and Lana had insisted it was just something she'd created out of curiosity, but Jen had noticed her since, staring at her reflection, pulling her skin about and looking as though she loathed the girl in the mirror.

Meg put the lid of the toilet down, sat, and closed her eyes. "Sorry," she said. "Sorry. I was being stupid. It must be the hormones. I'm fine now."

"Are you sure?"

She nodded, eyes still closed. "I need to wee."

"Okay." Jen let herself out of the cubicle. The woman with the ankle boots and mustard-colored tights was leaning over a sink, peering into a mirror while she flicked mascara onto her lashes. She smiled at Jen, amused, embarrassed. Jen smiled back, rueful, embarrassed. Meg came out and washed her hands, and they left.

The sky was nearly dark and it had begun to drizzle but, when Jen tried to pull her coat more closely around herself, she found it didn't fit. She'd picked up one of Lana's, and the joy and amazement of finding she could actually get her arms in it (if only her arms) was overshadowed by the fact that she was now out in the rain in inadequate clothing. She pulled up the hood and tucked it close around her face, hoping to keep the edge from falling over her eyes.

"Haven't you got a jacket or an umbrella?" she asked Meg.

"No, and I'm finding the rain refreshing."

"You can't afford to catch a chill in your condition."

"I'm not going to catch a chill from a bit of summer drizzle. Oh." She'd been swishing her head about and now put a hand to the side of her face. "My earring's come off." She went back the way they'd come, looking along the curb.

Jen followed and copied her, shining her phone light at the paving stones. Someone was whistling somewhere down the street, and it was haunting. She was peering vaguely through the railings of a house at the end of the road when her colleague Rupert walked around the corner.

"Shit, Jen!" Rupert said. "I didn't see you there. What are you doing, hiding out, waiting to scare people?"

"I'm not hiding out."

"You're dressed all in black. With a hood. Is it some kind of ceremony?"

"I'm dressed in navy blue, actually, and I'm looking for my daughter's lost earring."

"Ah," Rupert said, pulling his shoulder bag round so it made a barrier between them. "Surely you need some candles and a pentagram or two for that?"

Jen laughed.

"D'you want a hand?" He moved his bag again, pushing it onto his back, wearing it the way cycle couriers wore them.

"Thanks," Jen said, "but there's no point in us both getting cold and wet. What are you doing here, anyway?"

"I live just over there." He pointed.

"I never knew. We're practically neighbors."

"Fancy that. Well, good luck finding the earring. See you on Monday."

Jen felt the light from Rupert's hallway flash across her face as he opened his front door and went inside, and when the light was gone she felt a new appreciation of her own invisibility. It was definitely the super-power she would choose, despite knowing it was the wrong answer, the answer that made you a coward, unable to deal with the real world, not free enough in your soul to want to fly. She took a few steps along the pavement and stooped to look under a bench.

"Found anything?" Meg asked, catching up with her.

"No, sorry."

She stepped between two parked cars and pulled at the too-small sides of Lana's jacket, trying to cover the lighter-colored jumper, acting on the desire to blend into the night. When a lamp was switched on in one of the sitting rooms opposite, she turned her pale face away. The light bounced over the car bonnets and glinted in the puddles of rain, one of which she had a foot in.

"Shit," she said, like Rupert's long-delayed echo.

"It doesn't matter about the earring," Meg said. "You'd better get home and dry."

A shadow flitted across the puddle, once, and again. Jen looked up to see a pair of legs, visible below the blinds in a lit-up room. A man's legs, Rupert's legs, naked legs, blue against the yellow light, hairs curling shaggily from his skin. The ankles were reddish purple and Jen wondered if he was allergic to his socks. Then, as he moved, she saw he was completely naked, crouching slightly, as if he knew he could be seen and was trying, ineffectively, to shield himself.

Meg turned and caught her mother's eye. "I work with him," Jen told her.

"Not really?"

"Really. We'd better move before he sees us."

"Yes, we'd better. He's lucky we didn't take a picture," Meg said. "That's the kind of image that ends up on the internet."

#RAPTURE

The internet. Where a bad photo of you could live forever. Jen had once been interviewed by the local paper during a street party, and the picture had somehow made her look like an overfed toddler. And for years, it had been the first image that came up whenever her name was googled.

Occasionally, Jen looked at Lana's posts on Twitter and her photos on Instagram, to check there was nothing unfortunate there, to make sure she wasn't being bullied, or trolled, or sexually harassed. But since Lana's disappearance Jen had begun to look more closely, more frequently.

"Are you checking Lana's Instagram again?" Hugh said, putting a cup of ginger tea down next to her on Sunday evening. "Why don't you use your phone?"

"The pictures are too small on my phone. Oh, Hugh, it's like a different girl." Jen didn't look up from the laptop and tried to pretend the tea was after-dinner coffee, right up until the moment she tasted it and was disappointed. "She's like someone in another country, with another life. I don't recognize anything, or hardly anything. She doesn't even look like her."

"That's the point, isn't it?"

"Is it?"

"Yes. Be the best version of yourself, et cetera."

"Oh, of course," Jen said. "YOLO."

"Quite." Hugh sat down and closed his eyes.

"Not bothering with the reading stage of the evening, then?" Jen asked. "Going straight for asleep-in-chair?"

"As you see."

Jen went back to Lana's posts. Recent ones included a photo of a goldfinch on the garden fence (finally, something familiar), which must have been taken from her bedroom. *Birds inside and out,* Lana had written underneath. It had thirty-three likes.

Another was an image of a cave with writing obscuring it: *Don't pity me when I call myself a Nobody, I might be trying to defeat a Cyclops.*

"Very classical," Hugh said, as Jen read it out. "I wonder if she understands the reference."

"And there's a picture of a cake tin full of chocolate brownies here," Jen said. "When did she make brownies?"

"Are you sure they're hers?"

"Yes, that's my cake tin. And she's put: *Homemade brownies motherfuckers.* Hashtag *baking.*"

"Charming."

"Where're *our* motherfucking brownies?" Jen said, then looked up, shocked, in time to meet Hugh's eyes, shocked. "Sorry. I think I've been scrolling through for too long."

"Well," Hugh said, smiling. "That's woken me up."

"I am a bit annoyed at missing out on cake. Why weren't we offered any?"

"They probably had marijuana in them."

"Reassuring, Hugh. Thank you."

"You're welcome. Any other revelations?"

"She has a tattoo."

"A what?"

"Oh, no, that's Maya's daughter, Ash.

She's dyed her hair blond, and they all have the same haircut; sometimes it's difficult to tell them apart. Lots of pancakes and bacon, lots of photos of her own feet in shoes, lots of photos of her own face, close up. One with a cat. Hugh! It's *the* cat. The cat I saw on the stairs. I knew Lana had something to do with it. Those are our curtains in the background, too. I'm going to ask her when she comes down. If she comes down."

"Don't do anything hasty," Hugh said. "We agreed to tread lightly, remember. What has she written underneath?"

"Nothing useful. There are just a series of cartoon cat faces, one smiling, one pouting, one with hearts for eyes. Then hashtag *kitty.*"

"Maybe the cat ran in, she took a picture, and then it ran out again."

"Maybe." Jen began swiping quickly through the photos, letting her fingers flick up higher and higher on the touchpad with each sweep, until she remembered the impression Lana had done of her using Hugh's iPad and made her movements more conservative again. There were no more pictures of the cat, anyway, and she was about to close the laptop when she recognized the shape of the tor near the holiday center, a jumble of huge rocks which looked like a giant child's giant Lego project. The photo had been taken from a position that made the sun look as if it was sinking into a gap between the boulders. The toe of Lana's walking boot was just visible at the bottom of the photo.

Jen turned the screen around to show Hugh and finished the cold dregs of her tea.

"Last day on Earth," she read aloud from Lana's description. "Hashtag *rapture,* hashtag *beautiful,* hashtag *believe."*

There was a dark shape in the lower-left-hand corner, a peculiar shape that made Jen shrink back in her seat: it was out of focus and too small to be recognizable, but it looked like a person crouching slightly, as if trying not to be seen. The date of the picture was the day before Lana had gone missing.

NINE LADIES

That was the day the sketching group had been taken to the Nine Ladies: a Bronze Age circle of stones, no taller than knee height, in a clearing on the edge of the moor. The stones, misshapen and lichen-encrusted, seemed friendly and rather cozy in the middle of that scrap of woodland, and the English Heritage information boards by the footpath and the rainbowcardiganed people camping nearby only added to the feeling that any wildness was rather subdued.

However, there was a little flutter of excitement when someone realized there were nine women in their group (and two men), though this meant Lana wasn't counted and had to be demoted to "girl."

"They were once believed to be the remains of women who were turned to stone for dancing on a Sunday," Peny said, reading from an information board.

"Golly, let's hope we aren't turned to stone for sketching on a Thursday," said the Reiki practitioner as she set up her stool and portable easel.

The wood that surrounded the clearing was full of licorice-scented cow parsley, and the smell, expanding in the damp air, seemed absurdly strong for such delicate flowers. Everyone in the sketching group sat huddled under the birch trees in order to get the best perspective of the stones, but Lana wandered away and spent the session looking up at the oak tree that stood a few meters to one side.

It was strewn with offerings, from modern-day pagans, or perhaps just walkers who were moved by the place. Twigs had been tied together in various shapes (mostly triangles and stars) and hung from pieces of string, shiny ribbons were knotted onto branches, pinecones and shells were twisted around others.

"Matthew tied those there," Lana said, pointing to a collection of brown-and-white striped feathers which spun like a shuttlecock in the breeze.

"How did he get up there?" Jen asked, having laid down her sketchbook for a few minutes.

"Don't know. He didn't say. They're buzzard and kestrel and tawny-owl feathers. There's a way to tell the difference, but I can't remember what it was."

"The kestrel feathers will be smaller, surely."

"Okay," Lana said, as if even this guesswork were a kind of showing off.

She walked away, still looking at the tree. There were homemade dream catchers, and a yellow, knitted flower, and a bunch of tulips, quickly fading, and a woman (Jen assumed) had threaded her hot-pink thong around a cluster of leaves. Rather creepily, someone else had used a length of black chain to attach a stuffed pink washing-up glove to a central branch and the glove stuck up in the air like a dismembered hand. It seemed out of keeping with the rest of the things but, of course, Lana was particularly interested in it.

She took photos and drew some of the more unusual offerings (though these were gone from Lana's sketchbook when Jen looked the next day), and as they left the place a few hours later Lana ransacked her pockets for something to add to the tree, eventually producing her earphones.

"You can't leave those," Jen said, though the idea that Lana wouldn't be able to block her out with music was quite appealing.

"But you hate it when I have them in. You always say you hate it."

"That's never bothered you before."

"Well, I guess I thought maybe it's something I could do for you," Lana said, shrugging. "I could go without them from now on."

She began tying the white wires around a low branch, her voice changed by the angle of her throat as she reached up above her head. "I think it seems appropriate, anyway," she said. "Or, like, symbolic. I'm kind of saying we need to listen to nature, or whatever."

Jen supposed the modern pagans or druids, or New Age devotees, or run-of-the-mill hippies, would approve, and when the wires were secured she took a photograph of Lana standing with the earbuds in her ears, as if she were using a stethoscope and listening to the heart of the tree. Lana had put that picture on Instagram, too.

DISPLACEMENT ACTIVITY

Jen packed the laptop away in a hurry when Lana came down to watch TV, not wanting her daughter to know she'd been checking her social-media accounts. "Stalking," Lana called it.

"What d'you want to see?" Jen asked.

"Anything."

Hugh volunteered to put the kettle on again and came back into the room, muttering. "Everything gets lost in this house," he said, addressing the television rather than Jen or Lana. "What's this you're watching?"

"*Who Do You Think You Are?*" Jen told him.

"Not again?"

"It's that actress from *Upstairs, Downstairs* — you remember." Jen lifted the remote control but didn't turn the TV off or press pause or even lower the sound. She waited for Hugh to sit down or leave. He stayed standing, though, hovering over them, as the actress cried during the story of her ancestors' lives in a workhouse. Hugh's position didn't bother Lana, of course, who

185

wasn't watching the program.

"Shit," she said, her brows narrowed towards the screen of her phone.

"What's happened?" Hugh asked.

"Nothing. Autocorrect."

After a few minutes the program finished, the actress promising to learn the French horn, as her great-grandfather had been in a colliery band. Jen thought of Stephen's genealogy-inspired religious conversion and felt that someone should do a study on the influence of family history on the middle aged. The researcher could make up an interest or talent in an ancestor and see if the subject suddenly found they, too, were interested or talented in that direction. Should *she* go back to university, Jen wondered, and conduct the study herself?

In her imagination, she had completed an MA and a PhD and was about to present her results during an interview on *Woman's Hour.* If it went well, her thesis might get into the nonfiction charts; she might be asked to appear on a television show, or be offered tenure at a university (whatever "tenure" was).

Meanwhile, Hugh was still standing. "Do you want me to help look for whatever it is you've lost?" Jen asked, getting back to the TV's home screen and scrolling through the other ten episodes to see if there were any she hadn't seen.

"No, it doesn't really matter," Hugh said.

"Okay, then, do you want to sit down?"

"I don't know. I think I'm too restless now. I can't find my usual mug."

Jen gazed at Hugh. He didn't look quite like himself for a moment, or she was unable to recognize him. The shape of his face was heavier than it ought to have been, his nose wider. Then, a moment later, his face was too slight, the nose strangely narrow. It was as if she were seeing him in a circus mirror; the idea of him having a favorite mug had given her a new perspective on him. She looked at Lana, who had always known this about her father, trying to imagine what *she* saw, but their daughter was still staring at her phone.

"Which is your usual mug?" Jen asked in a quiet voice.

"It's a Cadbury's Buttons one. It's got a good wide handle, so I can get more than two fingers through it." He gestured holding a mug of tea with a firm grip.

"A few mugs got broken last week."

"Right. Well. Thanks awfully for telling me earlier."

"Oh. What a dickhead," Lana said.

"What did you just say?" Hugh asked.

"I didn't mean you, obviously."

"You're both very grumpy all of a sudden," Jen said. She made a mental note to find another Buttons mug on eBay and watched Lana for a moment, wondering what she was typing on her phone, wondering if it was something she'd be able to look at later, on Twitter or Tumblr or somewhere. In the meantime, there was television. She'd spotted another episode of *Who Do You Think You Are?* that she'd only seen once, and hit play.

An actor she vaguely remembered appeared on-screen; he was raking leaves while wearing a flat cap and wasn't yet in an archive or weeping over any sepia photographs. Jen turned the sound down.

"I'm not grumpy," Hugh said.

"I'm allowed to be grumpy," Lana said at the same time. "People can't help that. And I can't help it, can I?" She put a hand up to her hair and gave it a hard twist, the pink scar on her scalp tightening, distorting.

"Don't do that, darling," Jen said. "Actually, I might be able to help." Rushing to the kitchen, she came back with a Coke can and held it out. "Here you are."

"What's this?" Lana said, taking it. "Are you — are you joking? Or is this some kind of punishment?"

"Punishment?"

"Yeah, you give me a Coke, but the can's empty. Is it meant to be symbolic or something?"

"No, I thought you might like to crush it. For stress."

Lana looked at the can for a moment. "No, thanks, I'm all right."

"Are you sure?"

"Yeah," Lana said, handing the can back.

"Oh."

"I'd quite like to crush it," Hugh said.

"It was really for Lana, but okay, you go ahead."

"Why was it specially for me?" Lana asked.

"It's supposed to be a good displacement activity. So you don't take out your frustration on . . ."

"On what?"

Jen paused, for a second, less than that. "Sweetheart," she said, "it's just terribly hard for us, for your dad and me, when we see you . . . hurting yourself."

Lana looked back at her phone. It was a tiny movement, but it gave the impression of a large stone door banging closed.

"I know you don't want to talk about it, and that's fine, but you've got to let your scars heal properly."

Hugh sat down finally and sank well back

into his chair, staring at the muted television.

"You have to find other ways to cope with your feelings that won't inflict permanent damage on your skin." Jen thought of the other suggestions she'd read about in the handbook, suggestions which had seemed feasible on paper but which she now realized were absurd. Imagine advising Lana to hold an ice cube or suck on a little packet of wasabi paste. She wondered if the author of the book had ever actually met a teenager.

"We aren't blaming you, or judging you," Jen said. "We're just trying to give you better tools."

"Like an empty Coke can?"

"I know it seems silly, but it's just one of many ideas . . ." *Could* she tell her about the wasabi paste? "We love you very much. You know that, don't you?"

"Yes, fine," Lana said, and, grabbing at Jen's hands, she took the can, crunching the sides in and screwing the ends together. "There, happy now?"

No, Jen thought, of course not. But then, happiness was something from a past life; it was the opposite of life now, where you could try to do everything right and yet find you'd made things worse. Happiness was doing everything wrong and finding that things had turned out okay, anyway. Happiness was obliviousness, it was not having to read books about adolescent mental health, it was eating dinner in front of the TV without consequences, it was buying your children mobile phones and feeding them crisps and forgetting to check their homework. Happiness was everyone in the same room, captivated by their own digital device.

Baby animals

"Platypus," twelve-year-old Lana said.

"Oh, good one."

They looked down at their screens, typing. Already, in each person's search history, a list had formed: "baby pig," "baby panda," "baby panther," "baby penguin." They were doing the *p*'s.

"Sweet!" Jen said, as the series of images of tiny platypuses loaded: some wet, some dry, some asleep, some swimming.

"Have you got to the picture where it's curled up in someone's hands?" Lana asked, burrowing further into the sofa cushions.

"Have you seen the really tiny ones that are all pink still?"

"Funny creatures," Hugh said, holding his iPad at a distance. He didn't entirely approve of this activity and was yet to suggest

191

an animal for googling. "This is madness," he'd said, several searches ago. "What has human interaction come to? Surely we should at least be looking at the same screen."

"But we're looking at the same pictures," Lana had said (she'd invented the game, if you could call it a game), "so what's the difference?"

"They look so velvety," Meg said, turning her phone horizontal for a larger image of a baby platypus.

There was a collective sigh and then a pause. Jen's eyes strayed from the laptop to her family. It was a Saturday afternoon, and Meg was staying until Monday. They were all lounging back, gazing at each other, waiting, thinking. The winter sun came through the sitting-room blinds, the radiators whistled as they warmed up, bowls of half-eaten hummus lay on the coffee table. She gave thanks for comfortable furniture, for central heating, for chickpeas, for reliable WiFi. "Porcupine," she said.

"Ha!"

Another pause for typing.

"They are crazy-looking," Lana said. "Like mad scientists."

"Like they've been electrocuted," Hugh said. "But some of these pictures are definitely of hedgehogs."

This put a damper on the result, and they stopped scrolling.

"Possum?" Meg suggested.

"Oh, they're creepy, even when they're little." *Digital-native* Lana was always the first to get the images loaded. "They have weird ghost-faces."

"Yeah, you're right."

The game had run out of steam. In a moment, each of them would switch to Facebook or Instagram, a news site or a game app, and then they really would be separated by their screens. Jen tried desperately to think of one more animal beginning with *p,* but she could think only of pug or Pomeranian, and breeds of dog weren't allowed under Lana's rules. Someone reached for and crunched on a crisp. A cushion was adjusted. Feet were swung over the arm of a chair.

"Pangolin," Hugh announced into the silence, making each syllable especially clear.

The crunching stopped, the cushion was discarded, the feet dropped back onto the floor.

"Oh, Dad. Best one yet."

"Look at it hanging on to its mum's tail."

"Look at its funny little ears."

193

"Look at it snuggled under a blanket."

They smiled at each other. The pangolin had made the game feel like a success. Even Hugh was pleased, now he'd "won." Jen, with a sudden lucidity, a kind of premonition, realized she would look back on this moment and know she'd been happy.

PASSION

Nowadays, Jen had her own displacement activities, instead of happiness. She'd built a repertoire over the last year or so, taking comfort in small tasks performed perfectly: making a pot of coffee, wiping the leaves of a houseplant, flossing her teeth. In fact, the worse Lana's depression had seemed, the more careful and thorough Jen's dental care had become.

Sometimes, action, rather than distraction, was needed, though. After finding Lana with her bag of painkillers, real precautions had been necessary: all the knives and scissors in the house were supposed to be kept in a locked cashbox (bought for the purpose), and Jen had contacted pharmacists to ask them not to sell Lana any nonprescription medication.

The four days of agony in the Peak District had prompted other actions, too. Since

Lana's replacement mobile phone had arrived, Jen had been checking the bill, asking about any numbers she didn't recognize, asking Lana to explain who particular contacts were and where she had met them. And since she'd gone back to school, a week and a half ago, Jen had been getting to work late in order to chaperone her daughter to the gates. Lana was less than thrilled.

"I can walk to school by myself. I'm fifteen, not five."

"I know, but you have to understand, my mind runs riot as soon as you're out of sight."

"And I suppose that's my fault."

"Well," Jen said, knowing she should say, *No, it's no one's fault, it's just the situation we find ourselves in and we have to help each other through it,* but really wanting to say, *You're the one who's been threatening suicide for over a year, who ran off somewhere (you won't say where) and did something (you won't say what) — who else is to blame?*

She tried to come up with excuses to walk *with* Lana, offering to carry her PE bag or art project, but even the most gullible child would have been unconvinced, and three times in the last week they had had rows on the street: twice, loud, embarrassing, screaming rows; and once, a fierce under-breath bickering exchange, which had seemed somehow more undignified. And so Jen had stopped insisting on escorting Lana and had begun to follow her instead.

That was how, on a Monday morning in July, Jen found herself waiting for Lana to leave the house before following her at a distance, shadowing her own daughter, like some grubby detective in a hard-boiled crime novel.

But she wasn't going to give up like no weak sister, she thought, hearing Lana's footsteps in the distance; she'd just ankle to the main street then turn back for a cup of joe. If only she could get the girl to spill (Jen was warming to the noirish slang), but everything she said was hinky. Maybe she needed to put the screws on, though she'd have to make sure the girl didn't pull a Dutch act.

"What the hell are you doing?"

Lana was standing against a wall, her outline blurred by the monster growth of a passionflower vine that had climbed over someone's porch and was stretching up towards their first-floor windows.

"Are you following me?"

"Yes," Jen said. "Sorry."

"So, what now?" Lana asked. "Are you going to keep following me? Should I carry on, pretend you're not there?"

Jen shrugged, still a little dazed after being pulled out of her Chandleresque daydream. "I guess I'll take it on the heel and toe," she said, though her enthusiasm for the lingo had left her. There were dozens of flower heads open on the vine and something about them reminded her of Lana. It seemed fitting that she had hidden among them.

"You'll do what?" Lana asked, adjusting the bandana she wore to hide the tufty growth of hair and the scar on the top of her head.

"I'll go," Jen clarified. The flowers looked so much like eyes, she thought, with their purple-tipped lashes; uncanny eyes.

"Okay." Lana had her arms crossed. "Go on, then."

"What will you do?"

"What I was going to do originally."

"Walk to school?"

"What else?"

That was too huge a question, and Jen decided not to answer it. There was a faint smell coming from the passionflowers and she moved closer to dip her nose against the yellow anthers. It was the scent, she realized, that reminded her of Lana: sweet, slightly mentholy antiseptic.

197

She felt irritated. It should be a scent associated with childhood scrapes, bashed elbows, and scabby knees; it should be a wholesome smell, a competent smell, not a reminder of carefully sliced forearms and parental despair.

"Are you going, or what?" Lana asked.

"I'm going," Jen said, "but I'm going that way." She pointed towards the main road, towards the station.

"Fine."

Lana stood back to let her past, pushing herself further into the passionflower so that the leaves and tendrils formed a kind of crown. Jen moved, her feet heavy on the paving stones, but at the last minute she reached out and plucked a flower from the hedge — the owner wouldn't notice; there were so many — and tucked it above her ear. It was still there, still giving out its sweet smell, when she got to work. Rupert raised his eyebrows as she passed his desk.

THE FARMER'S IN HIS DEN

"Darling, you're distracted. Shall I call you back another time?"

Jen moved the phone from the crook of her neck. "No, sorry. Sorry, Mum. I do want to talk to you. I was looking something up."

The office was unusually empty. Rupert had gone to meet a new printer, and Jen had taken advantage of the quiet to call her mother but, beyond their initial greeting, she couldn't remember what they'd said to each other so far.

"Good to know I have your full attention," Lily said. "What were you looking up?"

"That farmer who found Lana. I just wanted to see if there was anything about him online."

"Why? I thought he was the Good Samaritan."

"He was. He is. On the face of it, anyway. But, I don't know, at the back of my mind, I suppose I'm also a bit suspicious. After all, how was it that he managed to find Lana when no one else could?"

"And? What have you discovered?"

"There's a Google result that says, *Farmer, Richard Crossley, charged with —*"

"Charged with what?"

"Well, that's just it. When I click the link, I get an error message," Jen said.

ANY ADVANCE

So Jen couldn't get any further than that, and she was looking forward to the police visiting, hoping she could get some answers from them. The officer who came to their house on Tuesday evening reminded Jen of Rupert. He looked small, bundled up as he was among the bulky accoutrements of his uniform. Hugh seemed more solid by comparison, despite the fact that he'd already changed into pajamas and smelled of her expensive rose-and-magnolia anti-aging cream.

"I'd forgotten someone was coming round," he said, grimacing as he came into the sitting room.

There was a moving of cold coffee cups and a gathering of magazines and a general shuffling about, a kind of welcome dance for a man who wasn't entirely welcome. And when that was done they sat perched on the edge of the sofa (Jen and Hugh) and the armchair (Lana), as if to sit back comfortably would be to admit to something.

The police officer had a lot of notes clutched tightly in his hand. He refused tea and chose to sit on a hard dining-room chair, which meant he was raised slightly above them. This arrangement made their sitting room feel more like a court, Jen thought: with a judge up on a bench, she and Hugh in the public gallery, and Lana in the dock.

"Just to explain, I'm from the Metropolitan Police. The Derbyshire Constabulary has asked me to come round to go over a few questions with yourself," he said, looking at Lana. "Just some follow-up questions. Is that okay?"

"It's okay."

"Great. Erm." He checked his notes. "So, Lana, can you tell me again what happened the night you went missing?"

Lana stared at one of the paintings that Jen had pulled out of her sketchbook to take to the framer's: a ruined section of medieval church with two peacock butterflies resting in an unglazed window. Jen was pleased with it, though the scene was perhaps a little too chocolate-boxy, and she could imagine the way her colleagues would dismiss the effort, the recent art-school graduates with their vagina paintings and sculptures made out of chicken skin.

"I got up to go to the shower block," Lana said, "and took a wrong turn on my way back. And that's it, really."

"Which way did you turn?" the officer asked.

"How d'you mean?"

"You came out of the shower block. Did you turn left or right?"

"Left, I think."

"Great, that's great." And he really did

seem to think it was great: his face lit up, and he beamed at them all. "Because when you were asked before, you said you couldn't remember which way you'd turned, so that's progress. Can you tell me any more? What could you see? Hear? Smell?"

"I might have turned right," Lana said.

"Okay." His smile dimmed. "Were you with anyone?"

"No."

"Did you meet anyone while you were lost? Anyone at all?"

"No."

"In four days, you didn't see a single person? It was a busy season in the Peak District, I'm told. Lots of walkers, holiday-makers."

"I didn't see anyone," she said, her eyes on the picture of the church. There were no people in it, and Jen felt responsible, as if she'd made those walkers and holidaymakers disappear, when Lana needed them. But adding figures to a landscape was awkward; hardly anyone on the course had put in the red- and blue- and yellow-jacketed swarms of middle-class tourists. They weren't picturesque.

"What were you wearing when you got lost?" the policeman said.

"Leggings, a fleece, a jacket, boots."

Finally, Lana looked away from the picture and met the officer's gaze. "I gave a list before."

"I know, but I have to ask, it's just how this process works. So. What did you have with you? Can you tell me that?"

"Phone, tissues, just stuff in my pockets."

"Nothing to eat?"

"I might have had a chocolate bar. A KitKat."

"No torch?"

Lana stared at him a moment. She seemed to be waiting for him to continue. "I had a tiny wind-up torch on a key ring. But I used my phone for light, until I lost it."

"And have you remembered where you lost your phone?"

She shook her head.

"So you had a light source at night."

"At night," Lana said, but it sounded like a question.

"Did you have anything to sleep on?"

"No."

"No sleeping bag, or blanket?"

"No." Lana had begun to raise a hand slightly with each answer, and Jen realized this was less like a courtroom and more like an auction room, Lana somehow increasing her bid with each denial.

"How did you keep warm?"

"I was wearing warm clothes. The weather wasn't that cold."

"But you did get wet?"

"Yes, but I don't know how. I must have walked into a lake or a river or something. I don't remember."

"What about . . . erm." He read his notes carefully, as if they were the details of an important lot: a Ming dynasty vase, a Raphael sketch. "What about condoms? Did you have any condoms with you?"

"No," Lana said. "No way."

"Did you use condoms at any time, or were you aware of the use of condoms?"

"No."

"Did you tear any of your clothing at any point?"

"I can't remember doing that."

"You hurt your head." He looked at the bandana she was wearing over her hair. "Did it bleed a lot?"

"I guess so. They said so at the hospital."

"Did you try and stop the bleeding?"

"Probably."

"What did you use?"

She shrugged. "Tissues?"

"You'd have needed a lot of tissues. You didn't use something else? A blanket, say?"

"No, I didn't have a blanket, so I couldn't have."

"Okay. Have you kept in touch with anyone from the holiday? I think you made friends with the center manager's son. Matthew's his name."

"I follow him on Instagram," Lana said. "He posts pictures of birds, mostly." She smiled, as though that was pitiable.

"No one else?"

"No."

"And you haven't arranged to meet up with anyone you met in the Peak District?"

"No." That hand gesture again, a half wave, a kind of demand to be noticed, despite the fact that they were all already intently focused on her.

"Right. I'm going to show you some photos that were taken of your legs when you arrived at the hospital. Do you remember the photos being taken?"

"I think so."

He fished them out from his bundle of papers and passed them to Lana. Her pale ankles looked mottled in the picture, but the thin bruise lines on the skin were unmistakable. "Can you tell me how you got those marks?"

"From my socks. I told the police that before."

"You didn't tie anything around your legs?"

205

"Again, no."

"Did someone else tie anything around your legs?"

"No."

"You're not protecting anyone?"

"No."

"And you're telling us the truth?" He said "us," as though he represented the whole of the British police force.

"Yes," Lana said. "The whole truth, et cetera, et cetera."

"We're not trying to get you into trouble," he said, starting to lean forward but finding his stab-proof vest got in the way. "We just want to make sure you've told us everything you can, for your own sake. *Our* job is to keep *you* safe."

"If you say so."

"I do. Are you sure there's nothing else you want to tell me?"

There was a moment of quiet while Lana smirked. The policeman looked at Hugh and Jen, scanning the room for any advance on the price: going once, going twice, sold.

"Okay, well, that's everything, then," he said. "Here is a number to call if you do remember anything new. I'll leave you to your evening."

Jen showed him to the door, her legs stiff from her perched position on the sofa. "So it was condoms, then," she said. "They found condoms. That's what made them send you?"

The officer fiddled with the set of accessories on his belt.

"She's supposed to be in my custody," Jen said. "How can I do my duty without all the facts? I need to protect her, don't I? And if there's someone else involved . . ." She dropped her voice. "I was told that the farmer who found my daughter has a conviction for something."

"Who told you that?"

"Why does that matter? Do you know what he was convicted of?"

"Look," he said. "All I know is what's written here. Apparently, a blanket, with some blood on it, and two used condoms were found on a Mr. Crossley's land. That's the farmer, right? But, as you heard, your daughter says they're nothing to do with her."

"You're just going to take her word? Can't you test the blanket for DNA?"

He half smiled. "Not unless we suspect it's linked with a serious crime. And there's no crime, insofar as we can ascertain. Forensic testing is expensive. We don't have the resources. We can't waste time and money. The condoms might be from some other member of the public and the blood might only be from an animal."

"Might."

"Unless your daughter says otherwise, we have to assume they're nothing to do with her case. And, like I said, there's no crime here that we know of. Her friends, classmates, and teachers were questioned, and her emails and social media were checked when she was missing. She hadn't been in contact with anyone of interest. Nothing, in fact, gave us any cause for alarm. Your daughter says there's no crime. Do you have reason to believe she's lying?"

"Just tell me. Is Richard Crossley a suspect?"

"A suspect? What would he be suspected of? I keep telling you, as far as we're concerned, there's no crime. If you can't give us a reason to investigate further, we have to leave it there."

He put his hat on, in a kind of universal gesture of farewell, and wished her goodnight. She closed the door and put her forehead against it, feeling the cool of the painted wood and trying not to feel anything else.

NUMBERS GAME

Two condoms were worse than one. That much was obvious. Two condoms meant two men or one man twice. It meant a longer ordeal, it meant more pain, it meant witnesses, but not the helpful kind, or it meant somehow keeping Lana confined so she could be hurt again.

Jen stood at the sink, scrubbing burnt sausage fat off a roasting tin, and rubbing the instep of her foot over her lower leg, as if trying to get something off. A tight sock, perhaps, or a piece of rope. The smell of the fat mixed with washing-up liquid was off-putting, but it was also familiar, domestic, safe. And although she was tired and could have let the tin soak overnight, she didn't want to leave the brightly lit kitchen; it was familiar and domestic and safe, too.

They'd all ended up in there after the police officer had gone; even Lana had renounced the solitude of her room for once, and sat through Hugh's long-winded account of his most recent (and nail-biting) piano exam. For Grade Two.

It was Jen who couldn't concentrate and who would ask later what "I'm an Old Cow Hand" meant, earning a tortuous and stilted recital of the piece. Instead, she was doing a terrible kind of maths in her head. Because it was about probability, wasn't it? It was about how likely you were to meet anyone in the countryside. How likely that the few people you did meet would be mad or bad. How likely that those mad or bad people would attack you. Or it was statistics: How many mad or bad people per hundred thousand? How many hundreds of thousands of people in that part of the country?

She had played this game at night when her daughters were small. How many child-snatchers in the population? How likely that they would live in London? How likely that they would live in her family's part of London? How far might a child-snatcher travel? How much time would they need to snatch a child? How long, therefore, would a child need to be accidentally left alone for all these things to converge?

The roasting tin was finally clean but, as Jen turned from the sink, Lana caught sight of her face.

"What are you thinking?" she asked, her jaw hard. "What are you thinking about me?"

"I'm not thinking," Jen said. "Or, at least, I'm trying my *best* not to think."

"Good, because everything you think is wrong."

That could be the tagline for their relationship, Jen thought with a grim smile as she made her way upstairs to bed.

TEMPTATION

She must have slept with her face pressed hard into the pillow because the next day Jen felt as if some surface were pushing back at her, as if the blood were only gradually returning to her skin. Her eyes were dry, and blinking was painful; she kept them closed on the train to work and found they were watery when she stepped onto the platform. She didn't recognize the promotions girl on the station concourse at first.

"Tortellini!" she was calling out, "tortel-leeeeni!" her voice like a little bell ringing among the shuffling feet and platform announcements. "Free tortellini."

"Bethany," Jen said, reading the sign above the stacks of pasta boxes: *Give in to temptation and a taste of Italy.*

"Jen," Bethany said. "Have a pack. They're new, and they're actually really good — well, we got to take some home last week, and my mum liked them, anyway. I'm only supposed to let people have one each, but do you want two? That'll be dinner sorted, then, won't it?"

"Thanks, yes. I won't have to go to the shops now." Jen slipped the plastic-wrapped pasta into her bag. "Shouldn't you be at school?"

"I've dropped French, so I've got a free period until eleven thirty, and this is, like, not bad money? I only work weekends, normally, but my boss offered me a couple of hours extra. I've been here since seven. Nearly killed me getting up that early, to be honest." She turned to take a breath and give her ringing call again (". . . a taste of Italeeeee"), and to hand out more pasta to the rushing commuters.

Jen watched for a moment, absorbed by the various reactions of the passersby: delight at an unexpected freebie, hawkish in their determination to get something for nothing, irritated at the obstacle on the concourse, angry to be asked how they liked their pasta at 9 a.m. on a Wednesday morning. She tried to find the child Bethany in this woman, with her perfectly painted face, her long, carefully buffed nails, the way she smiled and smiled again at each person, unfazed by their grabbing hands or bad-tempered brush-offs. She wondered if Bethany's mother ever asked herself who this spotless young lady was, whether she could connect her with the crisp-eating, knee-

212

scraping girl she'd been only five minutes ago.

"Sorry, but I can't really give you any more," Bethany said, looking around to find Jen still there. "I'd get into trouble."

"No, I know. I wasn't expecting . . ." She walked towards the Tube, calling back, "Nice to see you!" But at the steps down she stopped. Here was Bethany, without Lana. Here was Bethany, thrown into her path. Here was Bethany, grown up and sensible. And if she had any information, if Lana had told her anything important, then it might be enough to convince the police to test the blanket, to look again, to persuade Lana to tell them what really happened.

Heroine

Jen was a little late to work, but it hardly mattered, as the company's summer newsletter was a skeleton edition and there wasn't much for her to do. She spent the morning retrying the broken link to the article on Farmer Crossley, before flicking from Instagram to Facebook to Instagram again, feeling slightly nauseous. Somehow, she ended up scrolling through the comments section under an op-ed piece on

Mexican drug lords. People kept spelling "heroin" wrong, so that there seemed to be some other character, some heroine, in the struggle against corruption, some woman who would sweep in and solve everything.

"Tea, anyone?" Rupert called, waving a cup and a sachet of rooibos.

Jen shook her head, looking at the mug on her desk. It wasn't her mug, just one that had hung about the office kitchen for years, left behind by a long-forgotten colleague. But, somehow, it had become Jen's mug; people assumed it was hers because she apparently fit the description. *Supermum.* It felt like a nasty joke, considering everything she'd been going through with Lana. In fact, it was probably more of a comment on her and her family's taste. If the creatives in her team ever bought their mothers gifts (she suspected they didn't have mothers but had been constructed by a team of designers just like themselves), they certainly wouldn't choose anything as tacky as a Supermum mug.

On Monday she had filled it with water to keep her stolen passionflower in, though the water hadn't helped much. The flower had quickly closed its outer petals and wilted. There was a metaphor in there somewhere, she thought, about outside appearances and failed nurturing. And Jen felt something inside herself curl up in the same way when she saw Lana's school's number appear on her phone in the midafternoon.

She was missing from classes. They hadn't noticed at first. It had been several hours. Jen hung up and ran to the Ladies as nausea turned to actual vomiting, then dialed Lana's number, then Hugh's, then Lana's again.

At the sinks, she washed her mouth and began to splash water at her face, her head, her hair, letting it drip down her shoulders and over her chest. There was a part of her that saw how mad and exaggerated these movements were, that regretted the soggy, rat-tailed woman in the lighted mirrors, but another part relished her appearance because it matched the way she felt inside. Walking about with great stamps, she weaved in and out of every stall, tapping Lana's name, listening to the rings, hearing the first few words of the voicemail greeting, ending the call, tapping Lana's name again.

"I'm sitting under a bridge," Lana said, finally accepting the call. "Or, no," she corrected herself. "It's like an overpass or whatever."

Jen felt a dizzying relief at hearing her

daughter's voice but the emotion that came out was anger. "What the hell is going on? Why haven't you been picking up? Why aren't you in school?"

There was a pause, filled with the heavy sound of traffic.

"I wanted to go for a walk."

"Why? What's happened?" Jen asked, knuckling her left eye and feeling the makeup working its way into the delicate skin. "Where exactly are you?"

"I'm not sure. I can send you a screenshot from the maps app."

Jen gazed at her reflection in the mirror. She had been grabbing at her hair, though she'd hardly been aware of that. Now, the damp, dyed-dark strands stood away from her scalp, scarecrow-like. Her phone buzzed and she opened the image. "I'll call you when I get near," she said.

There must have been a reaction as Jen ran through the office, hair in a mess, makeup smeared. Worse, she had banged her knee against Rupert's desk as she ran and had exited limping slightly from the pain, but she'd been too intent to care, not knowing how long she had before Lana would move, would disappear again. The uncomfortable glances she got on the Tube gave her some idea of the way her colleagues might have looked at her, though, and by the time she reached her stop Jen was beginning to understand how she would feel once the drama of the situation had dissipated. It would be embarrassing (more than usually embarrassing) to walk back into work tomorrow.

Outside, Jen's appearance went unnoticed because it was raining hard. Lots of people had been caught without a coat or umbrella so she looked almost normal among them. An old woman handed her a plastic bag as she hurried past a bus stop, which was kind, but her clothes were completely soaked by the time she got to the overpass.

Lana was sitting on a small, dry patch of grass with her head down, not looking at anything. Jen didn't wait for the lights to change but ran across the road and in a moment of levity thought of herself swooping in to help, like her fantasy heroin heroine. Like a real Supermum. She sat down, too, folding awkwardly onto the ground, and watched the cars bump or zoom or sail up the ramp, the noise of them bouncing off the concrete surfaces and rumbling over their heads. It wasn't long before she felt trampled by them, slighted. Thick fumes, suspended in the damp air, engulfed her and Lana, coating the inside of their mouths and noses. Jen held her sleeve to her face. It was an unhealthy place.

She tried not to say anything to Lana, of course; talking wasn't allowed: all the books told you to become an ear, not a mouth. If Jen spoke, her daughter might get up and walk off, and this process would begin again at some other location. But the wet clothes hung heavily on her, the damp layer already making her skin buzz and itch, and she was cold now that the glow from her run across the road had faded. Taking off her jacket, she spread it over her knees, hoping to air it a little, and found Lana watching her, frowning at the jacket, as if she were offended by its style. It was denim, and buying it had been a mistake. Jen had known it was a mistake when she bought it six years ago, but she'd worn it anyway, and she'd carried on wearing it, because it hung on a peg in the hallway, because the pocket held a pack of tissues and her Oyster card, because it existed.

"Shall we go?" she asked, her voice shivering.

"You can go." The standard response.

"Why did you disappear like that? Didn't you think we'd be worried?"

"I just wanted to be on my own."

"But why? And why do it without telling

anyone?"

"Why do you think? I mean, you're asking my friends to spy on me, and then you say you don't know why I need to get away."

"You mean Bethany? I only asked if you'd said anything to her, I only asked her because you won't talk to me, you won't tell me what's wrong."

"There's nothing to tell!"

"Yes, that's what she said, too." The conversation had been frustrating, broken by the call of "Tortellini!" and full of shrugs.

"Look, I'm not stupid," Bethany had said. "The police questioned me, too. They thought someone might have taken her or, like, lured her somewhere. I told them I didn't know anything, and I wouldn't have lied. And, anyway, Lana's got, like, depression, right? So just because of that, even without everything else that happened, just because of that I'd tell you if she'd said anything weird or did something weird or whatever. I promise."

Jen sat and wondered about that promise. Whether she could trust it. There was a mysteriously growing puddle in the waste-land where they sat. It spread, despite no raindrops hitting it, fed, perhaps, from underground. Plane trees and nearby houses were reflected in the water, the houses no

219

one could want to live in, not this close to the noise and the dust. One tree in particular loomed over the puddle and seemed to reach for her and Lana, its mirror-self drifting under the road's barriers, feeling for them, sliding up their trouser legs. She leaned further back, onto the concrete wall, and brought up her feet, curling tightly away, and still she felt as if the watery branches were touching her.

Lana's limbs were loosely open, her body too soft, too close to the puddle, and Jen wanted to fold her into the position she usually sat in on the settee, twisted against the corner; she wanted to bundle her into an unbreachable package.

The hiss of the hard rain became a rhythmic tap as the weather began to clear up. Jen concentrated on this until a motorbike with its unbelievable crescendo roared along close to them.

"That tree is worrying me," Jen said, and this made Lana turn and look at her. It was a small victory, eye contact never normally won so easily. "It seems sinister."

"Sinister? The tree?"

"I know. Silly, I know." She should feel sorry for it, really, trapped in a tangle of concrete. She was reminded of the straggly tree in the hospital courtyard. "I can't help feeling that growing here would make any living thing evil."

Lana stared at her for quite a while, her mouth moving, as if she might say something, or was working out how to say something.

"Do you think it's possible for trees to be evil?" she asked at last.

"No, of course not. I said I was being silly."

"Even the really old trees?"

"I don't know. That one's not very old, anyway. London planes grow fast."

"But, like, those oaks that are all fat and rough," Lana said. "The ones with cracks in the trunks and branches that touch the ground. What about those?"

"I suppose they do *look* sinister," Jen said, "and like they contain ancient secrets, doorways into other worlds — fairy worlds, perhaps." She was warming to the subject. "There are stories, too. Did we ever read 'The Tinderbox' when you were little? In that, a witch asks a soldier to retrieve a magic box from the hollow of a tree."

"Did *you* read that thing about the drug smuggler who put cannabis inside Christmas trees?"

"Less romantic," Jen said, "although, to be fair, there's an alarming amount of cold-blooded murder in the Hans Christian Andersen story."

"I think they did it with heroin, too."

"Did what?"

"Hid the heroin in the trees."

"Oh, I see," Jen said, thinking back to the comments she'd been reading before the phone call and unable now to get rid of the mental image of a female superhero being concealed among branches. And there was something else that her mind kept going back to. A myth about a tree. She and Lana had sat like this, on a patch of ground, in the Peak District, and talked about it. Jen looked up at the London plane and just stopped herself from asking Lana if she'd ever heard the trees rustle in an enticing way.

LEGEND

"This walk is especially good for sketching," the tutor said on the third day of the holiday, "because we get a good view of Mam Tor. And then the church itself is particularly interesting because there's a ruin attached to it. We will be working in the tradition of Turner and Caspar David Friedrich."

There was an appreciative murmur at the

names of "real" artists as everyone got out of the minibus, laden with boxes of ink and fold-up stools. Jen, who had the same urge every morning to stay huddled in the musty minibus and have a sleep, was pleased to find that the day was already warm, and by the time they'd reached the churchyard they'd all tied their jackets around their waists and rubbed extra sun cream into their noses.

There was no point waiting for Lana, who was busy talking to Stephen, her voice quiet and then loud as she argued with him, so Jen knelt in the grass and began to draw the craggy half arch of what must have been a bit of cloister when the church was still a monastery. It was a perfect view, too perfect to get much out of it. No matter what Jen did, the picture came out looking sentimental or contrived. The sun shone too brightly on the weather-darkened stone and the frothy heads of the hogweed batted the buttresses too playfully; even the local wildlife conspired to make the place painfully picturesque, with a butterfly landing just where a spot of alizarin crimson would suit the composition.

Jen gave up and packed away her things. Lana's voice was drifting towards her again as she opened the door of the church; it echoed, somehow, through those skeleton rooms, even though there were no walls left to bounce the sound around.

"God is the ultimate mood-lifter," Stephen was saying.

"I think you're getting Him confused with Prozac," Lana replied.

"Very funny, Lana. But that's exactly my point. If people had more faith, they wouldn't need Prozac."

Jen closed the door on them and their voices and the bright light, and smiled at the small, elderly woman in a tabard who was stacking pamphlets on the history of the church and rearranging leaflets about their missions abroad. Perhaps she should have stayed outside to follow Lana about and eavesdrop, rather than leaving Stephen to it, but a moment later Lana was shoving the door open again. She walked straight past the tabarded woman, sat down in a back pew, and shut her eyes. She could have been praying, Jen supposed, but it seemed unlikely, and in fact it felt rather unseemly to pray in such an obvious way, to make a show of herself, especially in a church. The old woman certainly looked a little surprised. Jen bought a pamphlet from her.

The church smelled of lavender, which made Jen think of the South of France. At breakfast that morning everyone had talked about the weather being like the Mediterranean, but what was stranger was that it even sounded like the Mediterranean.

"Can you hear cicadas?" she asked, as she passed the pew where Lana was sitting.

"That's the radiator hissing."

"Oh, so it is."

The radiator was huge and brown and hot to the touch, despite the warm weather. Jen walked away from it, up the north aisle, and then down the south, looking at the monuments, reading bits of plaques, wishing she knew Latin. There was a rood screen which had been restored with Lottery funding, and she felt sorry for the scratched and bleached saints on the wooden panels. They looked rather surprised to be there, carrying their lambs and staffs and chalices.

The notice on the wall explained who the figures represented and described medieval church services: the priests hiding behind the rood screen to bless the bread and the ecstasy of the congregation when the Host was revealed.

A couple of other people came in, and there was a chink of coins as they bought postcards. Jen was enjoying listening to their muffled chatter when another voice began. "A–ma–a–zing grace," it sang. "How sweet hmmm–hmmm."

Jen turned, but couldn't see who might be singing. She supposed it could be a recording, but the voice was a bit rough for that. And wouldn't a professional singer know all the words?

"I once wa–as lost, but now a–am found. Was blind, but hmmm–hmmm–hmmm."

It was a flatish voice, breathy, slurring, and coming from the back of the church. Jen felt a chill descend over her. Could Lana be the one singing? Could she have found some strange voice within her? An unnaturally low and rasping voice? She moved around a pillar and flushed with relief. A large man with a sun-wrinkled face had his arms hooked over the back of the pew, one leg extended along the seat. He was drawing breath for the next line, but he didn't finish "Amazing Grace"; instead, he switched to "Silent Night."

"Doesn't he know it's May?" the course tutor said, catching up with Jen beside the tomb of some fifteenth-century grandee.

Jen smiled. "Perhaps he's practicing for Christmas. Or testing the acoustics."

"Well, I wish he wouldn't. What a terrible noise."

"I know. I think I'll go and join the others outside." She looked back at Lana, who made a face and got up, too. They crept out, and she felt quite sorry for the old woman in the tabard, stuck in the church with the terrible singer.

It was blinding to be outside again, and they didn't go far but dropped onto the grass near a bench where some of the other painters were starting on an early lunch. They sipped coffee from the lids of their thermoses and unwrapped rucksack-squashed sandwiches. The falling away of the greaseproof paper reminded Jen of the revelations of the rood screen, and she couldn't help thinking of the bread-made-flesh. She left her own sandwiches where they lay in her rucksack.

Stephen was sitting a little way off to do some reading, and Peny speculated that church grounds were difficult places to find potential converts.

"What do you mean? There are plenty ready to be persuaded," said the lady who was painting her own coffin, and she swept a hand out to indicate the sheep bleating on the hillside.

Jen laughed and flicked through the pamphlet so she wouldn't have to watch the others eating their sandwiches. The font was from another church, apparently; a green-man boss could be seen above the western door, though she hadn't spotted it; there was some ancient graffiti in the shape of a ship that had been carved into one of the pillars; and a tomb was adorned with a seventeenth-century depiction of a local legend. That last bit caught her attention, and she read it to Lana, who was lying down with an arm over her eyes.

"The legend is about a child who went inside a tree and found a staircase down into Hell," Jen said, bending back the pages of the pamphlet.

"Oh, yeah?" Lana said, her hair tangling in the grass.

"Isn't that something Stephen was telling you about?"

"Might be."

"Yes, it was something he told me, too," Peny said. "I didn't much care for the idea. What else does your booklet say?"

"In some retellings, it's an oak," Jen said, "and in some it's a yew. They think there was a great oak nearby but that it was felled in the eighteenth century."

"And why is the legend carved on a tomb in the church?"

"Well, it was a kind of talisman against going to Hell, because in the story the child comes back and tells all the people in the village what sins they must abstain from in order to avoid eternal punishment."

"I thought all that sort of info was already in the Bible," said the coffin painter. "Thou shalt not whatnot."

"There are several other instances around the church," Jen said, her back beginning to hurt from sitting on the ground. "A tree and a child in a section of stained-glass window, a tree with steps in the trunk on the end of a pew, and they think there's a reference in the rood screen, too. We'll have to go back and look, Lana."

"You go back and look," Lana said, her voice distorted by the crook of her arm. "I'll wait here."

"Some people think the tale was a sort of anti-'Jack and the Beanstalk,' " Jen said, still reading. "But rather than climbing up to steal from a giant, the child descends to bring back knowledge from Hell."

"I can see why the beanstalk one caught on better," Peny said.

"And occasionally, there is a bit added to the beginning of the story, where the child hears the wind in the leaves and follows the sound to find the tree. But this might have been influenced by the popularity of 'The Pied Piper of Hamelin.' "

She closed the pamphlet.

"Well, there we are," Peny said, though

they didn't seem to have got anywhere in particular.

Jen joined Lana, and lay back, shifting to find a comfortable position. Creeping thyme had crept into the lawn and each movement was greeted by a warm, clean smell which made her hungry for Hugh's roast lamb. Bees buzzed about the few tiny purple flowers, and the voices of the ladies on the benches took on the same lazy quality. Well, they could be lazy; they'd got the comfortable benches to relax on.

She lifted the pamphlet, intending to carry on reading from this angle, but her arms felt heavy in the heat, and it wasn't long before the cool pages were resting on her face, providing a square of shade for her to drowse under.

In her dreams, she ran down and down a spiral staircase which had thick and gnarly tree roots for banisters; the steps were covered in moss and she realized she had bare feet. The feel of the moss on her feet was so pleasurable she hoped she'd never reach the end of the staircase but, somehow, she knew she was nearly at the bottom. It was hot, getting hotter, and her skin was tingling, especially on her chest and arms. She wanted to stop and press herself against the damp moss, but she couldn't stop. The heat turned to a burn.

"Mum," Lana was saying. "Mum? Everyone's gone back to the minibus. They said you'll get sunstroke if you stay out here any longer."

Jen struggled up, unsteady with sleep, and followed her daughter along the footpath to the car park. As she passed the church, she wondered if the singing man was still inside and if the woman in the tabard was still trapped there with him.

Underground

When Jen had first come to London she'd found the experience of getting the Tube faintly religious. The gray platforms were like long, whitewashed, blue-lit naves, with worshippers standing facing the imminent deity, waiting the way medieval laymen once waited for the moment the Host was raised above the rood screen. The rush forward for the train had a tinge of rapture to it, and those passengers who stood against the wall reminded her of the statues of saints set into shadowed wall niches.

She didn't know whether to say any of this to Lana as they went down the steps into King's Cross Underground station. There were so many things she might be able to share now, thoughts and feelings. Lana might listen, might try to understand rather than deliberately mistake her tone; she might laugh kindly, she might answer with examples of her own. They'd had a not-totally-hostile conversation. It was a brave new world. Or, perhaps, a return to a half-forgotten one.

Smiling to herself, she was through the barriers and breathing the hot, dusty air of the Tube before she realized Lana wasn't with her. She felt immediately panicked; her fingers pinched and scratched at the skin on her neck as she checked around her and went back to the ticket hall.

"Lana?" she called, retracing her steps along the tunnel.

As Jen turned a corner, a plump, stylish woman came towards her, yawning extravagantly, not bothering to cover her mouth, and it seemed as if she were silently roaring at everyone walking past. Jen felt she was roaring, too, inside. But beyond the woman she caught sight of Lana's anxious face, peering down from the top of the steps.

"What are you doing?" Jen said, making her way up and holding on to the railing, her balance impaired by the sudden relief. "You gave me a fright."

"I shouted after you," Lana said, "but you

weren't paying attention, as usual."

"Sorry." Jen stood against the wall to let a huge group of French teenagers go by. "I didn't hear. You could have run after me."

"No. I couldn't."

"Well, what's wrong? We should get home before rush hour starts."

"You can go," Lana said, and the tone was so depressingly familiar Jen nearly wept. So much for getting back to their old relationship, so much for sharing her random thoughts with a receptive mind.

"What's wrong?" she asked again.

"I don't want to get the Tube. I don't want to go down into it. I'm not going to. You can if you want, but I'm going to walk or get the bus."

She turned and stepped away, and Jen had to follow her quickly along the Euston Road, catching breaths of her own bright perfume as she hurried.

"Why this sudden objection to the Tube?" she asked, as some sort of music started up across the street. It sounded like an organ but surely couldn't be.

"I don't like not being able to see the sky."

"What does that mean?"

She didn't get an answer, but she walked with Lana, of course. And it was a sweet walk in its way, the air heavy and jasmine-scented, the passersby appreciating the break in the weather with hand-holding and outdoor drinking. There were jugglers in Russell Square, and a homeless man's two Staffordshire terriers, bright bandanas around their necks, ran back and forth on Kingsway, their tongues flapping with happiness.

The sky, this sky that Lana was so desperate not to lose sight of, was lilac above them and colorless at the horizon, the sky of a foreign holiday. Everything looked better against it, the pale stone government buildings and the glass-veneered flats, the familiar red buses and the dark-leaved trees, and Jen was glad to have been made to stay under it for a little while longer.

DOUBLE

As they got closer to home, Lana took Jen's arm and hung on it, as if she'd suddenly sustained an injury, or aged sixty years. Jen stiffened her body to take the weight, feeling her daughter's hands crushing her through the damp jacket's sleeve as they walked. She tried to enjoy the proximity, this permission to be close, but holding Lana up was exhausting after the dash to the overpass and the long walk from King's

Cross, and she was relieved when they got to their local high street and Lana let go.

The hard rain had left puddles among the uneven paving stones, which reflected more of the lilac sky. And that after-rain smell filled the air, that grassy, soily scent, mixed with the petrol and tarmac of the city, and once, near the bus stop, some woman's perfume, lingering long after she'd caught her bus and been borne away.

A few minutes later they passed an unperfumed woman standing outside the chemist's, or they almost passed her. She moved as Jen got level with her so that she walked in front of Jen for a few paces, seeming not to notice anyone, her shoulder just ahead of Jen, her bulk between her and Lana. This went on long enough that Jen got nervous and wanted to barge past, reclaim the space nearest her child. Before she could, though, Lana stopped.

"What do you think the police think happened?" She bounced on her toes to look at Jen, intent on her own question, as if this stretch of pavement held no special memory for her.

Jen's thoughts, in contrast, had instantly returned to that moment a year ago when she'd found Lana with the stash of painkillers, found her filling her mouth with them, her chin wet from tears and the water she was using to wash the pills down. After the appointments and meetings and interviews this had prompted, the doctors and social workers had told Jen to take a photo of Lana into all the local chemist's, to take a photo and tell them never to sell her painkillers or anything she could use to harm herself. And Jen had done it, of course, but it was one of the worst days, the very, very, very worst days, admitting over and over that she couldn't keep her own daughter safe without the help of these pharmacists and shop assistants.

"I don't think the police know what happened, Lana," Jen said. "I don't think anyone knows except you. We're waiting for you to tell us." They walked on, finding that the woman had stopped again at the corner.

This time she turned to Jen with a half smile but didn't move aside to let them pass. The woman's face looked odd in the low sun, her nostrils lit up, her eyes blank with shine, her teeth a white mass inside her mouth, like a fat piece of chalk for drawing on gray paper, or a tube of titanium-white paint for spitting onto a canvas. They were at the exact spot where Jen had been standing when, having completed her task and shuffled the remaining pictures of Lana into her handbag, she'd begun to cry, to weep, on the pavement, in front of passersby. And Jen had the impression, she didn't know how, that this woman was herself, a version of herself, nothing alike in looks but still a double, and that she had been waiting here, would always be waiting here, to remind Jen of that time.

A moment later the woman had crossed the road and moved on, and Jen felt vaguely guilty. Perhaps she had just meant to ask for directions but, seeing Jen's horrified expression, had decided against it. Somehow, though, she couldn't quite rid herself of this sense of doubling, of a message, of a piece of herself standing guard at that spot.

FIELDS

"So, were you going to meet him today?" Bethany asked that evening.

"No, obviously. He lives, like, two hundred miles away."

"But he *is* your boyfriend? Have you told your mum?"

"Obviously, I haven't told my mum," Lana said, her voice full of hard vowels, "and he's not my boyfriend."

"But you had sex?"

There was a silence after this, and Jen

could only assume her daughter had answered with a nod or shake of the head. Please, she thought, her muscles aching from the need to sit still, let it be the latter. She hadn't opened the kitchen window, but it was open. She hadn't pulled out the chair, but she sat in it. She hadn't been trying to listen, but she heard. Was it someone innocent they were discussing? Matthew from the holiday? Or an older boy, a man? A bad influence, a creep, an advantage-taker?

Bethany had come round to find out why Lana had missed double drama ("You love drama, you never miss drama; I thought you wanted to be a director"), and Lana had insisted they sit outside in the evening sun. The weather had turned nice just as the day was nearly over, and wasn't that always the way? Their voices drifted in from the garden, competing with the buzz of the solitary bees which flew about the foxgloves near the greenhouse. There was a scent of sweet peas on the breeze, and Jen imagined it mingling with the girls' breath as she sat quietly, her hands flat on the kitchen table.

"And then what?" Bethany was asking.

"And then we walked up the road and went into a field —"

"A field?" Bethany interrupted. "What did you go to a field for? A field's where you go to get fingered."

A bark of laughter startled the bees into silence. "There are other reasons you go to fields, you know," Lana said. "Planting crops, for example. Rearing livestock."

"Oh, yeah?" Bethany said, sounding skeptical.

QUOTATION

"Farmer, Richard Crossley, charged with leaving sheep carcass to rot."

"I'm sorry?" Lily sounded slightly groggy, and Jen suspected she'd been asleep in front of the TV. Someone was talking loudly about Henry VIII while "Greensleeves" played in the background.

"That's the full headline. I found it." It had been the mention of fields that had reminded Jen, set her back on the electronic trail. And she'd only had to scrutinize twenty-seven pages of Google to find the answer.

"Congratulations, darling. Not what I was expecting, I must say." "Greensleeves" was replaced with silence.

"No, I know," Jen said. "This is the beginning of the article: *A local farmer has been ordered to pay over £1,000 in fines and costs after a sheep was found to be rotting on his* land. At the hearing, he pleaded guilty to the offense of failing to dispose of animal remains properly."

"Well. Rather unpleasant."

"And then this is an explanation: *I want to give some context for this news story. This is actually a real shame, as what the inspectors from the Animal and Plant Health Agency failed to understand was that the carcass was being carefully monitored by our community and that it had been deliberately left to attract a red kite.*"

"You've lost me."

"Okay. Well, Mum, this second bit is from a bird-watching blog. It says red kites are rare in the area, but one was apparently spotted feeding on a deer that had been hit by a car. So they tried to lure it back again with a dead sheep. *Red kites are sometimes known as the British vultures and, as such, feed on carrion. The sheep on Mr. Crossley's land had died after an attack by a dog and we asked him to leave the remains in the hope that the red kite would be attracted to it. Luckily, before the APHA forced the removal of the sheep, a young member of the club managed to get this photo.* And there's a picture of a red kite pulling the entrails from the sheep carcass."

"Bit grisly."

"Beautiful, though." Jen could see why they'd sacrifice a sheep to it, why they'd want to lure the bird down, to wait with cameras poised. "Anyway, I clicked on the picture and found Matthew's Instagram account."

"Matthew? That's the boy Lana had a little romance with?"

"Right."

"Excellent." There was a sigh on the line and the Henry VIII commentary started up again. "That's all tied up rather neatly, then. Are you feeling better?"

"No. The red-kite photo had a comment underneath, from Lana: *I should have fatted all the region kites with this slave's offal. Bloody, bawdy villain! Remorseless, treacherous, lecherous, kindless villain! O vengeance!*"

"*Hamlet,* if I'm not mistaken."

"*Lecherous villain.* Does she mean Matthew, d'you think? And *vengeance,*" Jen read again. "What does she want vengeance for?"

"It's Shakespeare, darling. All teenagers quote Shakespeare. They think they're the first ones ever to do it."

BIRDS

Now Jen had another checkerboard of Instagram pictures to scroll through in the evenings. Matthew's photos were all of birds, close-ups on trees, wide shots in fields, occasionally a whole flock in the sky, and, once, a picture of taxidermied birds in a glass case.

It's a real pity to think of these wild creatures being shot and stuffed and preserved with arsenic and other toxic chemicals. But on the other hand, these museum collections have been invaluable to those of us who are fascinated by birds.

What kind of sixteen-year-old wrote like that beneath an Instagram post? The spelling was standard, he'd used commas and full stops, and there weren't even any hashtags or emojis. Only four people had liked it. One of those four was Lana. This was the image Lana had shown Jen a few weeks ago, the one she'd chosen as a starting point for her Dr. Greenbaum–sponsored analogy, her fluttering feeling. It was Matthew who'd put the idea in her head. Perhaps that's what she wanted vengeance for.

Jen remembered the way Lana had shaken her head in pity at the memory of Matthew's posts. But it turned out she'd commented under lots of them.

Always looking for a shag, huh, Mattie? she'd written under a photo of a cormorant. This was followed by a laughing crying face, which, Jen assumed, was meant to take the sting off the words. She could imagine how embarrassed Matthew would have been at this sort of joke. A boy who blushed at the mention of a kiss. Unless that was an act. Might he always be looking for a shag? And not the bird variety? She'd thought Lana's tone was slightly bullying, but perhaps it was recriminating instead.

Jen thought about contacting Matthew. Would Lana object to that? Would she run off again if she found out? Would she run further this time? Jen dithered but kept an eye on Matthew's Instagram, kept an eye on the comments Lana wrote under his posts. A couple of days later she revisited the picture of the cormorant and found Lana had added another comment: *Satan now in prospect of Eden . . . sits in the shape of a Cormorant on the Tree of Life . . . to look about him.*

"There, that's Milton, not Shakespeare," Jen told her mother when she phoned.

"Well, they have Google now," Lily said, refusing to be impressed. "That's an unusual advantage."

"Vengeance and Satan. A bit concerning, isn't it?" Jen said to Hugh at lunchtime.

"I always rather liked cormorants," he said. "We used to go and look at them standing on the rocks by the bay, holding their wings out to dry." She left him to reminisce about idyllic childhood summers and tried Meg.

"You're reading too much into it, as usual," she told Jen. "You need some context."

"Is Matthew supposed to be Satan?" she asked Lana that evening.

"You're spying on Matthew now? Is no one safe?" Lana asked, with a dramatic flourish which Jen nearly smiled at. "I'm just winding him up, that's all. Butt out or I'll block you."

Jen promised she'd stop checking Instagram. She promised even as she scrolled back through Matthew's entire photo history.

One evening, she stopped on a picture of a buzzard. Lana hadn't commented under this, but something about the image gave Jen a chill. The shot Matthew had taken was wide, showing the foot of a tor behind. And in the background was what looked like a dark figure, crouching slightly.

Jen stared at it for a minute, wondering

why it was not only frightening but familiar, then she switched to Lana's Instagram and scrolled through her photos until she found the one hashtagged *rapture.* Here was the same tor near the holiday center and, in the distance, the same figure.

Mr. Crossley, perhaps, watching Lana, watching Matthew, creeping about in their wake.

ALIBI

Not Richard Crossley. He had been visiting his son in Edinburgh when Lana first went missing. But the police would look into the photos, they said, in case anyone remembered a stranger hanging about in the area or recognized the figure (unlikely, they thought, as he or she was just a tiny silhouette). In the meantime, Jen dug out the list of email addresses she and the other sketchers had exchanged and wrote to them, asking if they remembered anything, if they had any photos with a strange man in them, if they'd painted him into any of their pictures. She looked through her own paintings again, too, staring at the marks her hands had made, wondering if a bit of charcoal shading here or a blot of ink there was really a menacing miscreant or sneaking psychopath.

Framing device

Between two mismatched rectangles of grayboard, a church crouched, drawn too squat, and a river, heavy with brushstrokes, refused to run. A charcoaled cave had more darkness than depth, and the Nine Ladies were dowdy without their green moss coats, but butterflies, not yet pin-caught, provided a red splash.

The tors were unflattened, the trees unfolded, as the framer removed paper dividers, cut mounts, glass, colored woods, and a week later gave the landscape, ennobled, distinguished, back to Jen.

But at home, the necessaries couldn't be found: brass wire, hooks, nails, and a hammer. The tool drawers and boxes wouldn't deliver, so no pictures were hung on the wall. Instead the church sidled beneath the sofa, a silk fringe sweeping its pencil roof, a butterfly met a carpet moth, and standing stones were propped against the coffee table.

Copyright

One of the pictures was Lana's; Dr. Greenbaum had insisted that something of hers

246

be framed. Jen slid it out from under the bookcase and held it up to the light. Not the hint of a figure marred the surface. But in a corner, washed over with watercolor, and hardly readable, was a signature.

BREACH OF CONTRACT

"Hugh?" Jen whispered. "Hugh?"

It was four in the morning — *4:23,* the clock on the bookcase flashed dimly at her. She had woken to find she couldn't move her head and had immediately assumed it was paralysis. But after a moment or two of absolute panic, she discovered she could wiggle her toes and feel the broken spring in the mattress against one shoulder blade. Still, dark drowsiness kept the answer from her for a while longer and it was only slowly that she realized her hair was trapped beneath her husband.

She twisted her body about in an effort to wake Hugh, but her caught position left her weak, and he slept the way she used to: heavily, with no prospect of being woken before that inner clock had counted up enough hours. So, giving up, she relaxed back into the dip in the bed that her weight had been working on since midnight.

"I never told you about the man on the

train, did I?" Jen said. "I never told you who made me commit to the name Lana." She spoke into the warmth of Hugh's back, telling him the story of her own Rumpelstiltskin. "And I know you'd probably laugh if you were awake, but I really did feel I'd made a bargain with him. I really did feel I had to stick to the name Lana, that if I changed it something terrible would happen. Anyway, tonight I looked again at Lana's drawings, and found that the pictures in her sketchbook were signed *Alma.* She must have marked them all with that name, even the pages she let scatter to the winds. That gave me a fright. She'd changed her name, you see, Hugh. She broke the pact. And I thought, *He knows, he found the pictures, he came to claim her.*"

"That's bloody creepy," Hugh said, in a hushed voice.

"You're awake," Jen said.

"I don't know how you expect me to sleep with you rambling on behind me."

"If you're not asleep, you can get off my hair."

"And you've told me about old Rumpelstiltskin of the Railways before."

"Have I? Well, it's a good story."

"You just like frightening yourself. What exactly do you think he'd want with Lana?

It's not like she can spin straw into gold. What are you worried about? What does he symbolize? Is it something sexual?"

SOMETHING SEXUAL

That was the question. It plagued Jen day and night. She thought about the ripped condoms, discarded along a stony track, she thought about the shredded and sodden T-shirt, caught on a hawthorn tree, she thought about the bloodstained blanket spread over sheep-dung-dotted grass.

She studied the silhouetted man watching from the edges of photos. The police hadn't found anyone, or even heard of any other sightings. "To be honest, it's so unclear," the liaison officer had said, "we're not even convinced it's a person in the photos. It could just be the shadow of a tree or something."

She pictured the marks around Lana's ankles where something must have been tied tight, and she remembered the refused rape kit. She imagined Lana saying no to the nurse because she was ashamed, and then imagined Lana saying yes to a man. Saying yes and saying yes and saying yes and then saying no, but too late. One of the detectives had been convinced that Lana had gone to meet someone, seemed to expect to find an email exchange, a persuading message from a boy, or a man pretending to be a boy. She imagined Lana squirming in pain.

Somehow, it was all too easy to see her as vulnerable. When she pictured Meg, sturdily beautiful women came to mind — the Łempicka driver whipping along in her Futurist car, or a Judith holding a bloodied sword in one hand and a severed head in the other. But she couldn't help seeing Lana as an Egon Schiele drawing, one of those skinny and ragged girls, twisting and hungry and showing their vulvas.

Nude collection

"I think I've seen more naked men with you than I have alone," Meg said.

Jen, waiting just inside the café door, was startled out of her reverie by the sentence. She suspected this had been Meg's intention.

They met for lunch on Mondays whenever they could manage it and, since Meg had broken up with Kayla, they'd been going to a chain. The furniture matched and the baristas were fast and you could pay by card even if you were only buying a cup of tea for £1.60. It was full of people dashing about in suits. Her friend Grace wouldn't be seen dead there, and it was a relief not to be dragged to a chilly "characterful" café with chipped tin mugs and white, dread-locked waiters.

"I mean, not counting television, films, et cetera," Meg said. "In real life. I've only seen two men naked on my own. Tom and, well, someone else. Oh, and Dad, I suppose, but he doesn't really count. And anyway, that would have been with you, too, prob-ably." She eyed a Brie baguette, sighed, and picked up a chicken salad. "I had goat's cheese at Henri's last week and a woman told me off."

"Really? The cheek. Though you shouldn't really be eating soft cheese." She shuffled out of the way of huffing customers reach-ing for sparkling grape juice and hot wraps. "So what other naked men have you seen with me?"

"Well, when I was about nine, we went to stay with your friend Monica, and you spot-ted a man in the window across the garden. He'd been showering and was sort of silhou-etted against the bright light."

"Hardly graphic, then."

"I know, but I remember the rest of the evening being filled with whooping and laughing."

Jen smiled as she followed Meg into the café queue, not at the memory, which was missing from her mind, but at the idea of her and Monica getting some childish thrill from a half-glimpsed naked man. She missed Monica, who'd got a job in Glasgow and occasionally sent postcards but rarely visited.

"If you want something more graphic, well, d'you remember you used to take Lana on the train to get her to sleep? I came with you a few times. And once, we were stopped at a station for ages, and there were three shirtless men on the opposite platform. They were holding cans of beer."

Jen shrugged. She couldn't remember Meg ever coming on those train trips with Lana.

"You don't remember? We looked away and, when we looked back, they'd turned around, undone their trousers, and bent over."

"Had they?"

"Yes. Their beers were in a neat row on the yellow line. You told me off for making a gesture at them."

"What gesture?"

Meg demonstrated, pushing her tongue into the side of her cheek.

"Well, I can see why I told you off," Jen said, looking about to check if any of the other customers had seen. "Where did you learn that? You must only have been eleven. Good Lord."

"And then, we walked Scampi for Grandma once when I was about fifteen, we took him round the estate, and a naked boy leaned out of the window of a second-floor flat. You said it looked like he'd been about to take a piss."

"Did I?"

"Yes. He had his knob in his hand. Anyway, he saw us and shrank back into the room."

"That rings a bell. Didn't he have a dog, too? I mean, wasn't there a dog in the window as well?"

"With a waggly tail?" Meg asked, with a raised eyebrow. "I don't know, I wasn't looking at the dog."

A woman on a phone tried to push through the queue and stopped inches from Meg's bump. "God, sorry," she said, blushing. "I didn't see you were . . . When are you due?"

"Early October," Meg told her.

"Your first? Good luck."

Meg thanked her and turned to roll her eyes at Jen.

"Okay. So what's that? Five naked men," Jen said, moving aside to let an unsteady coffee-carrier past. "Not such a great number."

"Six: a couple of years ago, we were on the top deck of a bus, and d'you remember that man suddenly hunching over as he realized all the passengers, including us, could see into the first-floor bedroom of his gated mansion?"

Jen laughed. "I do remember that. The hunching didn't do him much good, it just made his genitals hang further between his legs."

Meg turned to the counter as the barista called her forward. "And then there was your colleague the other night," she said. "Bottom half only."

DICK PIC

Jen thought of Rupert's bare legs as she got home that evening, and was surprised to find she couldn't picture his penis. She'd definitely seen it, but then her mind had apparently wiped the image. It seemed especially peculiar, then, to be confronted, in her kitchen, with a photo of a large erection.

"Lana!" she said, peering over her daughter's shoulder at her phone screen.

"Oh!" Lana turned and nearly fell off the chair. "It's not what it looks like. Well." She laughed. "Actually, it is what it looks like."

"Whose penis is that?"

"I don't know. Some random dude's."

"And why do you have it?"

She shrugged. "It just popped up on my messages. Bethany gets them all the time."

"So you don't know this person. You haven't met him?"

"What's going on?" Hugh asked, pulling a pack of chicken from the fridge and stabbing it open.

"Lana has been looking at a strange man's penis."

"Mum! Jesus Christ. You make me sound like a pervert."

"Is the man a stranger or strange?" Hugh asked.

"A stranger," Lana said.

"He'd have to be pretty strange to send a photo of his genitals to a fifteen-year-old."

Lana shrugged again. "Like I told you, it happens all the time. People are always freaking out about it on the internet. But it's kind of interesting. Men's things are pretty weird-looking, aren't they? Bethany's got a collection on her hard drive. I've promised to delete it if she dies in a car crash, so her mum won't find the pictures."

"Good to know you plan ahead," Hugh said, grating ginger for a marinade.

"A collection?" Jen said, thinking of Meg's mental collection of nudes. At least some of those sightings had been accidental. "Can you report the men who send these images?"

"Yeah, we always do. I mean, you don't want little kids to end up seeing them, or whatever." She switched to another app and held her phone up. "Here, this is what Bethany got yesterday."

The large belly of a man filled most of the screen and at the top was a slightly curved, not especially impressive, member. Underneath, Bethany had written, *Hey Alma, some sugar for my sugar.* And then there was a series of winking faces and aubergines.

"Alma," Jen said. "Who's Alma?"

"It's just a name I made up when I was a kid. Bethany and Ash and me, we worked out anagrams of our real names when we were in primary school."

"I've been wondering about that, because you signed the pictures in your sketchbook with that name, too."

"I always sign my art Alma, it's like a private joke. And we still use our anagram names when we message each other sometimes. Bethany is Annette Shybib, and I'm Alma Axodd."

"Very suitable," Hugh said to Jen, nudging her with an elbow, as his hands were covered in yogurt. "She certainly *acts* odd."

"Yeah, really clever, Dad. That *is* the joke, though."

"Ah."

"What about Ash?" Jen asked. "What's her other name?"

"Well, she doesn't use hers. She doesn't like it."

"Why?"

"It's Ada Hianus."

"Hi . . . Oh, I see."

"You can understand why she's reluctant to hang on to that epithet," Hugh said.

"Wait a minute," Jen said. "Where's the *n*? Lana Maddox, Alma Axodd. You've missed out the *n*."

"Ugh, Mum. Trust you to notice that."

Hand-wringing

"Have you ever been sent a dick pic?" Jen asked Meg a week later. She'd decided she would be the one to say something surprising this time.

"No," Meg said. "I'm pretty careful with my privacy settings, and there are *no* dicks on my Tinder account. *Were* no dicks, I should say. I've deleted the app, as I'll probably never go on a date again."

Jen gave her a sympathetic pat and followed her from the counter, carrying their drinks. As they made their way between tables, a movement caught her eye.

Or perhaps not a movement, but a shape, a tableau. A man and girl were kissing on the small, hard settee at the back of the café, really kissing, their faces flushed, their flesh pressed out of place. The man was older — old, in fact — fat and bearded, and the girl was young, tiny, half his size, and her skin was painfully taut. When the man drew back, the girl coughed, and her cough, a thin sound which made its way through the café's chat and clatter and milk-steaming hiss, was young, too. It made Jen think of rubbing Vicks on Meg's and Lana's chests when they'd had infections as children, and a phantom eucalyptus smell rose in her nostrils.

Jen sat down and saw that the man had leaned back a little way and was meeting the other customers' stares, as if waiting for their applause.

"That's disturbing, isn't it?" she said, passing Meg her decaf tea. "What should we do?"

"What can we do? I mean, public displays of affection, even repulsive ones, aren't against the law."

"I wouldn't call that affection. How old is she, d'you think?"

"Could be any age."

"She's thirteen, if she's a day."

"She might just look young, Mum."

The couple began to kiss again and Jen looked around the café, hoping someone would come in and cause the scene to stop, hoping, she realized, for the girl's parents to storm through the line of caffeine-craving customers and drag the girl to safety. As if parents had the ability to do that. The next hope was that the baristas would stop it, but they were too busy, too efficient at their posts, to notice; the line of customers never thinned to fewer than three people and, once drinks had been served and money taken, their responsibility was at an end.

The girl's hands and feet were small and she leaned into the man, lying against him, as if she couldn't hold herself up. When the kiss was over, he had to hold her away from him. She coughed again.

"How do you think they met?" Jen said. "Do you think he sent her a dick pic?"

"I doubt it. Where's this obsession with dick pics come from, anyway?"

"Lana got sent one. She says it happens all the time. Can you believe that? Perhaps you can help her with her privacy settings."

"I can try, but I doubt she'll listen."

The back wall of the café was lined with maroon leather and the lights were dim; this should have hidden the couple, but somehow it made them glow brightly against the gloom. Jen was aware of them all the time she was getting through her too-bitter cappuccino, and the conversation with Meg was fragmented.

"Stop staring, will you?" Meg said. "If the girl's over sixteen, then there's nothing anyone can do."

That high cough sounded again, a lambish bleating. The couple went back to kissing, the man's swollen hands on the girl's upper arms.

"But she looks like a runaway," Jen said. "And he's obviously taking advantage. Maybe we should call the police?"

They didn't call the police, though, and no one else stepped in. The image of the small girl and the bulky man would haunt Jen for weeks; she couldn't help putting Lana in the girl's place, frightening herself with the thought. And she went back to checking Lana's Instagram again.

It showed the usual plates of food and feet

on grass, but there were more worrying things, too. That evening, she found a new post, a few lines of text over a faded black-and-white photograph of a Parisian street: *I like red wine that stains my mouth and men who leave bruises on my body.*

"It's just teenage posturing," Lily said, when Jen read it out over the phone.

But it terrified Jen. She thought of the bruises Lana had come back with after her disappearance; her daughter might have been a runaway, even if only for a few days. Could she have been with a man like the one in the café? It was an unbearable idea.

FALL ON DEAF EARS

Also unbearable was Lana's attachment to her earphones. A new pair had arrived with the new mobile, so the ones she'd tied to the oak tree hadn't been too great a sacrifice.

"I thought you were going to go without them from now on?" Jen said, reminding her of the promise she'd made at the stone circle.

"I only meant until the end of the holiday. Obviously."

Jen had a feeling this wasn't quite what Lana had meant but, either way, she was sorry that the things existed, as they allowed Lana to shut her out, refuse to engage in conversation, pretend she hadn't heard requests for cups of tea or explanations.

Her daughter often put the buds into her ears as soon as Jen got back from work, the wires like thick, white strands of hair announcing some past shock. The sight made Jen's shoulders slump, but what really disturbed her was the fact that, several times, she'd seen the end of the wire swing wide as Lana moved; no phone, no iPod in sight. The earphones weren't plugged into anything. And yet Lana seemed so completely absorbed, as if she were listening intently to a set of instructions.

CLIP-CLOP

Jen wished she could have worn earphones to the interview with Tori in Human Resources on Tuesday morning. Her absences had become worrying, apparently. Tori said they understood that it had only been two months since the incident with her daughter, but she'd left work unexpectedly too many times. They (who were *they*? Jen wondered) had noticed that her concentration at work had slipped, that some projects had had to be completed by other members of the team, and that she'd seemed distant in meetings.

"She asked me if there was a *before* me and an *after* me," Jen said, sitting down to watch Hugh heat up some black bean and pastrami soup that evening.

"Pardon?" he said, over the whir of the microwave.

"She meant, do I think of the time before Lana went missing differently?"

"And do you?"

"Not really. How could I?" But even as she said this Jen remembered pulling her suitcase towards the train station on the way to the holiday. The sound of the wheels as they clicked over the paving stones had made it seem like there was a little horse trotting behind her. She remembered indulging this fantasy until she began to suspect that passersby might be able to guess what she was imagining from her expression. And she'd stopped and waited for Lana to catch up. Lana, who wasn't talking to her that day, wasn't talking to her in an ordinary teenage way, or perhaps wasn't talking to her in a troubled teenage way. How were you supposed to tell?

"Who was this meeting with?" Hugh said, managing to send several airy boxes of Italian herb seasoning skidding out of the cupboard and onto the floor.

"A girl at work."

"You always say that."

"Say what?"

"A girl."

"Oh, sorry, a woman, then, a young woman," Jen said. "It's a habit, that's all. I know it makes me a bad feminist."

"I don't have an opinion on that," Hugh said, replacing the boxes. "It just gives me the impression that everyone at your workplace is school age."

"They practically *are* all school age."

Hugh laughed and transferred the defrosted soup into a pan.

"What about you?"

"Well past school age, I'm afraid," he said.

"No, I mean, is there a *before* you and an *after* you?"

"Can I have a third option? Can I have a *during* me? Because I'm still during, I think." He cut some limes into wedges and called up to Lana.

"God, I wish I'd thought to say that," Jen said. "Although she'd probably just have insisted I choose one of the two."

"What's the name of this person who was asking you foolish questions?"

"Tori," Jen said, taking the dish of limes and enjoying the clunk the thick china made on the scrubbed wood of the table. "She's in HR and is supposed to assess people who've had a lot of time off."

"And you didn't pass muster?" Hugh said.

He was joking, she knew he was joking, but she felt her face mismanage the smile and instead crumple into tears.

"Oh, Christ, Jen," he said. "I'm sorry, that was stupid."

She tried to answer him, but the words were too soggy or high-pitched and, in the end, the confused face he pulled as he tried to decipher her sentences sent her into fits of laughter.

"I think there might be an after me," she said, trying to catch her breath. "Only I think the after me might be a little bit cracked."

She'd expected him to say something like *That's nothing new,* but instead he slid into the chair next to hers, pulled her into his arms, and began to rock her. One of their chairs was a little unstable and a spindly wooden leg tapped on the floor tiles again and again with the movement. It sounded like a pony clip-clopping across the kitchen.

AT HOME

Tori had suggested Jen take a proper leave of absence. "Give yourself some time," she'd said. "Look after yourself for a bit, get your family issues sorted, and let us know when you're ready to come back."

Jen imagined Tori rehearsing the phrases in front of the mirror in the same way Jen had rehearsed the phrases from the books on teenage depression, and she wondered if Tori had been as disappointed by the real conversation as Jen had always been by her exchanges with Lana.

Lana's summer holiday had just started, so the next day neither of them left the house. The isolation seemed sudden, reminded her of those first few months after Meg's birth, when she was unprepared to leave the adult world behind, and she might have been half pleased when Lana refused to look for a summer job, or go out with friends or get out of bed. It was true that having someone else in the house pierced the claustrophobia, having someone to check on and worry about made her days feel less purposeless.

But she'd already found projects for

herself: repainting the bookshelves in the sitting room, taking the kitchen equipment they never used (two blenders, a sandwich toaster, a salad spinner, a coffee grinder, and three inexplicable pineapple slicers) to the charity shop, and vacuuming into the corners of every room. And with Lana around, which she frequently was, despite the arguments and threats and cajoling, Jen couldn't do anything creative. There were lots of *thoughts* about paints, but no paints were ever brought out; there were *plans* to sit in the garden and sketch, but no sitting out and sketching happened. Grace told her she was frittering away her opportunity for creative work, that she should be taking the time to "drop into the self," but all her energy was taken up with worrying about Lana or distracting herself from worrying about Lana. The hours alone together began to weigh on Jen.

Several times, she'd looked around while she was hoovering, to catch a glimpse of Lana as she darted away, or she would be vinegar-washing a path along the corridor to find her daughter sitting on the stairs, as if she were waiting for Jen, waiting to give her a fright.

"What are you doing there?" Jen would say, her heart heavy in her chest.

"Nothing," was always the reply.

Within a couple of days, this had turned into a constant menace. Either Lana was there, behind her as she loaded the dishwasher or changed the bedclothes, or Jen *felt* she was there, a prickle on her skin, which might or might not be from the scratchy linen tunic, a rash of goose bumps, which could or could not have been caused by the drafty hardwood floors. Sometimes, she deliberately didn't look round, not wanting to know whether it was Lana or her imagination that was causing this sensation.

QUESTION

"Do you think I could be a violent person?" Lana asked.

Jen didn't jump, because she'd suspected her daughter was behind her, but the dull tone of her voice was frightening, and when Lana's breath tickled the back of her neck Jen was filled with dread.

ROUGH WITH THE SMOOTH

On what would have been the day of the annual dinner (if she'd been at work), Jen crept barefoot along the landing, a washing basket bumping her hip. She held her breath, listening for Lana, trying to work out where she was in the house. The shower hissed as she passed the bathroom, but this didn't mean her daughter was in there (she'd made that mistake before), so she pushed Lana's door open with trepidation, and the flat of her free hand. She paused. She listened. She stepped inside. And gave a shriek.

A sharp stone had been left in the doorway, just where someone might place a foot, where a mother might place a foot, where a mother already nervous and trembling might place a foot. Jen backed out of the room, hobbling, and threw the washing basket down the stairs in a rage. The sudden pain made her feel violent and she wished Lana was there so she could scream at her.

A moment later, she was calm again and she was glad no one had been nearby. Still out of breath from the faded emotion, she bent to pick up the stone. It was familiar.

Last year, Grace had given Lana two stones about the size of plum kernels. One was a craggy sort of rock, gray, the other a polished white pebble, both nestled in a little velvet pouch with a gold drawstring. Grace hadn't given them to Lana in person but had entrusted them to Jen with a farcical formality.

"Tell her," Grace had said, closing her eyes and closing Jen's fingers around the pouch, "to keep them in her pocket. Tell her these are a meditation aid, they are powerful because they are symbolic. Tell her they symbolize life."

"Right, I see, sort of accepting the rough with the smooth," Jen had said.

"Oh, Jen, you love your clichés, don't you?"

"Absolutely. You can't judge a book by its cover, you know, Grace, especially as actions speak louder than words, and you're better safe than sorry, because what doesn't kill you makes you stronger and, as I always say, there's no time like the present, when the apple doesn't fall far from the tree, but the grass is always greener on the other side, and love is blind, but ignorance is bliss."

"Enough! Enough!" Grace had said, laughing.

"Well, I hate clichés," Jen had told her. "But I will use them against you. Consider yourself warned."

She passed the stones on to Lana and thought, *Who knows, it might be the idea that works, that gives Lana focus, that helps her gain perspective, that keeps her grounded* (it turned out Jen *had* become reliant on a lot of clichés from self-help books). As far as she knew, though, the stones hadn't yielded any results, they'd just sat collecting dust on a bookshelf in Lana's room. Until that morning, when the craggy one had been turned into a means of injuring her mother.

PULLING TEETH

Or perhaps the stone had fallen innocently from the shelf. Jen was aware of the hum of paranoia beneath her thoughts, a hum that rose in pitch whenever Lana and she were alone together. It became important to get out of the house while Hugh was at work, to get them both out, to find a different setting where other people would dilute the strange feeling that grew and grew each day.

A trip to the dentist was as good an excuse as any. Lana certainly needed to get her canine fixed but, as they waited in the reception, Jen began to feel she was taking her daughter to be punished, that this was an appointment made to serve her right, rather than serve her well.

"Do you want me to come in with you?" she asked, when Lana's name was called. She kept her voice low, because every sound seemed louder at the dentist's: the rolling of chair wheels towards a patient, the opening and closing of plastic boxes, the tapping of an implement on the rim of a metal bowl.

"Up to you."

"But what would you prefer?"

"I don't mind."

"Well, will you feel better if I'm there?"

"Not really."

"So shall I stay here, then?"

"If you want to."

Jen sucked in a breath, getting a mouthful of that dentist smell: mint and disinfectant and something sweeter, the traditional oil of cloves, perhaps.

"I don't want you to be on your own, Lana."

"I think the dentist will be there with me."

"You know what I mean."

"Yeah, I know. Okay, yes, please, come in with me."

"Right, great," Jen said, wondering if it would always be this hard to get a straight answer from her daughter, about even the simplest things.

And sitting through the procedure, she wished she hadn't offered. Especially as she didn't much enjoy watching as Lana had her mouth probed by latex-covered fingers. It was unpleasantly reminiscent of the sorts of things she'd imagined Lana might already have experienced while she was missing. And she couldn't shake the idea that she'd brought Lana there for interrogation, that she was squatting like some toad in the corner of the room, waiting for a torturer to soften up the victim and make her ready to talk.

The tooth only needed to be bonded with resin, though, so there were no needles or drills, and no pain as far as Jen could tell, and when the dentist snapped off his gloves Jen could only think about how dry his fingers were underneath the latex, as if he hadn't touched the inside of Lana's mouth at all.

SIGHTSEEING

"And this," Jen said, with a slow raise of the head, a long breath in, a flex of the toes, "is where your dad and I lived when we were first married."

A pause, convex on one side and concave on the other, slid between them where they stood on a rain-damp street. They'd left the dentist's half an hour ago and, not wanting to go back to being menaced from corners and doorways, Jen had suggested they walk up towards the common and "see the sights." Lana hadn't seemed enthusiastic but had agreed, as long as they didn't have to get the Tube.

"Obviously, this is the site rather than the actual building," Jen said. "The houses here were pulled down and replaced by these offices ten years ago."

"Oh. My. God," Lana said. "And I thought this couldn't be any more pointless. The house isn't even here now?"

"No, but the houses further down the road are the same as the ones that were here. So you can imagine what they might have been like."

"I could have *imagined* from home."

A line of traffic streaked past, the cars' tires making that long, whooshing, splashing sound of rubber on wet tarmac, as if to highlight the post-rain dismalness of the day and lend weight to Lana's argument that they should have gone straight home. They had missed a shower of rain by a few minutes, and Lana kept looking up at the sky as they walked, checking for any stray drops, glaring at the clouds.

"Okay, well," Jen said, determinedly bright, "that isn't the only thing I wanted to show you. There's a restaurant about five minutes away, less than five minutes away, where we had our first proper date." Her voice had begun to take on a pleading note.

"Is this actually still in existence," Lana asked, "or am I going to be *imagining* again? Will we be standing outside a betting shop this time?"

"It's in existence," Jen said, feeling a sudden exhaustion from the burden of the love she felt for Lana.

Why did she have to drag this love around everywhere when, sometimes, she'd like to leave it behind for a few hours? Without that love, she could float away, let her daughter's mood improve, let her put her frown and her sharp tongue back in their still-shiny packaging. Without that love, she could be light, untethered by their shared genetics, by the memory of Lana as a baby, or by the pride she felt in her wit, even when it was aimed fiercely at her.

Jen turned off the main shopping street, feeling the elastic connection tighten as Lana dropped further and further behind, feeling it vibrate when Lana stopped outside a curve-fronted shop on the corner.

"What now?" Jen called back.

Lana didn't answer but stared through the window.

"Why can't you at least answer me?" Jen said, retracing her steps on the dank paving stones and hating the whine in her words.

The shop was a Christian bookshop,

brightly lit and warm-looking, with cards and mugs in the window. At first glance, it could have been any bookshop, except for the slightly blurry covers on most of the books, the over-reliance on pastel colors. And of course, the special offer on glow-in-the-dark crosses, which bore the words "I will never leave you."

It had started to rain again, the first few drops like fitful needle pricks on the part of Jen's hair, the bridge of her nose.

"Can we go in?" Lana said, still staring into the shop.

"What for?"

"Just to look."

She pushed open the door and Jen followed, the smell of wood and new books replacing the petrol fumes she'd got used to on their walk. She didn't want to shadow Lana and annoy her but couldn't help hovering, trying to see what she was reading, what was catching her eye.

"Can you stop watching me?" Lana said, turning suddenly.

"I'm not watching you. I'm looking at this." Jen picked up a pamphlet from a carousel. It was entitled *Brethren Women* and on the cover was a photograph of three smiling girls wearing headscarves and long skirts. She flicked through the pages ostentatiously, catching sight of a sentence. *Every woman praying with an uncovered head causes herself shame.* She put the pamphlet back.

That was enough reading, she thought, wandering over to the Church Supplies section and finding packs of those cardboard hand-guards for candles that she'd seen used at Easter and Christmas. There were boxes of gluten-free wafers for Communion, too, and sets of tiny disposable Communion cups.

So some Christians *were* bothered by germs. And gluten allergies. It was reassuring and disappointing at the same time. Jen remembered a cathedral service she'd been to with Lana a couple of years ago, when they could still have a normal conversation, when she still felt like a real mother. They had been staying with relatives of Hugh's, who'd recommended they go sightseeing while Hugh signed some papers. Expecting just to have a quick look around, they hadn't meant to join a service but hadn't quite known how to say no when the smiling lady (a sexton? A lector?) had explained it was about to start.

It had been rather moving, and Jen treasured the memory.

"Shall we go?" Lana said now.

She looked vaguely disappointed, too, as if she hadn't found whatever it was she'd been searching for. But on the way out she dived for a soft toy and held it up, her expression suddenly bright, conspiratorial. The toy was velvety, a pale, closed-eyed bear wearing a nightshirt and cap. Its paws were sewn together in perpetual prayer and there was a push button on one side.

Lana squeezed it.

"I believe in God the Father and Jesus Christ," the recording began, "His only son . . ."

"Shall I get it for Meg's baby?" Lana said, laughing. "We could get a pink one because it's a girl. How much would Meg hate me?"

"Bless us, Lord, every day," the bear continued.

"I'm not sure she'd ever forgive you," Jen said.

"Amen," the bear finished, as if agreeing. It was tossed back onto the pile, and they left the shop.

CATHEDRAL

"Are you ready to leave?" the woman (an usher? A verger?) said, the light from her candles fluttering as she bent towards them.

"Yes, I think we're ready," Jen said, gathering her coat. "Lana?"

Lana nodded.

"Right you are, then. Follow me."

She was an elderly lady, and the candles she held were large and in heavy-looking holders. Jen deliberated offering to take one, but she didn't really want the responsibility. What if she dropped it and the flame lit on a pew and the whole Norman cathedral caught fire? Surely the church council, or whoever sorted these things out, wouldn't have entrusted this woman with such dangerous objects if they hadn't thought she was up to it. Still, as she and Lana walked behind her, Jen watched the pools of light sink ever lower in the gloomy, ecclesiastical interior and waver more unsteadily. She was relieved when they were at the west door and tiptoeing down the stone steps into the lamp-lit cathedral close.

The door closed quietly, but with a definite echo, behind them.

"Well, I'm glad we stayed," Lana said.

"It's not what I was expecting," Jen said, thinking she could have meant either the service or Lana's reaction to it. "It did feel sort of ancient, didn't it?"

Lana murmured in response, and Jen looked at the sign by the gate, checking that it definitely said Church of England, wanting confirmation that this was a service they were justified in attending.

"I really liked the lights all going off at the end," Lana said. "I suppose that was symbolic, but also it was just great and creepy to be in a huge church in the dark."

"Sorry I stopped you going up for Communion, only, you were never confirmed."

"That's all right. I wasn't really paying attention. I didn't know that's what everyone was queuing for. And no way would I have wanted to share a cup with tons of other people."

"I always think that. Not a very pious thought. They wouldn't have known about microbes when they started the tradition, I suppose. Must have been nice, not worrying about germs." She stopped on the high street. "Are we going in the right direction for the taxi rank?"

"Yeah, there's that Italian restaurant."

They crossed a road with no sign of traffic. It was that silent hour on an Easter Saturday, after everyone's stopped shopping and before the partygoers come out to take advantage of two days of hangover-recovery time. The incense from the cathedral had left its scent in Jen's clothes and hair; she could smell it around her and wondered how long it would take to wear off.

"I wish you could see the inside of more churches at night," Lana said.

"Yes, in a way, that's how they should be seen, mysterious and slightly frightening. Like God."

"Yeah. But also, it's just weird and like a vampire movie or something."

"Oh, I see."

"Also, it was really peaceful," she said quickly. "Maybe I should go to church more."

That's just what I need, Jen thought, someone in the family finding God. "The services aren't usually like that one, you know. Mostly, they keep the lights on."

"Pity," Lana said. "I'll have to stick to drugs, then." She gave her sarcastic smile and strode on to the taxi rank.

MODESTY

It was still hot, despite the rain, and Jen hadn't bothered to turn the lights on in the kitchen, lingering in the charcoal twilight after dinner and sitting with the French windows wide open. Overgrown nasturtiums poked their leaves into the room, and the rain hushed the garden beyond. Hugh was studying his music-theory books at the table, and Lana was lounging on a floor

281

cushion by the windows, occasionally reaching out to paddle her fingers on the round, flat leaves, as if doing an impression of the raindrops.

Jen had a hymn in her head, or a phrase of a hymn in her head, "Praise for the sweetness, Of the wet garden," and had to stop herself from singing it over and over. She suspected she wouldn't have thought of it if they hadn't been to the Christian bookshop. She suspected she wouldn't have started to find Lana's bandana so disturbing, either.

It looked like one of the headscarves the women were wearing on the cover of the *Brethren Women* pamphlet. It looked like a statement of virtue, of innocence or virginity, and made Jen ask herself if that was the real reason Lana was wearing it. *Every woman praying with an uncovered head causes herself shame.* Was Lana trying to avoid shame? Was Lana praying?

"Do you still need to wear that bandana?" Jen asked.

Lana didn't look round or answer but put a hand up to hold the fabric closer to her head, to flatten it to her scalp.

"Surely your hair's grown over the scar now."

Lana shook her head, still holding the bandana.

"And it looks a bit grubby. Perhaps I could put it in the wash."

There was a sigh. "Mum. It's fine. And it's not the scar I'm covering, it's the hair, the bit that the hospital cut. It looks stupid. I've tried a bun and a ponytail, but that bit just sticks up. I look hideous without the bandana."

"I'm sure it isn't that bad."

"You're disregarding my feelings again. We talked about this with Dr. Greenbaum."

"Am I? Sorry. So you're just covering that bit of hair. You're not wearing the bandana for any other reason?"

"It's not to show gang affiliation, if that's what you're worried about."

"Gang affiliation?" It hadn't been something Jen was worried about, but she'd add it to the list now.

"I wish I'd thought to wear a bandana when I was younger," Hugh said, making Jen and Lana turn to stare at him.

"Why, were you in a gang?"

"Hardly. No, I got some gum caught in my hair when I was young and had to cut it out, and then ended up cutting all my hair off."

"Cool story," Lana said.

"It's harder than people think, cutting your own hair."

"But you've carried on doing it, anyway?" Lana asked, giving Hugh's current haircut an assessing stare.

He laughed and rubbed a hand over his head. "I looked like Marc Bolan when I was younger. Do you know who that is?"

"No, obviously."

"He was a musician. The lead singer of T. Rex. He died."

"Sorry for your loss."

"It wasn't exactly a personal tragedy. And this was in the seventies. I was more into the Clash by then, anyway."

"Enough with the historical references." Lana pulled at a nasturtium leaf, snapping it off and releasing its peppery scent. Jen would have been annoyed, but she'd been meaning to thin the leaves out for weeks. "This is like being at school," Lana said. "You're not going to make me listen to the music, are you?"

"No, Lana. I was saying I had the same problem. I had long hair and ended up with a clump of it short."

"How long?"

"Past my shoulders."

Lana brought the leaf up to her eye, holding it there like a monocle. "Do you have any photos?"

"Somewhere. I'll have a look for them and

284

show you sometime."

"Great. That it?"

"How d'you mean?"

She dropped the leaf. "Is that all you wanted to say?"

"Erm. No, there's more to that story."

"Go on, then. You and Mum are both on a nostalgia kick today."

Jen found she'd been doodling on the edge of a newspaper, a series of birds wearing different sorts of hats.

"I did it over the bathroom sink," Hugh said, "and then, when I was finished cutting, and the sink was full, I thought the best thing to do was to wash the hair down the plughole." He turned to Jen. "It's sad to think that, now. I should have kept a lock of it, at least. What you don't appreciate when you're young, huh?"

"Dad, what is this, a midlife crisis in real time?"

"Okay. Well, obviously, washing the hair down the sink was a bad idea, because it blocked the pipes. A kind of soapy scum rose up into the sink whenever the tap was turned on. My mother was furious, but she didn't know what had caused the problem.

"Eventually, I knew I had to do something. It was only a matter of hours before she realized it was me who had done the damage.

I mean, I'd had hair and the sink had been fine, then I had less hair and the sink was blocked. It was only Mum's joy and relief at no longer having a 'long-haired oaf' for a son that had stopped her putting the two things together already.

"I tried vinegar and bicarbonate of soda while she was out at a WI meeting, but the effect was minimal, so I sneaked out of school the next day and went to the library and borrowed a book on plumbing and, when I got home, I sat under the basin with a bucket and removed the U-bend and poked a screwdriver up the pipe."

"Thanks for the plumbing lesson," Lana said. "What are you getting at?"

"There was a lot of hair in the pipe," Hugh said, "but there was also a ring. A woman's ring."

Jen gave one of her birds a smiling beak and put her pen down. "Your mother's ring?"

"Her engagement ring."

"From your dad?" Lana asked.

"Obviously, from my dad. Who else would it have been from?"

"So had she deliberately chucked it down the plughole?"

"No, Lana, she'd lost it."

"Oh oh oh." Lana knelt up on her cushion.

"And she knew she'd lost it down the sink. That's why she hadn't told you off about the hair. She thought it was just the ring that was causing the problem."

"Exactly," Hugh said.

"Would your dad have been angry if he'd known she'd lost it?"

"Livid, I expect. And anyway, she hates to lose things."

"So what happened when you gave it back to her?" Jen asked.

"Well, I cleaned it up first . . ."

"What a good boy."

"And I just put it down next to her while she was on the phone."

"Did she think you were proposing?" Lana said.

"I'm glad you're finding so much to amuse you."

"Sorry. What did she say?"

"Nothing. She just slipped it onto her finger and squeezed my arm."

Jen reached out and patted the first bit of Hugh her hand fell on. "No wonder your mother thinks you're her shining knight."

Hugh grinned. "What can I say? I have a habit of saving the day. You're lucky to be married to me, really."

"I know," Jen said, "especially as you're so modest, too."

SEEING THE LIGHT

Jen wished lying awake and worrying was an Olympic sport; that way, she would be training for glory every night and might have a chance at being hailed as a hero by her nation. If you needed ten thousand hours to become an expert at something, she was surely a senior apprentice, at the very least.

When being in bed became too frustrating, she wandered around the house, put their books into alphabetical order, made shopping lists, and kept an eye out for the housebreaking cat. Sometimes, she paced up and down the hallway, where the light from Lana's bedroom spread under the door — since their return from the Peak District, Jen had found her daughter's overhead lamp was almost always on at night. Once, during her pacing, she heard a repeat of Lana's words in the hospital.

"I'm here," she called. "I'm underneath."

But when Jen gently opened the door, she saw that Lana was sleeping.

"Can you stop creeping into my room in the middle of the night?" Lana said the next day, after breakfast. "It's really weird, and it's an intrusion."

"I haven't been creeping into your room,"

Jen said.

"Who's been switching off my light, then?"

"Oh, yes, sorry. That was me. But you need to stop leaving the light on all night."

"Why?"

"It's a waste of electricity. It's bad for the environment."

"It has an eco-friendly bulb, but if you're worried about money, I'll pay for it."

"I'm not worried about the money," Jen said, squeezing the remains of the satsumas to see if any were still edible.

"Then leave it alone."

Jen sighed. "I just don't like it, okay?"

"Well, I don't like the dark."

This admission seemed to have taken Lana by surprise, too, and she pulled the hood of her jumper up around her face.

"You said that in hospital. That's over two months ago. You're still finding the dark frightening?"

"Not frightening, exactly. I'd just rather not wake up in the dark."

"Have you been waking up a lot?"

"No, not really. I like knowing the light's on when I go to sleep. I like knowing it's going to stay on."

Jen tipped the satsumas into the bin, their brightness immediately dimmed by the dusty black bag, and decided to risk it. "Did something happen in the dark, Lana?" she asked, thinking of the broken condoms and the shredded T-shirt the police had found.

"I was lost at night, Mum. It was unpleasant, okay? I don't think that's so hard to understand."

Imaginary friends

It wasn't hard to understand. People had always been scared of the dark, of the things hidden by it, of the infernal imaginings which could be projected onto it. So, now when she lay awake, Jen had lots of choices. She could lie and worry that Lana had her light on all night, she could lie and worry that Lana had her light off and was frightened by the dark, or she could lie and worry that Lana was asleep and having nightmares.

The recurrent sound of the curtain rings shifting along their pole, clacking together, shifting again, became familiar, as Lana seemed not to be able to get the curtains wide enough to satisfy her. There was something else, too. Another noise, a murmur, that Jen wasn't sure if she was imagining. She was almost relieved when the murmuring carried on into the day and she could stand in the kitchen and catch the familiar rhythm of Lana's voice. *Almost* relieved.

"Who were you talking to just now?" Jen asked, when Lana came downstairs to make a raid on the fridge.

"No one."

"But you must have been talking to someone."

"Must I?"

Jen moved the fridge door to get a clearer view of her daughter. "Yes," she said. "I heard you."

"Did you?" Lana's tongue lapped the creamy residue from the lid of a yogurt pot, the smell of apricots on her breath.

"If you weren't talking to someone, what were you doing?" Jen asked. "Reading aloud?"

The lid was completely clean, but Lana continued to lick at it, keeping eye contact with Jen. There was something disturbing, sexual, about the action, and Jen was forced to look away. A few seconds passed, during which the neat, wet sound of Lana's tongue against plastic filled the room. Then the yogurt pot bounced into the recycling box. When Jen looked back, Lana's gaze was fixed somewhere over her shoulder and Jen had to contain a shiver, convinced suddenly that there was someone standing just behind her. Lana smirked, as if she could tell Jen was afraid, and then turned to run back up the stairs, but the feeling of another presence in the house didn't lessen, especially when the murmuring began again.

Jen was still rattled hours later, as she and Hugh walked around the supermarket. She'd tried to rationalize the incident, had taken refuge in Google and looked for explanations, read simplistic descriptions of child psychology, and waded through the comments of other worried mothers. There was one suggestion that kept appearing, and she mentioned it to Hugh.

"You think our fifteen-year-old daughter has an imaginary friend?" he asked, clasping a soil-covered, brain-like lump of celeriac in both hands.

Jen didn't say anything while she thought about her answer. She leaned on the push bar of the trolley until the front wheels began to spin.

"Or is she perhaps hallucinating?" Hugh asked. "Because I have a feeling that might run in the family."

"Oh, shut up," Jen said finally. "I've got a headache."

This wasn't quite true. What she really had was a strange, stretching feeling inside her skull, as if her head had expanded into a resonance chamber, a chamber which had been trying to catch the low sound of Lana's voice and bounce it about until it resolved into something understandable.

"Do you want some painkillers?" Hugh said, pulling the trolley away. "Should we get some?"

"I've taken two," Jen said, lying again. She didn't like to have any in the house now, and she didn't want her senses dulled.

All day, she had been certain that Lana was talking to someone in that constant murmur, pacing back and forth in her bedroom, pausing only to listen to whoever it was on the other side of the conversation. But whenever Jen went to the bottom of the stairs, the sound had stopped. She'd tried lifting the receiver to the landline quickly but had heard only the hollow noise of the dialing tone and, to make it more worrying, Lana's mobile had been charging by the microwave since breakfast.

Jen added a box of porridge sachets to the trolley and said the words "sandwich bags" to herself several times, in the hope she'd remember them when they got to that aisle.

"I thought at first she'd sneaked someone upstairs," she said, unable to help carrying on the discussion. "But if she had, he must have been there all night."

"He?" Hugh was laying a cardboard container of yogurt pots against the celeriac but, seeing her expression, he paused. "What's the matter? I thought you liked these apricot yogurts."

"I just think we should cut back a bit," Jen said. "They're very sugary, you know. Bad for us. And yes, *he*. Lana would hardly need to sneak a girl up there, would she?"

"Depends on the girl." Hugh put the yogurts back on the shelf. "And we made that mistake with Meg. Anyway, I thought you only heard Lana's voice."

"That's what it seemed like."

"And you couldn't hear a single actual word?"

Jen opened a carton of "happy" eggs and checked each one for cracks.

"Jen?"

"No, okay, I couldn't hear what she was saying, but it was *hours,* Hugh, she must have been saying something."

The eggs were all perfect and golden, and one had a soft, downy feather attached, as if to prove some sort of authenticity. She placed them on the plastic-wrapped toilet rolls for extra cushioning. The smell of the bakery drifted towards them, and Jen eyed a bag of doughnuts for a minute before picking up a loaf of brown reduced-carbohydrate bread.

She stopped as she was turning a corner, and Hugh walked into the trolley.

"What now?" he said.

Jen looked at him carefully. A jar of passata had been smashed nearby and the thick smell of tomatoes surrounded them; she wondered briefly when Hugh had last made Bolognese. "I can't get rid of the idea that Lana brought someone back with her," Jen said. "From wherever it was she went. Someone or . . . some*thing.*"

Hugh stared into the trolley for a second, tapping on the thin metal bars. "I know what we're missing. Wine. We definitely" — he looked up at her — "*definitely,* need some wine."

He dragged the unwieldy trolley after him and piled several bottles next to the vacuum-wrapped trays of mince and pork steaks. *Imagine if one of our children became a vegetarian,* he used to say with horror.

COMING OUT

MEG (*her willowy body very still, an exotic-looking young woman smiling at her side*):

Mum, Dad, I want you to meet Raffaella. She's my girlfriend. I'm gay.

295

HUGH (*leaping off the sofa to hug her*):

Oh, thank God for that. I thought you were going to say you were a vegan.

Spectrum

Jen called her mother while Hugh loaded the car. Could she tell her she was frightened of her own daughter and, if she could, what response was she hoping for?

"Jennifer," Lily said, picking up. "What's wrong?"

The craggy gray stone from Lana's bedroom floor had fallen from her pocket as she pulled out her mobile, and she bent to retrieve it. Suddenly, in the middle of a car park full of Saturday shoppers, Jen was explaining that something wasn't right with her daughter. She squeezed the stone tight as she mentioned the creeping about, the talking, the strange things on Lana's Instagram account, the cat in the house, but even as she listed everything she could tell they amounted to very little.

Opening her fist, she looked down at the stone and the red mark it had made on her palm. How typical, she thought, that she'd be the one who ended up carrying Grace's faddy meditation aid around with her, and how perfect, how symbolic, that she would only have the rough one. No smooth for her.

"Oh, sweetheart, teenagers are hard work," Lily said. "All they want to do is get a reaction, and they don't care which reaction it is. Frightening a person is as good as impressing a person. You were the same; your brothers were the same. Graham once got up on the roof and threatened to throw the tiles at us. And look at him now — hardly terrifying, is he?"

Jen laughed, thinking of her softly spoken, fastidious brother.

"Also, dear, you do have a tendency to worry unduly, don't you?"

"Do I?"

"Well, I sometimes think other people's emotions frighten you. You know, I was listening to a thing on the radio about how many women with autism have gone undiagnosed."

"Mum, I do not have autism."

"Don't get annoyed. We're all on the spectrum, darling."

"Okay. I have to go."

"Wait a minute. I was just going to say, don't you remember when you were, oh, nine or ten, I smashed a lot of plates? It had been a frustrating day — most of my days were frustrating, then — and I got to the end of my tether and I threw a plate at the wall, and then a couple more, and you ran to the telephone and called your dad at the office. 'Mum's gone mad!' you shouted. And you sounded so frightened your dad left work early to make sure everything was all right at home."

"I don't really remember," Jen said, thinking of the glasses and mugs she had let tumble to the floor. Had she frightened Lana? She hadn't considered that.

"No, well, by the time Robert arrived, we were fine. I had let off steam and then put the kitchen right. I was feeling much happier. A little sorry to have scared you, but pleased that I'd found such an easy way to get over my frustration."

"What's your point, Mum? I really have to go."

"Sometimes," Lily said, "you have to let someone act a little strangely, a little madly."

SECOND SKIN

Jen thought about this advice on Sunday when Meg came round to go through the baby clothes in the loft. After all, wasn't it a little mad to get pregnant at twenty-six?

"You were twenty-six, Mum, when you had me."

298

And wasn't it a little mad to end things with your girlfriend and ask for your friend's sperm?

"It was Kayla who ended things. And Tom has always wanted to be a dad. We talked about it for a long time. It's not like I just surprised him with a yogurt pot."

And wasn't it a little mad to hide the decision and the process and the early pregnancy from your (loving) parents?

"I'm sorry about that," Meg said.

"I know lots of people wait till the end of the first trimester." Jen dropped a black bag through the loft hatch and let it tumble down the stepladder. "But *five months,* that's an awfully long time to keep a secret."

"I said I'm sorry." Meg's voice drifted up to float about in the dark with the cobwebs and the insulation fibers and the smell of damp cardboard boxes. "I wanted to tell you I was pregnant as soon as I knew," she said, "but I waited a week, and then another. I wasn't sure what you'd think, how you'd react, and I was exhausted. I'd known it would happen, the tiredness, but it still hit me hard. I had to have afternoon naps and everything."

"How did you manage that at the gallery?"

"Sonya let me sleep in her office during lunch."

"Really?" Jen thought of the extremely thin and rather hard-looking South African woman who ran the gallery. She'd always been frightened of her, couldn't imagine her taking pity on a pregnant employee. "So you told *her* before me?"

"Only out of necessity."

"You mean you didn't *need* me."

"Of course I need you."

Jen carefully backed down the ladder, blinking the loft's dust from her eyes. Her hands were grimy, and she left a blackish print on the hatch cover when she replaced it. "Are you sure? I mean, what do you need me for?"

Meg, sitting on the landing carpet with her back against the wall, sighed and scratched her shoulder under the bra strap, releasing the smell of some honey-scented cream into the air. She'd been tired, but she hadn't had morning sickness, didn't get swollen feet or nosebleeds or dizziness (so far as Jen knew); it was just the eczema that seemed to plague her. "You gave me the name of that cream," she said. "And it's really helped my skin."

"That was your grandmother's suggestion."

"Okay, well, you reassured me that it was normal: you told me you got eczema when you were pregnant."

"Was that helpful?"

"It made me worry less," Meg said, scratching her shoulder again.

Jen nodded and wiped her hands on her jeans and picked up the bag of clothes. "You know, in some ways, the worst part of this whole thing with Lana is the feeling of being so useless."

"I get that, Mum. But you're not useless. I mean, look, you're about to give me a load of stuff for the baby," Meg said, her nails whispering against the roughened skin of her inner elbow.

"If any of them are suitable. They might have disintegrated in there, or be covered in mold."

"Well, you'll just have to take up knitting if they have."

Jen laughed. "I've tried that before. I'm not sure you'd want to dress your baby in anything *I'd* managed to create." She thought of the piles of crooked squares she'd painfully produced while pregnant with Meg, full of dropped-stitch holes and places where the wool had been pulled too tight.

"Actually, Dad said he might take it up."

"Knitting? Did he?"

"He read an article about some film star

who knits. It's *cool* for men nowadays, he told me."

"Ah, so I'm relieved of that responsibility, at least." She wasn't sure how she felt about the idea of Hugh clicking away with a pair of needles in the evenings. It conjured up an image of the woman in the hospital, hunched over her work and handing out unwanted wisdom.

Meg pulled the bag towards her and broke the plastic apart. A cold smell rose up, a muted sort of smell, like spices that have been sitting too long in their jars; nutmeg and cinnamon well past their shelf life. But the old clothes were intact, the flannel onesies and corduroy dresses, the soft cardigans and tiny cotton dungarees. Meg seemed quite moved by the sight. She was feeling through the bag with her right hand, Jen noticed, but her left arm was being surreptitiously scraped against the edge of the stepladder.

The reddened skin, covered in scratch marks, made her think of Lana's arms, of those similar scratches she had made on her otherwise perfect skin. How had both her daughters ended up with matching wounds?

"That cream doesn't seem to have been such a success as we thought," Jen said.

Meg dropped a gingham sun hat onto her

lap and looked at her hands. "Was I scratching?"

"Didn't you know?"

Meg shrugged, still looking at her hands. "I remember at school, or nursery maybe, thinking I had grazed my wrists and that the skin was flaking off, and then the teacher found I'd just got glue on them and it had dried and begun to rub away. I was embarrassed, about the mistake, because I'd gone crying to her, but I was relieved, too. Sometimes, I wonder if I couldn't just rub this away as well."

"You won't try that, though, will you?"

"No. I mean, it's tempting. When I look at the patches of eczema, I can imagine the skin underneath is perfect." She groaned suddenly. "I have to pee again."

"Shall I help you up?"

"No, don't worry," she said, inching up the wall and pushing herself off it.

Jen slid down onto the floor, replacing Meg. The sun was low in the sky and birds were flying into the tree beyond the landing window. Their sweeping movements made Jen think of crops being scythed, as if each bird were gathering something to it. The leaves shimmered in the light and could, just for a moment, have been a skin, shivering in a cold breeze.

"There are two new packs of condoms in a bag on the door," Meg said, coming out of the bathroom.

"Snooping?"

"Well, I thought I'd be helpful and put away your shopping." Meg was rarely daunted by any accusation of wrongdoing. "Whose are they?"

"Er, well."

"Surely there isn't much risk of you getting pregnant now."

"Because I'm too old, you mean? Thank you very much."

"Well, you've been through the menopause, haven't you? So what do you want condoms for? Are you having an affair?"

"No, of course not."

"Is Dad having an affair?"

"You'd have to ask him."

"So they're Lana's, then?"

"Not exactly." Jen watched a squirrel dangle awkwardly by its back legs and chew at something on the branch below it, before curling into the dense, concealing leaves of the tree. She could hear a shuffling on the stairs, the shaking of leftover sugar in a paper doughnut bag. Lana was listening.

Meg leaned against the stepladder and looked into Jen's face.

"They're for Lana, aren't they? Bloody

hell. *I* never got given condoms when *I* was a teenager."

"No, they're not exactly for Lana. I mean, unless she needs them. In which case, safe sex, you know, is very important." She was aware of the obvious message in her voice and imagined Lana rolling her eyes. "Did you *need* condoms as a teenager?" Jen asked Meg.

"I might have done."

Jen tried to stop her eyebrows from rising, but it was a struggle. "So there *were* boys, then?"

"Mum, for God's sake."

"Well, darling, if you won't tell me, how can I know?"

"Condoms aren't just for cocks, Mother, okay?"

"I'm aware of that," Jen said.

In fact, she had been thinking about this for days. Lana had insisted she hadn't had sex, so Jen had been looking up alternative uses, reading articles on survivalist websites. It turned out condoms could act as makeshift water bottles, could be stuffed with moss for pillows, could be made into slingshots for hunting, could be used to stop your matches getting wet, to stop lots of things getting wet.

Experiment

What you'll need:

One pair of walking boots (still muddy from
    your recent holiday in the Peak District)
One pair of thick woolen walking socks
One pair of shorts
A bath filled ankle-deep with cold water
Two condoms
Time on your own (without a daughter or
    husband to disturb/discover you)

What to do:

Change into the shorts (don't look in a mirror, this is not about how lumpy your thighs are). Put on the socks and walking boots and try standing in the bath. Make a note of how wet/cold your feet get.

Take off the boots and socks and see if it is possible to get them or your feet dry without the aid of a towel/hair dryer/radiator. Wring the socks out, squeeze the padded parts of the boots, shake your feet.

Now repeat the experiment, but before pulling on the damp socks and boots, encase each foot in a Durex Thin Feel condom. Note how your feet feel inside the condoms, both in and out of the water. (Try not to see your feet as two joints of vacuum-packed meat. Try not to think how long you'd have to stew those joints before they were edible. Try to focus on the task at hand.)

Once you have the socks and boots on again, walk about in the bath as much as you can.

Take off the boots. Take off the socks. Take off the condoms. Notice what marks the tops of the condoms leave on the skin around your ankles.

QUESTIONS TO ASK:

How wet/cold were your feet when you didn't have the condoms on?

Were your feet warmer/dryer when you did have the condoms on? Despite the socks being wet?

When you took the condoms off, how dry were your feet underneath?

Did the condoms successfully stop your feet from getting/remaining wet/cold?

Was it easy to walk about with a slippery latex layer between your feet and your socks? Was it pleasant? Were any blisters soothed by the material?

Did the condoms break when you pulled them off?

Could the marks that the tops of the condoms left on your skin be mistaken for ligature marks (especially by an anxious parent)?

COME ON

"So you think Lana used them as makeshift blister socks?" Hugh said. "This is a rather far-fetched excuse, if you're trying to cover up sleeping with someone else." He'd spotted the discarded condoms in the bin and the open packet in the bathroom cabinet, while getting ready for bed.

His tone was comfortable and Jen didn't bother to reassure him. She spat her toothpaste into the sink instead.

"It shows a certain amount of ingenuity, if you're right, though. Not that we should be congratulating her, obviously. Have you asked Lana whether your guess has any basis in reality?"

"No. I'm not sure if I could bear it if she said I was wrong. I'm not sure I can go back to imagining alternative explanations. And on the other hand, she might tell me I'm right because she doesn't want to admit she had sex with someone, or someone had sex with her."

"Hmmm." He rinsed his toothbrush under

the tap and turned the open box in his left hand. "I haven't looked at a box of condoms for a long time. D'you remember the old packaging? Men and women hugging and smiling. They looked like they belonged on the covers of Mills and Boon novels."

Jen shook her head and wondered, as she put the mouthwash away, if he was remembering their first meeting. It had involved a packet of condoms.

She had still been seeing the possibly-probably cheating boyfriend — the boyfriend who'd inspired the overnight drive — when she met Hugh. It was all a matter of chance and bad timing. A party in Oxford which Jen only went to because her boyfriend had left for a family wedding in Devon and hadn't invited her. A late arrival because she'd misjudged the train schedule. A lonely, lengthy hour in the kitchen, trying not to monopolize and annoy the host (the one person she knew).

On top of that, she'd been wearing a wide-sleeved blouse under a waistcoat, the sort of thing her London friends wore: not too girly, sometimes deliberately stained with a bit of oil paint or india ink, something to let people know you were an artist. But of course, everyone at the party had been dressed in proper party frocks with bows on the hip, or miniskirts with military-style jackets. Not a paint-splash to be seen.

She'd been wondering whether to slip away when Hugh introduced himself.

"I've been, I hope reliably, informed that you're the only other person here who is gainfully employed and so *has* to get the last train back to London. I propose we stick close so that neither of us forgets the time."

He'd had curly hair and a way of raising his eyebrows, as if asking her to laugh at the rest of the crowd (she found out later none of them were close friends).

So rather than leave early, she had stayed on, until it was just the two of them walking to the station, and he had stopped at a corner shop while she waited outside, listening to the whoops of Thursday-evening partygoers and watching the purpling sky and feeling part of the night, of the fun. She had appreciated her own youth (something she rarely did), and felt suddenly that she, too, would be engaging in a few whoops in the not-too-distant future.

And then, on the way home, as their train went through a tunnel and the lights briefly cut out, he'd put a packet of condoms on the table.

"Is that a come-on?" she'd asked, laughing.

"Do you know," he'd said quietly. "It is."

Which had made her laugh more.

"You said you had a boyfriend, but it's always difficult to know how serious . . . or what that means."

"It means a man I live with who I'd never knowingly betray."

He'd nodded and slowly drawn his hands back, taking the packet with them, as if by performing this action smoothly he could erase the last few minutes.

She hadn't been able to help smiling.

"Sorry," he'd said, when the box was safely out of view.

She'd shrugged. "At least you were planning on practicing safe sex."

They had both tried to look out of the window, but the train had stopped in the tunnel and it was dark outside and the glass had become a mirror, forcing them to gaze back into the near-empty carriage and narrowly miss eye contact over and over again. She'd raised the buffet-car beer to her mouth, the fizzing smell of it making her nauseous. The alcohol seemed necessary, though, so she'd taken a warm, painful gulp.

Wanting to repair the easy friendship they'd developed over the last few hours, she'd tried to think of something to say.

"If I wasn't already with someone —"

she'd begun.

"Yes," he'd said, cutting her off.

"Sorry."

"Don't be sorry. You're under no obligation. I'm not going to ask you to cover the cost of the prophylactics in recompense."

Relieved at his return to conversation, she had tried to carry it further into safer territory. "What's the most you've ever spent on a date?" she'd asked.

"What a very sexist question. Why not ask what is the most a date has ever spent on *me*?"

She'd laughed. "Because you wouldn't necessarily know that, would you? The most I've ever spent was . . . well, my boyfriend made me buy him dinner in a fancy French place in Soho when we were first going out. I didn't realize I was paying till the last minute."

"Charming."

"But it was half worth it. We were just starting on crèmes brûlées when Sophia Loren walked in."

"Ooh, and is she a massive hero of yours? Did you go all starry-eyed?"

She'd kicked him under the table. "No, but it's nice to be able to say I've eaten at the same restaurant, at the same time, just a few tables away."

"You could have said that without having to buy an expensive dinner."

"I suppose," she'd said, rolling her eyes, "but I prefer not having to lie." She had been enjoying herself, pleased they'd got over any awkwardness, any hard feelings about her refusal. But it turned out they hadn't left the subject that far behind.

"So, when you get off this train, will he be meeting you?"

"My boyfriend?" she'd asked. "No, he's at a wedding this weekend."

"I see."

And just like that they'd been back to spotting points of light through the black of the night, or she had been. He had settled further and further into his seat, sinking until his head was only just visible. Eyes closed, breath steady, he had promptly fallen asleep, fast asleep, relaxed enough to let his mouth drop open. She'd tried not to look — it had seemed rude to take advantage when he was vulnerable like that — but soon she was narrowing her eyes in the direction of his nostrils (downy), the under-side of his top row of teeth (unstained, as he wasn't a smoker), and his eyelids (paler than the rest of his skin, almost blue).

Feeling guilty, she'd drunk more of the unpleasant beer, raised the pages of her book, and tried to read, but had found it hard to concentrate and instead stole glances at the unguarded face. He'd begun to snore. To distract herself, she had looked directly at her own face, studied her own nostrils, teeth, and eyes, run a hand through her hair and wondered what it was he'd seen in her that had made him stop for condoms on the walk to the station (she knew now why he'd stopped).

The monochrome of the window's reflection was flattering and she liked herself in it, admired herself even, her dark, messy hair, her dark, liner-smudged eyes, her dark, red-wine-stained lips. She'd been drunkenly tracing her lips with her tongue when Hugh had woken, finally, with a start and blinked up at her.

"You look like a disembodied head," she'd said, teasing him before he could tease her. "On a plate."

He had laughed and wormed his way up the seat. "Like Holofernes?" he'd said. "That would make you Judith, wouldn't it? My seductress, my slayer."

She'd smiled and gone back to her book, pushing her beer can away, aware that he had taken it up to drink from. It was a shame, she had thought, because they were getting to be great friends, but she wouldn't be able to see him again. Except, of course, she had.

Corporeal friends

"Friendship is complicated, isn't it?" Maya said, putting the basket down on the kitchen table.

Jen agreed and poured hot water over Earl Grey tea bags and wondered what made people stay in touch, what made them feel close, why some people were with you for life while others drifted away. She felt she'd missed out on some of the best potential friendships just because of geography or scheduling, because someone had moved or because their working hours weren't compatible with hers. This seemed unfair, shallow, that the meeting of minds should be hampered by material concerns.

Once upon a time she'd thought she might be close friends with Maya but, despite physical proximity and similar timetables and children in the same class at school, they'd never properly clicked. It had been easy to drift apart when their daughters stopped being close friends. So Jen had been surprised to find her at the front door with a pretty basket full of food.

"Just some apricots and cherries, some

dates. And then a few other goodies. Biscuits and chocolate. I should have come round earlier. I thought you might need some cheering up."

Jen had invited Maya in, and the woman had looked around the kitchen in a way that made Jen glad she'd washed up all the pans and dusted the Japanese cups that morning. Maya was an oversized woman, tall and wide-hipped, with large hands and feet, and she wore crisp little bows or knitted flowers in her hair in a desperate attempt to seem dainty. She was also obsessively tidy, keeping her house and her person eerily neat. Jen imagined that someone had once called Maya sloppy because of her size and she'd spent the rest of her life trying to shake off that label.

"Teenage girls' friendships are especially volatile," Maya said now. "One minute they'd do anything for each other, the next they're clawing each other's eyes out, and then they're back to fierce devotion again."

"I suppose so." Jen opened the paper bag of dates and bit the flesh from the stone. It was delicious and melted like caramel. She could see the chocolate bars were the fancy kind, 85 percent cocoa with cinnamon, chili, or Madagascan vanilla, and the biscuits were Dutch stroopwafels in a little beribboned bag.

Maya sat down with her mug of tea. "And although Lana and Ash haven't seen so much of each other since Ash moved up to the top set for science, she still considers Lana a person she owes loyalty to."

"Well, that's nice." Jen was astonished. There had been a falling-out between Ash and Bethany last year and Lana had ended up in the middle, briefly hated by both girls. It had been a big source of tension, though that had been broken when Lana chose Bethany's side and stopped seeing Ash.

"And I know we haven't had many chances to get together recently, but I would definitely count you as a friend."

"Me, too," Jen said, but slowly, aware somehow that she was walking into a trap.

"So I was a bit surprised — more than that, disappointed — not to get a call from you."

Jen dropped the date stone into the compost caddy. "Maya, what are you talking about?"

"Okay. Okay, Jen, I'm going to come clean. I'm not here just to drop this off." She drummed her fingers on the side of the basket. "I also wanted to talk about Ash staying with you last night."

"Ash? I think you must be mistaken. I

haven't seen her in ages."

"Jen, I need you to be honest here."

"Maya, I am being honest."

Maya pulled at her bow so it sat a little flatter on her head. "I'm not angry, just a bit bewildered, really. You see, there's a sort of code, isn't there, between mothers? I'd have called you if Lana had been staying with us. I'd have called to check. I'm sure you understand — you of all people, after everything you've been through with Lana."

"I do understand, but, Maya, Ash hasn't been here. Perhaps she told you she was staying here and she was actually with someone else."

"My daughter doesn't lie to me. Don't look at me like that. She doesn't. She stayed here last night at Lana's request."

"Lana's request?"

"Yes. Lana told Ash she didn't want to be alone in the dark and that you won't allow her to sleep with a light on. She wanted Ash to keep her company overnight."

"I do let Lana sleep with a light on."

"Ash is a kind girl and so she agreed to stay, but she forgot to tell me what she was doing. Her father and I were going out of our minds with worry. Kiran and I are going through a difficult time at the moment — actually, we're about to start divorce proceedings — so our stress levels are already extremely high."

Jen felt a twinge of sympathy, knowing what it was like to find your child has been out all night, but she couldn't really concentrate on Maya's problems. Lana had sneaked a friend into the house, she'd said she was afraid of the dark, she'd admitted this to a girl who'd been her enemy for a year rather than sleep alone.

"The thing is," Maya was saying, "I was pleased, in a way, to find Lana and Ash spending time together. It's been rocky between them for quite a while. I blame that Bethany. But, look, I don't want Ash to stay overnight here, okay?"

"Fine." Jen reached for another date, barely listening.

"And I heard — Ash told me — that Lana still won't say what happened, won't say where she was when she was missing. So, well, we don't know what she's mixed up in, do we, or who she might be involved with?"

Jen froze, her hand hovering over the bag of dates. "What are you trying to say? You think my daughter is a danger to your daughter?"

"No, Jen, of course not. But I know Lana's been having problems for a while. Ash said she came back to school before the term ended, but I know that doesn't necessarily mean everything's sorted. And now I find you don't even know who's in your house at night."

Jen picked up the basket and dumped it in Maya's expansive lap. "I'll pay you back for the dates I ate."

Maya put the basket back on the table. "Don't be silly, Jen, this is a gift. Look, I think we've both got a bit overheated." She drew a breath in and the bow in her hair trembled. "I apologize, for my part. I'm rather frazzled. Ash didn't come home till this afternoon and, well, neither did Kiran."

Suddenly, Maya was crying. She grabbed at her handbag and pulled out a tissue, which she held to her face, as if the tears were obscene.

"Oh, Maya. I'm sorry you're having a tough time."

"I don't really want a divorce."

"Have you told Kiran that?" Jen asked, wondering how she'd managed to sound the least bit interested. *You've just accused me of being a bad mother,* she wanted to scream, *you've told me my daughter's dangerous and not good enough to spend time with your precious offspring. Meanwhile, my daughter has developed a phobia and is sneaking people into the house because she's so scared. I don't have any emotional energy left for your problems.* She patted Maya on the shoulder.

"I think he's already found someone else," Maya said.

"I see."

"I'm sorry. I should be going. We've promised to keep up normal family dinners till we tell the kids. But, can I just use your loo?"

Jen put the mugs in the dishwasher while Maya was upstairs, determined to leave her with an impression of neatness, of competence. It wasn't until later that she remembered the condoms in the bin. "Dammit," she said aloud. "God knows what she'll be telling the other parents now."

NOT IN FRONT OF
THE CHILDREN

"First sign of madness," Hugh said, coming through the door. "Talking to yourself."

"You're home early."

"Landlord canceled." He'd brought an unsettling sort of energy home with him and had a peculiar look on his face. "Lana not home?"

"No. She's out with Bethany."

"So we have the house to ourselves?"

Jen suddenly realized what the peculiar look was. She felt a little thrilling ache expand inside her. They went upstairs, and she heard the clink of Hugh's watch strap as he took it off. Once upon a time, they'd been noisy, vociferous, but since having children they'd got good at having sex in near silence, at closing the curtains and switching on the light and drawing back the covers with no discussion. She'd got good at communicating excitement by suppressed breaths rather than loud moans. She didn't remember ever caring what her parents or flatmates thought, but God forbid the children should know what was going on.

Jen giggled slightly, breathily, as she took her clothes off, and Hugh grinned. They'd never been somber lovemakers. He kissed her and she lay down and he kissed her again. Hugh was bigger now than he'd been when they'd met, and his weight pressed her legs wider, his skin was rougher and he sweated less, but the smell they made together was the same. Sharp, like sea salt and lemon.

Hugh had just guided her fingers between their bodies when the sound of the front door opening made them pause. Lana was home. And when Jen's head hit the headboard they didn't stop and shift down on the mattress because that meant they'd be on the creaking spring. Instead, Hugh just curled his hand around the top of her head and held her until they'd finished.

Jen laughed quietly again as she dressed and then ran downstairs, leaving her husband naked on their bed.

"Is Dad home?" Lana asked, pointing at his shoulder bag on the kitchen floor.

"Yes." Jen's voice was scratchy, and she cleared her throat.

Lana narrowed her eyes. "What have you guys been doing?"

If it had been her mother asking, Jen would have told her. Bold and unashamed. But it was her daughter.

"Nothing," she said.

"Well, you look weird."

Jen thought of Hugh, lying on their bed. "Well, apparently, Ash stayed here last night."

"What? Oh shit."

"*Oh shit* is right. Her mother's been round, so I know the truth."

"No, you don't. Nor does her mum."

"What I can't understand is why you felt you needed to sneak her in. I wouldn't have stopped you having a friend to stay."

"Good to know. But I didn't sneak her in.

She wasn't here. She was at Jonno's."

"Jonno's?"

"The guy Ash fancies. Her mum would freak out if she knew."

"Her mum is pretty freaked out as it is."

"Well, Ash didn't think she'd notice she was out. Her mum and dad are, like, divorcing, though they think Ash doesn't know. Plus, she thought her mum wouldn't check with you."

"Why?"

"Because she'd done this big speech about leaving us to heal or whatever, when we got back from Derbyshire." She spotted the basket on the kitchen table and started to poke through its contents. "Also, she didn't want to drop any of her *actual* friends in it."

"I thought you were *actual* friends."

"Not really. She's all nice one minute and then weird and mean the next. She's the one who told the boys to spell my first name backwards. Just because she didn't like *her* anagram name. Now they're constantly asking me if that's what I'm into. And she deliberately boasts about money in front of Bethany. And she says she's not dieting but keeps losing weight. And she's always telling everyone to get their eyebrows threaded. She's obsessed with eyebrows. Can I have some of this chocolate? Why is Dad still upstairs?" The chocolate wrapper fell to the floor. "Oh my God," Lana said. "You were having sex."

SUNFLOWERS

Candlelight was flickering along the hallway on Wednesday evening when Jen got home from her two-week see-where-we-are meeting with Tori in HR. The management team had suggested Jen wait until the end of Lana's summer holidays to come back. It was only three weeks away, but she wondered if she'd have a job to go back to by then.

Tea lights sat in jam jars and the kitchen was filled with a smell of toast. Lana huddled in one of the chairs and stared around the room, blinking at things as if she were taking a series of photos: the glass plant pots along the windowsill, the fish print above the microwave, the little Japanese cups on the dresser. Meg was setting the table for dinner, and obviously finding it difficult in the half dark.

"Do you think we could turn a light on now Mum's home?" she said.

"I like watching the shadows," Lana said, which wasn't exactly a no but certainly wasn't a yes.

"Are these the flowers from your room?" Jen asked, as she took her jacket off. There were three or four large sunflowers in a brown jug. Meg had made it her duty to replace the flowers every time they drooped, as if this act alone would correct everything.

"Lana thought she'd share them," Meg told her, smiling at Lana, as if to say thank you, though Jen was sure Meg didn't approve: the jug and the flowers didn't suit the kitchen; the rusticity of the jug was less charming among the mess of bills and unwashed crockery.

Lana made no effort to answer but hunched in her chair and blinked at a single yellow petal lying on the table. The flowers rather seemed like they'd been in the wars, with ragged leaves and quite a lot of petals missing. The seed-filled centers were marred with gaps, too, so that the flower heads looked like a bunch of rag dolls whose hair and faces had been battered, their mouths left with missing teeth. Jen couldn't imagine Meg had tortured them like that, and they seemed a slightly sinister gift.

"Well, it was a nice thought . . ." Jen began.

"They were just in my room, it's no big deal," Lana said.

There was a long moment of quiet then,

the oven timer ticking while they all looked at the ragged flowers, the bright yellow of the petals shaming the candles' watery glow. Jen wondered again how they'd got into that state and imagined Lana tearing them roughly from the vase, or even hacking at them deliberately.

"Can I do anything? Chop anything?" Jen asked Meg, helping herself to another of Maya's Trojan dates.

"No," Meg said, her back straightening suddenly. "But, oh, put the light on and come here. Mum, I think I can feel the baby kicking."

Jen pressed the switch and squinted under the glare of the overhead lamp. Meg bent a little and pulled up her jumper to lay a hand on the taut skin. As she did, her long hair swung dangerously near one of the tea lights still flickering in its little glass and Jen noticed several things at once: first, that Meg's hair nearly touched the flame; next, that Lana saw this; and last, that her younger daughter had no intention of warning Meg of the danger. Jen darted forward and swept the fall of hair away, tucking it behind Meg's ear.

"Careful," she said, though she knew her elder daughter hated to be told that. And then she kissed her twice, on the hair that had nearly been burnt. She kissed her deliberately, knowing Lana was watching, and she felt as though she were administering a punishment. Meg took her hand and held it to her bump, but Jen couldn't feel anything.

"It's stopped," Meg said. "She's stopped, I mean."

Lana stood then, unfolding herself, stretching. As she reached her hands above her head, Jen heard her spine cracking, a beat off the oven timer's tick. There was a smell of sweat — childish sweat — and a bright, expensive scent which Jen recognized as the perfume she hadn't been able to use since Lana's disappearance. She hadn't thrown it away because the bottle was the prettiest thing on her dressing table and because Hugh had been so pleased to have bought her something she actually liked, but she'd kept the top firmly on so she didn't have to smell it.

Lana let her arms drop, as if she realized she'd just given something away, but when Jen scanned her face there was nothing there: no guilt, no cunning.

"Sorry," Lana said to Meg. "I'm in your way."

She walked a few paces into the hall, where she stopped to lean against the doorframe. She looked exhausted, as though those few movements from the kitchen had been too much. Even her hair looked tired, and fell straight down from her scalp with lank weight, exposing the scarred pink skin. She was still wearing pajamas, and the top was very slightly grubby with a rip in the collar. She closed her eyes and held her face up to Jen, presenting a blank, a mystery. This, Jen felt, was her retaliation.

"Every day is a fight, isn't it, Mum?" Lana said, her eyes still closed. It sounded like something she had heard somewhere, not a sentence a London teenager would think of, but Jen couldn't ignore it.

"Is that how you feel, darling?"

Lana opened her eyes, but looked over Jen's shoulder, as if there were someone else standing in the hallway. "I thought it was for *you,* Mum," she said.

Finally pushing off the doorframe, she trailed her fingers along the wallpaper. The movement drew Jen's attention to a tiny scrap of petal, caught under her nail, and she saw that the creases of her daughter's hands were stained with yellow.

MOTHER'S DAY

For Jen, yellow became the color of worry, of dread, of paranoia, though Grace insisted she was wrong and that yellow gemstones in particular reduced panic and exhaustion. Which is how, after a chat over cups of rooibos tea and almond milk, she ended up wearing Grace's ridiculous citrine ring.

"Are you having an affair?" Hugh asked, when he saw it. And for a moment he seemed genuinely worried, which cheered Jen up considerably. She couldn't help torturing herself by looking at Lana's Instagram again, though, scrolling back through the months, half terrified at what she might find. (Was she imagining it or did there seem to be a lot of yellow in the pictures Lana posted?)

She reread the disturbing sentence about red wine and "men who leave bruises," studied again the photo of the housebreaking cat, let her mouth water over the chocolate brownies, and frightened herself with the sight of the skulking man in the corner of the *#rapture* picture. Her eyes were dry by the time she had scrolled back to March.

"I didn't even get a bloody card," Jen said suddenly, finding a familiar photo.

Hugh, dozing in an armchair, jerked

awake, his book thunking to the floor and his reading glasses coming to rest at a new slant across his face.

"From Lana," Jen said. "I got one from Meg . . . I think."

"What are you talking about?" Hugh's voice was groggy.

"Mother's Day. I didn't get a card from Lana."

"And you've only just noticed that now? It must be five months ago."

"No, of course I noticed at the time, or at least, I didn't not notice. I *know* she didn't even say the words 'Happy Mother's Day' to me, but now look at this." She turned the computer round so Hugh could see the screen, watching his face for a reaction.

"Oh, that's nice," he said, before righting his glasses and picking up his book.

Jen turned the laptop back round.

"Nice?" she said, looking at the picture.

It was an old photo taken when Lana was about two and showing a younger Jen, her hair still long and dark, her smile lines still characterful rather than craggy. They were standing in a garden, the shadow of a tree lying over their faces, the dappled sunlight highlighting the tip of a nose or the sharpness of a canine tooth. In the picture Jen was wide-eyed, on the verge of laughter,

331

surprised by a grubby-cheeked Lana, who had just tangled herself in Jen's long cardigan and was grinning madly. Jen could still feel the texture of that cardigan, a thin, buttery wool, and remember the weight and heat of the little body wrapped so close to hers.

"It's one of the photos from the album in the dining room," Jen said. "She must have scanned or photographed it specially. And it says: hashtag *Happy Mother's Day,* and hashtag *proud daughter* and *Words can't express how important the bond between mother and daughter is.*"

"You seem to be annoyed," Hugh said, not looking up from his book, though he hadn't turned the page in a while.

"Well, it's all just lies."

"Lies?"

"She posts these pictures, these sentiments, as if she's living them, as if they mean something, but in reality she couldn't care less about any of it. She wants her friends to think she's done something for Mother's Day, but not her own mother."

"Or" — Hugh rubbed his hands across his face — "that's what's going on in her head, and she can put it on social media but doesn't know how to express it to you directly."

He sounded very un-Hugh-like and Jen didn't know how to answer him. He didn't seem to know how to continue, either, and he balanced his book on the arm of the chair, where it rested for a moment before sliding off and banging to the floor again.

Jen stared at the photo for a few seconds then closed the window and the laptop. "Maybe you're right," she said, "but I don't see how much harder it would have been to write some of that in a card."

MAKING A SCENE

"Why do you care so much if she says one thing online and another at home?" Meg said on Saturday, as she removed the tomato from her artisan burger (what made it artisan? Jen wondered). "Most people give a false impression of their lives through social media; there are articles about it every day, usually *shared* on social media."

Jen laughed and bit at a very crisp chicory leaf. Having a daughter deliberately try to cheer her up cheered her up, and eating a perfect, peppery chicory leaf gave her joy, so why was the chief emotion she felt still sorrow? And was this how Lana felt at those moments when she was laughing, when Hugh thought perhaps she was "back to

333

normal"?

"You probably won't remember this, but when Lana was about nine she decided to be a director," Jen said. "A theater director."

"I don't remember."

"Well, you were at university then." Jen paused, wanting to get it right, to explain properly. "Anyway, at the time, there was a sort of craze at her school for putting on plays."

"Yeah, I went to one, a musical about space. She played a Lovebug."

"God, that was awful," Jen said. "She had about two lines and I had to make her a neon costume. I'd forgotten that."

"Here on planet Lovebug, every day is Valentine's Day," Meg mimicked in a high voice with a fake American accent.

"Oh, poor Lana, and she was so thrilled to get the part. I'm amazed you remember the line."

"It's the sort of thing that sticks. And I'm pretty certain she practiced it at least a hundred times."

"Probably. But that's not what I meant. That Lovebug play was arranged by the teachers, the music department. The plays I'm talking about were private."

"Private plays? Isn't that a contradiction

in terms?"

"Lana and her friends wrote and directed and starred in them themselves."

"When she was nine?"

"Nine or ten. She worked on the scripts at home, and she did talk to me about them, talked about the characters. She wasn't secretive exactly, but I could never *see* any of the plays because they were performed at lunchtime. The only audience was other children who didn't mind giving up their playtime to sit still in the main hall."

"They were allowed inside during play-time? The school must have changed since my day."

Jen shrugged. "I suppose she was part of a quiet sort of set, trustworthy."

"Oh, thanks. You mean I wasn't?"

"And everything was about creative ex-pression then."

"I'm not sure what you're getting at," Meg said.

"No, I'm not sure, either."

Meg turned on a sigh to ask the waitress for more ketchup.

"It's just," Jen carried on, feeling her way, "there was a kind of performance going on, a performance that took up lots of time and energy, and I suppose I was a little jealous, or hurt that it wasn't for my benefit, that it was for the benefit of other people entirely."

"Oh. I get it. And you feel like she's doing the same thing now, on Instagram or whatever?"

"Yes," Jen said, relieved. "That's it."

Meg shrugged. "That's probably exactly what she's doing. Not everything is about you."

Jen let her fork fall onto the plate. "You sound like Lana."

"Well, I'm beginning to see her point of view."

"Oh, don't say that." The words came out on a wail, which Jen hadn't intended, and the waitress looked shocked as she put down the ketchup.

"Sorry," Jen said.

"Sorry," Meg said, though Jen couldn't tell if it was for the waitress: a sorry-for-my-weird-mother sorry, or for her: a sorry-for-making-you-wail-in-public sorry.

A PLAY BY LANA MADDOX

DOWN THE PLUGHOLE

Act One

SOPHIE (*hands above her head*):

How did we get here?

336

CLAIRE (*looking up*):

We're all wet. I think we came down the plughole.

SOPHIE (*covering her eyes*):

Well let's go back. I don't like it.

CLAIRE (*with hands on hips*):

Wait a minute. Let's find out where we are first.

CHARLOTTE (*dreamily*):

Yeah, this bathroom is beautiful, I wonder whose it is.

SOPHIE (*pointing*):

Oh no! What are those?

CHARLOTTE (*kneeling down*):

What cute little doggies!

CLAIRE (*laughing*):

They are corgis. This must be the

337

Queen's bathroom.

CHARLOTTE (*hugging a corgi*):

Yes it is! Oh wow. Her toothbrush is red with a tiny crown on.

SOPHIE (*patting another corgi*):

I hope we don't get in trouble.

CLAIRE (*holding on to the basin*):

I don't think we'll be here long enough. We're being sucked down the plughole again.

ALL (*falling onto the stage*):

Here we go!

DAPHNE

After lunch, Jen and Meg went to see an exhibition. Meg was good at reminding Jen of the art shows she might otherwise manage to miss, at persuading her they were important, that the works were beautiful or meaningful rather than irritating or confusing. Mostly, Jen appreciated this; sometimes, she felt patronized.

"I'm not a child," she said, as they walked through a knot of tourists. "You don't have to monitor me."

"I'm not monitoring you, I'm waiting for you to catch up. I thought that was nice."

"Oh," Jen said. "Well, yes, that is nice."

She followed Meg off the long gallery staircase and breezed past the security guard after Meg's membership card. They read the bit of the artist's biography on the wall and looked at the first two early works, and Jen scrutinized the luscious brush marks with a sense of foreboding. She liked these pictures more than she knew she'd like the later ones. Artists always started, it seemed to her, to begin with beautiful paintings, pictures you'd love to have in your house, and end with incomprehensible and ugly monstrosities. She was careful to say none of this to Meg.

Instead, wanting to look more closely at a tender detail in one of the pictures, she rummaged for her reading glasses. But between bag and head she somehow managed to get them stuck. She couldn't move the glasses, she couldn't move her head. The problem converged just out of her eye line and involved an earring and some of her hair. She struggled for a moment before

Meg noticed.

"I've got something tangled here," she told her. "I can't see it. What have I done?"

"What were you saying about not being a child?" Meg said, freeing her mother.

"Yes, well, apparently, I'm heading for my second childhood. Anyway, it's good practice for you."

"In case my baby gets her earring and reading glasses tangled? What kind of a child do you think I'm having?"

Turning back to the pictures, they followed the walls around into the next room, and the next. As Jen had suspected, her interest in the work decreased the further they got, the longer the artist worked, the more fame he found. Feeling rather pally with Meg after the tangle incident, and in the final room of the exhibition (the door had those blessed words printed on it: *Exit and Shop*), Jen risked commenting on a picture. Lurid and scribbly, it wasn't even difficult to look at (she knew about art as challenge); it was, or it felt, meaningless. Perhaps she should have said that, but she didn't. She couldn't think quite how to begin.

"What on earth is going on in this?" She cringed as soon as the words were out of her mouth.

"It's meant to be Daphne," Meg said, moving closer to the painting, moving so close it looked like she might press her nose against the paint.

The gallery attendant, a small, round woman, got up from her seat and came towards them, turning back when Meg moved away again. She always seemed to play this game of dare in galleries, a more sophisticated, less thrilling form of chicken. It made Jen very uncomfortable.

"See, her hair is turning into leaves," Meg said, pointing too close now.

The attendant got up again.

"Yes, yes," Jen said, putting a hand on Meg's outstretched arm, "I can see. It was just the strange pose that confused me."

In the picture, Daphne seemed to be inside the tree, but she was bent over like a weeping willow rather than a laurel. Her head was upside down, her leafy hair spilling towards the floor. The painter had made an effort to show how the blood had run into her head, using lots of different shades of red, which contrasted with the green foliage. It looked uncomfortable, turning into a tree, not like the painting in the National Gallery, where the woman seemed to have suddenly sprouted branches in place of arms and was displaying them like jazz hands.

"It's interesting how there are these broad strokes throughout most of the picture but the bits where skin is turning into bark are really intricately depicted," Meg said.

"Hmmm," Jen said.

"It gives you a feeling of what it would be like to become a tree."

"Hmmm," Jen said again.

"Although I already know what that's like."

"How d'you mean?"

Meg rolled her sleeve up in answer, showing the red, scaly skin on her inner elbow. The eczema did look a little like bark.

"Oh, sweetheart," Jen said, horrified again by the similarity between Meg's sore and cross-scratched skin and Lana's careful, deliberately sliced forearms. "You must go back to the doctor about that. And you should keep your nails a bit shorter."

"I try, but my nails grow too fast. I didn't know that could happen, but it's because the baby is growing nails so there are extra nutrients, or something. Anyway, all the better to scratch with, huh?"

"But, darling, you've got to try *not* to scratch."

"Hmmm," Meg said.

She moved on, continuing the game with the attendant, who sighed every time she got up from her chair. Jen stayed by the Daphne picture, trying to work out what it reminded her of, or why it made her think of Lana. It was the red face that was particularly unpleasant to look at, which made her feel anxious, hopeless. After a few minutes she joined Meg, giving the last few pictures a cursory glance, knowing, relieved, that they were about to stop for coffee and pastries.

The girl in the courtyard café was the final hint. She was running back and forth between her mother and some railings, shrieking and refusing to sit still. Eventually, she hooked her legs over the bar of the railings and let herself dangle upside down. Her hair hung just as the woman's in the painting had, and the ends curled into a tangle of ivy, which grew along the edges of the courtyard.

At first, she laughed and shouted to her mother but, after a few moments, she let the smile fade from her face and looked out at the people sipping their lattes and picking at their salads with a solemn expression. Her face went pink, then red, and her mother called to her to get down. And Jen remembered an afternoon, a week ago, when Lana had refused to get off the sofa, refused to move from a position which left her head hanging over the edge, refused even when her face was nearly purple.

Jen felt the wail from earlier rise, like stomach acid, in her throat.

WASHING

Wailing, in public or private, was becoming a compulsion, though one Jen rarely gave in to. Instead, she looked for ways to soothe herself: listening to her mother describe, in her sibilant, telephone-tinny voice, all the irritating things Peggy had said or done; pinching off the juicy, leggy stems of peppery nasturtiums; exfoliating and moisturizing her hands until they were pink. At about this time she became interested in a woman, two doors down, who still hung washing on a line. She was the only person on the street to do this, as far as Jen could tell; everyone else presumably owned a tumble dryer. The garden and the washing line were partly visible from Lana's bedroom window, and Jen had taken to slipping in there every morning to watch the woman with her peg bag and basket.

She had first noticed the woman when she was checking on Lana in the days after they got back from the Peak District, making sure her daughter was still there and alive, and possibly, maybe, ready to talk. But now she couldn't be sure what her priority was, looking in on Lana or enjoying the calm that the woman's neat domestic actions inspired. The questions she asked the duvet-rolled lump in the bed had certainly taken on a routine tone.

"How are you this morning?" she said, while the woman pegged up a pair of men's striped pajama bottoms.

Lana's voice came through the bedding, low and muffled.

"Do you want anything? Tea? Juice? Breakfast?"

A series of tea towels was being hung. They were the kind that primary schools produce, with self-portraits of children on them, and they billowed bright and clean in the morning sun, making Jen forget the mustiness of Lana's too-lived-in room.

"I'm not hungry," Lana said.

"Or thirsty?"

"No."

"And are you up to anything today?"

She was rough with the line, the washing woman. It bounced and swung with each sodden addition and the pegs were pushed fiercely over the folds. She always held a peg in her teeth, which made her look, on first glance, as if she were smoking while she worked, and it gave her a grittier, roguish air, until she removed the cigarette and it became a peg again for a — what was it? A cotton handkerchief? Surely nobody used those anymore.

"I don't know what I'm up to," Lana said. "What are *you* doing today?"

"We could go shopping," Jen suggested.

There was a groan, as if Lana were having trouble digesting something.

The washing was nearly hung; the last task was to attach a central pole which changed the line from a shallow U to a shallower W. The woman was rough with this, too, and the washing trembled on its fastenings, the tea towels in particular. And then she was gone for the day.

Somehow, Jen always missed the moment the woman came back out to collect the dried pajama bottoms and tea towels and handkerchiefs. Occasionally, she missed the pegging-out, too, and was disappointed. She liked to keep a list of the items in her head: the blue-and-white bath towels, the fluffy oatmeal bath mat, the T-shirts with palm-tree prints and place-names: Key West, Lanzarote, Sharm el-Sheikh.

And once, hanging all day in the middle

of the line, there were just two long gray socks, like a rabbit's ears.

A CAVALIER ATTITUDE TO WASHING-MACHINE PROGRAMS

Jen's own washing routine was less clockwork, less calming. She was always behind and, although Hugh did his own, he'd become queasy about touching Lana's dirty clothes since she'd reached adolescence. So it was Jen's job to plunge a hand into the depths of Lana's laundry basket. She felt like a snoop every time she checked through the pockets of jeans and the pouches of hoodies to remove the tissues or sticks of gum or coins that had been forgotten.

There were often receipts in the pockets, too, which she flattened and read. But cans of drink, cheap makeup, and the occasional magazine didn't amount to much. The worst thing she'd found was a receipt for and then the actual pair of nail scissors. Jen had tried not to think about the reason Lana had bought them, why she had been carrying them about with her.

"Cutting her nails, perhaps," Hugh had suggested reasonably.

On Sunday, Jen turned out a pound coin, four twenty-pence pieces, and a pen with a charity logo on it. And then, in the zip pocket of a running T-shirt, she found a little velvet bag with a gold drawstring.

Inside were the two stones Grace had given Lana: rough and smooth. And Jen realized that the stone she'd trodden on in Lana's room, the one she'd been carrying around for nearly three weeks, was something else.

"Craziness," Lana said, making Jen flinch. She'd come into the kitchen and opened the laptop while Jen was staring at the stones. "Mum, what have you been reading? You spend way too much time on the internet, you know that?"

"You were using the computer last," Jen managed finally, dropping the velvet bag into the laundry basket and pressing any old button on the washing machine in the faint hope that it would start the wash cycle she was after, and regretting again the fact that she'd got the manual wet in the first week of ownership. Not that she'd have been likely to read it dry.

"Er, no," Lana said, her voice sharp, "I don't think so."

"Er, yes," Jen said, adopting the same tone.

As she got up from her position, crouched by the collection of washing powders and detergents, she realized Bethany was standing in the kitchen. The blood rushed from her cramped and swollen legs to her face.

"Oh, hi there," she said.

Bethany lifted a hand and smiled.

"We're just going to watch this video of a baby polar bear," Lana said, "because we've both run out of data and Bets hasn't seen it, and then we need to check when a film's on."

"Like, a film at the cinema," Bethany added.

"Oh, the cinema?" Jen said, only slightly sarcastic.

Lana gave a sigh-filled running commentary as she closed the "stupid" amount of tabs Jen had apparently left open and found that the film would be starting in twenty minutes. So they left immediately, taking one of Maya's fancy bars of chocolate with them, and Bethany missed out on the video.

The washing machine had begun to make strange noises, and Jen, worrying in retrospect about her cavalier attitude to program choice, asked Hugh, when he got home, what he thought.

"Google the model number," he said, scrabbling through the pockets of his raincoat for something.

Jen pulled the laptop towards her, but as she opened a new page she noticed the option to reopen all recently closed tabs and clicked on that instead. The pages that came up were on local newspaper websites, not local to them in London, but covering Derbyshire, Staffordshire, and Yorkshire. And every article was about a child who'd been reported missing.

"Have you been using the laptop to search the news?" she asked Hugh, raising her voice over the clunk of the washing-machine drum.

"That's what I have an iPad for." Hugh's voice was muted by the bag he was now rifling through.

"So you haven't been looking up missing children?"

"Ah," he said, discovering whatever it was he'd been searching for. He looked at Jen for a minute, as if listening to the echo of her question. "No. And, for the record, I never read anything on the laptop because it's plastered with debris from your cooking," he said. "Buttery fingerprints on the mouse pad, flour between the keys, dots of tomato sauce splattered on the screen. I don't want to even touch it."

It seemed more likely then that Lana had been searching for coverage of her own disappearance, but those articles weren't hard to find; they'd cluttered up the BBC News website and the national as well as local newspapers during the search and just after her discovery.

Jen read through every article: there was a teenage rock climber lost in bad weather, a boy who hadn't been seen since he jumped into a river to try to save his dog, a young woman with a history of drug abuse who might have been spotted in Leeds, and a toddler who'd wandered off. None of them bore any relation to Lana's circumstances.

Hugh took the prize possession he'd unearthed upstairs (Jen still hadn't understood what it was, and she suspected it was fictional, an excuse to duck any washing-machine dramas), and she sat thinking about the reasons Lana might have an interest in missing children. Had she met a child during those four absent days? Did she know where some of these missing children might be?

Jen was still thinking, blank-faced, in front of the computer, when Hugh came back downstairs in his DIY-worn after-work jeans.

"Stalking Lana again?" he asked.

"No," Jen said. "I was looking up . . ." She couldn't remember what she was looking up, and the possibility of remembering vanished as she spotted the last tab open on the page. It was one of those articles written as a numbered list.

7 Theories about Where Lana Maddox Went for 4 Days

Lana Maddox is the girl from London who went missing in the Peak District during the half-term holiday in May. She turned up again four days later, disorientated, cold, and covered in cuts and bruises and said she had NO MEMORY of the days she spent apparently lost in the countryside. Which begs the question: where did she go? Folks on the internet have been trying to work it out. Here are their theories.

1. The mermaid got her
Lana was really wet when she was found, despite the reasonably dry weather, so there's been a lot of speculation about which lakes or rivers she might have fallen into, and it's led to this great old myth resurfacing. There are lots of versions, some of which are listed on the <u>Myths of</u>

the Peak website, but our favorite story tells of a pool which is the bathing site of a beautiful mermaid who lures her victims to the edge and drags them down into the water. Almost no one survives, but those who do are granted eternal life. I guess our great-grandchildren will find out the truth of this if Lana is still alive in a couple of hundred years.

WHAT DO YOU THINK?

VOTE
Fantasy
Reality

See results:
90% Fantasy
10% Reality

2. Satanic cult in the woods

Okay, so this is a theory that crops up in nearly every list but, for once, there's a lot of backup evidence. There are the usual accounts of strange groups of weirdos in the woods, but one in particular is creeping us out. A cyclist was heading home at dusk around the time Lana was missing and he saw lights in the forest, got off his bike, and went to see where they were coming from and found himself in the midst of a satanic ritual, hooded men and everything. He ran away and only just made it back to his bike before they caught him. Afterwards, he swore <u>on his blog</u> that a girl had been lying in the middle of the circle, but police never found any evidence of the gathering.

WHAT DO YOU THINK?

VOTE
Same old same old
This time it could be true

See results:
78% Same old same old
22% This time it could be true

3. Foxhunters chased her
Now that foxhunting is semi-illegal, some people say the hunts have turned to chasing people instead, and not the cozy type with cuddly bloodhounds rather than foxhounds, where the human is allowed to put some distance between themselves and the dogs. According to theorists, the people, if they survive, are so traumatized and exhausted they don't remember anything about the experience. If you want to

know more you should check out this Tumblr with a list of all the other people who are supposed to have been chased, along with their stories.

WHAT DO YOU THINK?

VOTE
Sounds weird
I believe it

See results:
39% Sounds weird
61% I believe it

4. Stone-circle magic

There have been lots of accounts of lost time experienced inside one of the prehistoric stone circles in the Peak District. An American tourist found that she and her husband had spent seven hours inside the circle rather than the two they'd expected and had missed lunch and dinner. Read more on the Paranormalist blog. Another wanderer, from Belgium, decided to visit the circle one morning, leaving his group of friends at their campsite. Thinking he'd been gone about an hour, he was shocked to find his friends worriedly searching for him; it was nearly sunset and they thought he must have got lost. He could only remember being inside the circle. Could Lana have wandered into this same mysterious space?

WHAT DO YOU THINK?

VOTE
Too freaky
Too possible

See results:
64% Too freaky
36% Too possible

5. She was communing with trees

Mysterious human shapes have been found burnt into trees in the woods near where Lana went missing. They were only discovered after she was found and people in the local area have begun linking the two. The other explanation is that this is the work of art students from the nearby college, influenced by artist Ana Mendieta. See a photograph of one of her pieces: *Totem Grove 1985.* The students deny making the images, but they might be scared to admit to the act after the local authority promised to arrest the perpetrators for vandalism. So was it cowardly students or was Lana out there leaving the mark of her body on the bark of ancient oak trees?

WHAT DO YOU THINK?

VOTE
Totally the students
Lana fo defs

See results:
88% Totally the students
12% Lana fo defs

6. Abducted by aliens

Things just took an extraterrestrial turn. The theory of aliens out there on the moors has been gaining traction, especially as Bonsall, a village in the Derbyshire Dales, is the UFO capital of the world, with nineteen unidentified flying objects spotted in just two years, including this video recording of what looks like an alien craft. Bonsall is at the center of what is known as the Matlock Triangle, where there are often reports of strange lights, eerie noises, and things hovering in the sky, and one of the reports comes from the night of Lana Maddox's disappearance. Did aliens come down and kidnap

her before wiping her memory and dropping her back off on Earth?

WHAT DO YOU THINK?

VOTE
Makes sense
Doesn't seem right to me

See results:
28% Makes sense
72% Doesn't seem right to me

7. Descent into Hell
This idea's based on a local legend that a
Christian group is advocating on its website. The legend goes that one child in
every generation gets the opportunity to
go down into Hell and have a look around,
see who's down there, find out what sins
they committed, all that. Then they're supposed to come back and tell us lot on
Earth what we should and shouldn't do.
Eldon Hole might be the entrance, a
pothole which was once thought to be bot-
tomless. A goose was apparently thrown
down the hole (long before the RSPCA
existed to intervene) and emerged days
later with its wings singed by fires. So, if
Lana Maddox starts threatening us with
hellfire, we'll know this was the right call.

WHAT DO YOU THINK?

VOTE
Inspirational
Delusional

See results:
6% Inspirational
94% Delusional

Do you have another theory? Share it in the comments!

Break in hostilities

One of the article's links was broken, but Jen studied the photo of Ana Mendieta's carved and burnt tree trunks, looked at artists' impressions of the pool-dwelling mermaid, read ten other stories involving supposed satanic cults, and watched the UFO video in a trance. The stone-circle theory gave her a shiver, and she thought of the earphones Lana had tied on the tree by the Nine Ladies.

"Have you seen all these mad theories people have about where you went?" Jen asked when Lana got back from the cinema. ("The film was rubbish, I'm not letting Bethany choose next time.")

"Yeah," Lana said, drinking a glass of water and pouring another. "Dumb ideas, huh?"

"None of them are true, then?"

"Sure, Mum, I was abducted by aliens and then given eternal life by a mermaid."

Jen shrank into her seat, expecting a row, but Lana smiled and leaned towards the screen, putting an arm around her mother's shoulders. Jen didn't dare breathe in case she scared her away. A cold drop of water hit her on the back of the neck when Lana turned to drink again from her glass, but Jen stayed still and didn't complain.

"Weird about the Nine Ladies, don't you think?" Jen ventured.

Lana shrugged. "Someone at school asked me whether I knew if he was going to Hell. Obviously, I told him he was."

"Sweet of you," Jen said, risking the teasing tone.

"I know. I'm a sweet, sweet person." She put her glass down. "And some stupid emo shithead wanted me to describe the satanic ritual."

"He didn't really think you'd been involved in one?"

"Of course. I told you, he's a shithead. Have you looked at all the article's links?" Lana asked, bending so that their cheeks nearly touched.

Jen closed her eyes for a second. "Almost all. Why?"

"Just wondering how thorough your research of me is." She stood up then and laughed, as if they were playing a game, as if Lana had set a diverting riddle for her mother, or perhaps was performing in a murder-mystery evening and had come out of character for a moment to wink at the dinner guests.

Feeling as though she was being steered towards something, Jen went back to the article to see what she'd missed. There was just the Hell theory to go and she was surprised and not surprised to find that the link took her straight to the home page of the New Lollards Fellowship.

It was an ugly website, the kind that would make Jen's colleagues grimace. Busy with social-media updates and recommended books, there was an aggressive note for nonbelievers at the top, which said the site wouldn't tolerate abuse or blasphemy, and at the bottom an option to ask Google Translate to change the site into another language — anything from Afrikaans to Zulu.

"This is Stephen's church," Jen said. "Stephen from the holiday."

"I know. He's trying to cash in or what-ever, right? Cheeky fuck."

"To cash in?" Jen scrolled down and found a picture of Stephen standing outside a rather sad-looking brick building. *Our soon-to-be minister,* the caption read.

"Yeah. Not for like actual cash, probably, but publicity will get him more souls, right?"

"Do you think he's that cynical?"

Lana shrugged.

A page entitled "Correspondents of Hell" told the story she'd already read in the pamphlet from St. Andrew's church, only without the bits that suggested a reasonable explanation. At the end was a link to the local paper: Gerry and Stephen interviewed.

Jen followed this link, too, and found a large image of the stained-glass window in St. Andrew's.

HAVE YOU HEARD OF THE BOY WHO VISITED HELL?

By Susie Betts   @sbettsreporter

15 June 2015

There are references to this local legend in St. Andrew's, Middleton, and several other churches around the district. A young boy in the Middle Ages is said to have found an entrance to Hell and to have spent time there before resurfacing with a message for his fellow Christians. But how does that relate to a recent missing-persons case?

On 7 June this year, Lana Maddox, 15, a holidaymaker from London, reappeared after four days missing in the Derbyshire Dales. Thankfully, she was found safe and sound, if a little the worse for wear after getting lost, but it still isn't clear exactly where Miss Maddox was, or why searchers took so long to find her.

Now, a prominent member of the New Lollards Fellowship, which has its headquarters in Sheffield, is filling in some of the gaps as to what happened. Gerry Farnham, 68, claims Miss Maddox wasn't in this realm at the time of searching, and that the legend, alluded to in many of the churches in this area, is based on a real place that acts as an entrance to Hell.

Mr. Farnham said, "That boy in the legend wasn't the only one. My sister found the entrance, too, and went down into Hell as a child. She went missing in 1956, and she came back several months later, very changed. She, like this girl Lana, also refused to tell us what she'd seen, and denied where she'd been for a very long time. She needed guidance from our elders to recall it all."

Unfortunately, Miss Farnham passed away some years ago, so is unable to confirm or deny this story, but Stephen Laurie, 42, a minister-in-training at the same church, agrees. He said, "Lana needs to be encouraged to speak out. We could all benefit from what she knows and, equally, we might suffer if she keeps quiet.

"And it's not some mad theory. There are many accounts from children, or the guardians of children, who have taken the same journey, and also records made by the governors of schools or workhouses. There's a lot of evidence, going back hundreds of years, if you only look for it."

So could this be true? The Rev. Thomas Lasting, 54, Rector at St. Andrew's, doesn't think so: "These sorts of myths can be found all over the world, especially in regions where there are underground caves. They are interesting for students of the arcane but mustn't be taken literally."

LONDON ROAD

Jen was left thinking who might have information to add. She suspected that Gerry Farnham's sister had gone away to have an illegitimate baby, and she wondered if she should email Susie Betts with that theory.

Lana had just gone upstairs to have a shower (was she having too many? Was it a sign of something?), when the phone rang. Jen jumped at the sound and was glad no one was around to see. Her hand trembled slightly when she found a plate for the piece of toast she hadn't known she was eating and finally picked up the handset.

"Hey, Jen," said a high, soft voice with a London accent.

"Oh, hi, Bethany." The simple act of answering the phone to one of Lana's friends sent her back years, back to when things were easier, happier. "Do you want me to get Lana for you?"

"Erm. That's okay . . ." She was breathy. "I just wanted to check she's all right."

"Yes, I think so," Jen said, having to squeeze her own voice through a suddenly tight throat. "She's upstairs."

"Okay, that's good."

There was a shout in the background and then Bethany's voice, directed elsewhere for a moment: "Did I arks you? No. No. Well, then, don't give me your opinion."

Jen held the phone away from her ear to continue munching on the toast (when had she spread marmalade on it?) until Bethany's voice came through clearly again.

"What's going on?" Jen asked. "Have you and Lana had a fight?"

"No. No, nothing like that. It's just . . . Lana's been getting a load of tweets from randoms lately, and then today she seemed upset and she didn't stay for the film."

"Oh. She hasn't said anything about that to me." Lana had been out for hours. Where had she been, if not at the cinema? "What film were you going to see?"

"*London Road.* It's got Tom Hardy in it," Bethany said. "He's hot," she added, when Jen didn't appear to react.

"And you chose it together?"

"Yeah. But then she got really, like, twitchy as soon as we sat down and she didn't want her nachos, and then when the lights went off she kind of freaked out and said she had to go."

"And you let her? I mean, she just left?"

"I asked if she wanted me to come with

366

her," Bethany said, managing to pronounce "ask" in the usual way, now she wasn't shouting. "But she said no. She was like: *I just need to be outside.* Something like that."

"So you stayed and watched the film?"

"Yeah, though I wish I hadn't. It's like a weird musical about prostitutes getting murdered. Did you know?"

"Well, I saw it at the theater, before it was a film."

"And Tom Hardy's only in it for, like, two minutes, and they made his teeth all rank. I don't blame Lana for getting out of there."

"What time did the film start?"

"Four fifteen, but I like the trailers so we went in at four."

"And Lana left almost immediately?"

"Yeah. Like, less than five minutes after we sat down. It was kind of embarrassing. Especially because Marcus thought I'd arranged it so we could be alone."

Jen pushed her plate of toast away. Lana had got home at six thirty, which meant there were a couple of hours unaccounted for. Or, to put it another way, Lana had been missing for two hours. That sickeningly familiar unsteady feeling washed over her. She was floating up but her internal organs were rushing down, then her organs were rising but the rest of her was sinking.

"Did she say where she was going?" Jen asked, once her body had realigned itself. Had Lana left the cinema to meet someone, Jen wondered, someone she'd contacted on Twitter? Or was it the theme of the film that worried her?

"She didn't say," Bethany said. "But she's home now. You said that, right?"

"Right."

"Good. I was a bit scared, if I'm honest. I mean, creeped out, you know? It was like she'd seen something in the cinema, in the dark, that we couldn't see. Like a ghost."

"A ghost?"

A sigh came hissing down the line. "Yeah," Bethany said finally. "I'm sorry to scare you, and I feel bad, like, informing on her, you know? I mean, I shouldn't be calling her mum, really. It's just that . . . Lana's different since you came back from half term, since she was missing or whatever. She's all sorry for stuff all the time. Like she's scared I'm going to be angry with her or she's done something wrong. Have you noticed that?"

"Not really." Quite the opposite, Jen thought, searching for Lana's Twitter account.

UNWANTED SOCIAL-MEDIA ATTENTION

Lana Maddox @bananalanarama
Tweets & replies

The #dayofjudgment is coming. Are you ready? Do you want to burn in #Hell? Ask **@bananalanarama** what that is like. #rapture #Armageddon
Lana Maddox replying to **@lordgodn master:** No, don't ask me. I don't know anything.

@bananalanarama You're obviously mentally ill. I'd suggest getting help soon.
Lana Maddox replying to **@faithdust buster:** I already have a therapist, but thanks for your concern, dickhead.

@bananalanarama Can you please please please give us details about gehenna? It is essential we know.
Lana Maddox replying to **@eclipse heaven:** Can you please please please stop asking, I have nothing to tell you. It is essential you leave me alone.

@bananalanarama Really hope you're

ok. We are praying for you.

Lana Maddox replying to **@faithheals:** The burns have healed nicely now, thanks. Praying must have worked. I also recommend Sudocrem for all those post Hell injuries.

@bananalanarama I hope you liked what you lied about, because you WILL go to Hell for that lie.

Lana Maddox replying to **@jesusmy1 friend:** Thanks for the warning, but I haven't lied. I never said I went to Hell. Stop freaking out, freak.

@bananalanarama Come back daughter of darkness, we miss you. Sorry your ice cream melted, I'll get you another one. Promise.

Lana Maddox replying to **@satanmy satan:** Ha ha. Okay, but only if it's strawberry cheesecake flavor. #souls foricecream

An Old Woman Reading

There were pages of messages and replies. Jen was horrified by the vitriol some people had directed towards Lana, and angry that she'd been contacted by so many crazy or

370

threatening strangers, but there was nothing that revealed where Lana had been that afternoon.

Jen wanted to ask Lana directly, but they'd started to get on and she didn't want to risk an argument just yet. Instead, she planned a later conversation in her head while making an elaborate dinner, taking down her old cookbooks, glued shut with kitchen grease and dust, finding a motherly sort of satisfaction in gathering the ingredients from the fridge. It was nice to feel motherly in that way, in a competent way, rather than a failing, flailing way, and it was even better when Lana wandered in, saying the kitchen smelled nice.

"Why don't you give me a hand?" Jen asked.

"Maybe in a sec, I just want to read this," Lana said, making herself one of the protein shakes she'd been given at the hospital, and already absorbed in something on her phone.

Jen tried not to be disappointed, tried just to be glad that Lana was prepared to be in the same room as her for a while. The oily spatula glistened in the light, and Jen stared at it. When had it come to this? she thought. Since when was having her own daughter in the same room an achievement?

Lana gave a cackle of laughter, her canine teeth flashing at the corners of her mouth.

"What's funny?"

"Oh, nothing."

Jen went back to her cookbook, wondering if she really had to remove the chops or if she could just leave them in the pan while the other things simmered around them. A note had been written, in her own handwriting, long ago, but it was faded and gravy-spattered and illegible. She screwed her eyes up and held the page under the window and was still none the wiser. She wished she could go back in time and tell her younger self to write more clearly, but, she speculated, might that be a waste of the time-traveling process? If she got the opportunity to go back and give herself some advice, was there not something more useful she could say? It was worrying not to be able to think of anything more momentous than handwriting tips.

There was another grating cackle.

"Really, what's so funny?" Jen said.

"It's just something on BuzzFeed. Parenting wins–type thing."

"Parenting wins," Jen repeated. "Can I see?"

Lana passed her the phone and yawned and shook her protein shake while Jen peered at the screen. She seemed always to be peering at things now. Cookbooks, computers, the pores on her nose; she sometimes felt like a modern version of that Rembrandt painting of an old woman reading. She couldn't remember the title.

"People who are nailing this parenting thing," she read out loud.

Although she chuckled through the list, she felt more and more despondent the further she got. Had she ever "nailed" the parenting thing? Had she even *tried* to nail it? She'd certainly never deliberately embarrassed her children, and this seemed to be important. Accidentally embarrassed them, yes, but that wasn't nailing anything, that was just sad. Trying not to embarrass them and still managing to embarrass them was even worse. Perhaps she should get her face printed on a T-shirt, or start calling Lana a loser in texts — that certainly went down well on the internet. She couldn't imagine it going down well with Lana, though.

"Can I have my phone back?" Lana said.

"Hold on." Jen quickly looked up the Rembrandt painting she'd been picturing. She'd remembered how dark it was, and the way the woman rested her hand on an open page, but the subject was less bent-backed than she'd thought and there was a beautiful highlight on the cloak, a shine on the headdress, which her memory had left out. "*An Old Woman Reading*," she read. "Disappointingly literal. *Probably the Prophetess Hannah.*"

"What are you going on about?"

"Does this remind you of me?" Jen asked, turning the screen to face her daughter and holding it next to her face.

"No."

"Are you sure?"

The rich smell of the protein shake was on Lana's breath, and Jen had to turn her head away when she leaned towards her.

"Well," Lana said, considering, "maybe when you're trying to use Dad's iPad."

"Really?"

"No, not really. Can I have my phone now?"

Jen went back to her cookbook, brushing her hand over the page with that vague handwritten note.

"Oh. Right, then. You looked like that picture right then, when you did that," Lana said. "Oh, weird. Do it again, I'll take a photo, Instagram it."

"No, thank you," Jen said, shutting the cookbook. There was no need to go back in time, she decided; she'd deciphered the note: *Lana doesn't like chops.*

This was something else her memory had left out. And just at this moment when they were getting along, when she was beginning to feel she knew her daughter again, she had set them both up for a disappointment and proved she didn't know her at all. Her confidence left, her feeling of competence, and when Lana popped upstairs to the loo, Jen let herself slide onto the floor.

Do you believe in ghosts?

Jen's sudden lethargy, the severity of her disappointment, shocked her. She didn't remember giving up so easily before, or being so apprehensive, so instantly frightened. Was there, could there be, something else in the house with them, or was it just Lana who changed the atmosphere? Sometimes, Jen felt as though her daughter's emotions hung about in the air. Irritation, exhaustion, or despair lingered like a cloud of perfume, waiting to be walked through, the particles clinging to whoever passed by.

Grace had given her a book which suggested that moods — moods that couldn't be explained by other circumstances — were really caused by supernatural beings. It was based on T. C. Lethbridge's theory that ghosts were just traumatic memories stored in stone or brick and projected later, and Jen went about the house running her hand over the scratched paintwork in the hall and the bubbling plaster in the utility room, knocking at the baseboards and the doorframes.

"What are you doing?" Hugh said, finding her on all fours, her head in the under-stairs cupboard.

"Looking for something," Jen called back.

"I guessed that. What is it you're looking for?"

Jen backed out, shaking the dust from her hair and coughing the damp from her lungs. "A resonance, a change in temperature, an emanation. I thought I might know it when I came across it."

"And?"

"No luck yet."

"Shall I get the Hoover out while you're there?"

Jen nodded and went to make a banana pudding (something she *knew* Lana liked). She stared at the bowl turning round and round in the microwave and then, when that became dizzying, she opened the laptop and scrolled through the thumbnails of other Rembrandt pictures on Google. She stopped at *The Shell,* though she wasn't keen on the picture, having always found shells uncanny;

they were like empty houses, she thought.

When she was a child, she'd been sure they were haunted by the ghosts of the gelatinous creatures who'd once lived in them, and that the whooshing sound she could hear when she held one to her ear was the voice of the dead creature, moaning like ghosts do in stories. Rembrandt's shell was cone-shaped and spotted with pale teardrop markings. It sat, ominous, looming, with something eyelike about its coiled end, in a dark space full of cross-hatching, looking more like a haunted house than any image of an actual house Jen had ever seen.

WRINKLES

"I do look like that old Rembrandt woman," Jen said that night. "Even my eyeballs have wrinkles. I didn't think that was possible, but when I rub them like this, look . . . It's grotesque."

"Don't rub them, then," Hugh said, "and get some sleep."

"I'm trying! Do you think I'm not trying? I want to sleep, Hugh, I really do. I just can't."

"Getting into bed might help. You can't sleep at your dressing table."

"Hmmm." She rubbed her right eye one

more time in order to study the wrinkle again, a yellowish pleat of membrane near the iris which appeared and then smoothed itself out as she watched in the mirror. When it had gone, she packed away her lavender neck cream and verbena hand cream and honey lip balm and got into bed.

Hugh turned out the light and Jen shifted about, trying to get comfortable. She pressed play on one of Grace's audio-guided meditations, but concentrating on each part of her body in turn just made her skin prickle.

She stopped the recording and rolled over. "Okay, forget the eyeball wrinkle," she said. "But do your joints creak? I mean, audibly?"

"No." Hugh's voice was sharp in the clear dark of their bedroom.

"Oh. Mine sort of groan whenever I move. My shoulders especially."

"Groan?"

"Yes. I only notice it at night, but it's disturbing. Sometimes, the way the sound reverberates through the mattress, I think I'm hearing voices in the room below. People murmuring to each other."

Hugh turned the light back on.

"And you say *Lana* is trying to worry *you*," he said.

"I didn't say she was trying to. And I

didn't mean to worry you. Sorry."

His breathing was strangely quiet for a moment, and when Jen turned to look at him she realized he was listening out for something. She was about to ask what it was, but he threw the covers off before she could.

"It's no good," he said. "I'm going to have to go downstairs and check now, aren't I?"

"What for?"

"People who might be in the room below. Murmuring people."

Heavy-footed with fatigue, he walked from the room and she heard him trudge down the stairs. The door to the sitting room opened, the light switch was clicked on and then off, the door was shut, and then his steps creaked back up to the landing.

"All okay?" she asked, as he came back in.

"There's a cat on the sofa."

"Again, please."

"On the sofa in the sitting room. There is a cat. Asleep."

"Ah ha!" she said.

"What does that mean?"

"Well, I told you, didn't I?"

He leaned forward, resting his fists on the mattress. "You told me you heard murmuring voices, not a meowing cat."

"No, weeks ago, I told you about the cat.

I found it on the stairs in the middle of the night."

"Did you?" he asked. "How did it get in?"

"That's the question. I mean, in general, but also for Lana."

"And did you ask her?"

"Since when does asking Lana a question result in a comprehensible answer? She told me I was seeing things."

"Great," Hugh said, getting back into bed.

"What are you doing?"

"Well, that suits me. If the cat's imaginary, I can leave it where it is and go to sleep."

"But it's not imaginary, is it?"

Hugh took a moment to think. "I'm inclined to believe it is," he said. "I only saw it for a second, after all. It might just have been a vision."

"A vision?"

"Yes. A wrinkle on my eyeball, if you will. Good night."

The light went off again and after a few minutes Hugh's breathing became snuffly and regular. Jen lay picturing the cat curled up directly below her; she wondered whether to go down and let it out. All night, she listened for a meow, but heard nothing, and in the morning the cat was nowhere to be seen.

Jen brought up the imaginary cat the next morning at their family-therapy session with Dr. Greenbaum.

"Ah, but cats are like that," he said. "They sneak in where they're not wanted." He told them to google *People who don't actually have a cat.* "It's a series of photos, for instance one of a fluffy tabby in a kitchen sink, and the text reads something like: *Came home to find this, oh and by the way I don't own a cat,* and so on. So, you see, you are not alone. I doubt you are imagining it."

Afterwards, Jen and Hugh and Lana went to a pizzeria, their customary treat after a session, where Lana inevitably chose to sit at one of the high tables with bar stools so they had to eat with their feet dangling in the air. Some students had crowded into one corner, dragging chairs across the floor and shouting to friends as they came in, and a chef kept throwing disks of pizza dough into the air to the customers' applause.

Usually, the buzz of the place made Hugh cheerful, but he seemed distracted while he ate his Fiorentina, and he absentmindedly put chili flakes on his garlic bread, even though he disliked spicy foods.

When Lana went off to the Ladies, Jen asked what was wrong.

"There's a man staring at you," Hugh said.

"Which man?" Jen didn't look, but sat a little straighter, as if her back could feel for eyes.

"Blue shirt, sitting with a woman."

Jen made a show of adjusting the cardigan on the backrest of her bar stool, managing to catch a glimpse of the man Hugh had indicated.

"No, he isn't," she said. "He's just facing this way, we're in his line of vision."

"He has caught my eye approximately sixteen times in the last twenty minutes."

"Well, maybe he thinks you're staring at *him.*"

Hugh used a pizza crust to mop up some egg yolk while he thought about that. "No," he said finally, "it's definitely you he's got his eye on. And he's a bit odd."

"I suppose he'd have to be, to be eyeing me."

"I don't think that. You know I don't think that."

"How's he odd, anyway?" Jen said. "Just because he looks around the room? It would be odder to keep your eyes shut throughout lunch."

"Why are you taking his side?"

"I'm not taking his side."

They sat quietly for a few minutes, the smell of basil filling the space, the vinegary tang of the wine the only thing that passed between them. Then, unable to resist any longer, she swiveled on her seat to get a proper view of the man.

She felt immediately that he couldn't have been staring at her. He had a swollen and blistered face and was nearly deformed by some skin condition. This convinced Jen of his innocence. No one, she thought, with such an inflamed and unattractive face would draw attention to himself by staring. She ate the last few bites of her pizza in peace, her fingers oily and her lips sore from the salty tomato sauce.

"Ah, now, that's interesting," Hugh said, as he folded his greasy napkin. "I mean, I thought it was funny he wasn't talking to his wife."

"What?"

"Well, she obviously wasn't his wife. She just paid and left, not a word, not a look. They were just strangers, sharing a table."

"It *is* very busy in here."

"Or . . . he was using her as a front. A decoy."

"Hugh, why would he do that?"

"So he could stare without making us suspicious. Oh." Hugh smoothed his shirt-front and peered out of the window. "He's coming over."

Jen turned just as the man got to their table.

"Hello," the man said.

It was Stephen. He said hello, but Jen heard him badgering Lana about Intelligent Design on their holiday, heard him telling Lana that Jesus could cure depression, heard his words in the newspaper article, calling for Lana to "speak out." Her fists curled involuntarily; a rush of anger made her breathless.

"You probably didn't recognize me just then, did you?" he said.

"No," she admitted.

"Hogweed."

"Excuse me?"

"Hogweed's what did it. My face, my hands."

"How did hogweed do that?" Hugh asked.

"I brushed against the broken stems when I was clearing litter from the side of the road, and of course I was in the sun. The blisters came up within a few hours. They were the size of conkers, but they've gone down quite a bit. I'll have the scars for months, the doctors say. I'm having to wear a hat when I go outside now."

"Dreadful."

"Yes, so you mind what you touch in the countryside."

"Well," Hugh said, obviously at a loss as to how to respond to this advice.

"Were you doing some sort of community service?" Jen asked. "Was it punishment for a crime?"

"I'm not a criminal, Jen, I just like to try and do my bit. It's disgraceful how most people treat our environment. God's green earth. Is this your husband? We met on holiday in the Peak District," Stephen explained to Hugh.

"It's Stephen who believes that Lana visited Hell while she was missing," Jen said.

"I see." Hugh shifted off his bar stool. Jen had the impression it was a masculine move, rather than a polite one, that Hugh was measuring himself against this man. "Did you want to join us?"

"Thank you, but I should be getting back. I'm here for a conference, New Lollards from all over the world. Atlanta, Chelyabinsk, Monrovia, Copenhagen. We're certainly growing. To think, when my great-great-great-uncle was a member, there was only the one congregation. It's wonderful, really. Before I go, though, tell me, Jen, how do you think Lana is doing?"

Jen felt herself flush, and thought this must give them a resemblance. She pictured them red-facing each other across the table, and thought of those videos of exasperated atheists, making themselves look unreasonable next to placid believers, arguing until they were purple, with unmovable opponents. Lana had been drawn into arguing with Stephen. Jen wanted to avoid that.

"I ask," he said, "because we developed quite a rapport on holiday, and I took a particular interest in her."

"I know that. I saw that. All the other people in our group saw that. There are witnesses."

"Witnesses to what? To my talking to her? Have I done any harm?"

"Harm? Of course you've done harm. Where do I even start? You tried to lure my daughter into joining your cult, you've encouraged her to cut herself, and on top of that you've talked to the press about her, told everyone she's had a supernatural experience. You've opened her up to internet trolls and cyber-bullying. Made her a target of any nutcase who might google her in the future."

Stephen nodded, as though he were listening to a list of grievances against another

386

person, as though he were moderating rather than being accused. "I have to say, I wish I hadn't talked to that reporter. I've had unwanted mail myself since the article was published — people suggesting that I have mental-health problems, or that I've been brainwashed. It hasn't really had the effect I'd hoped it would. Perhaps we could ask the newspaper to take the article down?"

"I've already asked the newspaper to remove the article."

"Well, good. What else can I say? I'm sorry."

This sent another wave of angry heat through Jen's body. She stood, rubbing the backs of her thighs where the bar stool had cut into them. She was furious, and his apology only made it harder to express that fury.

"You're sorry," she said, trying to match his calm tone. "You're sorry you picked on a vulnerable girl and attempted to convince her that dinosaurs never existed, that her self-inflicted wounds were divine, that she'd visited Hell while on holiday in the Peak District."

"I don't actually know *where* Lana was," Stephen said. "But I suspect there is more to her absence than she is admitting."

This was something they could agree on,

Jen thought. She didn't like finding that they agreed about anything.

"I also never encouraged her to hurt herself or suggested her injuries were a positive thing. I just wanted to help her with the guilt, the shame she felt for having made those marks on her body."

"She doesn't feel shame about that."

"She told *me* she does."

Jen tried to sit down but misjudged the height of the bar stool and slipped. Her cardigan slid to the floor and she knelt next to it, as if it were an injured child. She studied the sagging where her elbows had stretched the wool, the gap where a button had come off; she stroked the bobbly nap. Had Lana really chosen to confide in Stephen rather than her? Did she think this mad stranger was more trustworthy than her own mother?

"So you know she's had depression," Hugh asked Stephen, as he offered Jen a hand.

"Yes, I know. I know because I had it myself once. And do you know what helped me?"

"Let me guess. The New Lollards Fellowship."

"I was going to say faith, but yes. I think, when we're feeling low, it can be a sign that

God is preparing us to receive him. I didn't want Lana to miss that window, miss that chance at healing."

"You're a conservationist, then, a concerned citizen. Cleaning the highways and byways and trying to save the souls of passing teenagers." Hugh looked amused, but Jen noticed he was gripping the back of his empty chair. He was angry, too. She felt a rush of love for him.

"Let me ask you another question," Jen said, pulling on her cardigan. "Did you tell Lana to cover her hair? For modesty? Did you make her cover up?"

"No, certainly not. We don't believe in any particular dress code. Though it's a good idea for all women not to invite the glances of men."

Jen sighed in relief, pleased to find she could hate him again. There was no need to challenge him, to get into an argument, to ask why the onus should be on women. She caught sight of Lana across the restaurant, walking back from the Ladies, head down, phone out. Somehow, Jen had forgotten her daughter was there, that they had come to lunch as a three.

"There's something else you should know," Stephen said, his feet shifting. "I've studied this for quite a time, and one or two of the accounts suggest the children returned with . . . a friend."

"A friend," Hugh repeated, in the blandest tones. "D'you mean you?"

"No, no, I mean something else, a *being*," Stephen said, glancing round. "From their travels."

Jen felt a sort of shiver pass over her body, and she grabbed at the collar of her shirt. She'd said nearly the same thing after hearing Lana talking alone in her room. *I can't get rid of the idea that Lana brought someone back with her.*

"And what do these *beings* do? What are they for?" Hugh asked.

"They continue to guide the children in some way," Stephen said. "Listen, you live with Lana. Have you noticed any unusual behavior?"

Jen thought of the creeping about the house, the questions about violence, the imaginary cat that Dr. Greenbaum said wasn't imaginary. She scanned the restaurant, surprised Lana hadn't arrived at their table yet, and spotted her standing half hidden by the counter, watching them.

"This is ridiculous," she said, urgent, wanting to get her venom out, but wanting to get it out quickly, before Lana decided to join them. "Next, you'll be suggesting an exorcism, and I've seen documentaries about those. Mothers in Italy being told to touch holy water to their daughters' genitals."

Stephen seemed slightly taken aback. "I'm not suggesting you do anything like that," he said, dropping his voice so low it was hardly audible over the clatter of the restaurant. "But I can help her."

"Ah, right, I understand now. You mean it would involve *you* touching her genitals with holy water."

STILL WATERS

They had bought some holy water on holiday in Norfolk last year, scooped from an ancient well and decanted into a little bottle. Jen had carried it around in her handbag for weeks, wondering what she should use it for, wishing she had an ailment she could test it on.

Then, during the train journey to the Peak District, she'd gone to the loo and, wanting to clean up afterwards, had covered her hands in a sugary-scented liquid soap, only to find there was no water in the tap. So it was the holy water she'd used to wash away the soap. There had been no discernible difference to her hands afterwards — her nails were just as likely to break, her skin was still vulnerable to a casserole-lid burn — but she *had* noticed since using the water that every time she'd tried to hail a cab she'd been successful.

"That's a new one," the cab driver said, looking at her in the mirror. "I never thought picking up fares had anything to do with God."

"Nor did I," Jen said.

"When have you taken a cab in the last few months?" Hugh asked.

"Just a few times with colleagues when we would have been late for a meeting."

"So your company paid?"

"Wow, Dad, tight, much?" Lana said, turning from the window. "Mum has her own salary, you know."

"I know."

Did you just defend me? Jen wanted to ask Lana, but instead she said, "That was Stephen we were talking to in the restaurant. Stephen from the holiday."

"Oh, right."

"Didn't you recognize him?"

"What was wrong with his face?"

"He'd got a kind of burn from a plant. Hogweed."

"Oh, hogweed," the cab driver said. "That's terrible stuff. I read about that in the paper a few weeks ago. You have to be careful to keep kids away from it."

"He looked really gross," Lana said.

"I'll bet. People get blisters and everything."

"Yes, I almost felt sorry for him," Jen said. "Is that why you didn't come over, Lana? Because of his face?"

"I just didn't expect him to look like that."

"Expect him? How could you? It happened recently."

"I know, but it was a shock."

"A shock?" Jen felt her phone buzz in her pocket — an email arriving — but she didn't reach for it because she was remembering Stephen's question. Not *How is Lana doing?* but *How do you think Lana is doing?* As if he already knew and just wanted Jen's opinion. Had Lana found Stephen handsome before? Had she wanted to see him, arranged to meet him at the restaurant, and then changed her mind when she'd seen his face?

"He looked frightening," Lana said.

"Perhaps he needed some of that holy water," the cab driver said.

BAD PRESS

From: Queries@pdnews.co.uk
To: maddoxfamily@hotmail.com
Subject: Re: Boy who visited Hell
  article

Dear Mrs. Maddox,
Thank you for the email you sent to Susie.Betts@pdnews.co.uk.

After careful consideration, we have decided not to remove Lana's name from the article of 15 June, nor to take down the article altogether. There was extensive coverage in the paper during the time your daughter was missing in which her name was already mentioned, and we only remove names and articles as a very last resort, or if we think that not taking action will lead to extreme consequences, for example, if someone's life is in danger.

We were contacted by members of the New Lollards Fellowship and chose to pursue an interview because they had a different angle on Lana's story. That story was, and still is, of great interest to our readers, and, as you'll acknowledge, our initial coverage did help to locate her — it was seeing our article that made Mr. Crossley of Yew Farm contact the police when he saw a young woman on his land. I would also remind you that you did give us several interviews yourself, as well as permission to use photos of Lana.

I'm sorry to hear she has had a few unwanted messages on social media, but I'd be very surprised if that had anything to do with us. There have been several more lurid articles online, on websites which (alas) attract significantly higher numbers of readers than the Derbyshire and Peaks Gazette.

I hope Lana is adjusting to life after her ordeal. If she does want to talk publicly about her experience and set the record straight, we are here for her.

Kind regards,
Luke Boyle, News Room Assistant
On behalf of Susie Betts, Reporter

ONE OF LIFE'S
LITTLE MYSTERIES

Jen missed the woman hanging up her washing the next morning, but there was only a pair of men's boxer shorts on the clothesline, swaying in the wind, and as a mist of rain swept the garden, a straight-backed, white-bearded man came out of the house to retrieve them. Jen stared at him from Lana's window. He wasn't the washing woman's husband.

ASTROLOGICAL ARGUMENT

"Lapis lazuli is what you need," Grace said. "Especially worn near the throat or the third eye. It unlocks mysteries."

Jen had been persuaded into accompanying Grace to a rock-and-gemstone fair in a community center on the outskirts of north London, so there they were at three o'clock on a Monday afternoon, strolling between the stalls and surrounded by displays of bead necklaces and great hunks of phallic-looking pink rock.

"And get Lana to wear some silver. And you should take more zinc, because it binds copper, and women produce too much copper."

"I didn't know," Jen said. "If I had, I'd have kept my crop of copper to sell to a scrap-metal yard."

"*Scrap* metal? Don't be so down on yourself, Jen."

Grace brought out a shopping list and

began to buy a series of lethal-looking crystals, ticking them off the list. "Metals and minerals, that's what you should concentrate on, what we should all concentrate on," she told Jen. "You know, the microbes that live in underground caves subsist entirely on minerals that percolate through the rock? Pure nutrients. And they have lived down there for millions of years, have survived every kind of global catastrophe. They're stronger than humans in so many ways. We could learn from them."

Jen tried to imagine a lesson taught by a microbe, and she wondered, not for the first time, what it must be like to see wisdom, or the potential for wisdom, everywhere. It must be exhausting, surely, but Grace never seemed to tire.

"It's a pity you didn't go caving while you were in the Peak District."

"Why, what was I supposed to do? Lick the rock?"

Grace laughed. "I'm only saying there are minerals we don't get enough of but that are available in caves. Imagine if you ate like an underground microbe for a week."

"You'd certainly lose a lot of weight." Prompted by this thought, Jen suggested they stop for coffee and cake.

Grace sat down near the tea-serving hatch

and arranged her collection of lumpy crystals on the table — fluorite, pyrite, hematite — explaining how each one would help absorb negativity, guard against manipulation ("I'm particularly thinking of my mother, of course"), and balance energy. Jen bought the coffee and, when she put the cups down, saw that Grace was also unwrapping a piece of gritty-looking chocolate cake. The texture of the cake seemed designed to fit in with the theme of the fair, to be mimicking the rocks and crystals on sale around them. It was gluten-free, made with sweet potatoes or beetroot, or diabetic chocolate, or almond milk, and Jen wasn't expecting to want more than a bite.

"And this" — Grace took a bracelet from a paper bag — "is agate."

Jen slipped the bracelet onto her wrist, the movement sending a sheaf of paper napkins to the floor. "Lovely," she said, studying the variations in the color of each bead, red to yellow to green.

"Oh, that's typical of you, Jen," Grace said, gathering the napkins and setting them back on the table.

"What's typical of me?" Jen scooped up a bit of cake with a plastic fork and found it tasted better than it looked.

"You weren't interested in the things for

you but immediately take a fancy to the necklace for my cat."

"Your cat?"

"Yes. Agate acts as a sort of surrogate for the natural world. And Milo's a house cat, so he needs that."

Jen slipped the beads over her hand, doubting very much that Milo would think a weighty collar made up for not climbing trees or chasing birds. She took another forkful of cake, and then another, and realized with a shock that she hadn't eaten all day.

"Remember that personality test I got you to take last year?" Grace said. "I thought at the time it was so accurate it was frightening. You're a contrarian, Jen. Through and through. You have to be careful you're not becoming passive aggressive, though. Actually, one thing that might help with that is concentrating on your heart chakra . . ."

"Do you remember that conversation we had, ages ago, about your cat and the fact that I needed perspective?"

Grace looked blank. "We had a conversation about Milo?" She unwound a sheer-silk scarf from her neck, sending a cloud of her expensive jasmine perfume Jen's way.

"About shutting his tail in the door."

Grace winced, her eyes shut.

"Sorry," Jen said. She gave up corralling the crumbs that danced about the foil wrapping. "I just thought I'd tell you, we have a cat now, too. Kind of. Not that you were actually telling me to get a cat, I know — that's just a coincidence."

"Kind of? You mean you got a cat for Lana?"

"No, not quite. It's sort of an imaginary cat."

Grace picked up a spoon and spent a long time stirring her coffee (though she didn't take sugar) and not making eye contact.

"An imaginary cat," she said at last.

Jen nodded. She had thought it was a funny thing to say, endearing, quirky, but saw now that Grace thought she was making fun of her. Jen never seemed to get the reaction she expected from other people. It was as though they didn't think she was the person she thought she was. When Grace put down the teaspoon, Jen picked it up and looked at the tiny version of herself in the back of it.

"What you were saying about perspective," Grace said. "When I talked about shutting Milo's tail in the door, you know, that's a technique for dealing with anxiety, not a solution for family problems. Also, it didn't really happen . . ."

"How d'you mean?"

"Well." Grace shifted in her seat. "Like I said, it's a technique."

"But you winced just now, when I mentioned it."

"I've imagined it many times, it feels real to me, but that's the point: the realer it feels, the more useful it is."

Jen sat and stared, her coffee growing cold. "But you told me it had happened. I believed you. I did what you said. I listened to meditations and wore a citrine ring and ate cashew nuts and drank moon tea and I've carried a bit of stone about in my pocket. And I thought about your technique for perspective, tried to learn from it, only it turns out that was a lie."

"It wasn't a lie. I'm trying to help. I'm always trying to help, Jen. You know, I was talking to my astrologer, and something else you can do is get Lana to give you flowers and sugar and also things made from white cloth on Mondays."

"Oh," Jen said with a laugh. "Brilliant. I'll tell her that when I get home."

"You're not really going to tell her, are you?"

"No, Grace. No, I'm not. Have you any idea how hard it is just to get her to talk to me? The likelihood that she'd be interested in giving me gifts on a Monday, or any other day of the week, is slim, to say the least."

"But it's worth a try, surely? I mean, *I* would try, if it was me."

"What the hell would you know?" Jen said suddenly. "She's *my* daughter, not yours. And she's real and her depression is real and I've never shut her tail in a door, fictional or otherwise."

This was not the brilliant finish she'd been working towards and, somehow, the ideas and the words had become rather jumbled, but she stood and picked up her bag anyway, sweeping the napkins to the floor again.

For the next few minutes, as she walked through the fair, she kept catching sight of Grace, waving at her and gesturing. Jen's anger had dissipated, but she wanted a break (just a tiny break) from Grace's endless prescriptions, so she pretended an interest in the lapidary-club activities, watching someone polish a stone, and then another.

It seemed unnecessary to make anything else shiny — there were so many light-reflecting surfaces in the room already, including the lapidary's fingers: wet from the polishing machines. And, amid all the glitter, she found herself drawn to a table of duller textures. The fossils on display were still rough and chalky, and smelled of earth.

Here were things that had some meaning, Jen felt. Not a meaning for those born in July or those hoping to find a cure for lovesickness, but a meaning for every human, their history preserved in stone.

Her knowledge of evolution was a little vague and so she wasn't sure humans were actually related to the creatures whose forms had been carefully exposed by fossil hunters, but she silently greeted them as if they were ancestors.

She nodded at the ammonites as she traced their tight whorls, and smiled, rather ridiculously, at the beetlish trilobites; she raised her eyebrows at the huge megalodon tooth, and half waved at the delicate traces of an ancient fern. She wondered what Stephen would say about this spectacle. That they had been created by some conspirator to test their faith, perhaps.

"I've got more information about each piece, if you're interested," a voice said.

Jen jumped. A man in a checked shirt had been sitting between a great slab of stone which held the graceful white shape of an ancient sea lily and a framed tuft of gingery woolly mammoth hair. She hadn't noticed him and hoped he hadn't noticed her greeting his merchandise.

"Everything's so interesting," she said, just

to say something. "Do you find them your-self?"

"Some. Some I buy. A lot of it comes from America now. They've got bigger and better everything there, haven't they? That includes fossils."

"They're amazing. So detailed. Some of them hardly look real."

"Real enough, I promise you."

"Oh, I wasn't really doubting that," Jen said, looking at the smaller things in little paper boxes at the front. There was a basket at the corner of the table full of what looked like broken fossils, or chipped bits of rock. "What are these? Flints?"

"No, no. Those are what's left of an extinct species of oyster, if you can believe it. You find fossilized oyster beds in cliffs and inside caves."

"Really?" Jen said. "Only it's funny. I have something similar." She took the stone she'd found on Lana's bedroom floor out of her pocket and offered it to the man.

"Oh yes." He turned it in his fingers. "That's one. You can just make out the shape of it, and what they call the beak. See? Where did you get it?"

"I'm not sure."

"Been to the Dorset coast?"

"No."

"What about Yorkshire? Or Derbyshire? You'd remember if you'd picked it up in a cave, I suppose."

"In a cave?"

"Yeah, there's a few places underground where old oyster beds have been exposed, but you'd have to have proper equipment to explore them. You wouldn't want to wander down there, it'd be too dangerous."

He held the fossil out to her and Jen took it. Grace had stopped waving at her, but Jen could see her thin figure through the glitter of the fair. She wondered if Grace would recommend that she suck on the fossil if she knew it came from a cave. She gave a small, slightly hysterical laugh and thanked the man, knowing her face had gone slack, that she must look slightly dazed.

"Underneath," she said.

TRIPPING

It wasn't like a real cave, nestled, as it was, high up in the side of a hill. The sketching group had had to walk and then climb for about an hour to find it, but the path was furnished with sweet-smelling hawthorn bushes, and boulders to rest on, to briefly sunbathe on, to lay your art equipment on, which made it easier. The cave itself wasn't that impressive, only about six feet deep, and the crucifix carved into the wall (the reason it was worth visiting at all) was only a vague shape, best seen on the screen of a flash-enabled digital camera. It had suffered from the effects of the weather over the years and there were no edges to it, no way to bring it into sharper focus.

Surprising, Jen thought, that it was apparently still so exposed to the elements, despite being sheltered by the mouth of the cave. But then, people — walkers, tourists, pilgrims — had rubbed at it, and the rain could be fierce and sly here. It came down almost sideways sometimes, the tutor said, soaking a walker or tourist or pilgrim even in full waterproofs. An immobile stone carving didn't have a chance.

Modern hermits still attempted to stay in the cave, and they'd left blankets behind and charred circles on the ground from cooking fires. Beyond these, right at the back, was a narrow opening into the ground, a bit like a well. Someone suggested it was where hermits had gone to the toilet in the past, but according to their tutor it was just a natural chimney from the underground tunnels beneath the hill.

As they moved about the cramped space, one of the blankets got tangled up and kicked into the chimney. Jen saw it slip into the darkness. She knelt to see if it was reachable, then dipped a hand down, feeling for the blanket. She only managed a few seconds before pulling away with a shudder. It had been frightening to lose her arm to that black space, even for a few seconds.

The day was hot and sunny, but the ground, even outside the cave, was dark, due to a great yew tree growing by the entrance. Its roots dug into a narrow strip of land with a sheer drop down to the road below. It wasn't a friendly tree; it made the place gloomy and damp, the sun barely reaching through the branches. Passing close to the outside of the cave wall, Jen was confronted with the huge, gnarly girth of it, the twisting, crevice-filled, woody belly. To get anywhere, she was forced to edge along, needles catching at her clothes and hair.

The tree had an animal smell, she felt, not like a plant at all, as if it were sweating in fear of something, hiding out in that narrow space, praying not to be discovered. And out of spite it tried to attack the visitors: several times, Jen tripped over the roots, which had concertinaed against the weathered stone.

She worried about Lana, about that sheer

drop, and tried to keep an eye on her, but the tutor kept coming to check on their sketches, and tourists kept arriving to take photos, and Lana kept disappearing into the shadows. One minute, Jen could see her, balancing on the arches of the roots, stepping nimbly from one to another; the next, she was gone.

Matthew had come with them that day. On the hunt, he said, for a red-backed something, or a gray-tailed something, or a bearded-and-spotted something. Jen suspected he was really there because of Lana, but that had seemed simple enough, sweet enough, on the walk (and she had to admit she was pleased it had displaced Stephen from his usual position by Lana's ear). Only now, in the gloom, it took on a more sinister aspect. And when their faces emerged from the cave, pale, almost luminous, in the blackness, she wondered what they'd been doing.

Matthew was panting as he sat down beside Jen and the hems of his trouser legs were wet. "Weird smell around here, isn't there?" he said.

"Peny just told me yew trees can cause hallucinations," Lana said, sitting, too. "It releases a toxic gas on hot days."

"Oh, yes?" Jen looked up and noticed

Lana had dirt in her fingernails.

"She said that's probably why this became a holy site. Hermits seeing things."

"Makes sense, I suppose."

"It's pretty hot today," Lana said. "It can only be a matter of time before we start tripping."

"I've done enough of that already," Jen said, rubbing her ankle.

"Not that kind of tripping, Mum."

"I know. Joke."

"Anyway, I don't think it's quite that easy."

"Still, we probably shouldn't take the risk, should we?" Matthew said, moving to sit on the edge of the drop, where the air was clearer. "That might even be what's given you a headache, Lana."

Jen was amused by how genuinely worried he seemed by the idea of an unasked-for high, and she caught Lana's smile as she turned back to her sketch. Several times, she'd heard Lana tell Matthew she had a headache, and she wondered if it was an excuse, if Lana's generation was still using that excuse to avoid intimacy.

Her picture had come out too dark, too muddy, and she was packing up her things ready for the walk back down the hill when a large flock of birds suddenly appeared, flying through the tree's canopy, their wings batting at the branches and sending a shower of needles down over the people below. Matthew wasn't interested, didn't even seem to notice, and Jen was surprised. Later, she wondered if she'd hallucinated them.

And she wondered about the tear in Lana's leggings, too, and the scrapes on her knuckles, and the bit of stone Matthew and Lana had tossed between them on the walk back to the holiday center. Had these things been real, or just the effect of the yew's taxine?

BEHIND CLOSED DOORS

The journey home from the rock-and-gem fair seemed never-ending, and Jen remembered why she avoided visiting any station so close to the end of the Central Line. The motion of the Tube made her dizzy and she gripped her hands between her knees as the train plunged into the first tunnel, the sudden blackness beyond the windows giving her a sense of panic.

By the time she got home she was exhausted and, relieved to find there was no one else in the house, she shed most of her clothes inside the front door. She was thirsty but couldn't face a trip to the kitchen on the way upstairs, so she drank the dust-skinned water from the glass next to the bed, wrapped herself in a dressing gown, and went straight to sleep.

When she woke, the house was dark and her head was thumping. She bumped off the wall as she left the bedroom and staggered along the hallway. Her headache seemed to be affecting her ears, she couldn't get her balance, and the usual floorboard creaks were muted, the traffic outside oddly muffled. Crouching on the landing, she wasn't sure at first if she could really hear voices coming from Lana's room.

"Did you speak to her earlier?" her daughter seemed to ask someone.

"I tried, but she wouldn't talk to me because she said I was being aggressive."

It was Hugh. He was in there, too, and they were discussing something, discussing *her,* in low tones. A blue computer glow shone under the door, but there was no other light, as if they had gone into the room when it was day and hadn't noticed the light failing, hadn't thought to put a lamp on because they were so intent on something else. Something on a screen.

Jen looked at her hands, pressed flat to the carpet. The blue light just touched them, making them ghostly and smooth, making them look like long cylinders of selenite. "That's good for mental clarity," Grace had said. Mental clarity felt distant at that moment. The voices carried on, but Jen could catch only half of it and couldn't guess at the meaning.

"Doesn't she understand that everyone can see what she's done?"

"I think she's beginning to realize now."

Jen crawled to the other side of the landing, wanting to press her ear against the door. The smell of Lana's honey shampoo came from the bathroom, which meant her daughter had only just had a shower. She tried to work out why Lana would have showered at that time of day. She tried to work out what time of day it was. Her watch wasn't on her wrist, she'd left her phone somewhere, there was a distant ticking, but no clocks visible from her position on the floor.

Jen felt she'd been curled up by this door for hours, or that she'd fallen into some space between time. She had a feeling that something important had happened but couldn't remember what it was.

Lana's laugh rang out, then, and Jen suddenly understood. She was being mocked. They were standing behind the door laughing at her, perhaps looking through the keyhole. They hated her, they despised her, they wanted her to go mad. Jen began to crawl away. If she could just get back to the safety of the bedroom, she would be all right. If she could just stop hearing their voices, she might be able to forget, to forgive them.

PROVOCATION

The next day, Jen wasn't sure what *had* happened and what hadn't. She woke early and roamed the house. Her clothes had been picked up and hung over the newel post, the newly identified oyster fossil was on her dressing table, Hugh slept with one hand tucked behind his head. Jen watched the flicker of his eyelids.

She had had a bad dream, a migraine and a bad dream, and her mind had invented a whispered conversation between her husband and her daughter. This was what she thought and what she needed to think. Her brain had conjured it from a muddle of impressions.

But the image of that blue light washing over her hands made her feel grimy, even after showering, so to counteract it she went into the garden and sat with the backs of her hands tilted towards the sun. Her brain

413

seemed to have been replaced by a lot of air, a familiar feeling the day after a migraine, and she moved her neck about, as if it were the string of a helium balloon.

Remembering the glow of the computer leaking into the hall, she got the laptop and set it on their patio table. The screen was almost invisible in the glare of the sun and she had to wait for a passing cloud to check the internet history. It was blank, had been cleared. She leaned into her chair and waited for another cloud, and perhaps another idea, to pass. She was still waiting when Hugh came to find her.

"What are you doing out here?" he asked.

"What are *you* doing out here?" she countered, lowering the laptop screen. "Shouldn't you be at work?"

"I've taken the morning off. You weren't well last night."

It was the dream's fault that Jen wasn't touched by this, was instead instantly suspicious. "Just a headache," she said.

"You were very groggy, though. I could hardly wake you for more than a few minutes, even to drink some water. What brought the headache on, d'you think?"

"I forgot to eat breakfast, and then lunch. I only had a bit of a cake that Grace made."

"Ah, well, that might explain it," he said,

opening the parasol over the table and adjusting it so she was in the shade. "You're sure Grace didn't put cannabis in the cake?"

"Oh God."

"Only a joke, Jen. It was probably just full of some awful health-food supplement that isn't fit for human consumption. Anyway, don't get sunstroke."

She nodded.

"Shall I make some coffee?"

She nodded again, and he went away and came back with coffee and a large glass of water and a bowl of raspberries, and a little later, a *pain au chocolat,* which he must have gone to the bakery to fetch.

"I don't want you to go hungry again," he said, bringing out more coffee and sitting down to eat his own pastry, pulling the heavy iron chair into the shade next to her.

"Thanks," she said. And she was grateful for the food, but she couldn't shake the feeling that he was monitoring her, monitoring her use of the laptop, especially, as if there was something on it he didn't want her to find. The machine began to whir then, a rising note, and for a moment she thought it was in on the plot, alerting her husband to the fact that she was using it. But a moment later the noise stopped. It had just been a big bumble bee buzzing under the catmint.

"Where's Lana?" she asked.

"In the shower, I think. What are you going to do today?"

"Nothing. Sit here," she corrected herself.

"Shall I put the laptop back inside?"

"No, I might want it."

"Okay."

They sat quietly, eyes following the small movements of the garden, the flicker of a flying insect, the ruffle of a leaf in the breeze. After a few minutes, Lana came to join them, standing on the lawn for a moment with her eyes closed, holding her face up to the light.

"Well, I think I'll tackle that yarrow," Hugh said, getting up and going to the shed. He stopped to say something to Lana as he passed her, and she nodded and turned to look at her mother. Jen watched them both for a while after that, watched while Hugh brought out bamboo stakes and various tools and pushed the bamboo into the earth, and cut a bit of twine off the spool, and tied the flat, yellow heads of the yarrow to a stake. She watched while Lana sat on the grass and ate a croissant and held her limbs out to the sun.

A storm was coming, which was perhaps another reason for the migraine. The air was full of buzzing, but the big bumble bee crawled along the ground, its buzz more like a croak, a groan. It came every few seconds, along with a sporadic liftoff, a few inches of flight. You were supposed to feed tired bees sugar water, but she had none out here, so instead Jen picked a stalk off the catmint bush, which was covered in other, smaller bees, and held it down to the bumble bee.

It leaped on it, pushing its sucker into every purple flower head, and then flew off, high and distant. Soon, though, it was back again. Dragging its heavy, round body along the patio under the buddleia. Jen knew it was the same bee because its buzz was bassier than the others', was distinctive to her ears, as if she were a mother who could distinguish the cries of her own newborn. She held another stick of catmint out before turning back to the computer.

Scrolling through files in various folders, she checked the recently opened documents: a list of their cousins' addresses, which she'd checked to send a birthday card, a sleep log she'd been keeping on Lana's behalf, a couple of essays that Lana had begun and abandoned — nothing caught her eye. She clicked on the trash, but it was just the usual collection of screenshots and blank documents. She opened applications at random, but they didn't lead her anywhere.

The bee's mournful buzz made her sad, desperate, and she checked her emails just to have something to click on, finding an update on the petition she had signed asking the government to stop pesticide companies killing bees. Life was all of a piece, she thought.

Hugh came over with a floret of feathery leaves which had broken off as he'd tried to tie them. "Don't forget to drink your water," he said.

"I won't." She ran the leaves through her fingers and sniffed at them. The camphorous scent of the yarrow was comforting, addictive.

Hugh seemed reluctant to leave her alone, looking at her, looking at the computer screen, and he waited until Lana had replaced him at Jen's elbow before going back to the shed. Jen shut the laptop lid and smiled at Lana. Perhaps worried that her mother was about to begin a serious conversation, Lana bounced out of her chair and offered to take the computer inside, just as Hugh had.

"Why? Do you want it?" Jen asked.

"Only if you're finished with it." The casualness seemed studied.

"I'm not finished with it."

"That's cool." Which wasn't a phrase Lana used. And she kept her eyes on the computer as she drifted back over to Hugh.

So Jen began to play a game. Each time Hugh got up the ladder into the pine tree, she opened the laptop. That seemed to cause him to drop down the rungs onto the grass, or to come over and ask her if she wanted anything. And whenever Lana went to resume her position on the lawn, Jen would tap noisily, randomly, at the keyboard, making her daughter sit up and look at her.

Then she'd close the lid or turn the screen so the impartial home page of the BBC was visible and note the way Hugh would relax, returning to his gardening, and how Lana would sink back into her sunbathing.

This went on for a long time. It stopped being amusing and became tiresome. Jen closed her eyes for a while, trying to think, trying not to think, and when she opened them again she saw her husband and daughter, crouching among the summer greenery, half hidden by the monster-growth of a global-warmed garden. They were whispering. They were working together, conspiring. Perhaps they had been from the beginning. There was a special closeness between them that she hadn't noticed before, though the signs had been there. Lana had known that Hugh had a favorite mug.

Jen dipped the yarrow stem into her glass of water and kept it on the table beside her for the rest of the morning, crushing the leaves between her fingers every time she was about to type theatrically into the computer, every time she wanted to make Hugh and Lana focus on her again. The medicinal scent of the leaves lingered on the keyboard for days afterwards.

HOLY COW

If there *was* some sort of relay monitoring going on, then Jen's mother was in on it. Hugh had barely left for his afternoon at work when Lily phoned.

"Anything wrong, Mum?" Jen asked, squinting in the relative dark of the sitting room after her hours in the bright garden.

"No. Does something have to be wrong? I just wanted to catch up. Shoot the breeze, as Americans would say."

"I'm not sure they really say that."

"Don't they? That's disappointing. Anyway, what have you been up to today?"

"That's a funny question." Jen sat down on the sofa. The house smelled of dust and faintly of the salmon they'd cooked two nights ago.

"It's not especially funny. How was your crystals-and-whatnots fair?"

"All right. Actually, Mum, I had a stone with me that I found in Lana's room and this man identified it. He said it was a sort of fossil that's found in caves. So it's made me think, or it's made me wonder, where Lana got it."

"Oh, well, caves are interesting," Lily said, not sounding particularly interested. "Lots of religious connotations. And Lana does seem to be curious about religion all of a sudden, doesn't she?"

"Does she?"

"Haven't you noticed? She asked me about my *beliefs* when I spoke to her last week. Rather a personal question, I thought. And, it's funny, really, because Peggy's been making me go to church with her. I think she's trying to boost the earnings from the congregation, not that I ever put in huge sums. But it's all come at the same time so I feel I'm being rather battered by the Bible from every side. Perhaps that's what's made me think of it."

"Think of what, Mum?"

"The parallels, darling. Between Lana and Jesus. A spell in the wilderness — well, you

421

could call that depression — and then being presumed *gone* for a few days before reappearing, and now the idea that she was in a cave at some point, though presumably not one with a boulder rolled over the entrance."

"What are you trying to say? That Lana's the Second Coming?"

"No, of course not."

"And, I mean, she's not exactly the soul of kindness."

"Well, Jesus wasn't that kind to his own mother, was he? What's that bit? *Woman, what have I to do with thee?* Though I suppose she was harassing him about wine for a party, so you can understand his frustration."

"I haven't been harassing Lana about wine."

"I wasn't suggesting you had been."

"Good. Sometimes, Mum, I think you're deliberately trying to wind me up."

SKYLIGHT

Hugh came home that evening with a box of chocolates. "Thought you deserved a treat," he said, before going upstairs to ask Lana what she wanted for dinner. He had stayed in her room for a long while and

Lana hadn't come downstairs since.

"What do you think she's doing up there?" Jen said, letting another chocolate wrapper drop to the floor.

Hugh glanced at the lean-to's skylight, through which the yellow-lit window of Lana's room could be seen. "Reading?" he suggested.

"Reading what?"

"A book?" He went back to the book *he* had been reading with a slight smile.

"Sorry for disturbing you," Jen said.

"Not at all."

"I just happen to be worried about our daughter."

"I know."

"But you aren't worried?"

He sighed and tucked a bookmark between two pages. "Would I like to know what happened? Would I like a better idea of what's going on in her head, day to day? Yes. Do I think we will find out eventually? Quite possibly. Do I think we will find out sooner by pestering her? Certainly not."

"What if when we do find out we find out too late?"

They stared at each other for a couple of seconds, Jen waiting, the remains of the chocolates rough on her teeth, Hugh seemingly trying to make sense of her last sentence. He looked up at the window again and this time spent a while studying it. This was encouraging. She'd finally got him interested, she could feel it; his gaze was focused, he was thinking about something.

"What is it, Hugh?"

"Do you think the wood on the right side of the window is slightly warped?" he asked, not moving his eyes from the skylight. "It looks warped from this angle. But do you think it's just the light? We did have all that heavy rain at the beginning of the year. That could have damaged it."

Jen waited for him to bring his gaze back to her before she got up. She heard him calling after her as she mounted the stairs, where she found a tiny sliver of glass nestled in the carpet. It disturbed her that she immediately blamed Lana, thought of it as an act of hostility. Especially when it might just as easily be a tiny shard from one of the glasses she broke two months ago. Sharp fragments always managed to travel across the house and hide from the Hoover or dustpan and brush. It was a worry that had kept her awake when the girls were small, that a smashed glass in March could lead to a sliced toe in June.

Lana opened the bedroom door before Jen could knock and, for a moment, Jen couldn't help but imagine Hugh had sent some sign to her through that skylight, a warning, an alarm. *Your mother's on her way! Watch out. Achtung!* She had heard the noise of the curtains being pushed back yet again; Lana had been at the window.

"I was just coming downstairs," Lana said.

"Can you see your father from here?" Jen asked, slipping in past her daughter. The room smelled of floral deodorant and worn tights and the rotting banana skins which had piled up on the desk. Above the desk, the oblongs of press cuttings curled away from the corkboard and Jen tried not to look at the dozen or so smudgy replicas of Lana's face.

"I just wondered, because he's probably asleep in his chair." She made a noise which she thought might pass for a laugh and raised a hand to cover her mouth, as if she couldn't stop a smile.

Lana didn't move. Her lip curled slightly.

"I'll just look quickly," Jen said, still attempting a jokey sort of attitude, hunching her shoulders in a way she imagined was mirthful. Peeking around the curtain, she found she could see Hugh's chair, but Hugh wasn't in it. She let the curtain fall heavily back into place and turned, grinning, to her daughter.

"Well?" Lana said.

Jen shrugged. "Well," she repeated.

"You're being weird."

"Oh, weird, weird. Children are always calling their parents weird. You'll have to do better than that."

"Have to do better?"

"Come on, think of something. What might send me scurrying away?"

"Mum, really . . ."

"Surely you must have something up your sleeve. You've managed not to talk so far, you're not going to let me get close now. An insult wouldn't be too much; if you hurt me enough, I might leave you alone for good."

"I don't want to hurt you," Lana said, looking bewildered.

"So you say." Jen sat down on the bed and slid her hands over her face, only to discover she was crying.

"Shit, Mum," Lana said, moving about in front of her. "Don't cry."

Jen felt a hand brush over her hair, then four kisses were placed quickly on her head. She looked up and dried her eyes, feeling they'd been soothed. "With kisses four," she said aloud, not remembering where the line came from.

"Are you okay now?"

Jen shook her head, making Lana sigh.

"What is it, then?" There was a hint of impatience.

"It's just, why *have* you pinned up those newspaper clippings? How can you want them there?" She stopped herself. "Unless it's some kind of joke to you."

"It's not a joke, Mum," Lana said, her teeth gritting. "Look, you really want to know why I keep them? Okay." She went over to the board and leaned in.

". . . a bright and popular student," she read, *"well liked by teachers and classmates . . . a caring, loving daughter and granddaughter . . . the sort of girl who lights up a room . . . she means everything to us . . .* That last quote is you." Lana walked to the curtain and carefully pulled it back so she could look out at the dark. "It's nice to know what people think of me. It's nice to know, to be reminded, what *you* think of me. I understand people *have* to be nice when they think you're dead, but I still like reading the descriptions — your descriptions — of me."

"Oh, sweetheart. Do you really need an article in a newspaper to know you mean everything to me?"

"Sometimes," Lana said, and then she turned. "Dad *is* asleep in his chair. Look. Mouth wide open and everything. I never realized you could see him from here. I

427

should take a photo. He looks hilarious."

"Oh, your poor dad." Jen was breathless with relief, with love, with the headiness of this unexpected conspiracy. Hugh did look unfortunate in that position, vulnerable and older. She felt tender towards him and stopped Lana taking a picture. "I'll go and wake him for *Newsnight,*" she said.

"Okay. I'll definitely come down if there are still some chocolates left."

Jen didn't answer, tasting the last of the chocolate in the crevices of her mouth.

"Oh, and, Mum," Lana said, "I think the wood around the skylight might be a bit warped. You should probably tell Dad about that."

PRIVATE CONVERSATION

She was getting really paranoid. Seeing conspiracy everywhere: the neighbors were having extramarital affairs, her husband and daughter were communicating in code, Lana was harboring something evil. She had even suggested to Hugh that the imaginary cat might be some sort of familiar.

"And who's the witch in this scenario?" he'd asked, exasperated.

There was a murmuring from the hallway now.

"What did you say?" Jen called, muting the television.

"I was talking to myself," he said, "if you don't mind."

"Oh, sorry to intrude. Secret, was it?" She didn't wait for his answer but put the sound up on the TV. Then she muted it again so she could think.

Hadn't there been other times, recently, when he'd seemed to be having internal conversations, as if some part of him were talking to another part? And weren't they visible, these dialogues, apparent on his face somehow, in the twitch of a cheek muscle, the narrowing of an eye? Was he . . . could he be hearing voices? Jen thought of Lana and her unplugged earphones.

"Tea?" he said, putting his head around the door.

"Is that addressed to me? Or should I pretend I haven't heard?"

"Do you want a tea or not?"

"Not."

"Fine."

His head disappeared from view again, and she could hear him filling the kettle and unloading the dishwasher, innocuous enough sounds. And yet, was there a whispering just detectable beneath the domestic clinking and rumbling? She tried to breathe quietly, to eliminate all rasp in her mouth and lungs, to angle one ear and then the other, making the space into a kind of sievable entity, a liquid she could pan for golden noise.

"Practicing your lipreading?" he asked, as he came back in with his mug.

"What are you getting at?"

"The sound's off."

"Oh, yes, sorry." She pressed the volume button on the remote but, although she was aware of the voices of the on-screen comedians, she couldn't quite grasp what they were saying; their words didn't fit the shapes their mouths made. She felt they were hostile, especially the six men on the panel show, and at moments the one woman seemed in danger, wedged between them, harangued on both sides and penned in by the long desk. Hugh laughed intermittently, the noise jerking from him, though each chuckle extended a little more each time, as if he were making a point of laughing, a way of proving his affinity to these men. Proving he was alien, malicious, proving he was an enemy.

"I don't blame you for not finding it funny," he said, startling her. "It's got very childish, this program. Shall we turn over?"

"I thought you were enjoying it."

"Not really. You can guess the punch lines by now, can't you, and so I suppose I was just laughing at my own cleverness in guessing right."

He took a big slurp of tea.

"What were you saying to yourself?" she asked. "Just now, in the hall?"

"Oh." He looked sheepish. "I was just checking my phone. You're not going to like it. Mum's joined Instagram, or someone's joined it for her. Some meddler at the library, I imagine. I thought you might have seen already?"

"Seen what?"

"She's been commenting on Lana's posts."

Jen opened the laptop. Under a picture of Lana pouting next to Bethany, Carolyn had written: *Don't forget to smile in photos, dear. You have a beautiful smile. You don't want to end up squinting at the camera like your mother always does.* And under a photo of a stacked sandwich from a local café: *I suppose your mother's too busy to make a home-cooked meal.* Jen shut the laptop.

"For Christ's sake," she said, allowing herself to breathe loudly again.

"Lana's already called to ask her to delete the comments and told her not to say anything about you. And she's said, if there

431

are any more comments like that, she'll block her."

"Has she?" Jen was unable to stop a grin. "Lana's told her grandmother she'll block her? Really?"

"She's promised to."

"How did your mother take that?"

"Not well," Hugh said.

Social media never sleeps

Overnight, as if to test her power, Lana had posted a new photo on Instagram, a tropical island with a quote over it. The quote was from Keats (Lily still refused to be impressed):

> . . . the cave is secreter
> Than the isle of Delos. Echo hence shall stir
> No sighs but sigh-warm kisses . . .

She wondered who Lana was hoping would give her sigh-warm kisses, but was relieved (and perhaps just a little triumphant) to see that the only comments beneath the picture were from other teenagers. They waited all day, but there was no sign of Carolyn.

She lay in the dark and remembered a night about a year before, when the family had attempted a mass gathering in Norfolk. It had been a disaster: Hugh had been away for work so his calming presence was missing, Graham and David had argued fiercely about whether to skin the tomatoes for the pasta sauce, and Lily had gone and eaten the whole ball of mozzarella while they were distracted (just to infuriate them, Jen suspected). On top of that, the cottage, which David's wife had booked, didn't have enough rooms for them all, so Jen and Meg and Lana had had to share a chilly attic room full of narrow single beds. Though, in a way, that had offered them a refuge. Up at the top of the house, they could hide away from the drama. The only problem was filling the time, as there was no TV, no WiFi, and very little light.

"We could tell ghost stories," Lana had suggested.

"I don't think I know any ghost stories," Jen said, turning over to find a better location for her stiff limbs amid the bumps and wrinkles of the mattress and sheets.

"Well, any kinds of stories, then."

"Okay. I've got a story."

"Oh, wait. Is it about a little girl whose shoes pinch?"

"Oh, God, yeah," Meg said. "And her mother has sent her out for a pint of milk with their last bit of money?"

"And she sees some new shoes in the window of a shop and wants to buy them?"

"But they're so poor that buying the shoes means they'll go hungry?"

"But she buys the shoes anyway?"

"Because if it's that story, then we've heard it."

"Like, a billion times."

"Good to know she recycled the same material for you," Meg said.

"Recycled? It was a straight-up hand-me-down," Lana said.

"Fine, then." Jen was annoyed, because she *had* been about to tell the story about the girl whose shoes pinched. "Do *you* want to tell us a story?"

There was quiet for a minute or so. The door rattled slightly in the wind and an animalish rustling started in the eaves. A worn-socks smell had expanded in the dark, making the room both stuffy and familiar at once. It felt like their space. It felt safe.

"Okay. Once there was . . ." Lana paused.

She paused for so long that Jen began to drift, gratefully, off to sleep, but Meg laughed.

"I can see you were really burning to tell *that*."

"Fuck you," Lana said.

"Lana," Jen said, feeling herself pulled awake, the sensation sickening and irritating.

"Well, I got nervous, and she's not helping."

"Don't be nervous. And, Meg, don't be mean. Right, Lana, tell your story or go to sleep. Decide now."

"Okay," Lana said, choosing the opposite option to the one Jen had been hoping for. "It starts with a girl."

Another pause. There was a stifled giggle from Meg, but Lana either didn't hear or chose to ignore it.

"She was just an ordinary girl with normal comfortable shoes," she said. "She lived with her family and went to school and everything, but one day she woke up with a song in her head. It wasn't a song she knew very well, though she must have heard it before, in a film or on an advert or something, but it was catchy and it turned out she could remember all the words, though she usually couldn't remember the words to songs, even the ones she really liked."

"Sounds like Mum," Meg said.

"Ha, yeah," Lana said, her sheets whispering as she got into a better storytelling position. "Anyway, this girl, she couldn't get rid of the song. She tried to distract herself with games and shopping and seeing her friends, but she kept finding herself singing the lyrics or humming the tune. She listened to other music, but as soon as she turned it off the song was there underneath, waiting."

"It's called an earworm," Meg said.

"Are you going to keep interrupting?"

"Yes."

"Fine. Anyway, it wasn't an *earworm,* because it seemed more like she was hearing, rather than remembering, the song. Like it was the light, bright, real thing, rather than a shadowy mental version. And it didn't go away, even at night. Weeks passed, and the song got louder, growing inside her head. She couldn't sleep, or concentrate on reading, and when she spoke she said the wrong words a lot, substituting the lyrics for the sentences she meant to say.

"Her parents thought she was being difficult and her friends thought she was mocking them or not listening, and people began to avoid her because she seemed weird. This was kind of a relief, because the song eventually drowned out all other sound. When her teachers asked her something in class, she couldn't understand them, and she ended up in detention every day. The sound of traffic was deadened and she had to be careful crossing the road. She was cut off from everyone, in her little bubble of music, in the middle of a constant loop. Her head was heavy with it, and it felt like it would burst open from the pressure.

"Then she was walking home from school one day, hardly able to see because of the insane volume of the song in her head, when she stepped off the pavement and was hit by a bus. Her head cracked open on the curb and, as her blood leaked out, the music leaked out with it, and finally everyone else could hear the song.

"That's it," Lana said. "The end."

There were a few seconds of quiet, and then Jen sat up and switched on the lamp. "Is that how you feel? Is that what life feels like to you?"

Lana looked caught in the sudden light, her eyes puffy and squinting. She shrugged and wriggled down under her covers. "I don't know." Her voice was muffled by the duvet. "I don't want to talk about it."

"Why not?"

"You're not supposed to analyze it. It's just a story."

"A pretty freaky story, though," Meg said. Lana flipped a corner of the duvet away from her face. "Did it freak you out?"

"Yes."

"Good," Lana said. "Night night."

VISITOR

Jen, lying in her own bed, in her own house (and with her own ball of mozzarella downstairs in the fridge), found *she* had a song stuck in her head. Something from the eighties, or possibly two somethings that her mind had blurred together. She twisted about, trying to untangle the lyrics, to work out where one tune became another, but it was no good. At last, after determinedly recalling a third song, the phrases seemed to fade (and, thankfully, without the need to crack her skull open).

But when she thought she might actually finally sleep, she realized there was someone — something — in her bedroom, crouched by the curtains. Jen could hear breathing, could feel a stare cutting through the dark. She tried to focus on the figure, decide how — why — it should be there, but her mobile was buzzing, distracting her. It was strange to feel it buzzing there, against her face. She shifted slightly on the pillow, coming

438

out of sleep but not quite ready to open her eyes. Why was the phone slightly wet, she wondered, and how was it tickling her cheek? She gazed into the shadows around her, finding a little pink nose hovering over hers, a set of whiskers feathering her skin, a cat dipping itself towards her as it purred.

"Hello," she mouthed, wavering a hand up to stroke it, her eyelids heavy. There was something cozy and calming about waking to a cat, even if it wasn't your cat, even if it was imaginary. There was an unfamiliar smell, slightly composty, rich and warm.

"What are you doing here?" she asked, with a sleep-stuck tongue. "Where did you come from?"

The cat put out its tongue and licked her nostril with a rough stroke that made Jen hold her breath.

"Hello," she said again, as if the lick had been a greeting.

The cat turned and jumped down from the bed with a thud, trotting across the floor. It hadn't left the room, but it had slipped into the shadows. There was a heavy rustle of curtains and Jen was suddenly, properly awake. She slid out from under the covers quickly and almost fell onto the floor. Lana was kneeling in the corner of the room, looking as though she couldn't decide whether to run at, or away from, her mother. The cat had curled its tail around her hips.

"So it *is* you," Jen said, "who's been letting the cat in."

HAVE YOU GOT THE BAG?

They had each gone back to bed, Jen feeling this discovery couldn't be dealt with in the dark and silent hours. She didn't want to wake Hugh, and she felt she was likely to attribute some extra significance to Lana's actions among the shadows and unfamiliarity of nighttime.

But in the morning, it seemed almost indelicate to raise the subject. And she had become so used to second-guessing herself that she wondered if she hadn't dreamed the incident, dreamed the cat entirely, and she was reluctant to make a fool of herself.

She watched the woman hang out her washing. She waited for Lana to shower and dress, she made coffee and poured it away and made it again. She walked through each room, looking for a good place to talk, a neutral space, but unsurprisingly, there wasn't one. So they went out to lunch.

"If you wanted a cat, you could have said," Jen told Lana, when they'd sat down. She kept her eyes on the menu so her daughter

440

would understand that nothing about this exchange would be accusatory.

"It's not that I really want a cat."

"So why have you been letting it in?"

Lana lined up the salt and pepper shakers, spun the cornflower in its little vase, tugged at the bandana over her hair. "Someone at school saw my scars."

"On your head?" Jen kept her voice low, because another customer, a man, was reaching for something behind his chair and looking at them as he did so.

"No, the scars on my arms. The ones I did, you know."

The man got up and walked out of the café, with a big paper parcel, turning his face away as he sidled past their table.

"Have you still got that shopping bag?" Jen said suddenly, feeling sure that the man was a thief rather than a real customer. "The gray one?" She tried to look under the table, but passing waitresses kept getting in her way.

"Yeah, it's by my feet," Lana said. "So, anyway, this boy — his name's Simon — he asked me how I'd got the scars, and when I said I didn't want to talk about it he started telling everyone to check out my arms."

Jen looked around the café to see if anyone else had noticed the man, or lost a bag, but

441

they were all tucking into their pulled-pork buns and smashed avocado on toast.

"I thought about saying I'd been gardening," Lana said, "but, like, no one is really going to believe that . . ."

"But I can't see the bag, Lana," Jen said, knowing she shouldn't be focusing on that, knowing she would anger her daughter, but not able to help herself. "Are you sure you've got it?"

"Yes, Mum. Here, look." She lifted the bag up over the table then dropped it back down between her knees. "Happy?"

"Thanks. Make sure you hold on to it, won't you?"

"Yes, Mum."

"Can I take your order, ladies?" the waitress asked, appearing next to their table. They both tried to speak at once but, as they were ordering the same thing, it hardly mattered. "Like peas in a pod," the waitress said, not seeming to notice the gritted teeth behind their smiles.

Lana continued to look down at the table, even after the menus were taken away. She spun the cornflower again.

"Go on," Jen said. "Tell me what happened."

Lana didn't look up, she didn't speak.

"Please, Lana, I'm sorry."

No answer.

"I really am sorry, but I don't see why you're quite so upset, I only wanted to check —"

"I'm *upset*," Lana said, "because you asked me to explain something difficult, but you don't really want the explanation. I'm *upset* because you assume I'm incompetent, you can't imagine I'm capable of holding on to a bag and not losing it or having it stolen."

"That's not true, it's just that I've been with people when they've had bags nicked in cafés, and it's done so easily, believe me. I don't think you're incompetent. It's silly, I know, but I do the same thing with your father."

"That doesn't make me feel much better. The way you talk about Dad like he's hardly got two marbles to rub together."

"Two marbles?" Jen said. "I'm not sure that's the expression."

"Seriously? This is what you're going to focus on?"

"Sorry, it just sounded funny. I know that's not the point. I knew what you meant. And I don't think your father is incompetent, either. Oh, here comes our soup."

Two big bowls of goulash were put down in front of them and they ate in silence for

443

a while, the steam clinging to the lower half of Jen's face.

"So, if you can't say you've been gardening, what can you say?" Jen asked, halfway through her bowl. "How did you explain the scars?"

Lana stirred the chunks of beef and potato, apparently considering. "You *were* listening."

"Of course. Was this Simon bullying you, Lana? Because we can talk to the school about that."

"He isn't important enough to be a bully," Lana said. "He's just such a lowlife that he has to find stuff to tease you about. I wouldn't have cared but it's, like . . . some boys find it weirdly . . ." She looked at Jen, as if she were trying to decide whether to finish her sentence. "Sexy," she said finally.

"That's rather disturbing," Jen said, wondering if Lana meant boys or men, wondering if there was a particular boy or man she was thinking of.

"Yeah. So I told this idiot that the scars were scratches from my cat."

"Good thinking."

"Only Bethany let slip I didn't have a cat. It wasn't her fault; she didn't know I'd lied or why I'd lied. But Simon was going to have a field day, so I thought if I lured a cat

444

in and got a photo of it, with me, then I could say Bethany didn't know or, like, I think of it as my cat but, really, it's my grandma's or whatever."

Jen looked at her daughter, amazed at the level of subterfuge, pleased somehow that she could make these sorts of plans, worried that she could make these sorts of plans. How many schemes might she have used to throw her parents off?

"Honestly," Lana said, "it made me wish I'd never done it. Cut myself, I mean. I know you and Dr. Greenbaum are always telling me it's terrible and everything, and to be honest, that's never had any effect on me."

"Good to know. Thanks."

"But having to, like, cover it up is a proper deterrent, you know?"

"Are you ashamed of the scars?" Jen asked, quietly. "Stephen said you'd told him you were ashamed."

"Stephen? You mean on the holiday? I don't know. I don't know about ashamed. Embarrassed, maybe. I didn't want everyone knowing. Is that the same as shame? Anyway, then the cat started coming round all the time. I was feeding it at first and I guess it wanted more food. I couldn't get it to go away, or I would think it had gone out into the garden and then I'd find it under my bed, or it would be outside meowing and meowing and I was worried it would wake you and Dad, so I'd have to let it in again."

"But did it work? I mean, you put pictures up on Instagram, didn't you? Did this boy believe you?"

"On Instagram, right," Lana said, narrowing her eyes at Jen. "And, yeah, basically, it worked. I don't think he believed me, but he'd look like a weirdo going on about how I'd cut myself when I could show everyone the cat."

"Well, that was, I mean, I don't condone . . . I mean, I'm glad you sorted it out," Jen said.

"Me, too. Only then the stupid fucker asked me out. Crazy, huh? As if I'd touch him with a . . . cat's claw."

HEARTFELT WORDS

After lunch, they went shopping and, despite the fact that most of her questions hadn't even been asked, let alone answered, Jen felt as though the air was clearer between Lana and herself. One step at a time, one query a day, perhaps one every other day, perhaps one each week; the important thing was not to fall out again. She would just talk about frivolous things in the meantime, and not choose each word carefully; she would be honest and foolish and let Lana make fun of her if she wanted.

"Is it a sign of age, do you think," she said, as they queued in a clothes shop with too-loud music, "that I find myself admiring an elderly woman's tidy moustache?"

Lana stared at her. "Admiring it how?"

"The way it fits neatly between the lines at the corners of her mouth. The way it lends her an air of capability."

"Capability?" Lana looked about the shop, her arms dropping and dropping until the ruffle-sleeved top she held brushed the floor.

"Or wisdom, perhaps." Jen guided her daughter's hands up again so she didn't get dust on the silky hem.

"I don't think it's a sign of age," Lana said, still trying to locate the moustache and its venerable wearer.

"Oh, good."

"Insanity, though . . ."

"Yes, yes." Jen waved her comment away. "Is my lipstick bleeding?"

"As in wounded?" Lana asked carefully.

Various bags knocked together as Jen turned to her. "No, Lana. I am not con-cerned for the welfare of the tube, I am worried that the color is making its way along the lines at the edges of my lips so that I'll look like an old lady who can't apply her makeup properly anymore. Okay? Reassured? Canceling the psychiatrist?"

Lana nodded, and Jen tried not to smile too heartily, her insides squeezing with relief, with pleasure, at their silly, teasing, *normal* conversation. She'd managed to climb out of the hole of suspicion and desperate anxiety she'd been digging for months. She realized that, as long as they were getting on, no questions were necessary — there was nothing she needed to know.

"Actually, I would much rather be the sort of person who thought her lipstick had been injured in some gory way. That would be less depressing than finding it in my wrinkles."

"Can I help?" The girl behind the till leaned out to peer at the queue of shoppers and Jen counted the number of people who were ahead of them: three.

"Where's — where's the woman?" Lana whispered to her mother.

"Who?"

"The woman with the moustache."

"She's not here — she was at the exhibition I went to last week. I just suddenly thought of her because of that poster." She pointed to the image of a lizard advertising a range of desert-inspired clothes.

"Right."

"It's a bearded dragon. And it made me think 'bearded lady,' and that made me think of the woman with the moustache I'd admired."

"Oh, perfectly logical when you put it like that."

"Who's next?" another shop assistant called.

They were two places from the front now.

"Do you really think this is the right thing?" Lana asked, shaking the top and making the sleeves flutter.

"Yes," Jen answered, in the tone of someone who has answered the same question in the same way many times before, and very recently.

"You're right," Lana said, not in the tone of someone who'd repeated this phrase many times over the last hour, though she had done just that. "I think it's the smell that puts me off. That chemical they soak the clothes in to stop them getting moth-eaten or whatever."

She wafted the top towards Jen's face, coming rather close to swiping her with it.

"Watch out. I wanted you to tell me if my

lipstick was running, I wasn't expecting you to blot it with your new shirt."

"It smells, though, doesn't it?"

"I'll wash it when we get home."

"Thanks."

"Can I help?" the first shop assistant said, and the young woman in front of them shuffled forward with two armfuls of clothes.

"It'll be us next." Lana stood up on her toes for a few seconds then let herself sink down again. This meant some heartfelt words were about to be said, Jen knew. "You never look like you can't apply your makeup properly," Lana said, rushing the sentence, her voice breathy. "And you don't have lines around your mouth."

"That's kind of you. Thank you."

"And you shouldn't think about age all the time, and you shouldn't feel depressed about it."

"I know."

"And I've been using your perfume."

"Oh," Jen said, surprised at the sudden confession. "Yes, I know. I'd noticed."

"I thought you had. I'm sorry." She rolled the sleeve of the top around her wrist then let it unfurl again. "Actually, I'm not sorry."

"Right. Okay." Jen laughed a little, not sure what to say.

"Because, I used it in Derbyshire, too, and smelling your perfume, well, sometimes it's the only thing that makes me feel better."

The shop assistant called them then, and Jen got out her card and typed in her pin and refused a bag, and found she'd fallen straight back into the hole, that once again, she felt she needed to know everything.

Knickers

"Oh, Jesus Christ!" Lana yelled from her room the next morning.

This is it, Jen thought, whatever has been coming, whatever has been lurking, waiting for a time to strike, it's finally here. She snatched her dressing gown from the end of the bed and ran across the landing.

"What is it? What? What's happened?" she said, shoving Lana's door open and not worrying for once that she was asking questions.

"These," Lana said, turning, "were in the sleeve of my hoodie."

She held a pair of Jen's knickers in her fingers, touching only a tiny section of fabric, as if they were diseased.

Jen said nothing while she tried to get her breath back.

"I mean, it was so weird, putting my arm

in and feeling *something else* in there."

Jen took the knickers from her hand. They were slightly stiff from having been washed and then dried inside the jumper. But they were clean, so Lana could stop looking revolted. "Is that it?" Jen said. "I thought something terrible had happened."

"Er, yeah." Lana gestured to the knickers. "Something terrible *has* happened. But I'm going to be late for meeting Bethany so I'll just have to try and get over it."

Her feet had rumbled down the stairs and she'd slammed the door before Jen had thought about putting on clothes and following her. She slipped on the knickers and tied the dressing gown more tightly around her waist. Although Lana had left her in the room, although Jen hadn't entered deliberately, she felt guilty being there alone.

She shouldn't stay a minute longer, she shouldn't flick through the exercise books on the desk, she shouldn't rummage in the gym bag or open and shut every drawer in the bedside table. And if she did, it was her own fault when the words in the books were confusing or the empty plastic sachet seemed ominous or the box of condoms made her uncomfortable.

The board of newspaper clippings seemed less sinister today, and Jen lifted up the various scraps of translucent paper, reading some of the sentences again: . . . *so smart and always there for me . . . my best friend in the world . . . a truly beautiful person . . .* Jen could understand why Lana might enjoy reading the tributes, even though they did make her sound like a dead person, but most of the sentiments seemed empty to Jen: they could have been about anyone.

As she flattened the cuttings back against the cork, she felt another thin scrap of paper and uncovered it, unpinned it from the board. It was a receipt printed in pale blue ink. The items were all listed in an indecipherable code: BK Fir Con 14.99, BK Ant End 9.99, BK Vis Joh 5.50, BK 23 Min Hel 6.99, BK Sin Ang God 4.00, BK Dan Div Com 4.99, GF Bib Bea 15.99. The list meant nothing to her but, when she looked at the date at the bottom, she saw it had been issued the week before, that the things had been bought during the hours Lana was supposed to be at the cinema.

Bless us Lord, every day

Jen went to sit down on Lana's unmade bed, still puzzling over the receipt, and knocked her anklebone against the sharp corner of a pile of books. The stack was half hidden under the bed, the spines facing away from the light, and Jen felt a flicker of anxiety as she knelt down to get a better look.

The top book was called *23 Minutes in Hell*, a memoir of one man's experience of the afterlife; the next book, *Sinners in the Hands of an Angry God*, was an eighteenth-century sermon with extensive notes. BK 23 Min Hel and BK Sin Ang God. Jen had begun to check through the others when Hugh came home to pick up a file he'd forgotten.

"Have you seen it?" he shouted up the stairs. "My meeting's in an hour. Where are you?"

She thought about scrambling out of Lana's room, but her legs were stiff and Hugh was there before she could do more than brace her hands on the carpet.

"What are you doing?" he said, finding her kneeling on Lana's floor.

"There are all these books, Hugh, about Hell. Describing it, explaining it."

"You've been searching her room? I thought we were supposed to respect her privacy and everything."

"I've had enough of that." She held the books in her hands and read the titles. "*The Fire That Consumes.* Look, *Anticipating the End Days,* and this one, *Visions of John Bun-*

454

yan. Hugh, I *know* there's a chapter on suicide in this one."

"Well, I'm assuming the book's against suicide," he said. "Surely that's sort of positive. And I see she's got Dante's *Divine Comedy* there. I mean, that's a little precocious perhaps, but it's not damning."

"Damning?" Jen repeated.

Hugh had kicked off his shoes at the bottom of the stairs, and Jen watched him wiggle his socked toes as he thought of what to say. "How d'you know the books aren't for school, for religious studies or religious education, or whatever it's called now?"

"She dropped RE last year. Where did she get them, do you think? *Why* did she get them? I wondered if, perhaps, someone might have bought them *for* her. Stephen . . ."

"Jen, whatever questions we ask now, they're pretty meaningless without Lana here to answer them. And she's not going to be all that happy to explain if she finds we've — or *you've* — been searching her things." He fluttered a hand about as if to indicate the insubstantiality of a teenage girl's possessions. "Try to put everything back where it was and then we can go downstairs and talk properly."

"There are condoms in her drawer," Jen

said, naming the one item that might shock him. "I think she's had someone up here. Doesn't that concern you?"

"Do you mean she's been sneaking a boy in for sex? Yes, I suppose it does concern me, though it also seems reassuringly normal."

"Is that all you have to say?"

"Put the books and everything back."

Jen looked up at him for a moment then down at his toes. Even his toes were sensible, reassuring. She pinned the receipt back on the corkboard and shoved the books about Hell under the bed.

"But we should talk to her about this, don't you think?" Jen began, only to fall silent as Hugh shushed her.

A voice was coming from under the bed, a murmuring, male voice, the words not yet discernible. Jen immediately imagined a man lying on his belly like a lizard. She could picture his eyes, shining in the dark, his mouth open, his lips almost kissing the floor. He had stayed flat and still while Jen had searched the room and found the books and talked to Hugh. Waiting, hiding, spying.

Hugh knelt carefully, wincing as his knee cracked, obviously regretting the noise more than any pain. He tilted to the side, trying to get a better look.

"I *told* you she'd got someone up here," Jen whispered, getting onto all fours.

Hugh shushed her again as he got hold of the bed frame and, breathing hard, tugged it suddenly away from the wall.

There was no one there.

"Bless us Lord, every day," the voice said. It was the teddy bear from the Christian bookshop. "Amen."

"What the hell?" Hugh said, his voice loud as he let the air in his lungs escape.

"Bible bear," Jen said, reaching for it. She took a long breath in and then out, making dust balls float about. There was a smell of shoe leather and damp, a monkish sort of smell, and Jen felt as if it were coming from the bear. "Lana joked that she was going to get it as a gift for Meg's baby."

Hugh didn't make any comment and they sat side by side on the floor for several minutes, as if waiting for the voice to continue, or for some other voice to begin.

NOT EVERYTHING
IS ABOUT SEX

Lana's voice wasn't heard that evening. She was tired, she ate a bowl of cereal at the kitchen counter, she went to bed.

Hugh had made Jen promise not to say

anything about the books. He didn't want her to admit searching Lana's room until they knew that the books weren't for school or some other legitimate activity. Jen argued because she felt she must but, after the unexpected affection Lana had shown her while they were shopping, she was reluctant to do or say anything that might push her daughter away again.

She had been worried Lana would notice that her things had been moved, and when Jen went to wake her daughter the next morning her gaze darted about, checking that she hadn't left anything out of place, left any clue. The books were hidden, the talking teddy bear had been sent back into the dark and dust beneath the bed, the cuttings on the corkboard lay flattened over the receipt. Lana didn't seem to suspect anything. Instead, it was Jen who was suspicious.

She would have missed it if the washing woman hadn't been hanging the contents of her basket, if Jen hadn't been so keen to watch the calming domestic scene, if the curtains hadn't been half closed, if Lana hadn't got out of bed to pee as soon as Jen entered the room, if the curtains hadn't puddled on the bedclothes.

It was the way the bottom of the curtain

dragged across the mattress that caught her attention. Something in the hem was weighing it down. Jen felt along the fabric and found an oblong lump and a tuck held together by a clothes peg. When the peg was released a phone tumbled onto the bed. The toilet was flushing as Jen picked it up. The water in the basin was running as she walked out of Lana's room, and Jen was downstairs in the kitchen by the time the bathroom door was unlocked.

"Will you bring my tea up here?" Lana called down the stairs.

"Yep."

"Great. I'm going to have five minutes more sleep, then."

Jen put the kettle on and turned the phone in her hand. It was a small thing, a cheap thing, not like the all-singing-all-dancing model Lana usually used. A secret phone. A burner phone, they called it on the television. Hidden in the curtains. No wonder the rings were always rasping along the pole or clacking together. But what did Lana need a burner phone for?

There was no password, and no wallpaper; the background was the one that had been set at the factory. And when Jen opened the messages app, there was nothing there, either. Deleted, perhaps. The call log was the only thing that showed the phone had been used at all. One number repeated over and over: missed, received, made, twenty minutes, forty-five minutes, an hour and twelve minutes. It was a landline, not a mobile number, and although there was no name attached to it, the area code was familiar.

Jen found the laptop and typed the number into Google. A website was suggested. The New Lollards Fellowship. Stephen's face was just appearing, above a web form and a jolly *Contact us!*, when Lana came in. She'd pulled on a fleece dressing gown and scraped her hair into a bun. She picked up the last stroopwafel and bit into it. "Go on, then," she said.

"Have you had sex with him?"

"Oh, Jesus. I knew that'd be your first question. No, Mum, I haven't. Not everything is about sex, you know."

"But you *were* with him. When you were missing."

"Again, no."

"So. What, then? What's going on?"

"We've been talking, over the phone."

"Just talking? Just on the phone? He hasn't been here? You haven't met him?"

Lana sat down heavily, the chair squeaking on the tiled floor. "He got in touch after we came home. He emailed me and said if I wanted to talk about anything . . . He said he thought he knew what I'd been through."

"What you'd been through?"

"I mean, obviously, he didn't know anything, but I suppose I thought it would be funny to stay in touch, because he's kind of mad. But then it turned out he'd had a breakdown when he was younger, he knew about depression. And it was just nice, I mean, it's nice to talk to someone who wants to talk to you."

Jen felt herself start to pant. "But *I* want to talk to you."

"You say that, Mum, but you don't want to listen."

"Yes, I do. I've asked you so many times to tell me what you're thinking, what you're feeling, what's happened."

"Ugh. That's what I mean. You don't listen. You just want me to answer a bunch of questions. And maybe I don't want to answer your questions, maybe your questions hurt and make me feel bad, maybe I want to talk about something else."

"Okay. So tell me. What have you been talking to Stephen about? What's been so interesting?"

"If you're going to be like that . . ." She

tied the dressing-gown belt tighter, about to get up.

"No, Lana, really. Please. I *am* listening."

"Fine. It was all, like, religious, and you'll get annoyed, but fine." The ends of the belt were dropped. "We talked about the cutting and stuff. He said maybe God was, like, making the marks on my arms, like working through me. Like stigmata."

"Oh God. I knew it."

"Don't freak out. I'm not stupid, I told him he was mental. Like I said, it was kind of funny. I mean, you and Dad and Dr. Greenbaum, you're so bloody reasonable. All trying to work me out, trying to manage me like I'm crazy. Sometimes, it's nice to talk to someone you *know* is madder than you. Like, however weird I might be, I know I'm not as weird as Stephen. Right?"

One corner of her mouth lifted in a smile, and Jen tried to smile back.

"But, Lana, what I don't understand is, how could any of this help?"

"Well, right back at you."

"What do you mean?"

"All that crap Grace talks. You complain about it, but you keep meeting her, buying shit, reading dumb books on mindfulness or whatever. Drinking water with, like, a molecule of nothing in it. You know it's rubbish, and you tease her, but you like it. You like the way she gives you a solution to every problem, and you like feeling superior."

"But Grace is kind, and she doesn't take herself too seriously, and her ideas aren't dangerous."

"Well, Stephen is kind and his ideas aren't dangerous, either."

"How can you say that? He told you God made you self-harm."

"But I didn't believe him. So it doesn't matter."

Jen felt stiff from anger and rolled her shoulders to calm herself, to make sure her voice came out evenly.

"Why the burner phone?"

"Burner phone? I'm not cooking meth."

"You know what I mean. Why all the secrecy?"

She shrugged and stood up. "You get sent my phone bill for my proper phone. And I knew you'd be weird about me talking to him. He told me you accused him of wanting to molest me with holy water or something."

"That was in the restaurant. He was here. Did you meet him? Did you tell him to come?"

"No. He really did have a nutcases' conference. But I think he might have planned to

463

bump into us. I told him I had therapy that day and that we usually go for pizza afterwards. I didn't think he'd just show up. I was kind of pissed off about that because it stressed you out."

"So, when you hung back . . ."

"I was worried he would say something, that you'd guess we'd been talking."

Jen nodded. "I can't say I don't feel betrayed. So many lies."

"Okay, if you're going to start with the emotional blackmail, I'm going for a shower." She was at the kitchen door.

Jen gripped hold of a mug. "I found the books about Hell."

Lana turned back. "You searched my room?"

"No, not really. I just came across them. Are you going to tell me you bought them because they were funny?"

"Stephen said he'd pay me back, if that's what you're worried about. I just have to send him the receipt."

"Well, that's very generous, I'm sure."

"When did you find the books?"

"Yesterday."

She nodded.

"Your dad was there, too."

She nodded again.

"So, why do you have them, Lana?"

She took a deep breath. "Because I was in Hell," she said.

Something collapsed inside Jen. Her daughter was lost, she thought. She could pretend Stephen hadn't influenced her, hadn't persuaded her, but really, she *had* been taken in by these fanatics. This is what happened to vulnerable people: cults took advantage, sold them lies, cut them off from their families.

Then there was that smile again. "That's what Stephen thinks." Lana had deliberately left a pause, Jen realized, for maximum effect. She genuinely thought it was funny.

"His weirdo church all believe that children can visit Hell. And, even though you think I'm shagging my way around the country, Stephen still counts me as a child and tells me that's where I've been."

"Yes, and he told a newspaper that, too. He talked about you in the press. You were annoyed. You said he was cashing in."

"I wasn't really annoyed. I mean, who cares? It's stupid. I'm going to keep the article to scare my niece with."

"And the books?"

"He said I might recognize something from one of the books."

"Have you?"

"No, obviously." Her look asked Jen if she

were mad. "Although I haven't read any of them all the way through."

"So, you've been — what? Pretending to go along with it? Why?"

"Well, it was comforting in a way, to imagine I'd experienced something meaningful, something significant."

"Why? What *did* you experience, Lana? Tell me. Tell me now. What *did* you experience?"

"Nothing," Lana said, suddenly shouting. "That's the point, Mum. Nothing."

WOMAN OF SPIRIT

Nothing was supposed to be good. Nothing was what you were aiming for in the meditations Grace recommended. A state of oblivion, which allowed you to engage in deep self-care. So said Grace. Grace who had sold Jen lies about cats' tails, and made her perform rituals, and tried to persuade her to come on retreats away from her family. Perhaps it was *she* and not Stephen who was the truly sinister one, and only Lana had noticed.

Jen had hardly known Grace at art college, and they'd only met again by chance a couple of years ago. She'd been walking along the high street one day when she'd caught a glimpse of green leather shoes and a yellow jute bag through a shop window. That was just before she heard the thud of a woman's head hitting the glass.

The woman had been Grace.

A sales assistant in the shop's uniform had run noiselessly over as Jen had stood watching from the pavement, replaying the shock of the thud, observing Grace being attended to, wondering how she hadn't realized she was heading towards a window. Had she, like an insect, not recognized the glass?

"I was having an epiphany," Grace said later.

An embarrassing thing to say, Jen had thought, putting it down to mild concussion. But of course it wasn't the concussion. And since then, Jen had sat through lectures on every kind of fad, had nodded and smiled and teased Grace for her ideas. And afterwards, she had almost always walked home feeling more competent than usual, feeling superior, as Lana had said. Because, if nothing else could be said for her, at least *she* hadn't walked into a plate-glass window.

COMPARTMENTALIZING

Jen thought of Grace as she knocked on Lana's door the next morning. She thought she would tell Lana she was right, that her friend wasn't so very different from Stephen. She thought it might be something to discuss, maybe even to laugh about. There was no answer, so Jen called through the door.

"If you don't want me to come in, say so now."

She waited a moment before entering the room. And then it was as if all information had to be corralled into lists, every sensation or action logged carefully and distantly, if she were to keep sane.

WHAT WAS GONE:

Any residual warmth in the depths of the mattress.
Lana.

WHAT REMAINED:

Silence.
The overhead lamp, left on all night.
The curtains, open, no longer weighed down by a hidden mobile phone.

The books on Hell, brought out into the light and set on a shelf.

The smell of Jen's expensive perfume.

Sunflowers that had contracted into brown fists in the jug.

The bandana that Lana used to cover the scar on her head.

Long chunks of light-colored hair, curled in the wastepaper basket like snakes, and still showing the scissor marks where they'd been cut from Lana's scalp.

WHO WAS CALLED:

Lana (seventeen times); no answer.

Hugh (once); he said he'd come home from work immediately.

REACTIONS:

Dizziness which forced her to lie down.

The need to turn every room in the house upside down.

A tendency to bite at her own hand.

An urge to run down the road, to race across the common, to scream Lana's name at the top of her lungs.

A compulsion to take off her clothes and put them back on again.

An ability to notice, unaccountably, that

the hand wash had nearly run out in the bathroom, that one of the little Japanese cups in the kitchen was broken, that Lana had left a half-eaten packet of Hula Hoops by the kettle.

An unexpected appetite for slightly soft BBQ-beef-flavored Hula Hoops, finished in two large mouthfuls.

SNACKING

She had tried. She had tried everything. Reading books and keeping diaries and talking to professionals and spending time with family and being there and not being there and Western medicine and homeopathy and crystals-and-metals-and-astrology and staying home and having a change of scene. What was there left but superstition, bargaining?

Jen's mind went back to a Saturday, months ago, when she'd been chopping parsley. She'd felt she had been chopping parsley for a thousand years, and had been annoyed at herself for agreeing to cook what Meg suggested for dinner. Tomato juice was dripping over the edge of the chopping board, a paper cut on her thumb stung from squeezing lemons, and damp bits of herb clung itchily to her skin from fingers to

470

elbow. She wasn't even certain how to pronounce "tabbouleh," which syllable was supposed to be emphasized.

Meanwhile, Lana had sat at the kitchen table and helped herself to the pomegranate seeds that were waiting to be sprinkled on top. She'd seemed unaware that she was eating at all, the movements of arm, hand, and mouth mechanical, automatic. And something about the action, the sleepwalking quality of it, had made Jen uneasy.

"Stop eating those," she'd said, and Lana had stopped for a few minutes, looking at the bowl as if she'd never seen it before. But the sound of teeth crunching the flesh-covered seeds had soon begun again.

Jen had poured a packet of Thai-red-curry-flavored crisps into another bowl, wincing at the slightly fetid smell of them, and swapped the bowls around in a smooth movement. Lana had continued to eat, as if she hadn't noticed, though she obviously had because, after a couple of mouthfuls, she'd asked Jen if she was trying to make her fat.

"You've swapped the healthy option out for the unhealthy one."

"Well, I need the seeds for the recipe," Jen had said, but really thinking that no maternal deals had ever been made over curry-flavored crisps.

RELIEF

She was at Meg's.

GRAPEVINE

"She arrived about ten minutes ago."

Jen gripped the phone and sank onto a kitchen chair, imagining Meg's flat — peaceful, beautiful, and full of odd things that would seem ridiculous in anyone else's home. The dried seed heads of alliums dropped into square candleholders, a vase filled with porcupine quills, a string of bright silk scarves suspended above the window, the wall of artists' palettes encrusted with a thousand shades of paint.

The things were always so pristine, and Jen suspected that her daughter dusted, and not only that, took the scarves down and hand-washed them, ironed them, and hung them up again on a regular basis. She had once watched as Meg took about a hundred corks out of a huge glass jar, cleaned the jar, brushed fluff off each individual cork, then put them all back in again. *Whose child are you?* she'd wanted to ask.

472

"Is Lana all right?" she said now, leaning on the table and finding butter on her sleeve. "What's happened?"

"Apparently, she set off early this morning, but it took her a while to get here because she doesn't like using the Underground. Did you know that?"

"Yes," Jen said, turning at the sound of Hugh's key in the lock. And then he was there, filling the kettle, getting down mugs, pinching chamomile tea into them. The room immediately felt calmer, more comfortable, though he hadn't yet taken his jacket off.

"Meg," Jen mouthed at him, pointing to the phone. "Lana's there."

He nodded then sat down, looking at the phone, concentrating.

"Mum?" Meg said. "You knew? That Lana doesn't like the Tube now?"

"She told me. But what's she doing there?"

"She's asked to stay."

"With you? For how long?"

"We haven't really discussed it yet."

"Okay. Look, I realize this is a pain, but can you hang on for an hour? Your dad and I will set off now." Hugh nodded again.

"No, Mum. I think it's best if you give her some time alone."

"Alone?"

"Or, not alone, but just some space, you know?"

"You mean, away from me?" There were crumbs on the table, and Jen gave the phone to Hugh while she swept them into a hand, smearing more butter onto her sleeve as she did so. Getting up to throw the crumbs away, she noticed that the fruit bowl held only the remains of a bunch of grapes, mostly knobbly stalks, and that the glass in front of the fish print was covered with speckles of grease. No wonder Lana would prefer to be at Meg's, she thought, fetching a cloth and some vinegar from under the sink.

"Lana's cut off all her hair," Hugh said, holding the phone away from his cheek for a moment.

"I know. I found it in the bin."

"Yes. She found the hair," he said into the phone.

"Why did she do it? Has she said?"

"Sick of having to cover the short patch over her scar, apparently."

Jen tipped some vinegar onto the cloth and then rubbed at the grease over the fish print. "So she's okay?"

"Yes. In pretty good spirits."

The glass was clean. She dabbed at her

sleeve. "But, I mean, why did she leave without a word? Why did she go to Meg's?"

"Did you hear that?" he asked the phone. "Right." He looked up. "Meg doesn't know. Oh, *really*?" He held the phone closer, his mouth open. "Is that what she says?"

"Says what?" The strong smell of vinegar made Jen's eyes water.

"Wait a minute." Hugh covered the mouthpiece. "Lana says she's always thought of Meg as a second mother."

"*Has* she?" Jen dropped the cloth in the sink.

"Not that I was aware. Meg certainly doesn't feel like her mother. Perhaps she just means because of the age gap."

"Well, it's news to me. How long has she felt like that?"

"About five minutes, I expect. Just long enough to make a case for staying at Meg's."

"Ask her when we should come over."

"When d'you want us, Meg?" Hugh asked.

"No, not *when d'you want us?* When should we come?"

Hugh turned his face away to better hear the voice at the other end of the line. "Right. Jen, here's the plan. The summer holidays end in six days. Meg says Lana can stay till then. She's editing a catalogue and can work from home till next week. So maybe this is a good time for everyone to have a rest."

"A rest? As if I will be able to rest with Lana roaming London."

"She won't be roaming London. Meg says she'll keep an eye on her. She promises." He laughed into the phone. "She says, think of it as one in the bank for your future babysitting duties."

"Oh." Jen stopped a moment, cheered by the idea of looking after her granddaughter. Meg couldn't think she was so terrible a mother if she was willing to leave her child in her care. "Will we have babysitting duties, then? That will be nice." She looked around the kitchen, at the flakes of onion skin that skittered about under the cupboards, at the tea stains around the kettle, at the limescale on the taps and the burnt sauce on the hobs and the soil under the plant pots. "But the place is such a mess. You couldn't have a little one here."

"Well, it won't be for a while yet."

"I know, but I should get started," Jen said, dumping the mushy grapes into the bin and squirting washing-up liquid into the bowl. Hugh tried to hug her as he left the room, but she wriggled out of his grasp and began to fill a bucket with bleach.

Hugh was in bed, asleep, by the time she had finished scrubbing the toilet and moving furniture so she could hoover under it, and washing the cushion covers and shining the windows and cleaning the baseboards and disinfecting the floors and running every piece of crockery and cutlery through the dishwasher.

"I thought nesting was meant to be limited to the mother-to-be," he'd said, as he went upstairs.

In the morning, after he'd left for work, she started again, gouging at the mold in the bathroom sealant. But she was distracted. The cleaning seemed less urgent today; the impulse had turned into a general restlessness. She tried to call Lana and then Meg, but they didn't pick up (she imagined them smirking at her name flashing on the screens of their phones) and, when she got a text a few minutes later, it was just Meg telling her they'd call that evening, that she should relax. A dismissal.

She tried to feel anger but didn't have the energy for it, and she wondered, rather desperately, what to do with the day, how she might pass the time in the house. Then came a sudden awareness of her solitude, her freedom. There was no one here to watch out for, to wait for, to manage. If she was restless, she could leave the house, she could go anywhere she liked. At first, she couldn't think where to go. It was a blazing-hot day, the sort of day to share with other people, only no other people wanted her.

But perhaps she could visit her mother, she thought, and she got into the car. There was a sense of unoriginality in her actions as she set off, that she was following Lana's reasoning, Lana's movements of the day before: leaving the house without telling anyone, running away and seeking sanctuary with the only family within reach. Except that Lily really *was* Jen's mother; she didn't have to rewrite their relationship to justify the visit.

Once on the road, though, Jen felt reluctant to drive to Suffolk, to end up in a garden center admiring dainty fuchsia trees in glossy pots and bending to read out the labels on each plant. She felt too wild for that, too willful. And it wasn't long before she found herself heading northwest, rather than northeast, exchanging the gentler landscape of Suffolk for the tors and moorland of the Peak District.

It was inevitable, she realized, that she would end up back there; this had been where she was heading, in her mind (in her soul, Grace would have said), for months. Something had been lost there, something had gone awry, and she needed to feel the soil under her feet, to retrace her steps, her daughter's steps, and see if the landscape would reveal any secrets.

She pulled into a service station for a toilet trip and a coffee, for petrol and another bag of Hula Hoops (she had developed a taste for them), and remembered the overnight drive from Scotland she had attempted in her twenties. At least this exploration, though vague, at least this search, though it was for something unnamed, wouldn't require her to sleep in her car (she hoped).

And it wasn't cold. It was, in fact, the most beautiful day. The heavy summer foliage that lined the motorway seemed to have taken on its own light, as if the sun had splintered into a thousand pieces and hung, glowing, on the trees. The whites of things, of dresses and china cups and tablecloths, was dazzling. Only there weren't so many dresses and china cups and tablecloths along this way, there were more road markings and empty billboards and VW vans, but somehow, the weather still suggested the former objects better.

The light printed patterns of whatever was

above her onto the ground: birds flying low enough were accompanied by their shadow selves and the branches of trees created crisscrosses on the tarmac. If you closed your eyes, the light would flicker and falter and make you sick. (Though Jen kept her eyes open, as she was driving.) Her sight was slightly impaired, all the same, was bleary and smudged with tears. She was disappointed to be crying, to have been crying for forty miles.

There had been a Japanese man in the service station, who'd taken his baby daughter on his knee while the mother ate McDonald's from a paper bag. It had seemed like the loveliest thing Jen had seen in years. The man had sat on a chair in the food court and pointed things out to the baby, hugging her to his chest and smiling down at her and looking so blissful. The baby's little feet in their little socks had bounced once on the seat of the chair, and the father had pulled his coat around him and tucked it under the feet so the fabric cradled them, protected them from the grubby upholstery.

Why cry at that? Why cry at the way he held up a knitted doll for the baby to see? Why cry at the rosy cheeks of the mother as she pushed fingerfuls of chips into her mouth? Why cry at the way light filtered

480

through the service station's skylight to fall on those three figures alone?

Well, if she cried enough, Jen thought, at least she might not need the loo again for another forty miles.

FIRST SIGN OF MADNESS

It was lunchtime when she arrived, and she ate a currant bun she'd bought from a supermarket and felt quaint and rustic. There was a car park in a little hollow about a mile from the holiday center and, when she had finished eating, Jen slipped off her shoes and pulled on the wellingtons she kept in the car.

She walked uphill, not really sure where she was going but sensing that high ground would be a good start. Perhaps, if she could get a good view of the valley, she would spot someone, hiding, following her. But the hill was densely wooded and there was no view to be had. It was difficult to know which way to go next, and the ground was littered with sycamore keys, crazy arrows pointing her in every direction, mocking her.

The creaking-door sound of a woodpecker echoed through the trees and Jen turned towards it, taking a path which led her along the edge of a field to another small wood where there was a tree with bulbous points on the trunk, and a strange root form, like the legs of a child-sized nymph curling out, limboing out of the earth. She thought of the child who was supposed to have found a door to Hell in a tree, she thought about the painting of Daphne she'd seen in the gallery, and she thought about Meg's baby. She'd had a dream some nights ago about the baby turning Meg into a tree from inside — her lungs becoming branches and foliage, her intestines roots, her skin bark — and the horror of it came back to her only now.

She spread her toes in her boots, feeling the uneven ground beneath the thick soles. People were always telling you to "plant yourself"; they talked about it in self-defense classes, being moored in the earth, like a tree, unbreachable. But what if all women had a propensity for turning into trees? What if pushing your feet too hard into the ground was dangerous, caused you to sprout roots and stay stuck there forever? She moved on.

Half an hour later, Jen finally admitted she was lost. She frowned at the mouth of a rabbit warren, she frowned at the rabbit droppings stuck to her boot, she frowned at a row of shotgun cartridges littering the path. The countryside was disturbing. Everywhere you went there was evidence of people shooting things.

"Probably rabbits," she told herself.

Poor rabbits, she thought.

"Or foxes," she said aloud.

Poor foxes, she thought.

But it was normal here. In the country, people weren't so cut off from death, they accepted it as part of life. She rolled her eyes at her own lecture.

"It's not some otherworldly culture, Jen," she said. "Country people watch *EastEnders* and shop at Waitrose just like you."

But, thinking about it, she didn't actually do either of those things.

She trudged on. The fields were mostly bare earth, and the boundary hedges ragged; it was like an approximation of the countryside rather than the real thing: there weren't any discernible smells, except a thick waft of manure, or similar, which hit her every few minutes. Not a bird called, not even a crow; she hadn't even seen one swoop overhead. *And no birds sing.* The phrase seemed significant, a continuation of another thought, and though she couldn't remember where it was from, she knew it had something to do with sedge, whatever that was.

A kind of moss or succulent, she guessed, as she ducked under a trail of ivy and watched out for a person to ask for directions. But no buildings rose up, no cars rattled by, and no people appeared, despite the evidence of their existence in empty cartridges and discarded beer cans.

And a saw.

"Oh God," she said, fully giving in to the urge to talk to herself, and even pointing at the saw, as if this gesture would draw the attention of another soul. The saw was a blue-handled, slightly rusting wood saw, hanging on a branch at about thigh height. Hanging there, in the middle of nowhere.

"You're telling me that's not disturbing?" Jen said. "I might be about to get eaten."

Then silently: You're not in Texas and it's not a chainsaw.

"It'll just be for normal farmer-type things," she said. "Cutting back branches and things." She looked around as she spoke, though, and couldn't help imagining figures in the trees.

When a movement caught her eye, it took Jen a few moments to realize that her gaze had fixed on something across the next field. For a minute, she thought it was the crouching man from the Instagram photos, but it was a girl.

She stood far enough away that Jen couldn't see her face, and she held her head slightly bent, as if she were looking at Jen under her brows, scowling at her, tracking her. The girl's shoulders were bowed and her arms hung down in front of her, the sleeves swamping her hands. It was a pose not unlike Lana's in a bad mood, a petulant stance, childish. But also menacing, unreasonable, beyond reach. The girl's hair moved in the wind, flapping about, masking and unmasking her face, but she did nothing to stop it, to brush it away; she only stood and stared at Jen.

Dry-mouthed, Jen tried to say something to herself, to come up with a reassuring phrase, but the words wouldn't form. She felt trapped, unsure whether to flee. The girl hadn't moved, seemed to be concentrating, and Jen had an idea that Lana had sent someone after her, an eerie double, a rage-filled stand-in. Could her daughter's hatred have followed her, somehow?

She felt a brush across her face, as if some ghostly fingers had touched her skin, and jerked away so quickly that she fell against a fence. But the "fingers" were just clumps of feathery seeds which had detached themselves from a spike of rosebay willow herb. The white fluff bobbed along the ground, carried by the breeze, a disembodied rabbit's tail, and Jen pushed herself up and followed it, not checking to see if she was still the subject of the girl's intense stare.

And as she got over a stile she bumped, quite literally, into Matthew.

He had been on one knee, as if waiting to propose, and a collection of straps hung around his neck, connected to cameras and camera bags, which bounced against his waist as he got up.

"Hello," he said, his clear face so normal, so ordinary. "Hello, Lana's mum." That slight catch in the middle of his sentences, the repetition. Could you call it a real stutter?

"It's Jen," Jen said.

"Yes, sorry, I remember. What are you . . . What are you doing here?"

Jen didn't know how to answer him. She hadn't banked on meeting anyone she knew. "I was trying to find the cave with the crucifix in it," she said, picking a landmark at random. "But I've only managed to get lost. What about you?"

"I was hoping to catch sight of a red-backed shrike, but I think the original sighting was a fairy tale. Anyway, all the birds seem to have been spooked by something. You, probably." He smiled.

"Sorry," Jen said, smiling back. "So, you know where we are?"

"Yes. We're not far from the crucifix cave. You're not as lost as you think. I can show you, if you like."

He led her back the way she'd come, and her breath caught as they passed the girl, still standing in that same unnerving position, but as they got close, Jen saw it wasn't a girl at all, that what had spooked her was a cleverly lifelike scarecrow. Perhaps the crouching figure in the pictures was a scarecrow, too.

"No wonder there are no birds," she said.

BINGO

"Is . . . Is Lana with you?" Matthew asked, as they crossed a field of sheep.

"No, it's just me."

"You're not going to visit the center? You haven't come to talk to my dad?"

Jen didn't answer. Taking her eyes from the landscape and focusing on the boy, she was aware of a panic in Matthew's voice, aware of a calm that she could fake and he couldn't muster, aware that her silence was more effective than anything. It occurred to her that Matthew had the answers.

"Please don't tell my dad," he said. "I . . .

I know I shouldn't have taken the vodka. Or any alcohol. It just seemed a good . . . a good idea, because it was our last night together. Mine and Lana's."

"You drank vodka?"

"Well, no, we didn't actually drink it —"

"Matthew," Jen interrupted, "did you have sex with my daughter?"

His blush was immediate and fierce. "No, no." He unscrewed the chunky lens from his camera and packed it into a bag. "We, er, we kissed. But no. I promise we did not do that."

"Explain about the vodka again."

"I took some from the bar at the center, but neither of us wanted it and then Lana said she'd hang on to it, because I was scared my dad would catch me trying to put it back."

"And you think I'm here to tell your dad that?"

He looked at her, a long, studying look, the kind that Jen imagined the birds in these hills must be familiar with. "No, I suppose it's a long way to come for that, isn't it?"

"Quite a long way."

"Is it Lana, then? Is she all right?"

"She's all right enough."

"What about her headaches?"

Jen felt a bit sad that he'd been so easily

put off with such an obvious excuse. "I think her headaches are gone now."

"That's good. She was having a terrible time when she was here. I had to get her painkillers from town."

"She asked you to get painkillers?" Jen wondered how easy it would be to smash all the camera lenses in the padded bags he carried. "So, when you left her, Matthew, the night she went missing, she had a bottle of vodka and lots of painkillers?"

He nodded.

She might have shouted at him then, asked why he hadn't told anyone that at the time, but there were other things to think about. The mouth of a cave had made her stop.

"Matthew, I think I'll have a rest here," she said, thinking of the #*rapture* picture, of Lana's sleep-talking ("I'm underneath"), of the oyster fossil.

"Oh." He walked a little way and then ran back to her, as if he were attached by a piece of elastic. "I can't really stay with you. I have to help my dad with a kayaking tour."

"I know. That's okay. Have a good time." She wanted him gone, but he kept turning as he went, that piece of elastic bringing him up short over and over.

When he was finally out of sight, she

turned back to the cave. She had a powerful sense of recognition, though she didn't know why. It was a dark opening, partly hidden by a mass of fern, and she walked towards it, waiting for some meaning to materialize. Halfway across the field, it came to her. From this distance, the shape of the cave's mouth looked like the figure of a man, crouching slightly.

CRABWALK

The first bit was too easy, that was the trouble. You just had to walk in. It was dark, but there was a torch on her phone, and the ground was a bit treacherous — covered in loose stones — but the slope was very gradual and the walls were dry to the touch. A dozen yards in, she had to turn sideways to get through, but that seemed an adventure, a safe sort of an adventure. She scraped her knuckles, grazed the side of her head as the tunnel varied in height, and she caught her shoulders and elbows on outcrops of rock, but the pain was pleasing and she felt it would be appropriate to emerge from the depths of the earth with a few war wounds.

SUMP

People had said caves were dangerous, but it wasn't as if you could die. There was just one way in and one way out, and although it was dark — so dark that she had to keep checking there really was a floor ahead of her — you could feel your way along well enough. The only cause for alarm was a hole at the end of this stretch. A wide hole, full of fast-moving water, which a person might fall into if they were moving too fast. But she hadn't been moving too fast and her torchlight had found it before her feet did. The shiny, slippery stone at the edge had only been under her boots for a second. She was fine. She began to walk back again.

ROUND CHAMBER

She had ducked to avoid a stalactite and discovered an opening, low down on the right, black in the gray, a crawl space that, when she shone her light through, held something which glinted at her. She squatted and edged forward, inelegant, creaky, glad no one was there to see, and soon came out into a roundish chamber that she could kneel in (if she didn't mind the stones pressing into her kneecaps). It smelled of incense.

But perhaps the smell was just associative, because the place resembled a church crypt; no one could have been burning incense down here, could they?

No, but it seemed someone had been drinking. The glint she'd caught sight of came from an empty vodka bottle. So this was the place. Lana had come here after leaving Matthew. And had she sat and waited while they'd been frantically searching for her? Had she heard their calls? Had she imagined how desperate things were above ground? Jen felt a sick sort of anger and took a photo of the cave, the vodka bottle, with a vague idea that she was gathering evidence.

As she crawled off, though, she knelt on a blister pack of Tylenol. Also empty. A few inches to the left was another, crushed flat, and two more were wedged between some stones. Jen curled against the wall and shuffled the foil sheets together. Thirty-two pills at least. More than enough to end your life, if that's what you wanted to do. The chamber took on a different aspect. It wasn't a hideout, but a condemned cell. She sat awhile, waiting for the emotion to leach from the rock, for some sense of her daughter's rage or despair to materialize. Nothing happened. So much for T. C. Lethbridge, so much for human suffering being stored in stone. She put the pill packs into her pocket and squeezed back towards the main tunnel. Except it wasn't the main tunnel she found herself in. It was another narrow space, slightly lower. She stretched a hand out to stop herself falling and her sleeve got soaked to the elbow.

RIVER PASSAGE

She would have to be more careful. She didn't want to get lost. And she wondered if she should tie her shoelaces into a guide rope, or unravel her jumper and plait the wool into a ball of string. A nice idea, if she hadn't been wearing wellingtons and unwoven synthetic fleece.

Back in the main tunnel, there was a sort of ringing in her ears, or else a singing in the rock, which could have been water, an underground river whistling along somewhere nearby. She hadn't noticed the sound before. It seemed colder here, too, and she could see her breath cloud in front of her.

She walked (stumbled, fumbled, tripped) for a while, a long while. Long enough that she realized she'd made a mistake, that this wasn't the tunnel she'd been in, the tunnel that led to the entrance. That this was some other passage, and God knew where it went. She turned back. But it was soon apparent that this was hopeless as well. She couldn't find the entrance to the round chamber in the dark, though she diligently shone her torch into each crack and fissure, and even poked her head through some of the openings.

The stones carried on with their wet ringing, which she thought for a moment might be rain. Down here in the gloom, it was possible to imagine the Peaks awash with every kind of weather and, despite knowing the reality was blazing sun, she pictured the sheep in the field, huddling under wind-battered trees, sheltering from hail, blending, white on white, into a wintry landscape.

ECHO CHAMBER

"Hello?" she called, her voice bouncing off the stone and dispersing, half drifting towards the ceiling, half slipping into the dark recesses ahead of her. There wasn't exactly an echo, but it was a lonely sort of sound, and she regretted it.

CHOKE

She dithered, didn't trust herself to make a choice, started one way and then changed her mind, stood in one place then moved about frantically. Finally, she took a chance, working her body into a small opening. The air was heavy here; she could smell her own breath (sour from the junk food she'd eaten on the drive up). And the tunnel narrowed too quickly to be right, so quickly that she got stuck, unable to move in either direction. Her breathing was loud, her ribs pressing against the rock; she seemed to be swelling in the stone tube. There was nothing to get hold of, nothing to push against, her feet sticking out, an arm crushed to her body. She wriggled uselessly, her clothes bunching around her hips, then gave up (the despair of that moment, the hopelessness). Her lungs deflated. After a moment, she found she could move again.

HOLLOW

Things she remembered about caves: that they were the only places left that Google Earth hadn't mapped, the only places left to explore. That the plaques that form in the lungs due to tuberculosis were made of the same material as limestone caves (which meant that, when Keats was writing "Endymion," he might already have had the beginnings of his own tiny cave system inside his chest). That the constellation of the stars was meant to be somehow mirrored by a network of tunnels under the ground, as if the straight lines between stars on a star chart were pathways. What Jen always wondered was what the tunnels underground were supposed to link — what was the earthly equivalent of a star? A clod of mud? A rock? Some sort of precious mineral?

None of this was of any use. She had never been able to get the hang of celestial cartography, and quoting Keats was hardly likely to get her anywhere (however much she felt like a "lamb strayed far a-down those inmost glens"). Even Google couldn't help her.

Blanket shaft

There was an opening in the ceiling, and a blanket hanging from it, just out of reach. She stopped and looked up and thought of the wannabe hermits and their discarded camping equipment. Could the crucifix cave be above her? Might someone be up there?

"Help!" she shouted. "Please, help me!"

She shouted for a long time, but no answer came. Even if they heard, she thought, they'd probably dismiss it as a yew-induced hallucination.

Low crawl

It started at crouching height, but soon she was on her belly, the phone pushed along in front of her, or held in her mouth. Either way, she could hardly see. Rock constantly grazed her skin as her jacket rode up again and again, and she got a cramp in her neck from holding her head up. Her wrists were hurting, a shooting pain in one of them, and every movement was laborious. She longed to walk upright again. The noise of her breathing was brittle and carrying; it seemed dangerous, alerting anything predatory to her presence. How fast could she really move along on her belly if someone or something came up behind her? Which was nothing to the idea of something appearing in front: there was no room to turn around.

The fear was so sudden and physical that she had to stop moving, despite her better instincts, and lie still in the tight space. Her limbs were ticklish with exhaustion (she wished she hadn't done so much cleaning the day before), her heart's thudding was like a heavy stone dropping over and over.

Moving again was an effort — it suddenly seemed almost embarrassing to keep trying — but Lana had made it out, so there must be an opening somewhere. Jen just hoped it wasn't three days away.

COLD DROP

She sat at the edge, letting herself down slowly. The opening began with coarse boulders arranged in a descending circle like a natural spiral staircase. Each step was waist height or taller, and Jen slid from shelf to shelf on the seat of her jeans.

Her first steps at the base of this chamber echoed, and Jen felt again as if she were in a holy place, though the holiness wasn't re-assuring. It made her think of Stephen, of the children he wished so much to send into Hell. He hadn't been entirely wrong, she realized. For what was this like, if not Hell? There were no fiery pits, no devils, but be-ing stuck here, alone, in the dark, with no way out, was close enough. She wasn't surprised Lana latched on to the idea, an idea that gave the experience meaning, that located it, related it to something bigger.

Her throat was cold, her lungs, too; in fact, most of her body was stiff and freez-ing. She was frightened. Suddenly, she was desperate to get back up to the tunnel she'd just left.

Half lying on the lowest boulder, she scrambled up, scraping her shoulder as she stood. The second ledge was narrower and she scraped her elbow and both knees, tearing her jeans. The next jut of rock was almost out of reach. She broke a fingernail trying to get a handhold, then swung forward, hitting her cheek and finding herself hanging against the rock, with nothing below her.

She swore, then remembering her desire for battle scars, swore again and called herself names. Stretching her legs back, she found the ledge opposite and pushed herself onto solid rock.

If she made it out of here alive . . .

If she made it out alive? She laughed — a mad sound, peculiar and unfamiliar, which made her shiver. To dispel the fear her own voice had caused, she began to talk to herself, repeat things which were ordinary and unthreatening, things that were from the world she knew.

"Washing machines live longer with Calgon," she said, trying to get the intonation exactly right, trying to get the volume right, to match it to the space. She restarted several times, and thought of Lana's not-quite-stutter. She could imagine, after this, it would be hard to get used to the way her voice sounded in the outside world.

The Calgon jingle was vaguely unsatisfying and she tried to think of something longer. The Lord's Prayer, perhaps. She attempted to recall it, but got caught up wondering if it was "*who* art in Heaven" or "*which* art in Heaven." This reminded her of a children's book she'd read to Lana once, where a girl sang hymns to keep her courage up. The only hymns she knew were Christmas carols. She tried a few lines, but they seemed sinister down there in the dark.

SQUEEZE

There was something coffin-like about this section of cave. Her breath caught at the comparison. Had she died already? And was she now suffering her punishment?

OCTOPUS CAVE

Her phone's torch lit on something, a creature, reaching out for her in the dark. It took up the whole width of the passage, and she recoiled, dropping the mobile. The blackness was so deep that it hurt her eyes, and she felt newly vulnerable without the light.

For several minutes, she was too frightened to search, blindly, for her phone, but just kept still and tried to tuck herself against the wall, hoped that whatever it was — cave squid, kraken — would pass without guessing she was there. She tried to breathe quietly, to stop the thudding of her heart. She sat for a long time; she couldn't tell how long. When she couldn't stand it any longer, she stretched out a hand and felt for the phone. Something hard and slimy met her fingers, but it didn't move and she soon came across the smooth, flat oblong she needed.

When she switched the torch app back on she saw that what had spooked her was a pale, shining rock formation, a ghostly octopus with stubby tentacles. "Cave," in Latin, she remembered now, meant "beware." *Cave canem!* Cave octopus!

The walls around it were black and water spilled off a jutting layer of rock. She put her tongue to it, gratefully, thinking of Grace's microbe diet. It was a relief, though she had hardly known she was thirsty. Hunger was another problem, but there was no way of solving that, unless . . . Scrabbling through the pockets of her jacket, she found one chew sweet, wrapped in pink paper, and she put it in her mouth, feeling like Persephone surrendering to the temptation of a pomegranate seed.

A wider bit of cave was visible up ahead, and she dragged herself along with renewed energy. The trickle of sweat inside her jacket was comforting; the idea of her body working gave her strength. There was a short drop, which she went into hands-first, her mobile in her teeth. The air was damp and smelled like old grass cuttings, which made her think the outside world was close, but the only light came from her phone, and that was running out of battery.

DRIED-LEAF CAVERN

This was narrow, filled with dried birch leaves, souvenirs of the outside world. She stood and shone her circle of light over every inch of the rock, but couldn't find how the leaves had got in. Perhaps they'd been carried here by water.

She was so tired, and the never-ending dark was so heavy and it all seemed so hopeless. Perhaps the best thing was oblivion. Sleep would be a respite, a way to blank out the world. It was something she had seen Lana do and, if she made it home, she promised herself she would never drag Lana into the waking world again.

She lay down among the leaves; they made for a comfortable mattress, and if she kept still for a moment she could convince herself she was somewhere else, somewhere familiar and safe. She trawled her memories for moments which might fit into this dark. A night in the old flat, in their old bedroom with the swirling popcorn ceiling and the big, plasticky windows. She pictured it, felt it. She was pregnant with Meg, and the duvet, which she'd pushed down to her thighs, rested too heavily on her. She kicked it off entirely, lying splayed on the damp mattress.

Hugh was next to her on the bed, the air thick and soft, the air of a hot summer, dense enough to carry the smell of the lime trees in through the window. The woman downstairs was shouting in a companionable, irritating way, and they were trying to decide what her complaint was, repeating any words they made out: finances, handle it, useless, dinner. Laughing into their hands.

Jen opened her eyes and had a brief moment of panic. In the past, she had been warm and safe and loved. In the present, she was tense, cold, alone, and there was only the bleak, icy sound of water somewhere beneath the rock. She got up and carried on.

TRAVERSE

She found she was thinking of Rembrandt, a series of etchings of Christ's entombment, each one blacker than the last. In the first you could see the detail that you'd never know was there in the final, darkest picture. It made you imagine all the things you could miss in that darkness. The crumpled mourners and discarded skulls you might stumble over.

There was a hole in the floor; she nearly didn't spot it. The only means of getting past it was to wedge her feet into the narrow ledges on either side, brace her hands against the walls, and hope. Halfway along, though, she wondered if it wouldn't be best just to let herself drop, rather than carry on struggling like this. It was the trying to survive that was torturous; ending things now might be preferable.

LOW CRAWL

Her mind was wandering, she realized, remembering bits of dialogue from old sitcoms and odd moments from meetings at work. She worried a little that this was a sign she was delirious or crazy, but made no effort to halt her thoughts. Occasional dripping and echoing still made her shiver, the idea of someone grabbing her foot, but it was almost cozy here and part of her wanted to wait and not move until someone came to rescue her. Only who would know she was here?

Guilt flooded her. She was going to leave Meg and Lana motherless, she was going to make Hugh a widower. She would never meet her granddaughter. How could she have been so reckless, so unthinking? To walk in without any preparation, without safety gear, a guide, or even a map. To walk in without letting anyone know where she was. She was going to disappear, just as Lana had disappeared, only it would be for good. The image of Hugh, alone, miserable, was unbearable. Although it was worse (disgracefully) to think of him with someone else, a second wife, a woman with long, dark hair and a wardrobe full of tight-fitting velvet dresses which made her irresistibly strokeable (where did these details come from?).

The woman would be unsympathetic to Lana, would be one of those people who didn't believe in depression. She would tell her to "pull herself together" or stop seeking attention. And she would want to go out and show off all the time and would never let Hugh fall asleep with a book in the evenings. And she would be homophobic.

Picturing the woman made Jen angry. She started to feel as if she'd been tricked. It was that velvet-clad harpy who'd led her down here, lured her away from her family, got her trapped. Well, she wasn't going to allow it. She was going to get out, get back.

STREAM

After a narrow fissure, which scraped her body on both sides, came a wide, low space half filled with water. She had to wade through it, on her hands and knees, her boots submerged, her jeans getting heavier and heavier. She hurt her knees on sharp bits of stone hidden under the water and dribbled as she carried the phone in her mouth. She took off her shirt and tried to rip it apart to make bandages, to make kneepads, but the shirt was too well made, the material wouldn't tear, and so she put it back on again.

She was in pain and suspected her head was bleeding, though it was hard to tell because she was so wet all over. Her hands were cut and blistered, but she couldn't save them as she moved and had to accept the feel of rock biting into her skin. She was sorry for herself and wept at the pain, but amid the self-pity and anguish was a kernel of satisfaction. Her suffering would leave a mark, and this infernal journey wouldn't exist only in her head.

The images of Lana's red-scored wrists came into her mind and she felt for a moment a tiny fraction of what Lana must feel when she sliced at her arms, a desire to show what was happening inside on the outside of her body.

CROUCH

She couldn't remember if she had turned left or right, her mind wouldn't focus on the question; the low roof in this stretch of cave forced her into a permanent stoop so that her back ached with every step. She felt the way she did after a migraine. Unable to find the energy for anything, unable even to find words. She had begun talking to herself again, but the sentences went unfinished. She could hardly remember what she was doing there, what she was hoping for.

River passage

Was she still human? It was a question that came to her all of a sudden. Down here, was she some other being? She remembered something about the insides of caves being the closest parallel to the environments of other planets and found she could believe the comparison. The caves certainly looked like part of an alien landscape.

Grotto

There were midges. She was so pleased to see them, dancing in the torchlight, that she didn't slap at them when they bit her. They had to mean an entrance somewhere close. She looked around wildly.

Lana's phone was propped up on a high shelf in the rock, a flat, shining object. Completely dead, of course, but definitely Lana's. Recognizable from the stickers on the case, a collection of brightly colored cartoon characters and fashion logos. Jen realized she had seen nothing with any color since she entered the cave, that she had existed in black and white.

She held the phone in her hands as if it were a tiny Lana, a fragile creature. To find something so associated with her daughter, to see it now, when she might never see her again, was overwhelming. She rocked it and held it to her cheek and kissed it before she put it in her pocket.

REVIVAL

It was the sudden gust of air that told her she was near the surface, and the temperature change and, finally, the thin, pale gray shaft of light. She had to turn and turn and turn again to get up, corkscrewing out of the ground. She banged her mouth in her rush to gain height and had to wait a moment for the pain in her lips and teeth to subside. Then, cramming her toes into too-narrow gaps, she kept worming up towards the surface, until at last she could get her arms out and grab on to the roots of some nearby tree and pull herself into the world.

She gulped down breaths as if she'd been drowning, and lay flat for a moment, her wet clothes stuck in creases around her knees and middle. The sun shone and she looked at it, not caring to save her eyes, so happy to see it, so grateful for its warmth, its presence. As she stood up, the breeze caught her hair, her scalp stinging in response, and she found there was blood on her fingers when she put them to her head.

Her neck ached from hunching her head into her shoulders and she stretched as far as she could, grateful not to be cramped, grateful for the ability to move wildly without hitting rock.

There was no one around, and Jen briefly believed — really, *really* believed — that everyone had vanished, every human on the planet. Perhaps it was the fresh breeze after the airless tunnels, or the light on her skin after the darkness, or the feeling of rejoining the landscape, but there was a wonderful sense of newness to everything. A Garden of Eden newness.

The car park was only a few minutes' walk. She had walked and crawled and squirmed for hours but had come no distance at all. It seemed impossible. She was out of breath and dizzy, soaked through and freezing, and shivering only made her ache more. Her jeans were torn through at the knee and the skin was bruised and bloody. She staggered to the car, her muscles still cramping.

It was stifling inside, but she was grateful for the heat, and the dusty smell which made her think of family picnics when the girls were little and, before that, with her own parents. She fell on the other three currant buns in the packet.

There were some tissues in the door bin, and she began dabbing at the cuts on her head and knees and hands. She pictured the chunk of scalp that had been missing when Lana reappeared, obviously lost to the jagged ceiling of a tunnel. The first-aid kit was half empty, but she rubbed some antiseptic cream over her wounds and stuck plasters on her knees, then she took off her jeans and her shirt and her socks and spread them on top of the burning-hot car.

She sat in the driver's seat in her underwear, finally comfortable, not hungry, not wet, not bleeding. After a minute, she started the car battery, plugged in Lana's phone, and waited for it to come back to life.

CONFESSION

I've heard that, if you die down here, they just cement your body in. I hadn't thought about it before, I guess I hadn't meant to be found. But I don't want to be left here, even if I am dead. I don't want to be left in the dark forever.

My battery is really low now. There isn't much time to write a message, and I can't work out what I want to say. My head hurts like crazy.

Two things: I feel stupid and I'm sorry.

511

I thought, when I came down, that this was the best way, that I wouldn't traumatize anyone. I didn't want to make someone else, like a train driver, cause my death. I didn't want to be found all gross-looking, or for my dead face to haunt someone forever. I didn't think about changing my mind. I didn't think about the pills not working. I didn't think I'd be stuck here, alone, for so long. I didn't expect to wake up.

When I did I couldn't stop puking. I must have thrown up everything I ate this whole week. The leftover pills were floating in the water, dissolved to mush in their packets, useless. I hope the chemicals don't hurt any wildlife. There doesn't seem to be any wildlife down here. A couple of times I thought I saw a mouse. I'd give anything to see another animal. But it was just a trick of the light of my torch and a drip from the ceiling.

Ironic that I came down here to kill myself and now I don't want to die. Or not ironic — embarrassing. I'm really, really embarrassed. As soon as I realized I wasn't dead I felt like an idiot. I just want to get out and never tell anyone what happened. Ever. But I've tried to find my way back to the entrance and I only got more lost. It all looks the same, every tunnel. I'm wet through, and my knees are torn from crawling. I've hit my head and it's bleeding. My hands are numb. I'm not sure I could get back up the shaft I came down, anyway.

A few hours ago, I thought I heard someone above me, and I shouted and shouted till my throat hurt, but if there was anyone there I don't think they heard. So maybe no one will ever find me, maybe no one will ever find this phone, this message. If they do, then please tell my parents and my sister that I'm sorry. Please tell them I love them. Tell my mum that she was right, that life is worth living. If I was given the chance to live now, I'd never do anything so stupid again. I'd never take seeing the sky for granted, I'd never not appreciate having dry feet, I'd never eat another KitKat (maybe). I've got one in my pocket, and I've been saving it but

HEARING THINGS

The note ended there; her battery must have died at that moment. Jen's throat was tight, and her heart was hammering by the time she put down the phone. Her hands were shaking too badly to drive. Instead, she got out of the car and peeled her shirt and jeans from the car roof. They were stiff and ripped but warm from the sun. Taking her lead from Lana, Jen looked up at the sky. That calmed her a little. Not wanting to leave sight of it for a while, she put on her dry shoes, locked the car, and walked towards the moor.

After a moment, she realized her phone was ringing.

"Where are you?" Hugh asked. "Have you had your phone off?"

"No, there's no signal here. I'm in Derbyshire."

There was silence for a few seconds.

"Dare I ask why?"

"I'll explain when I get back. Sorry. I didn't mean to come here. It just sort of happened."

"Well, something else has happened. Meg's gone into labor."

"Oh God. But she's not due yet. Is she okay? Is the baby okay?"

"Don't panic. The baby's several weeks early, so they'll probably have to stay in the hospital for a while, but yes, it all seems to be going okay in general. Meg would like you to be here, though."

"Of course. I'll come back straightaway. I mean, it'll take me a few hours."

"All right, love. I'll tell her."

She said goodbye to Hugh and gripped the phone as she walked on. In a few hours, she would have a granddaughter, and she should be rushing back, but she was still shaking from the tiredness, the shock of the day, and currant-bun-induced sugar rush. So she carried on across the moor, hoping the air, the sunlight, the scenery would steady her.

When they'd visited in May, all the monster rhododendron bushes had been in purplish flower. Now, it was the heather that added color to the moor. The bilberries were ripe, too, so the whole landscape seemed rather decadent, a swathe of softness filled with fruit. She was tempted to lie out over the soft tufts of heather and fill her mouth with whatever berries she could reach.

Instead, she went through a little gate, and along a sandy path — where the catkins that had fallen off the birch trees wriggled underfoot — and came to the Nine Ladies. The stones seemed like old friends. She went and stood in the middle of them and noticed a patch of bare ground there, where everyone came to stand. She took a photo, thinking she might start her own Instagram account, then slipped the phone into the top pocket of her shirt.

Hanging on the great oak tree were Lana's earphones. They shone in the golden afternoon light, and Jen moved under the branch and held the buds in the palm of her hand.

The back of one had come off and a few tiny wires poked out. She thought of them nestled in Lana's ears, how intimate these objects were, how much a part of her daughter, and she lifted them to her own ears.

At least she finally knew, for certain, what had happened. Despite the miles between them, she felt close to her daughter in a way she hadn't in months, so much so that she almost thought she could hear her voice, as if the earphones were connected to Lana. "Mum," she could hear her call. "Mum?"

The voice came from the direction of her heart and Jen smiled at the sky for a moment before realizing it wasn't her heart but her shirt pocket that the voice was coming from. Her top pocket, where her mobile was. She fished the phone out and dislodged an earbud.

"Hello?" she said.

"Mum, for fuck's sake. This is the third time you've pocket-dialed me. Where are you? Dad says you're on your way."

"I *am* on my way."

"Good," Lana said. "Because we need you."

ACKNOWLEDGMENTS

For the help with research, thanks to:
Jon Daniels, at Dolomite Training (with special thanks for getting us out of the caves alive)
Martin and Sarah Falkingham
Christopher Healey
Cora McKechnie

For the useful conversations about writing, thanks to:
Oonagh Barronwell
Jack McDavid
Priya Parmar
Sarah Perry
Shai Sendik
Alice Slater
M. O. Walsh
Catriona Ward

For the feedback on early drafts, thanks to:
Andrew Cowan

Hannah Harper
Kathryn Healey
Debra Isaac
Charlotte Stretch
Louisa Theobald
Rowan Whiteside
Lucy Yates

For the support and insight, thanks to:
Venetia Butterfield
Karolina Sutton

For the meticulous copyediting (on this book and *Elizabeth Is Missing*), thanks to:
Sarah Day

For the encouragement, thanks to:

Everyone who contacted me via email and social media, wrote me letters, or spoke to me at events after *Elizabeth Is Missing* was published — your kind words kept me going throughout the writing of this book.

For all of the above and much, much more, thanks to:
Andrew McKechnie

ABOUT THE AUTHOR

Emma Healey grew up in London, where she studied for her first degree in bookbinding. She then worked for two libraries, two bookshops, two art galleries, and two universities before completing an MA in creative writing at the University of East Anglia. Her first novel, *Elizabeth Is Missing,* was published to critical acclaim in 2014, became a *Sunday Times* bestseller, and won the Costa First Novel Award. She lives in Norwich, England, with her husband and daughter.

The employees of Thorndike Press hope you have enjoyed this Large Print book. All our Thorndike, Wheeler, and Kennebec Large Print titles are designed for easy reading, and all our books are made to last. Other Thorndike Press Large Print books are available at your library, through selected bookstores, or directly from us.

For information about titles, please call:
(800) 223-1244

or visit our website at:
gale.com/thorndike

To share your comments, please write:
Publisher
Thorndike Press
10 Water St., Suite 310
Waterville, ME 04901